THE REIGN OF BLOOD

KC KEAN

The Reign of Blood
Heirborn Academy #2
Copyright © 2024 KC Kean

The moral right of the author has been asserted.

Without in any way limiting the author's, KC Kean, and the publisher's exclusive rights under copyright, any use of this publication to "train" generative artificial intelligence (AI) technologies to generate any works/images/text/videos is expressly prohibited.
The authors reserve all rights to license uses of this work for generative AI training and development of machine learning language models.

Cover Design by Dark Imaginarium Art
Interior Formatting & Design by Wild Elegance Formatting
Editor - Encompass Editing Service
Proofreader - Sassi Edits

All rights reserved.

No part of this publication may be reproduced or transmitted by any means, electronic, mechanical, photocopying or otherwise, without the prior permission of the copyright owner.

ISBN: 978-1-915203-48-9

The Reign of Blood/KC Kean – 1st ed.

To everyone at Wild and Windy 6 who welcomed me to the US for the first time with open arms. You were all a dream. Thank you.
I don't think there's much else to say except...
PENISES!!

I thought being a fuckboy was fun, but learning every inch of her body is even better.

– Brody

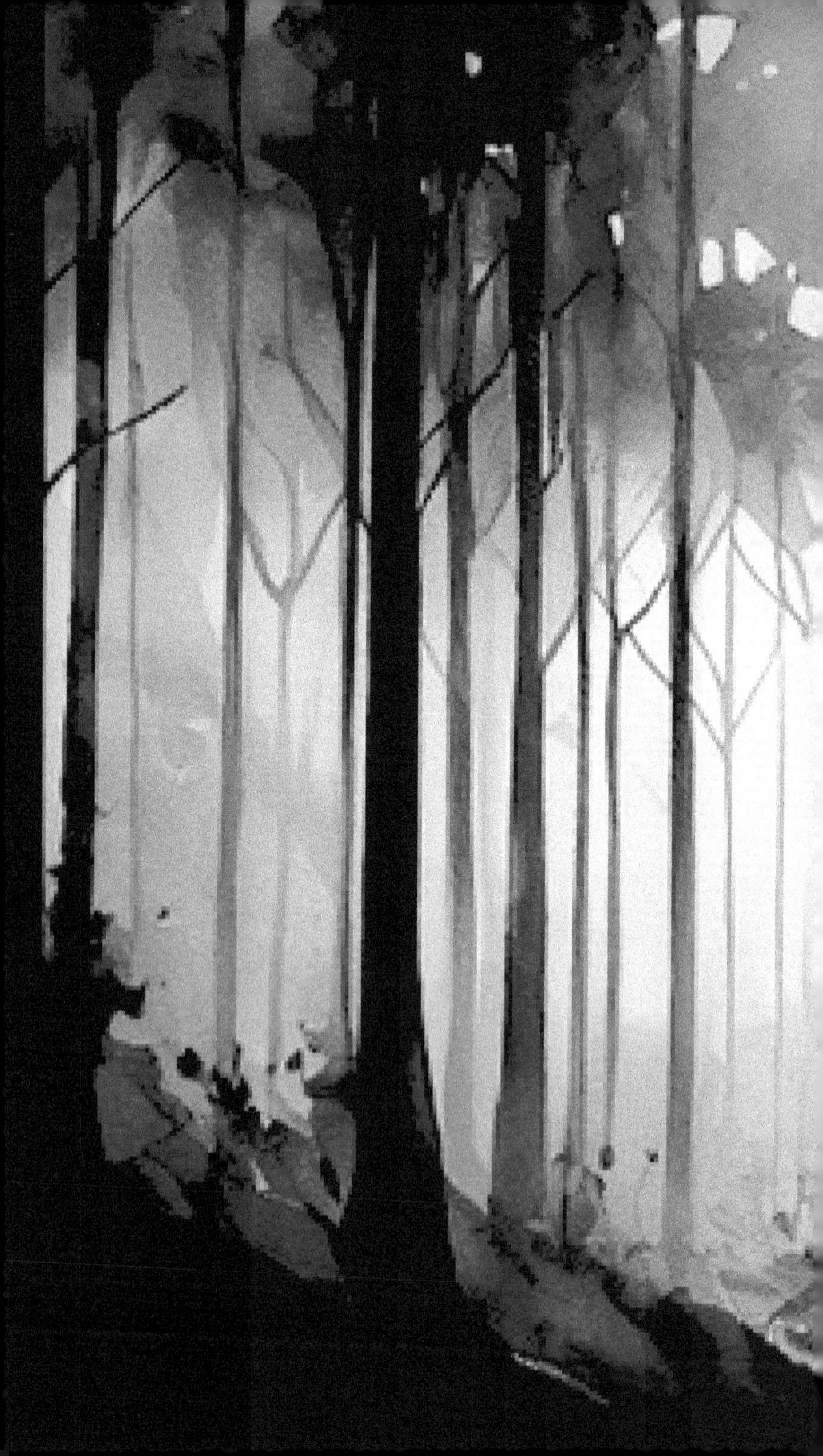

RAIDEN

1

My fingers tingle the way they always do when I know I'm going to do something rash and possibly stupid. My usual collected and calculated manner disappears into the thick of night, leaving me to crawl from the derelict depths with my own blood, sweat, and tears fueling me.

Only this time, as the world unravels before me, I'm not making the decision for myself.

Standing, my seat at the table is long forgotten while Brody and Kryll remain in their spots with a silent Janie, who is blinking up at her alpha like he's going to tear her throat out. He just might if that snarl on his face is anything to go by.

The moon party seems to have found the highlight of its entertainment, and I'm not the least bit surprised that it involves the lowly fae that continues to survive in such settings. What puzzles me most is the fact that I can't seem to turn away.

I blink, my eyelids shuttering in slow motion as I hear the treacherous words swirl around the trees, gathering us in and holding us captive.

"I've sliced the ears of a Fae before." … "A small girl." … "Not just any small girl…you."

"Me." The word is barely more than a whisper from Addi's lips.

I frown, noting the horror on her face as a sickly feeling ripples down my spine. I knew the leader of the Kenner pack was insane, but this is something else entirely. He's ruthless to the core. In another setting, it might be inspiring, but the way my muscles bunch together tells me that's not what my subconscious is taking away from this little speech.

"Somebody spell it out for me." Cassian's growl pisses me off. He knows his father better than anyone, or maybe not, considering the truth seeping into the night air around us, but he should know better. He wants to hear it said out loud because he refuses to believe the weight behind the words. Words that have his father beaming with pride, a salacious grin splitting across his face.

Maybe Cassian should just put the girl down so we can see what she can do. The stiffness to her arms, the coiling of her fists, it's a little exciting. She'll fail against Kenner, but watching her direct her rage is a source of entertainment I'm growing fond of.

As if sensing my thoughts, Addi growls. "Let go of me, Cassian. He needs to pay." Her green eyes narrow at Kenner. "What you did to my sister…" Her pain is thick and her heartache is true. I can feel it in the air, echoing in my ears like my own pulse.

"Ah, little Nora, right? Was that her name? I can't remember."

Hmm, a sister? Two of these maniacal handfuls? Please tell me there's not. One of her is more than this world can handle.

"She was just a baby."

My head tilts at Addi as she spits the words out. Her ears have been an unusual feature this entire time, and learning who is the cause of her sliced tips is doing something to my chest. My jaw clenches and I internally berate myself. I just ridiculed Cassian for not paying close attention, yet it slowly washes over me that it didn't just happen yesterday; it happened when she was small—her sister seemingly even smaller.

I don't like that.

I don't like that at all.

"How is she?" I'm certain Kenner can't smile any wider, but he makes a liar out of me by tipping his smile up another inch.

"Alive, no thanks to you."

Alive? What did this fucker do?

I peer at Brody and Kryll out of the corner of my eye, intrigued to see how they're reacting to all of this. It's no surprise to find their jaws slack and nostrils flared. It seems an attachment is growing to the irritating little fae among all of them.

"How are her legs?" Kenner is having too much fun. *Way* too much fun.

"What the fuck is going on?" Cassian repeats, ignoring the growing audience as he snarls like a pup having a tantrum over his favorite toy. I'd say that's all this is, but a ball of anger at the revelations falling around us is continuing to expand through even *my* veins.

A cry echoes from behind Kenner, drawing his attention away from the little fae, leaving trouble in her wake. Dalton, his right-hand man and keeper of secrets, parts the gathered crowd, pulling along a woman.

The woman in question looks tired and worn, her eyes darting around frantically like she hasn't seen so many faces all at once in a long time. She's not concerned about any of us though, just one person in particular. I catch a flash of her green eyes and my chest tightens.

Her lips part and she half sobs a single name from her lips. "Adrianna."

Murmurs echo among the gathered wolves and I speak the words on everyone's lips.

"Is that Queen Reagan?"

I regret them the moment they leave my mouth when I realize I played straight into Kenner's hands. "That's right, everyone. Please gather 'round and meet Queen Reagan." His gaze isn't on the fallen queen, though. No, he's settling in on the troublesome fae with wide green eyes and a jaw so tight she could cut through steel. "And Adrianna Reagan, daughter of King and Queen Reagan, the fallen king and ruiner of the fae origin. Which makes her the rightful yet despised heir to the kingdom."

Gasps ring throughout the crowd, holding everyone captive as they piece together the slivers of information Kenner provides. The queen bows her head, a single tear tracking down her face. Cassian's hold on the little troublemaker slackens, but he doesn't release her completely. If he did, I'm certain she would fall on the spot, lost to the truth, bringing her mother to her knees.

It seems there's a lot we don't know about the wicked fae whose lowly life just became a tad more interesting. She holds me captive, but movement to her left catches my attention.

Dalton.

He's no longer hovering by the queen like the good little lap dog he is. He's inching toward the named princess.

My lips purse, my fingers flex, and the rash and uncalculated side of me takes over before I can even consider my next breath.

Putting one foot in front of the other, I quickly eliminate the distance between Cassian and me, retrieving the little doll from his grasp before he can even fathom what's happening.

And before I can think better of it…I run.

THE REIGN OF BLOOD

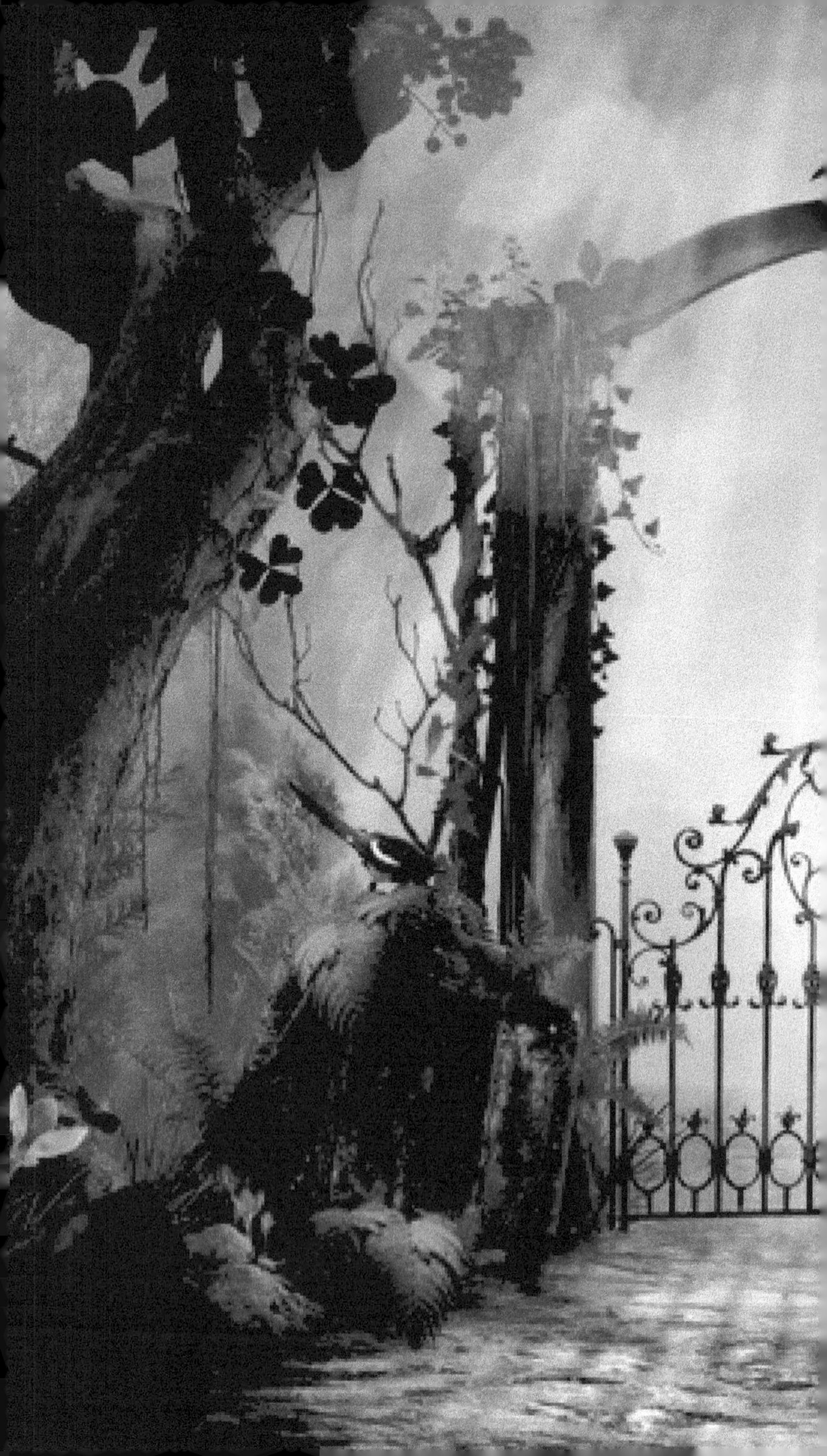

ADRIANNA

2

The strong arms banded tightly around me fall slack, giving me enough space to squeeze my daggers in my fists. But before I can use the leverage, another set of arms close in around me.

We're traveling at supernatural speed before I can bark my anger at the new person man-handling me. Unfortunately for me, I'm distracted by the nausea that curls through my stomach, taking me hostage and leaving me at the will of the man pinning me to his chest.

Even with my back pressed against him, I know exactly who it is. The world shifts around me, my secret exposed and raw, yet the familiar scent flutters at my senses, shooting a sharp vision of a chiseled jaw and perfectly styled black hair into my brain.

Raiden.

Of course the vampire comes after me first. Despite the sickly burn up my throat as my insides threaten to spill, I still berate myself for not being prepared for his onslaught amongst the madness. But in my defense, laying eyes on my mother, who disappeared without a trace so many years ago, has left me completely off-kilter.

Vomit tickles the back of my throat and I'm certain I'm going to puke, but as suddenly as the initial thought enters my head, we stop. The strong arms around me disappear a moment later and Raiden takes a step back. My vision is blurry, my balance completely off, and as much as I want to glare at him, I'm left to fend off the effects of gravity. My arms flail at my sides as I fall backward and my mouth opens, but not a single word comes out before I slump into a chair behind me.

I grip the armrests like my life depends on it, silently relieved there is something to break my fall, but it does nothing to aid the nausea still churning in me. My chin drops to my chest as I try to rid myself of the feeling by taking a few deep breaths, completely aware that I'm alone with the vampire at the top of my foe list.

Once the feeling starts to subside, my mind whirls to life, unsure what fact or revelation to clutch onto first, but I have to put all of that aside and deal with the problem at hand.

Looking up through my lashes, I instantly frown when

I don't spot the vampire where I last saw him. Stiffening in the armchair, my fingers curl around the material as I slowly lift my head, trying to listen for anything I'm not seeing, but I come up empty.

I peer around the room, lips pinched, as I vaguely recall the space from the only other time I was here. Raiden's room. I passed through here when I stormed from his bedroom with a tattered shirt and the aches and pains from the duel Leticia subjected me to. The plush leather sofa sits across the room, a huge television on the wall, and there's even a mini kitchenette in the far corner opposite the doorway to his bedroom. The crown jewels of the room, however, are the huge arched windows that look down over the campus like he's tall and grand, above it all.

At least I'm back on campus and not in some dark and dingy lair he might have, but it's still too far away from the wolf I want to get my hands on.

Retribution is necessary. Avenging my sister… paramount.

Rushing to my feet, the room spins around me and my arms begin to flail again.

"Sit your ass down, Troublemaker, you're only going to make it worse."

I snarl at Raiden as he steps into the room with measured steps and a cloth in his hand. Standing taller, despite his command, I wag my finger at him. "You know nothing about me, asshole. Don't tell me what to do." I'm acutely aware that my finger isn't quite as aimed at him as I would like it to be, and the way he cocks his brow confirms it. Fucker. "I would be fine if you had just left me there. It's your fault I'm close to puking my guts out," I add, my hand instinctively clutching my stomach as it rolls at the words leaving my mouth.

"Are you done?" he asks with a sigh, giving me a pointed stare, and my eyes narrow at him.

"No."

Another sigh, paired with his lips pursing in distaste, escapes him. "Spit it all out then. The quicker you finish your ranting, the quicker we can get to the good stuff."

Good stuff?

There is no *good stuff.*

My nostrils flare, anger getting the better of me, and my hands clutch the handles of two daggers strapped to my chest.

"This is exactly why you're a dangerous troublemaker," he states, waving a hand at me. "Always quick to be vicious with those little blades of yours." He strides toward the sofa and sits with purpose, holding his hands out wide in a show of surrender. "How about you sit the fuck down, chill the fuck out, and we'll go from there?"

"Wait, do you think I'm going to discuss what just happened back there… with you?" I scoff, my pulse ringing through my ears in disbelief as my jaw sits agape.

"I don't think. I know." His voice turns harder, the promise etched into his words.

I really don't need this shit on top of everything else. Pinching the bridge of my nose, I take a few deep breaths before peering around the room in search of the best possible exit plan I can muster.

As if sensing my thoughts, Raiden clears his throat. "There's no escaping, Troublemaker. We're going to talk. *Then*, you can leave."

I scoff again. "Do you really expect me to believe that you're going to just let me leave once we're done talking?" I know he thinks I'm a dumb fae, along with the rest of my origin, but he can't truly think we're *that* dumb, can he?

Another pointed look, and this time, it's paired with his hands clenched together. "I swear it. If I wanted you dead, I would have done it already, regardless of who or what you are." I gulp at the truth in his words, but I'm quickly overwhelmed by the resilience that forever burns through my veins. "Before you start another rant about how strong and brave you are, I'm sure you would put up a good fight, but let's cut the bullshit and discuss what the fuck just happened back there."

Do I need to go over everything that happened? Yes.

Do I need to get my ass back there and kill that fucker? Definitely, yes.

Does this asshole need to be involved in any of that? Absolutely not.

As I begin shaking my head, I can tell he already senses my refusal, and he cocks a brow at me. "What was that about your sister?" I instinctively take a step toward him, my shoulders tensing and hands balling into fists, and he grins. "Touchy subject, as I guessed. What's that about?"

I purse my lips, my breaths coming in short, sharp swells as I rack my brain over his approach. He's asking about my sister first. Not my heritage. That doesn't make any sense at all.

Clearing my throat, I force my body to relax. "I'm not discussing my sister with you."

"Why is that?" he pushes, my body desperate to eliminate the distance between us so I can fucking hurt him. "Adrianna?"

He's trying to kill me. He's trying to fucking kill me with words alone, and it's going to work.

"Don't call me that," I rasp, my chest so tight that I'm almost certain I'm going to implode.

"Why? It's your name, your birthright."

So he did hear it. I know he did, but hearing the confirmation from his lips makes my body ache with tension. My secret is out there. It was always going to be, eventually, but I was hopeful it would be on my terms. Once my strength and willpower had proven my worth.

When the crown was back in my possession. But alas, I'm powerless to the strength of the darkness that wreaks havoc on our kingdom.

I need to get out of here. I need to get as far away from these four walls as possible so I can think and process by myself. I take one step toward the door, and he's crowding my space in the next breath. His fingers wrap around my upper arms, pinning me in place.

If he knows my secret, there's no need to hide myself or the powers anymore.

Sinking deep into my core, connecting with the air around me, I take a deep breath and thrust my hands toward him. The air whips around us, blasting him into the wall beside the door with a grunt. A sigh of relief passes my lips as I feel the tingles of my magic I haven't touched since I arrived here.

Raiden's effortlessly back on his feet within a blink of an eye, hands clenched at his sides as he glares at me. "I'm trying to help you, Adrianna. Use your royal magic on me one more time, and I'll consider that a declaration of war."

"Help me? Why the hell would you want to help me?" He's lying; he has to be.

"What was Kenner referring to when he was talking about your sister?" He repeats the same question from earlier, making my teeth grind together in agitation.

"I'm not discussing her with you," I snap, eager to get

the hell out of here, but his threat of war feels far too real for me to act without caution.

"Tell me about your ears then."

"No."

"I've got all night, Adrianna. Do you want this discussion with just me, or would you prefer we wait until the others finally figure out where we are, and then we can have a group chat?"

Fucker.

"I'll tell you about my ears, and then you'll let me leave?"

He assesses me for what feels like an eternity. What he's considering, I don't know, but eventually, he nods. "Tell me, and I'll let you leave, but you're going to have to be prepared for further bargains down the line."

I don't know what that's supposed to mean, and I should probably ask, but truthfully, I just want to get the hell out of here as quickly as possible.

"Fine," I grumble, folding my arms over my chest so I can discreetly wrap a hand around a dagger. Just in case. "The night the castle was overthrown, my father—"

"King Reagan," he interjects, eyebrows raised as he waits for me to clarify.

"King Reagan," I repeat, the words heavy and pained on my tongue. "Gathered me and... gathered his children and took to the secret passageways. He had fought as hard as he could, used his magic until there was no chance for him to regenerate it in time, and declared that saving his beloved daughters was his top priority." Silence falls over us as I try to find the right words, but recalling the events of that night causes more pain than I care to admit. I've packed it away for so long, wearing my untipped ears with pride regardless, but it still hurts to remember the feelings that ran through my body, the smell of earth and singed plains, along with the taste of copper in my mouth. "My father—"

"King Reagan," he corrects again, and I glare at him.

"King Reagan or not, he's still my father, and I'll continue to refer to him that way," I snap, anger consuming me once again.

He shakes his head. "He is your father in the comfort of your own surroundings. In public, in conversation with any soul not in your immediate bloodline, he is King Reagan. Addressing him as anything else is, at best, a display of your poor knowledge of the ways of our kingdom. At worst, it could be interpreted as outright contempt for our traditions and way of life."

My brain freezes. His words aren't acid or lecturing; he's being... helpful? I can't be certain.

Fuck.

Shaking my head. I focus back on the story. His proximity isn't aiding my thoughts. "King Reagan told us to hide in the caverns as we awaited our transportation, but we were overwhelmed by a pack of wolves. He told me to keep my eyes closed and sing my favorite poem in my mind to fight off the pain and panic, so I did, just as he had always taught me, even at such a young age. I didn't see the faces of the attackers. I barely felt the slice along my ears until we somehow made it to safety." The rest threatens to spill from my lips, the inability to correct the damage that had been done, both to me and to Nora, but I quickly shut it all down and clear my throat.

"That's not as gruesome as I thought it was going to be."

Asshole.

"Fuck you. Are we done?" I snarl, inching toward the door. He doesn't move at first, eyes narrowed on me as he considers his next move. I've played his game long enough. My irritation is at an all-time high, and if he doesn't get his shit together and let me leave, a war between us will be the least of his worries.

My magic thrums to the surface, ready to act, but as I step within an inch of him, he moves to the side, clearing my path. I grab the door handle and swing it open so fast I can barely breathe, but his parting words stay with me far beyond exiting his room.

"Don't forget, Troublemaker, you're going to tell me everything I want to know. Unless you want this little secret to get out."

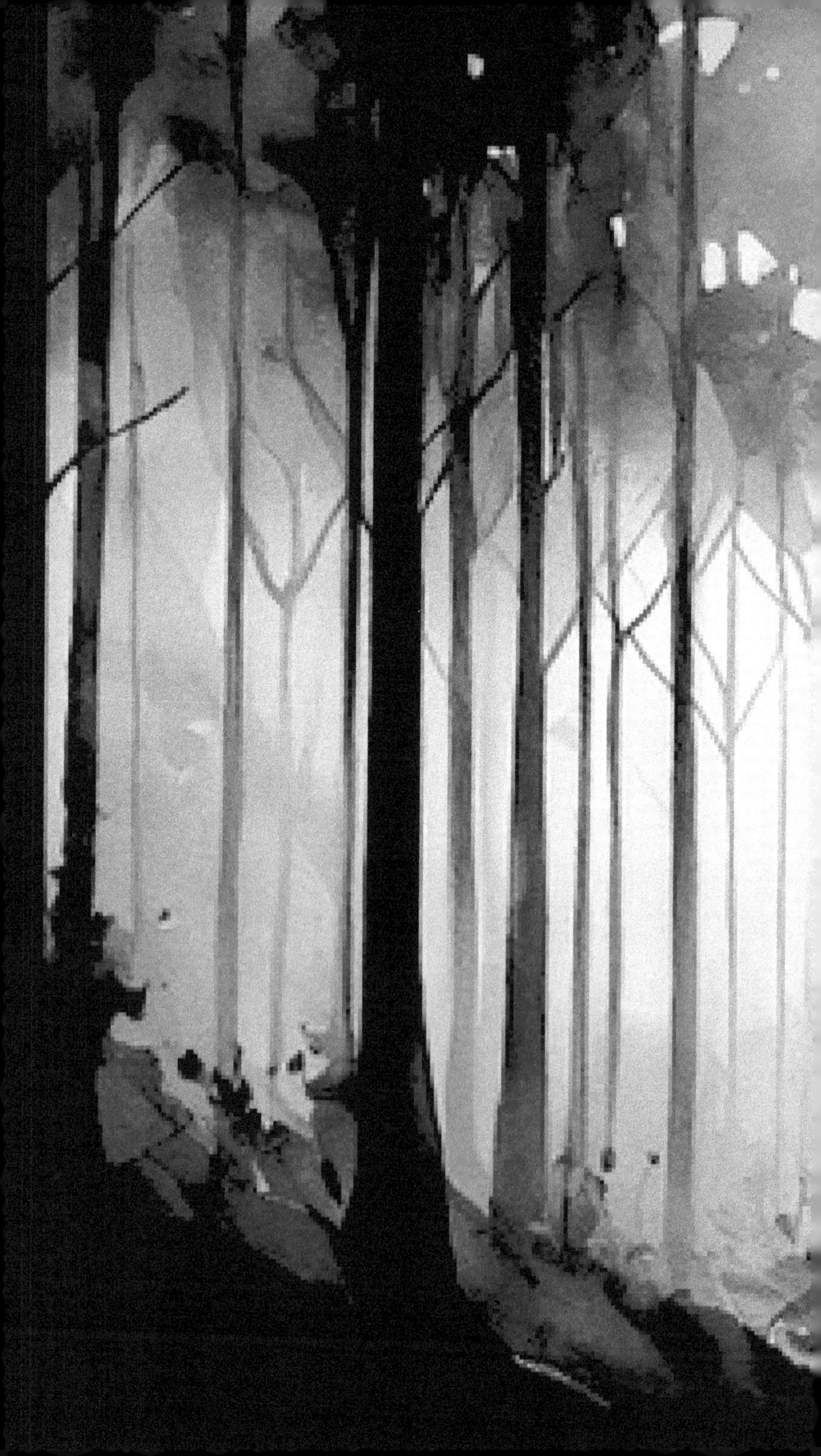

CASSIAN
3

Anger courses through every fiber of my body as my wolf itches to take over. I can feel him pushing against my flesh from the inside, ready to cause havoc and demand answers to questions we haven't even thought of yet.

"Everybody fuck off," I snarl, my breath whooshing with every inflation of my lungs as I struggle to remain calm.

"You don't get to order them around anymore. You're not the alpha heir to the Kenner pack, or even a measly pack member, remember?" My father smirks, a sense of accomplishment spreading across his lips as he stares down at me. My nostrils flare as I strain against my wolf, who is desperate to lash out, father or not.

If my father notices my inner turmoil, he doesn't

mention it, and he turns away from me to find Dalton. He doesn't see me as a threat at all. One day, I'm going to have the pleasure of correcting him on the error of his assumptions. Right now, though, I need to understand what on Earth is happening.

"Get rid of her," my father grunts, and Dalton yanks on the queen, still on her knees. My jaw ticks as I turn away. I don't know what the fuck is happening, and my gut already knows that my father isn't going to share anything with me, but that doesn't mean I can't try.

Looking down at my bare hands, I try to calm my rising fury as I consider the past few minutes. One moment Addi, or Adrianna, or whoever the fuck she is, was in my grasp, and the next, she was gone. With Raiden. I should be concerned about what he has planned for her, but I can't seem to move from the spot I'm in, my father turning back to me with that familiar-yet-sinister look in his eyes.

I'm not naïve enough to refuse to consider that I'm completely out of my depth in this moment. My mind swirls with hints of betrayal as my emotions threaten to get the better of me.

"What have you been up to, old man?" I ask, fingers clenching at my sides as I assess him just as hard as he's assessing me, until my gaze cuts to the former queen crying out in the distance.

"Please, please. My daughter! Please!"

The wolves around us remain frozen in a mixture of intrigue and horror as they watch the mess unfold before them. Forever my father's sycophants, they won't object to any of his decisions; that's always been my job. But it seems he was making moves before I was old enough to understand my role. Moves that can't be reversed.

"The party is over," my father bites, earning a few gasps and grumbles from the pack around us.

"But the full moon," someone begins to protest, and he waves his hand dismissively, effectively cutting them off.

"Can be celebrated elsewhere." The firmness in his tone isn't to be questioned and everyone knows it. Silently, the gathered wolves begin to disperse at his command, except one, who stalks toward me with purpose.

Leticia.

Fucking Leticia.

"I'll still be declaring a challenge against that disgusting fae," she bites, eyes narrowing as she glares at me, and I roll my eyes.

"I wouldn't bother," I grunt, my gut twisting slightly with concern for the intoxicating fae that is now in the grasp of my vampire friend, but I tamp it down, making sure it's not noticeable to the outside world.

"I can do whatever I please," Leticia retorts, hands on her hips as she attempts to peer down her nose at me.

"You can, but I don't want you. Whether you win

or not. You just can't seem to get the message," I snarl, pushing further venom into my words as I glare back at her. I don't feel an ounce of guilt as she turns with a huff and storms off. She's never going to learn, no matter what I say or do.

"Your way with women is… interesting."

I turn to my father. His raised eyebrow and judgmental gaze only makes my wolf harder to restrain. Instead of letting him know the difficulties I'm facing, I scoff at him. "Says the man holding Queen Reagan captive."

"She's not a queen anymore," he snarls, revealing his own emotions as the muscles at his neck bunch together. It seems I've definitely hit a nerve.

"And why does it feel like you had something to do with that?" My chest tightens at the accusation I already know is true. He doesn't bother with a response, though. Instead, he tilts his head up to stare at the moon, but I don't miss the smirk that ghosts over his lips.

He's always been like this. Elusive. Holding all of his cards closely to his chest. It makes it hard for anyone to predict his next move. It's half of the reason I left. I want transparency and truth from my leader, and he's incapable of either of those things. That's how I knew the pact with my friends was my future. My father will never be an alpha I believe in, so I'll be my own leader, my own alpha, with my own pack instead of waiting for him to die.

"Why the fuck do you have Queen Reagan anyway?"

"That's none of your concern," he retorts, not bothering to look away from the moon.

"I think it is," I push back, finally earning his deathly stare again.

"Are you a part of this pack?" he grunts, jabbing a finger at the ground as he takes a heavy step toward me. Even with only the moonlight glittering down on us, I can still see his cheeks reddening with anger.

Fucker has me there, but this is about more than the pack and he knows it.

"I'm going to bring this to The Council." The words are out of my mouth before I can even consider them, but the scowl I expect is nonexistent as he tosses his head back with a dark and wicked chuckle.

"You think they don't already know?" he muses, eyes returning to me once again.

"Bullshit." There's no way. There is no *fucking* way.

"Think about it, Cassian. I've done what I want, when I want, for years now. Why do you think that is?" His grin doesn't reach his eyes as the feral side of my father rushes to the surface. "It's because I hold all of the power, and you turned your back on all of that for a Kingdom that doesn't care what it does to its subjects, thinking *you* can change it. You can't." His words become gravely and choppy as he turns his jabby finger toward me, pushing at my tense chest with every syllable before sauntering off without a backward glance.

Fuck. Fuck. Fuck.

Maybe out of my depth is not a true representation of where the fuck I'm at. Scrubbing a hand down my face, I take a deep breath that does little to calm me.

My father's secrets are more than I could have anticipated. Queen Reagan is in his grasp; she has been for more years than I care to decipher right now, and that obviously leads me back to one person.

Addi Read. Or, more specifically, Adrianna *fucking* Reagan.

A hand lands on my arm, pulling me from my thoughts, and I whip my head around to find Janie looking up at me with concern swelling in her deep eyes.

"Are you okay?" she whispers, and I sigh. There's no real answer to that right now. Not one I can truly wrap my head around and swear it to be true.

"I've been better."

She nods in understanding as we both watch my father shift into his wolf form before darting through the tree line in the distance.

"That was a lot."

"That feels like an understatement," I grumble as she drops her hand from my arm.

I press against my temple with my fingers, trying to

will the growing pain away, but it's pointless. Turning to the table that was full of my friends earlier, I find it empty now.

"I told them to leave. That it was pack business and they weren't welcome." Janie's face twists, hating the lie she gave, but she's only trying to protect them, whether they see it that way or not.

"Thanks," I mumble, bracing my palms on the table as I take a few deep breaths.

"You might not be pack anymore, Cassian, but you will always be my family."

I tilt my head to look at my oldest friend, the big sister I never had and, for a big portion of time, never wanted. Yet she's the purest soul and strongest person I've ever had in my corner. Confiding in her has always been easy, and that won't ever change.

"Seeing all of this makes me wonder if leaving was the best idea," I admit. It was the first thought to enter my mind when my father declared the woman at his feet to be Queen Reagan, while staring triumphantly at her daughter.

"Why, because you want this dark kind of power like your father?" Janie asks, surprise lilting her voice as I shake my head.

"No, because it's harder to put a stop to it from the outside."

She hums in understanding, her hand finding its way

to my arm again as she squeezes in comfort. "It seems it's been happening behind all of our backs for a long time, Cass. If anything, you might be our only savior."

I scoff, but the softness of her words leaves me a little breathless. She believes it to be the truth, yet I'm filled with more doubt than ever.

"I need to get out of here."

"Go. Think. Check on your girl," she rambles, pulling me in for a half-hug that I don't have time to reciprocate before she takes a step back.

"My girl? That's not my girl, that's a fucking princess," I grunt, and she shrugs like the weight of that sentence doesn't matter all that much.

"She's always looked more like a warrior to me."

I stand with my jaw slack, staring at the empty spot she had occupied moments ago as she takes off toward Jake, who is standing by the tree line. She can't just say shit like that and disappear into the night.

Addi.

My alpha.

She has been worming her way under my skin, yet the lies, the deceit, it's all there. I can't even begin to consider how I feel about it all, but I'm not going to figure any of that out here.

Shifting into my wolf, I take off. He's eager to go in search of my father, but relents on heading back to the academy.

We're back on campus quicker than I'd hoped, and I shift back into my human form at the fountain. I take a moment to stare down each path, leading to a different origin building. I start at the fae path first, but the anger that radiates through me has me taking a step back.

I have to trust in my gut that Raiden hasn't hurt her while I consider whether I care or not.

My cell phone vibrates in my pocket, pulling me from my indecision. Suddenly I hate the fact that I shift back into a human fully clothed and with all my belongings. To shred it all and leave it all behind would have been an excellent excuse to not look.

Raiden:

Meeting. My room. NOW.

It's directly to me and not in the group chat, which tells me the others are already there. If he has Addi with him, I'll be at a complete loss as to my feelings, and I need time to figure them out for myself first. She might intrigue me, but right now I can't see through the fog of information tainting my vision.

I'm not in the mood for any kind of meeting right now. They can discuss whatever it is between the three of them and I'll wade in with my thoughts tomorrow.

Marching down the pathway that leads to the wolf building, I continue to glance out of the corner of my eye at the vampire building that stands even taller than ours, but every thought that makes me consider heading over there is rebutted with another that tells me I'm doing the right thing.

As I approach the front door, I know I've made the right decision, and as my hand wraps around the handle, I sigh with relief until a whooshing sound echoes from my left, signaling movement, but before I can take action, a sack is shoved over my head and everything goes dark.

THE REIGN OF BLOOD

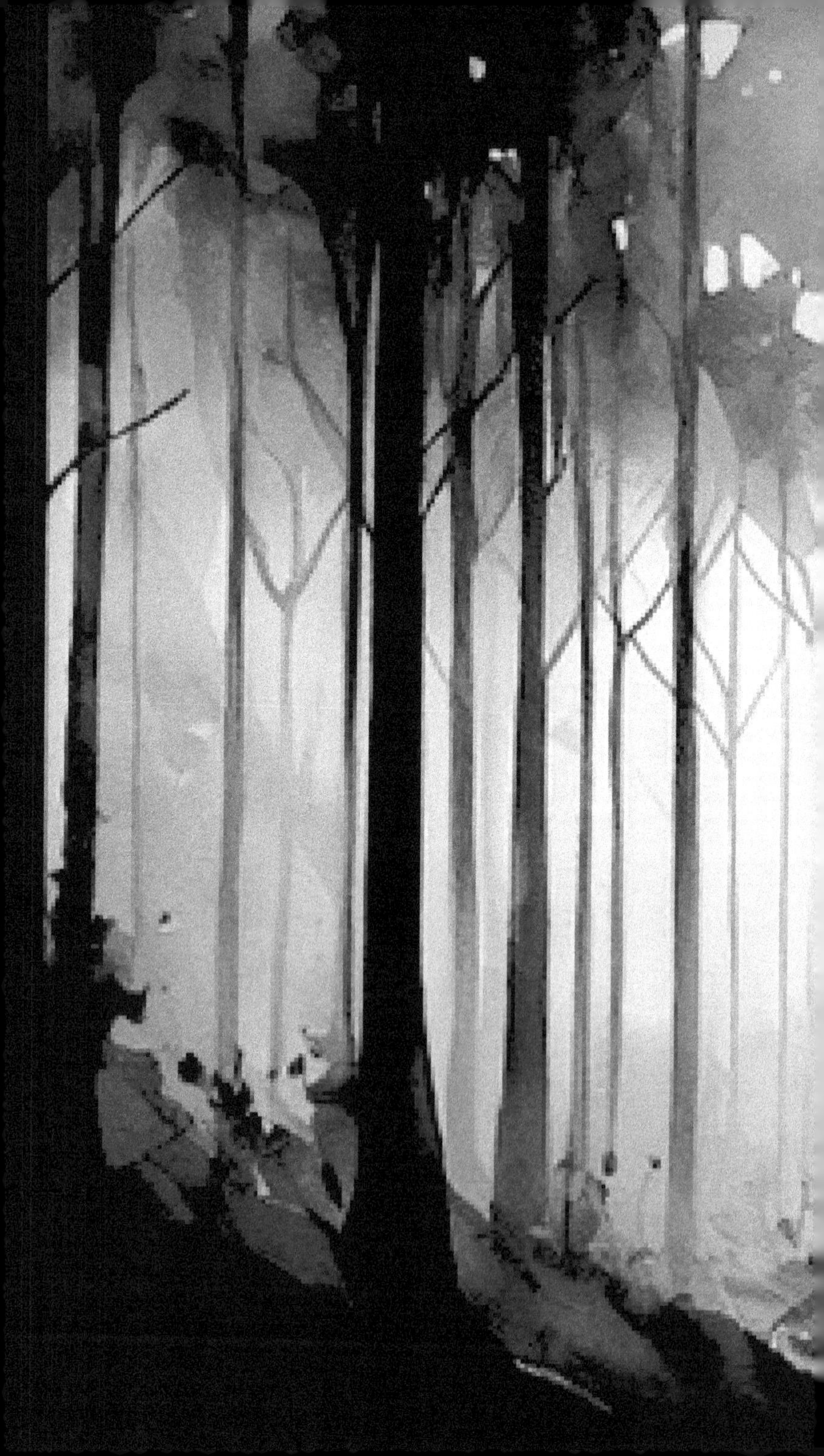

RAIDEN

4

I stare down at the filled seat, disgruntled by the efforts we have to go to, but it's really no surprise, not when it comes down to it. Which is exactly why we were waiting in place. It doesn't stop the irritation from coiling through me, though.

Fucker.

Not willing to waste any more time, I whip the sack off Cassian's head and glare down at him.

Brody takes the signal, and his chants no longer fill the room as he releases his magical hold on the wolf.

"Was any of that actually necessary?" Cassian grunts, his hands balling in his lap, but he doesn't make to get up even though he can move at will now.

Cocking a brow at him, I push back with a question of my own. "Were you making your way over here like my message said?"

His eyes narrow. "I think you know the answer to that."

"Then it was necessary," I explain with a shrug, which makes him scoff.

"To get what *you* want?" he retorts, the bite clear in his tone.

I wave my hands out at either side, pointing toward Kryll to my left and Brody off to the right.

"To get what we *all* want."

His head twists, slowly peering around the room for the first time. He knows where he is. He's been in my room enough times, and the two men present are our closest friends, so when he continues to search, I instantly understand what he's hoping to set his eyes on.

"She's not here."

"What did you do to her?" His eyes darken as his jaw tics, his irritation rising to the surface as I grin.

"Ah, so you *do* care." I know I'm goading him, and I know it's working.

"What. Did. You. Do?"

Sometimes it's too fun. "Nothing," I admit, and he rears his head back in confusion.

"Nothing?"

"What did you want me to do to her?" I push with a pointed look, and he bares his teeth.

"You're the one who took her." He's right about that

part. I can give him that, but he doesn't need to know my motives. Yet. When all I offer him is a shrug, he sighs. "Why did you do that?"

"Do what?"

"Take her."

"Why not?" I shrug again, annoying him even more, but before he can try and chew my ear off, I redirect the conversation back to the point of this gathering. "You're the one in the hot seat, Cass. You're the one supposed to be answering questions here, not me."

His eyebrows furrow in confusion. "About what?"

"Dumb doesn't suit you, wolf."

Brody clears his throat, garnering Cassian's attention while I continue to stare at him. "He's referring to everything that just happened on the Kenner compound, Cass." His words are soft, but the confusion is still prominent.

One of us has to be the mediator; it's only fitting it's the mage that regularly helps us navigate our conflicts.

Cassian wipes a hand down his face, clearly trying to piece together a response. "I was heading home to give myself a minute to wrap my head around it all. So, I don't know what you want me to give you right now when I have no clue myself."

It makes sense, but this is also Cass. He can't hide away for days when we have things we need to discuss right now.

Kryll takes a seat on the coffee table, offering a soft yet tight smile to his friend. "I'm going to assume you didn't know about Queen Reagan."

There it is. The elephant in the room. The surprise that knocked us all off our feet and has us not thinking clearly.

"You would assume right," Cass bites back in response, his jaw ticking, and my eyes narrow.

"What did your father say?" He said something. I can see it in his eyes, and honesty is the only way forward.

He runs a hand through his hair as he subtly shakes his head. "He talked in circles. Even after openly admitting what he did to Addi, he—"

"Adrianna," I interject, immediately feeling three sets of eyes swing my way.

"What?"

"She's royal. Her name is Adrianna, and that's how she should be addressed."

"I'll call her whatever the fuck I want," Cass snaps, and I shake my head in distaste.

"Your kingdom protocol is lacking."

His eyebrows knit together in confusion. "My kingdom, what?"

I hold my hands up in disbelief. "You're such a wolf." The grumble falls effortlessly from my lips.

"Can we get back to the point?" he grunts in response, eyes wide, but his pupils are dilated.

"Fine, you were talking about Adrianna," I prompt, making him heave a heavy sigh.

"He openly admitted to attacking *Addi* but declined to admit if he was a part of the kingdom's demise. He also advised me that his control over the queen is entirely why The Council never gives him any pushback."

"They know," Kryll breathes, looking at Brody, and I follow his line of sight. His father sits on The Council. Does that mean *he* knew?

Fuck. This is getting messy, and I'm certain it's only just begun.

"So he says," Cass confirms, and I can't deny that a piece of me sees the sense and logic behind it. His father gets away with far too much shit for him not to have something over the governing body of our kingdom.

"Anything else?" I ask, but the defeat that radiates from him confirms his answer before he even speaks.

"Nothing."

I know he's telling the truth, but I can't help but push. Maybe it's because I'm getting tired, or maybe it's because of all the revelations Kenner unraveled tonight. "Do I need to check if you're lying?"

As predicted, Cassian rears back like I've punched him in the face. "You've never had to question my loyalty before. Why now?"

"Because your father—"

"Is no extension of me, just as each of your bloodlines are not extensions of you. That's what we committed to one another when we made this pact. Is that changing?"

"No."

He searches my eyes for a moment before rising to his feet. "Good. Now, where is she?"

I should have known he would want that piece of information sooner rather than later. "In her room."

"Her room? You let her go?"

It's my turn to frown at him in confusion this time. "Why wouldn't I?"

"She lied," he snarls, and I roll my eyes at his dramatics.

"And that means we should keep her captive?" I clarify, watching as he peers at Kryll and Brody for backup but comes up empty-handed.

"I don't know. Maybe."

Taking a step toward him, I try to push down the disappointment threatening to rise within me. "I took her from the compound because I could see it in your father's eyes."

"What?"

"Your look is the same now. He wanted to keep her, too." His gaze narrows on me, but he doesn't deny it. Instead, he curses under his breath. "Maybe the apple doesn't always fall far from the tree."

"Fuck off, Raiden. She lied," he bites, but I see the hurt

in his eyes from my words. Not because I said them, but because they could be true.

"Technically, she omitted," Brody interjects, and I have to bite back the grin from my face.

"And why the fuck would she tell us anyway?" Kryll pipes in, fueling the anger emitting from the wolf.

"Because we have a right to know."

"Do we? All we've done is wreak havoc on her life," Brody pushes back.

Kryll holds his hands up. "I haven't." Silence descends over us because the same can't be said for the rest of us. "What do we do with this little snippet of information then?"

"We dangle it over her head until we learn everything there is to know," I reply with a shrug. I might not want to hold her captive, but I still want the information. Color me intrigued.

"We won't have long then," Cassian murmurs, wiping a hand down his face.

"Why?"

"Something tells me my father will use the confirmation of who she is to his advantage." That's true. That's truer than true.

"This isn't his territory," Brody states, which is also true.

"Nothing is ever his territory, remember?" There's

a sass to my voice as I take a swipe at Cassian, but the fact still remains: his reach is greater than most. Sighing, I consider what I learned from her already. Which really isn't much. "She wouldn't tell me anything about her sister that Kenner mentioned, but before I let her go, she told me about her ears."

"And?" Kryll nudges.

"It happened the night they escaped the castle." Cassian's hands ball into fists as a solemn reality washes over us. "How does that make you feel?" I ask him, intrigued to see the truth.

"Mad as fuck that I was blindsided."

But not mad as fuck that it happened. Should I read into that? Something about it pisses me off, and once again, I find myself making uncalculated moves.

"Now imagine how she feels," I rasp, making the others frown at me.

"What's that supposed to mean?" Cassian grunts, and I shake my head.

"You're such a fucking wolf."

"Spit it out."

Cocking a brow at him, I sneer. I don't know whether I'm simply intent on hurting him today or if it's merely a coincidence.

"Do you really think she's going to go anywhere near you now? She's been fucking you. The son of the man who hurt her."

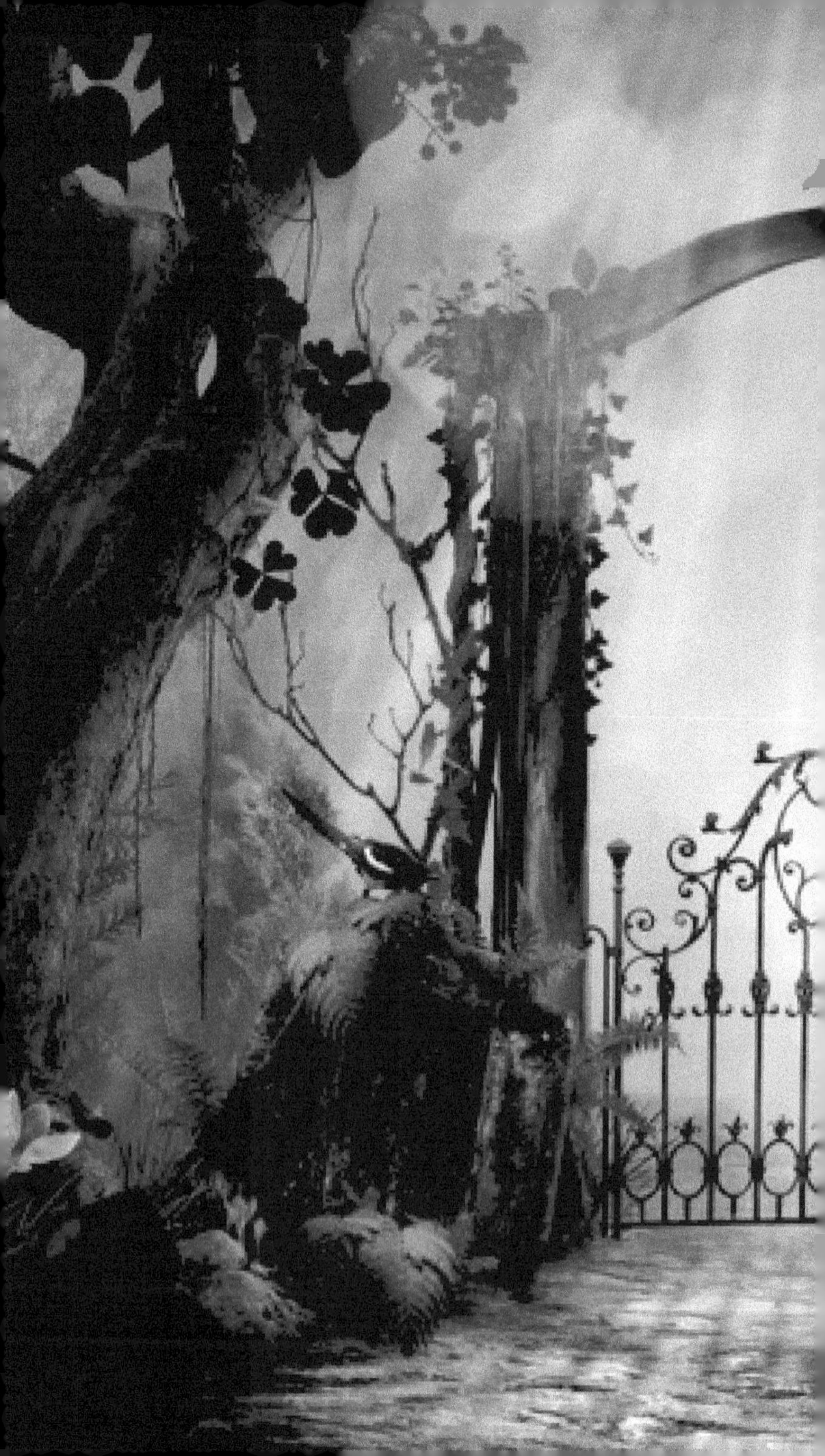

ADRIANNA

5

Darkness sweeps around us, my heart racing in my chest as I try to breathe past another hiccup.

I'm scared. So scared, but Daddy's hand wrapped around mine promises me he's right there.

"Come, Addi. Keep a hold of Nora's hand, too. We must hurry," Daddy whispers in a worried voice that I don't really recognize. He's always so calm and collected; this is nothing like him at all.

My dress is heavy, weighing me down, and I can see Nora is struggling too, her little fingers tangled with mine as our father drags us down the darkening corridors. I know every inch of our home. I could walk it with my eyes closed and come out unharmed, which is why my tummy twists with worry when we take the right corridor.

"Daddy," I breathe, the panic evident to my own ears

too.

He glances over his shoulder with a sad smile on his face. "It's going to be okay, my love. It's all going to be okay."

Something about my vision is grainy, my eyes struggling as the castle grows darker. I know how many steps to take in the right direction, the issue is, I really don't want to be here.

My father comes to a stop at the hidden doorway that leads to the secret passage. It's my least favorite. I've taken it only once, leaving my parents panicked, but I vowed never to do it again when I reached the other side. It's scary out there.

"Daddy," I murmur again, my bottom lip wobbling with worry as I look up at him.

His free hand rests on the access point while he squeezes my fingers firmly with his other. "Addi, I promise you, everything is going to be okay, but we're no longer safe here, and keeping you and Nora safe is my number one priority. Always."

I stare deep into his eyes, the blue pools brewing with unspoken words, and despite the fear that continues to cling to me like a second skin, I nod. His crown glistens in the darkness, his clothes dirty and stained red. I don't understand what's going on, but I trust him with my whole heart.

Shouts ring out from behind us, echoing through the halls, and Nora cries out in panic.

"Mama!"

I feel my father's hand slip as he releases me to console Nora. "She'll come soon, my love. Soon."

Frowning, I tilt my head at him. He said it the same way he always says things that aren't true. He's been teaching me how to tell a lie. That was one right there. I open my mouth, ready to point it out, when a deathly snarl looms around the corner.

"Quickly, girls, quickly!" he orders, opening the latch and edging us through the passageway.

It's pitch black in here. The uneven floor makes it difficult to take each step as the feeling of cobwebs brushes against my arms. My tummy turns as I bite back a sob. A glimmer from the moonlight peers through the opening at the other end of the passageway, and as much as I fear it, I fear the snarl of the creature just as much.

Holding on tightly to Nora's hand, I stay at the front, leading the way, while my father holds up the rear to make sure no one is following us. Pressing my foot onto the open ledge, I steal my breath as panic tightens in my chest again.

The choppy water laps at the rocks below, beckoning us to take the leap and feel the fall. Nora tugs at my hand, clawing with her free hand at my wrist to release her, but if she thinks my hold is too painful, she has no idea what could happen if she falls.

Keeping to the edge, I take a deep breath, pressing my back against the wall behind us. Nora follows suit, but her fighting against me doesn't stop.

"Daddy," I call out, my words far quieter than I would like, but he manages to hear me over the howling wind. He doesn't respond; he simply signals for me to take the steep slope to my right.

I'm cautious and careful, taking one step at a time. Although I'm probably going too slow for Daddy's liking, he doesn't rush or hurry me. Hope blossoms in my chest as I see the ridge of the meadow at the top of the incline, safety steering us closer.

"Let go of Nora's hand, Addi. Then I will lift her up to you, okay?"

I peer at my father before dropping my gaze to where Nora's hand rests in mine. My gut tells me not to let go, to keep her at my side and protect her at all costs, but despite my protectiveness, there's no way we will get up into the meadow otherwise.

Nora sniffles, her eyes puffy, tired, and full of tears. My nose twitches with a burn that I know means I'm going to cry too, but I can't. Not yet. I have to keep it together for her. Lifting her small hand to my lips, I press a little kiss to her knuckles, and the corner of her mouth tips up. She does the same, as we always do. I take another deep breath and release her hand.

I don't want to waste a single moment, so I turn for the ledge and curl my fingers into the top, using the exposed tree roots to push up as fast as I can. The second I'm perched on the edge of the meadow, relief flooding my body, I turn and outstretch my arms, ready to help Nora.

Daddy does most of the work, lifting her up high, but I still wrap my little arms around her waist and pull tightly. So tightly that we stumble backward in a heap, a giggling pile of mischief as we forget our circumstances for just a moment.

Her big blue eyes shine under the moonlight. She is my sister, my best friend, my everything. If we just lay here like this, then all of the darkness will go away.

As if hearing my thoughts, Daddy appears a moment later, hovering over us with his hands planted on his knees as he glances around the open space. A curse breaks past his lips, and even in the thick of night, with only the moon to guide us, I watch as the color drains from his face. His eyes latch on to mine as he reaches his hands out to cup both of our faces.

"Run, hide, I'll find you," he whispers, a solo tear tracking down his face. "I love you," he adds. Before we can even offer a response, he takes off.

Frowning, I roll in the grass so I can lift to my knees and get a good view of what he's doing, but when my eyes latch on to the glint of my father's crown, horror claims me.

There are wolves, and wolves, and wolves. Every color, every size, and all with their snarls snapping at my father. My father who is charging toward them.

The ground beneath us rumbles as he connects with his magic, and the air around us whips tighter and harsher. Nora moves beside me and I clutch her to my chest. She hasn't had any magic training yet, it's supposed to start in two weeks, so she's going to need me to guide her.

Father said to run and hide; that's what we have to do.

With my arms around Nora, I take tiptoe steps toward the outer tree line, away from the castle. Grunts and howls echo in the distance, but I refuse to look. My focus is protecting Nora, and Daddy's magic is making it almost impossible to move with the wind going crazy around us.

The tree line slowly gets closer, my heart racing in my chest, and just when I'm certain I've completed my task, a snarl rumbles through the night, but this one is much closer than the others. My eyelids fall closed as panic clutches at my chest.

I tilt my head to the left to find a jet-black wolf with storming hazel eyes and deathly white teeth inching closer. He prowls toward us, his intention clear as he licks along his pearly whites and narrows his eyes.

Clutching at my own magic, I whisper into the wind

and direct the little bubble of knowledge directly to my sister without concern that the wolf will hear. I don't look at her, and I don't wait for confirmation. We've talked like this many times before; it has to work in this moment, too.

My tummy twists, a sickly burn making its way up my throat, but I fight against it and release Nora's hand. She takes off running, her feet padding along the grass in time with my thudding pulse in my ears. I'm so focused on her escape that I don't react quickly enough when a giant paw comes flying toward me.

A scream threatens my lips, but it's lodged in place as I'm pinned to the ground.

I can't breathe with the weight of the paw against my neck. I can't see with the tears quickly flooding my vision. I can't do anything but lie frozen in shock and fear. The glint of a claw on the wolf's free paw shines under the moon, looming over me, before I feel excruciating pain consume my left ear, then my right. Despite the claws framing my throat, an almighty scream of terror burns from my lips.

It's too much.

It's all just too much.

I'm certain the wolf is going to carve away at me until there's nothing left, but something seems to distract them. He's gone a second later, leaving me to curl into a ball, shielding myself from the high winds and pain consuming every ounce of me. The sobs rack my body, taking everything from me no matter how hard I try to wish it all away.

A scream fills my ears and I frown for a second, certain it's not from my own lips. My heart stops, realization dawning over me as I fight past my own pain in search of the source.

Nora.

Scrambling to my feet, I blink a few times, clearing my vision to find the same wolf who hurt me looming over her, too.

Her legs are...

She screams again, the anguish thick, and despite my need to ease my own sorrows, I push my feet into the ground beneath me, letting my magic whip through my body, but when the time comes to harness it like Daddy always tells me, I don't. I let it consume me, I let it take everything I am to protect my best friend, my sister, my everything.

My body stiffens as the air, earth, water, and fire magic warring inside of me tries to get out. They create a bright light from my palms as it illuminates the sky and stops the awful wails coming from Nora.

As quickly as the bright sky appears, it dissolves into darkness once more. My eyes land on Nora first, finding her cowering alone in the grass. My jaw tightens and my nostrils flare as I turn in search of my father.

There's no wolf in sight.

Not as I take a relieved breath.

Not as Nora's sobs slowly return.

Not as I watch my father's golden crown fall to the ground.

Swaying, I mutter my three favorite words into the wind for Nora. "I love you."

The world shifts beneath my feet and the darkness seeps in.

I jolt awake, my ears burning and my throat tight. I'm not sure if it's from the memory or the fact that I may have been crying out. Sitting up, I lean back against the headboard before wiping a hand down my face. Tears stain my hands and cheeks as my heart continues to hammer in my chest, leaving me breathless.

Pain consumes me as it does every time I have the unfortunate pleasure of reliving that nightmare. It doesn't matter if I gave Raiden a condensed version; the facts aren't his concern. My nightmares still have a way of reminding me, it seems.

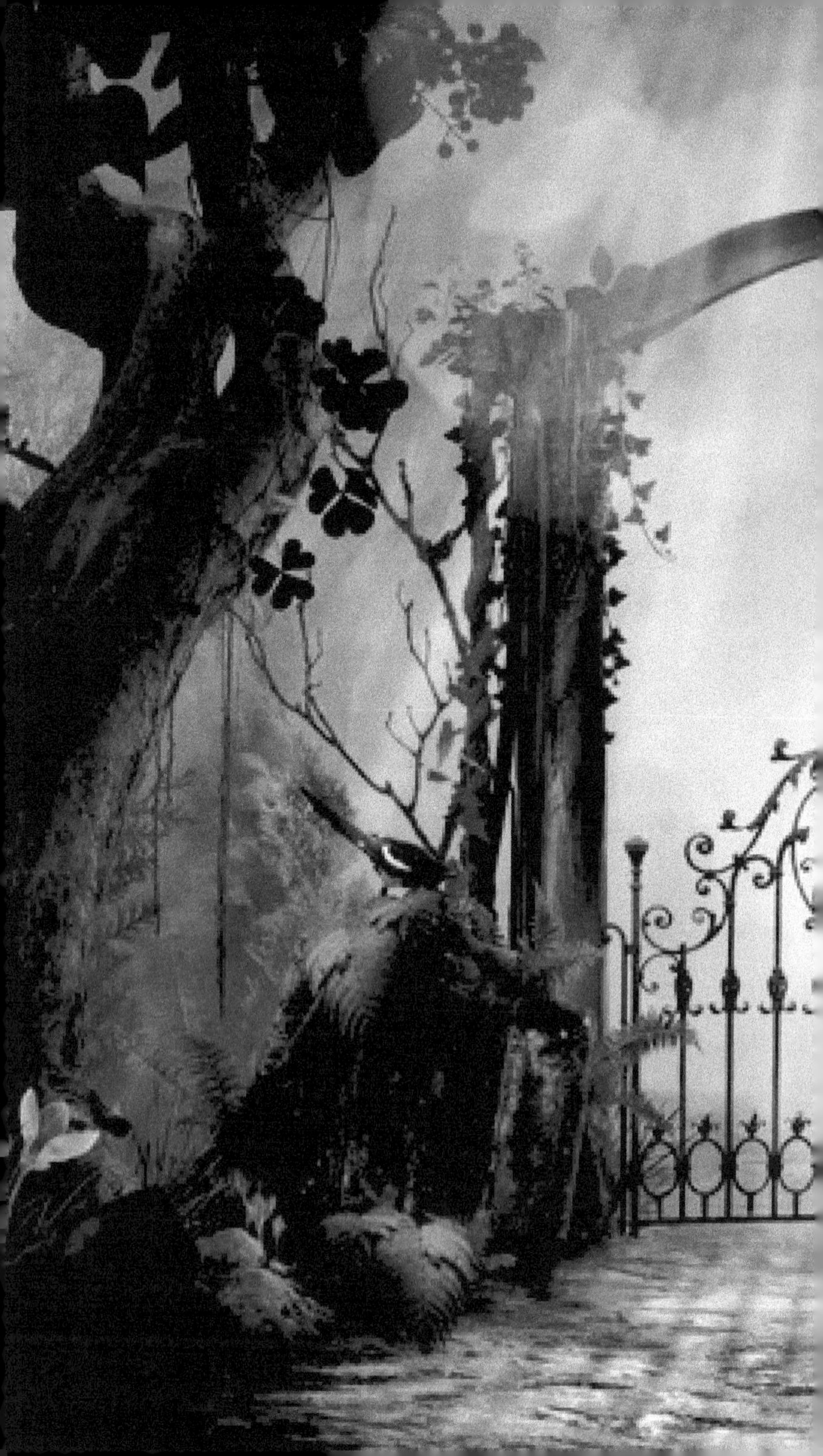

ADRIANNA

6

The steaming hot water pounds down on me from the shower, washing away the lingering pain and heartache as my chest refuses to ease. Tilting my head back, I embrace the droplets, giving myself a moment to let the tears mingle with the water so the truth of my pain goes unnoticed.

I'm accustomed to hiding my emotions like this. My penchant for being ruthless, brutal, and unwavering is harder to cling to than I care to admit. Sometimes, my deeper emotions get the better of me, and I refuse to share them with the world.

They're for me and me alone.

I don't think it helps that last night was such chaos, and the nightmare on top of all that only cripples the horrors that I bury deep inside. They haunt me at night when my barriers are weakened, and my feelings always end up visible through the cracks. Otherwise, they're tucked away in the far corners of my mind where I prefer them to be.

Counting down from ten, I let it all out.

Ten.

Nine.

Eight.

Muted screams.

Seven.

Six.

Silent sobs.

Five.

Four.

Three.

Two.

Pent-up anger that will forever fuel me.

One.

I lean back, wipe the water away from my face once more, and focus on washing my hair. It's done with now. I don't have any more time to waste on it. Festering in the dismay will only distract me, and I think I've allowed that to happen far too much since arriving here.

Rinsing out my hair, I turn my attention to my body and run through the mundane task of cleaning away the rest of the grime that still clings to me.

It's Saturday. I have the whole weekend to survive now

without any classes to distract me, and I don't know how I'm going to make it through. I know I need to process everything that happened yesterday, especially since I flopped on my bed last night and effectively passed out. I need to analyze it all, whether I like it or not, but I can't do it here.

Switching off the water, I swiftly dry myself off and get dressed. A plain black t-shirt and matching yoga pants. Blacker than black to match my mood and my heart.

The hallway is empty when I step out and shuffle down to my room, leaning back against the door as I close it. My bed terrorizes me, a reminder of the state I woke up in earlier. I need to avoid it at all costs. The desk doesn't look much more inviting either.

I sigh, knowing what I need to do. As much as these four walls are the safest place for me right now, I can't stay cooped up. That only makes things worse. Using my magic, I connect with the air around me and effortlessly dry my hair. It loops into a braid, pinned to my head before a few loose tendrils frame my face.

Despite my distress, the warmth that travels through my veins makes me smile—just a little. When I first used magic on campus, I channeled the earth, making everyone believe I was an earth fae. Fear constricted my throat and left me tangled in the lie, so I couldn't bring myself to dare use any of my other abilities.

Until last night.

Raiden. I can still see him sailing across the room with surprise etched into his features before he berated me.

People know. They know my bloodline, my true origin, and I don't know how long my secret will last, so there's no point worrying over small things now. Braiding my hair by hand was becoming a task, so I'll take this small favor. Not only is this easier, but my magic vibrates inside of me, relieved to be let out.

With that in mind, I roll my shoulders back and shake off the worry that continues to cling to me before I head for the door. I need to run, I need the fresh air, and I need to think.

Swinging my bedroom door open, I startle when something falls from the handle. My defenses rise, my heart hammering in my chest, but it's all for nothing when I see what it is.

A rose.

A single blood-red rose.

I frown down at it for what feels like an eternity before I peer down the hallway. There's no one there, just the flower. Wetting my lips, I crouch down and loosely hold the stem. When nothing jumps out, I take a step back and close my bedroom door.

Admiring its beauty, I also can't help but stare at its prettiness, but still… nothing happens. Why would someone leave it there? *Who* would even leave it there?

I don't need to be worrying about this on top of everything else.

Placing it on my desk, I head back for the door, my initial intent still set on getting out. I rush out into the hallway and let the door fall shut behind me before hurrying down the stairs.

Arlo is sprawled across the communal sofa, fast asleep, but there's no Flora in sight, so I step outside and take a deep breath. As I exhale, I focus on relieving all of my stress along with it.

While I'm out here, I need to think about everything that's happened and attempt to process it all. Once I step back inside, I will focus on my plan. Just like my emotions in the shower, I can't allow myself to be weighed down by all of this. Not when there's so much at stake. I have a legacy to uphold, a crown to win, and a kingdom's future to solidify.

Tilting my head up to the sun, I let the rays warm me from head to toe, and my eyelids fall to half-mast as I let the weight of the world fall from my shoulders.

With my mind made up, I start toward the main fountain that connects all of the origin pathways, stretching out my muscles as I go because once I get there, I'm sprinting until my lungs burn and my body can't take it anymore.

Determination and adrenaline come to life inside me,

adding an extra bounce to my step as my focus sharpens. Which is everything I want and need until I stumble, head still tilted and gaze not set straight ahead, falling into the arms of a mage. Not just any mage. *The* mage.

Brody.

THE REIGN OF BLOOD

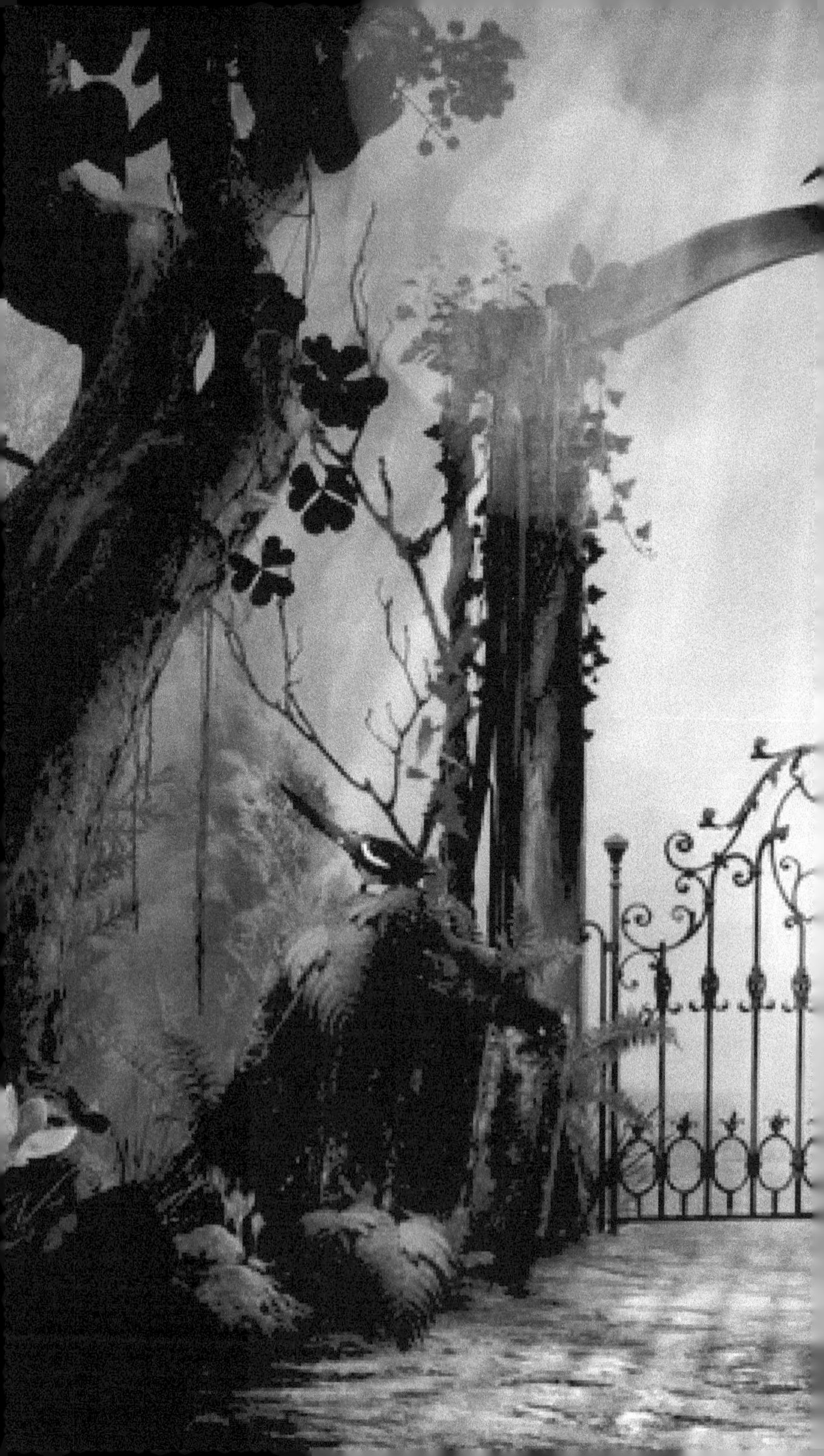

ADRIANNA

7

His fingers wrap around my upper arm, denying me the embarrassing fall that was likely coming. It would have been mortifying, but at least it would have put some space between us. Deep-blue inquisitive eyes search mine as we stare at one another before I come to my senses and try to take a step back.

His eyes narrow, but his hold relents, and I take a larger-than-necessary step back.

"Hey, I was hoping to find you," he breathes, tipping the corner of his mouth up, and I shake my head.

"I can't say the same," I mutter, not waiting around as I start down the path away from the fae building. I sense him hot on my tail, and as he goes to grab my arm again, I turn my deathly glare his way.

"Hey," he protests, lifting his hand away quickly,

raising it in surrender. It takes a few moments for calmness to settle back over me and for the anger burning in my eyes to dissolve.

I'm acutely aware that he's not technically the target of my pent-up emotions, but he has a connection to it all and that seems to be enough to put him in the line of fire. "Go away, Brody."

He pouts like a toddler preparing for an almighty tantrum. "But I come in peace."

In peace? He doesn't know the meaning of the word. Why is he even out here?

Wait…

"Was the rose from you?" I blurt, folding my arms over my chest as I narrow my eyes at him.

His head rears back, his brows knitting together as he subtly shakes his head. "Rose?"

It definitely wasn't him. He'd be boasting about it if it was.

"Nevermind," I grumble, turning away from him before setting off on my run.

Despite his close proximity and my desire to put distance between us, I keep to a jogging pace, not wanting to injure myself when I don't know what awaits me behind any turn. Between the up-and-coming challenges from the academy and whatever else Kenner may throw my way, I need to be alert. Losing my shit over some guy being near me while I'm out for a run is a waste of stress and energy. Especially if he's not actually causing me any harm.

Which he isn't…yet.

Deep down, I know I'm not really surprised when he falls into step with me. His footsteps are in sync with mine as we keep pace, our arms moving at our sides, but to my shock, his mouth remains shut.

Peering at him from the corner of my eye, I consider his threat levels and come up blank. As we round the fountain focal point and head off toward the outer perimeter, I can't help but break the silence.

"I don't need company, Brody." He doesn't respond, which makes me frown, forcing me to turn and look at him. He offers me a full-blown smile and a wink, getting under my skin in a way only he seems to be able to. "What?" He presses his finger to his lips, making my eyes narrow further. "You're giving me a headache."

"I haven't said a word," he blurts, gaping at me.

"Exactly," I grumble, shaking my head to try and rid the growing tension.

He's persistent and slightly annoying, but if I pretend he's not there, it will all be fine. With my mind made up, I take a deep breath and focus on my rhythm. He remains silently at my side as we cover the grounds of the academy, and I manage to run without him being a distraction.

As we round the bend and the forest comes into view,

I feel somewhat lighter and a little less stressed as the world brightens up around me. Out here, with nature, I can sometimes find more perspective, and now that my mind is clearing, I can focus on everything that's happened in the past twenty-four hours. My only issue is figuring out where to even begin with it all.

Our pace naturally slows as we move between the trees, the familiar fallen log reminding me of the memories I already have out here, even though we haven't been on campus very long. As we near the spot where my jogging companion fucked me, he comes to a stop altogether. Much to my irritation, I slow beside him.

I'm a sucker.

A true fucking sucker.

He turns to me, his hands firmly on his hips, as his head tilts ever so slightly to the side. "Last night was a lot, even for me as a spectator. I can't imagine how it was for you in comparison, and I guess I just don't like the idea of you being alone right now."

I frown at him as he waves a hand between us, attempting to explain why he's running with me. "I can handle myself just fine." It's all I can muster. I'm the one who takes care of others, not the other way around, and I can't say I feel comfortable with it.

"I'm not doubting it."

Now that we've come to a complete stop, the familiar

ache runs over my limbs, so I stretch my arms and legs as I work on my breathing, hoping we can fall back into comfortable silence since he's made it clear he's not leaving.

Any hopes I had are shattered as he takes a step toward me. "What was the hardest part?"

My heart flutters, just once, as my chest clenches. That's some deep shit right there. I don't know if I want to even venture into that territory by myself, let alone in a conversation with someone else.

"Of what?"

My attempt at playing dumb falls flat when he cocks a brow at me. "Of last night."

I shake my head despite two initial thoughts coming to mind. One thing I know for certain is Cassian had no idea.

Not. A. Single. One.

The hold he had on my waist was laced with panic, uncertainty, and distress. He was as much in the dark as I was.

Learning who I am is no surprise to me, and I knew it would happen one day, so as much as my secret is out there in some capacity, it doesn't scare me as much as other things do.

The two things it comes down to are threaded with so much horror and uncertainty, I don't know where to begin.

My mother and Kenner.

Simple words, yet they carry so much weight. My nightmare is just the tip of the iceberg.

"I can sense your mind going a mile a minute, but you're not sharing," Brody murmurs, breaking my train of thought.

I clear my throat, looking off into the distance for a second before turning back to him. "Just because you're asking questions doesn't mean I have to answer them."

Disappointment flickers in his blue eyes with a hint of sadness. My mind comes alive, my magic fluttering between us despite my better judgment, revealing the genuine feelings behind his questions and actions.

Fuck.

Quickly pulling my magic in, I sigh. "I think you learned some things about me last night that should explain why I'm not into this whole talking shit," I state, and he offers me a weak smile.

Without a word, he saunters over to the fallen tree, getting comfortable in the center of it with his elbows braced on his thighs. "For sure. I mean, you're… you." He waves a hand at me, and I know without a shadow of a doubt he was about to say something with the word *princess* in it. Yet he didn't. "I can't imagine what it's like having to hold everything so close to your chest." He shakes his head, his eyes drifting off as if he's truly contemplating it.

What the fuck is going on right now?

Before I can think better of it, I inch closer, dropping down on the log beside him as I stare off into the distance. His words fill the air around us a beat later.

"My father is on The Council. Trusting people is difficult for me. That's why I stick to the guys and don't really tolerate anyone else, because their intentions are always unclear." I try to imagine what that's like. If the kingdom didn't fall and everyone knew who I was, what would my friends be like? Would I have any? Or would it still be just Nora and me?

I huff at the thought. If it were up to my sister, she would force me to be so sociable my eyeballs would bleed. But deep down, I know in my core I would have the same regard for outsiders. The issue is that I've spent the past sixteen years *being* the outsider, happily enjoying my place, and now, everything is shifting.

It comes with being at the academy. I guess I knew that, but acknowledging the fact now that I'm at the center of it all feels different. I truly have lived a different life than what my birthright declared, and reclaiming it isn't going to be so easy when it changes every fiber of my being.

My mind races with thoughts and feelings, just as it did in the shower, but thankfully, there's no threat of tears springing to my eyes this time. Now, it's with the burning desire to get them off my chest. I can't talk to Nora about it, not when I'm trying to shield her from everything.

Maybe Flora?

"It's okay, Adrianna. I get it. I'm highly aware that I promised to fuck you and be gone, yet here I am, like a puppy desperate for more of your attention. I can't even begin to explain it myself." He wipes a hand down his face, but I'm left gaping at him.

"What did you call me?"

His eyebrows furrow. "Adrianna?"

"Why?"

He gulps nervously before sweeping his tongue over his bottom lip. "Because Raiden said you're of… because you are who you are, and you should be addressed as such."

I frown at him for a split second before I laugh, truly laugh. I cover my mouth to no avail as I try to calm myself down. I don't know what it is, but when I turn to look at him, seeing the uncertainty in his eyes, I manage to soften just a little.

"I'm sorry, I just… please just call me Addi because that's so unnecessary it makes me cringe."

"But—"

"Your dick was inside me before you knew anything, Brody, and you literally just said yourself about how people treat you differently because of your birthright. Are you going to do that to me?" It's my turn to offer a pointed look, and he shakes his head.

"No, that's what I'm trying to say—"

"But your actions aren't quite meeting with your words."

Silence descends over us as guilt creeps over his features. He's right, it is strange. The guy sitting beside me isn't the same person who took me to the diner on Kenner land two weeks ago. Technically, if I wanted to point fingers, I could blame him, but that just feels like an excuse.

He doesn't deserve a single thing from me, yet I feel a desire to say something, anything, about last night.

Staring off into the distance, I run my hands over my thighs and sigh. "The worst part about last night is the fact that my history is creeping up to haunt me in the most public way possible, and I don't know how to feel about it."

He clears his throat beside me. "Your mom or your attacker?"

"Both," I admit with another heavy sigh.

She looked well, at least. Pulled along like a pet by that guy named Dalton, sure, but I'm certain she could have looked worse. I believe so, anyway. I haven't seen her for so long because she abandoned us—just like the stories said—so I can't be certain.

But *did* she abandon us? Knowing what I know now, could that be a lie too?

"Am I supposed to just go and save her now?" I blurt

before I can think better of it, a new weight on my shoulders that I'm unsure I can shake off.

"Is that what you want to do?"

I turn, blinking at him as I feel the question deep in my bones. My adrenaline kicks in and uncertainty wars inside me as I let the situation consume me.

"I don't know. It's taken everything in me to put myself on the path I'm on now. I've spent forever hating her, and as much of a surprise as it may be, that doesn't change overnight." The truth rolls from my lips, not burning my tongue like I expect it to.

"Then do what's right for you," he replies with a shrug, like it's really that simple.

But what about my father... Nora? My chest tightens at the thought of her with regard to our mother.

"It's not just about me. It's about my father, my family, my people, the entire kingdom," I rattle off, avoiding Nora's name, but it's like he's drawn to the fact as his eyes settle on mine.

"What did Kenner do to your sister?"

"It doesn't matter," I grunt, sharper than necessary, as I shake my head.

"Is she okay?"

"She's better than the rest of us," I answer honestly.

"You're a royal. Princess Adrianna Reagan of the Floodborn Kingdom. You can do what you want. You can make him pay, you can save your mother, you can do as you see fit and no one is going to challenge that."

My chest clenches as the title falls from his lips, but the belief that he thinks I can just do whatever I please is almost laughable.

"I am, but Addi sounds just as good, too. My title doesn't make me who I am, and it's never going to simply get me what I want."

He offers me a half smile. "I can agree to that, but there's so much more to you than what meets the eye, Dagger."

I bite back the desire to grin at his nickname for me. I'm sitting here letting him worm his way under my skin again when I vowed to put distance between us.

My brain is a wreck, my mind isn't focusing like I want it to, and the desire to run and hide from it all is embarrassingly overwhelming when I pledged to myself that I would destroy anything in my way.

"What's going through your head?"

There he goes, trying to get deeper again.

I shake my head, not wanting to share anymore. "So much that I just want to pretend it doesn't exist right now," I admit instead.

"You can only pretend for so long."

I turn to look at him. He's right. Pretending only lasts so long and gets you so far, but I could combine the need to do so with the other desire that runs through my veins. It's probably a bad idea, but not one I can see biting me in the ass, so I go with it.

Sitting tall, I turn to face him properly. "I know, but given the chance, I would give everything I am just to forget for five minutes. You could help me with that."

He shakes his head, denying my offer, and despite the sucker punch to the gut, my head tells me it's the right thing.

"I won't fuck you as a distraction, Dagger."

Sighing, I stand. I need some kind of distraction, despite how weak it makes me feel. Then, I need to refocus. "Thanks for that chat, Brody. I'll see you around."

I make it two steps.

Two. Fucking. Steps.

"But I'll fuck you because it's what we both want, Dagger. You just have to say the word."

THE REIGN OF BLOOD

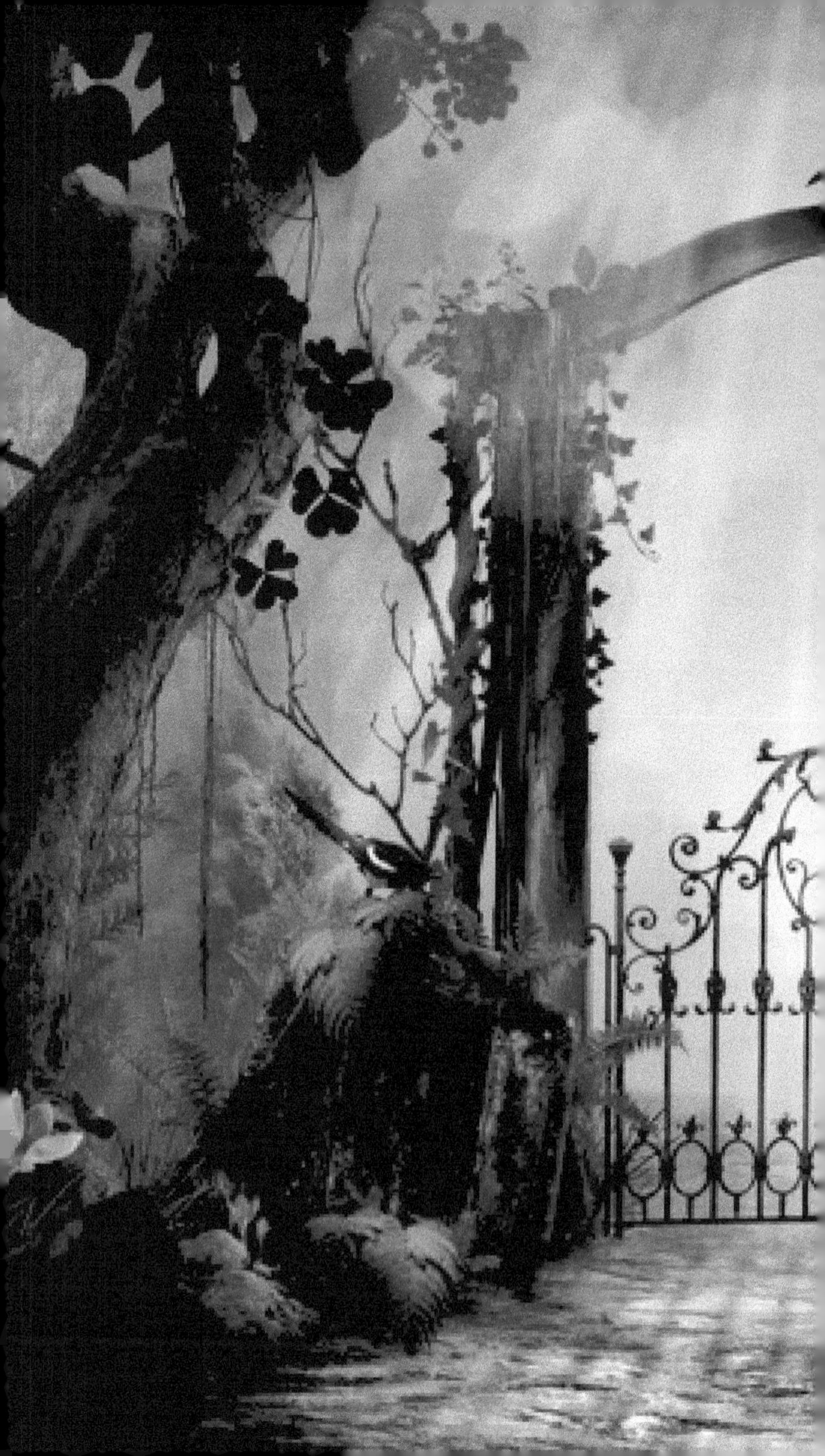

ADRIANNA

8

Just say the word.

Just. Say. The. Fucking. Word?

Who the fuck is this guy?

Irritation claws through me, and I can still sense his eyes along my skin as I get the fuck out of there. With a shake of my head, I back up, and take off in a sprint.

That's way too serious. I could hear it in his voice. If he said it in the carefree fun way he usually says everything else, I would have likely brushed it off and jumped on his dick, but that was far from the Brody I'm used to. My usual interactions with Brody are funny, but that was bordering on commitment, and I'm not here for that.

Shit, he had me talking about myself, which is far enough outside of my comfort zone as it is.

My muscles relax a little as I follow the path and

turn so I'm no longer visible from the forest, his gaze disappearing along with it. My ovaries are disappointed, but my head isn't.

Stupid fucking men with magic fucking dicks.

I keep my head high and my gaze locked ahead as I stomp down the path back toward the fae building. I pass a few people, but I pay them no mind as I have my sights set on my destination. I've got my hands full with last night's drama, the annoyingly hot guys that continue to appear in my way, and life itself. Not to mention the looming crown I refuse to allow anyone else to win.

I don't need to add any issues with anyone else along the way. Not when I've still got Vallie and the majority of the female wolves to contend with too.

Stepping through the front door, I spy Arlo still passed out on the sofa, but nobody else seems to be around. Heading straight upstairs, I exhale with relief when I reach my floor, but my steps falter as I near my door.

A rose.

Just as crimson as the other.

Balanced on my door handle.

What the fuck is going on?

Glancing around, I see nothing, hear nothing, and sense just as much.

"Who the fuck is this?" I call out, getting nothing in response as I grab the thorn-free stem and peer down at it.

"Stop being a weirdo and show your damn face," I push, my irritation growing, but I still get no reply.

Assholes.

It's annoying that the flower is so pretty, though. It calls to the earth magic inside of me, and the desire to nurture it takes over.

Stepping inside my room, I kick the door shut and place the flower beside the one I found this morning. It's a pity there's nothing to put them in.

I could probably steal a glass from the dining hall, or if I can get my hands on some sand, I could make something myself with my fire magic.

That's a thought for later, though. A distraction of a good kind when I may need it.

As much as I want to nurture the flowers, I need to take a minute and nurture myself, even if it's simply in a mental capacity. Life is sucking big giant monkey balls right now, and I really need to get my head on straight. It's one hurdle after another, and my body is feeling the ache.

I almost consider rushing back to Brody to let him fuck it out of me, but the reminder of his words has me standing firmly in place. I need a release, not another layer of madness to add to the pile.

The familiar sound of my cell phone vibrating on my nightstand makes me jolt and I whirl around to face it like it's sent from the devil himself. Apparently, I'm a little jittery this morning, which only serves to irritate me even more.

With a sigh, I cut the distance and retrieve the device, watching as my sister's name flashes across the screen.

I should have known. It wouldn't be anyone else, but how can I talk to her like this? After last night? Today? There's so much going on, and I'm not ready to tell her any of it.

But if I don't answer at all…

Shit.

Taking a deep breath, I muster the best smile I can, knowing full well she will be able to tell the difference if I don't.

"Hey." The word breezes past my lips effortlessly, and a rush of relief runs through me.

"Hey, how's your weekend going?"

"Boring," I lie, flopping down on the bed, and she scoffs.

"That's because you have no academy stuff to do. You need something to do outside of that, Addi. You need to live a little."

I roll my eyes even though she can't see. "I don't have time to live a little." Or, more specifically, every time I *do,* something goes drastically wrong. Like last night, for example, or my birthday, for another. Nothing good comes from veering off track.

"Video chat with me, Addi. I'm bored and I miss your face."

Dammit.

How does she have such an ability to wedge me between a rock and a hard place?

If I decline, she'll only push and know something is wrong. If she notes a single ounce of uncertainty on my face, she'll grill me until she pulls the truth from my lips. If it's going to go wrong, it's out of my hands, so I opt for the latter. If she does see right through me, at least we took the shortest journey to get to my demise.

Clicking the video chat button, I wait a few seconds until her face appears on my screen. My heart warms at the sight of her. I can't describe how much I miss her. Everything I do is always for her, even being here, but the distance between us makes it harder. If she were here, I wouldn't be dealing with all of this mess. I'd probably be dealing with more.

"Where's Dad?" I ask when I notice she's sitting in his brown leather armchair.

A look flashes in her eyes before she answers. "In the barn, fixing up my wheels."

Panic strikes through me and my eyes widen. "Why? What happened?" I rush, and she rolls her eyes at me.

"Quit worrying. It just broke on the way back from the market. See? I'm fine." She aims the cell phone farther away so I can see more than just her face.

Her feet are settled on the carpet, a blanket over her lap, and she's wearing one of my hoodies. She's such a menace. I don't call her out on it, though. I like that there's a piece of me there with her.

Despite the happiness I feel when I see her in one piece, as she promised, my heart still aches.

I know it's because of me that she couldn't be healed. I'm the reason she looks perfectly kept together, but her legs are deceiving. Her wheels, as she likes to call them, are the only way she can get around. It's because of me my sister is confined to a wheelchair.

I didn't know at the time. I was so small and scared that I didn't realize what I was doing, but the knowledge remains inside of me, and it will do so forever.

"I know that look on your face," she states, and I gulp, trying to widen my eyes and smile.

"What look?"

"You know exactly what look," she retorts with a cock of her eyebrow.

"I love you, Nora."

She shakes her head. "Yep, definitely that look that is always followed by those heartfelt words."

"What?" I'm terrible at faking innocence with her, and she knows it.

"Don't *what* me. You're just jealous that I get carted

around like an extra special princess and you don't." We both have knowing looks. Just as she points out mine, I can see hers. She loves to make light of the situation like this. She's forever my savior, the good in this world, and it only makes me love her harder.

"You're wicked," I state, and she chuckles.

"And you love it."

"I do," I admit with a nod.

"Any guys we should be excited about?" she asks, veering away to lighter conversation. In her opinion, at least. In mine, it's a loaded topic.

"Definitely not," I grumble.

"You're boring, Addi." If only she knew.

"Maybe, but that's my life goal. One of us has to be boring so the other can bask in all of the epicness," I state, making her grin grow wider.

"And you can't have any of my epicness. I'm not good at sharing," she retorts, and I shake my head at her.

"I have permanent bruise marks to confirm that statement."

"You're welcome." She preens, making me snicker, when a knock echoes from my door.

I glare at it before turning my stare back to her.

"Why is it, whenever you call, someone knocks on my door? Are you drawing people toward your awesomeness without even being here?" I quiz her, despite the uncertainty

I feel. I'm not all that keen on opening the door right now.

She giggles. "I just can't help myself."

I stand, swallowing down the concern in my throat. "Of course you can't. Talk soon?"

She nods. "Talk soon. I love you."

Those three words from her fill my heart with so much love I can't even find a strong enough word to describe it.

"I love you too."

She disconnects the call and I slip my cell phone back into my drawer as another knock sounds from the door.

Why is there no patience in this place?

With a heavy sigh, I place a palm on my door, trying to read who is on the other side. I can't seem to decipher their thoughts. Reluctantly, I grab the door handle and pull it open.

Ah, fuck.

THE REIGN OF BLOOD

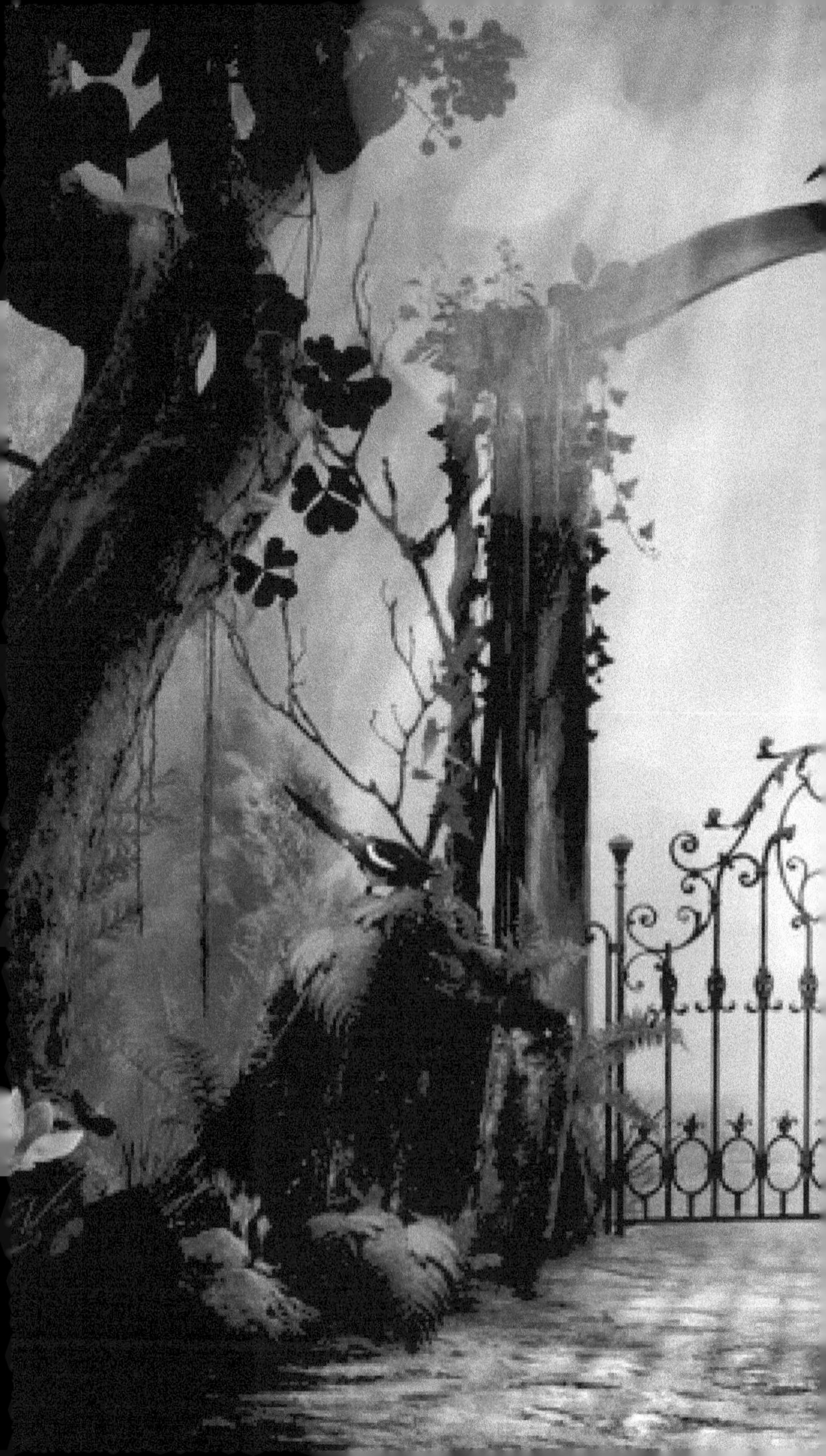

ADRIANNA

9

My hand flexes on the edge of the door, my fingers eager to slam it shut again, but the anger brewing in the gaze across from me has me locked in place, helpless to his rage.

"Let me in." His voice is gravelly, his jaw clenched so tight I'm sure it's going to snap. His hair is ruffled and unkept and his clothes are the same ones he was wearing last night.

It looks like we've both had a fun time. At least I'm not the only one.

Slowly shaking my head, I keep my gaze fixed on him, watching as he bares his teeth.

"Let me in, Addi, or I swear—"

"You swear what, Cassian? You. Swear. What?" I snap, refusing to let him show up here and give me hell without pushing back. Any frustrations he has can be taken out elsewhere because I'm not dealing with it.

His head droops, his gaze locking on the wooden floor at our feet as his arms stretch out and his fingers wrap around the edge of my door frame.

He looks defeated, exhausted, and as lost as I feel. But when he looks up through his lashes at me, I know we're far from done.

"We can have this conversation out here where anyone can hear how you lied, or we can take it somewhere private." He raises his voice, encouraging others to listen, and right on cue, the door next to mine swings open, revealing Flora's bright red hair.

"Is everything okay?" She peers at me with wide eyes, which narrow on the wolf filling the hallway.

I muster the worst smile, but it's the best I've got. "I'm good, Flora. Thank you, but it's nothing I can't handle." My smile might be fake, but my words aren't.

Before I can think better of it, I grab his arm and haul his ass into my room. He kicks the door shut behind him, and as soon as it's just the two of us in my personal space, I regret it. I think I'd rather have Flora know everything than deal with this asshole in my space again.

He consumes it, sucking the oxygen from my very lungs.

Besides, if these fuckers know, Flora deserves to know

too. Hopefully, she won't react like this.

Folding my arms across my chest, I take a step to the side. "What do you want, Cassian?"

My attempt to put space between us is obliterated by him turning to face me head-on. I instinctively take a step back to feel the wall right behind me a moment later.

Framing me in, his eyes are wild. It's disgusting how hot he looks. Truly irritating, but if he thinks I'm going to falter under his rage, he's come to the wrong place.

"You're not going to intimidate me with whatever stare you think you have going on," I point out, and he takes a step closer.

Fucker.

"I can fucking hear the racing beat of your heart telling me something different," he grunts, hands clenching at his sides as I shake my head.

"No, you're hearing it pounding. It's not in fear. It's adrenaline. There's a difference."

He inches closer again, only this time, we're chest to chest. My stomach clenches as my eyes narrow, but before I can give him a piece of my mind, he lowers his face to mine.

"You lied."

"You've already said that," I retort, trying not to roll my eyes at him.

"Aren't you sorry about it?"

"No."

His eyes narrow, but I'm being honest with him. What more does he want?

"It's good to see where we stand then," he grunts, his irritation flowing off him in waves.

"Stand with what?" I can't think straight when he's this damn close to me.

"Us." Two letters, one word, and a million implications.

"What *us*?"

"Don't play dumb."

Calling me dumb is the equivalent of setting off a detonator.

"Oh, I'm not playing. We fucked, and you made no objections when I was forced into a duel. None of that is on me. Well, maybe the winning, but that's just who I am. I won't submit, admit defeat, or die at the hands of someone when it's just not my time." I punctuate every point with a jab of my finger at his chest.

His eyes search mine, looking for fuck knows what, until he finds the question he's eager to explore.

"And there was no part of you that thought I should know the truth?"

I can't decide if he's delusional or just that self-centered.

"When it was one of your kind, your father no less, that ran me out of my home and scarred me for life? No, I don't think I owed you the truth. Not for a second."

My chest heaves with every word, the truth falling between us as our short and heavy breaths mingle.

He stares and stares and stares.

Cassian Kenner, speechless? No way.

As if sensing my disbelief, he finds his tongue.

"My father's actions aren't a representation of me."

I rear back, my head knocking against the wall as I frown at him. "I didn't assume they were."

His gaze narrows as the tension around us rises. His hands lift, planting against the wall on either side of my head. He leans closer, so close our noses touch. "Raiden said you would blame me."

I scoff. "Raiden doesn't know me well enough to make that assessment."

He runs his tongue over his bottom lip as my pulse quickens. I can feel it vibrating through me.

"You're a princess."

"I'm a fae." That's what's important here. My origin overrules my status—it always has, and it always will. If my father drilled anything into me the most, it was that.

"A fae princess."

"You're a wolf prince."

My chest rises and falls with every breath between us. His pupils dilate as he searches deep into my eyes. I catch a glimpse of the storm brewing in his, but before I can attempt to decipher it, our lips crash together.

I don't truly know who moves first, but my fingers are clinging to the neckline of his tee for dear life. My body pulls him closer, despite my mind being eager to push him away. The internal battle won't stumble into a war, not with how he's claiming my mouth.

My body wins every time.

It may be a huge mistake, but that can be tomorrow's regret. Right now, I'm desperate to lose myself in his touch and forget all of my problems.

Fighting for control, I nip at his bottom lip, forcing a growl from his throat that resonates deep inside of me. He moves one hand to my throat, flexing with precision, just how I like, while his other hand lands on the familiar spot between my legs.

It should not be this hot when someone grips your pussy, but he makes it the perfect possession and I can't bring myself to deny it.

I groan as the heat between my thighs increases from him pressing his palm against my clit. His lips tear from mine, his breath ghosting over my cheek in short, sharp puffs, forcing me to pry my eyes open.

My breath lodges in my throat as my eyes meet his.

Feral.

It's the only word to describe the glint in his dilating pupils.

His lips part as if he's about to say something, but they quickly slam shut before his eyelids fall closed and his nose swoops over my cheek and down my throat.

Fuck.

I pout when his hand moves to accommodate his lips, pressing against my pulse with purpose, but the second he sinks his teeth into my flesh, my tantrum dissolves and desire ignites even deeper in my soul.

My eyes roll back as the thud from my head hitting the wall echoes around us. I can't see, I can't think, all I can do is feel.

A tear rips through the air, and before I can realize what it is, Cassian speaks.

"You ripped my fucking t-shirt."

A ghost of a smile curls over my lips as I run my thumbs over the separated fabric. Blinking my eyes open with utter reluctance, I find him gaping at my hands. His muscles flex as he slowly drags his gaze to mine.

The familiar heat between my thighs disappears as he grips my black tee and offers the same to me. Our arms fall to our sides in sync. Breaths heave with every rise and fall as we stare at each other in our reckless states.

We shouldn't. We really shouldn't. This should be our warning sign to stop, but we sailed past that too long ago.

One breath, two breaths, three… we collide.

Lips, fingers, skin.

Everything. Everywhere.

It's not enough.

Clothes scatter at our feet as he inches backward, and I move with him. I don't shiver when there's no longer a single piece of fabric touching my skin. My body is on fire.

His fingers wrap in my hair, gripping tight as he pulls me toward him. Our lips soften, the urgency ebbing slightly, but as soon as I think that, his movements become savage. Hands grapple at my waist, hoisting me in the air, tossing me toward my bed, and I tumble off the side. He catches me just before I hit the floor, but he only adjusts us enough to maneuver me into position.

My feet press into the carpet as he pushes my head against my comforter. My fingers instinctively grip the sheets in anticipation of the force about to come from him, but to my surprise, he strokes a single fingertip down my spine.

Freezing in place, my nerve endings zap through me from head to toe as my thighs clench together. When he reaches the globes of my ass, I glance back, eager to feel him, as he ghosts the tip of his finger between them. A smirk spreads across his face when I shiver and gasp, but he doesn't utter a word, as if he's locking the reaction away for a later date.

My mouth opens, ready to blast him, but I'm rendered speechless when he brings his palm down on my ass, the echo of the smack vibrating through me. He repeats the motion on the same spot, making my back arch, and he uses that slight movement to his advantage.

I barely get a chance to appreciate the weight of his size lingering at my core before he slams inside me. All the way to the hilt.

I can't breathe.

I can't fucking breathe.

His hand winds in my hair again, making my back arch even further as he rolls his hips, letting me feel every inch of him inside me.

Fuck. Fuck. Fuck.

My body protests as he pulls my head toward him while pinning my waist and thighs to the bed, but it's the most delectable discomfort I've ever felt. There's no moment of reprieve, no time to adjust, but with how slick my walls are, he doesn't need it.

Retreating, I feel the loss of him instantly before he snaps his hips and fills me once again. I'm certain he's determined to break me, but that's simply foolish of me because, after three thrusts like that, his tempo rises.

I grip the sheets for dear life as he takes me over and over again. My body is alight, on the cusp of euphoria, as he takes everything he wants while giving me exactly what I need in return.

I succumb to it, to him.

My breasts bounce, my ass cheeks still tingle from his harsh touch, and my core clenches around his length desperately.

"Come for me, Alpha. Drench my dick in your juices. Prove to me how much you want this while your words still deny it," he rasps, making my muscles clench even tighter. "That's it. Just like that," he growls, slamming into me with more force and relinquished desire than I thought possible.

His words start the detonation inside of me, leaving me helpless but to fall apart at the seams from his touch. My jaw falls slack, my spine stiff, as the world melds into a technicolor mirage on the back of my eyelids.

Pleasure claims me as he slams into me one final time. His release has his cock pulsing against my walls as they clench around him, extending my own climax as I fall limp against the bed.

Holy fuck.

Holy fuck.

The world shifts around me as he slips from between my thighs, and his harsh hold leaves my body. I can hear movement behind me, but it takes forever to turn and look. When I do manage to focus my eyes, it's to watch the back of his head just before he slams my bedroom door shut behind him.

THE REIGN OF BLOOD

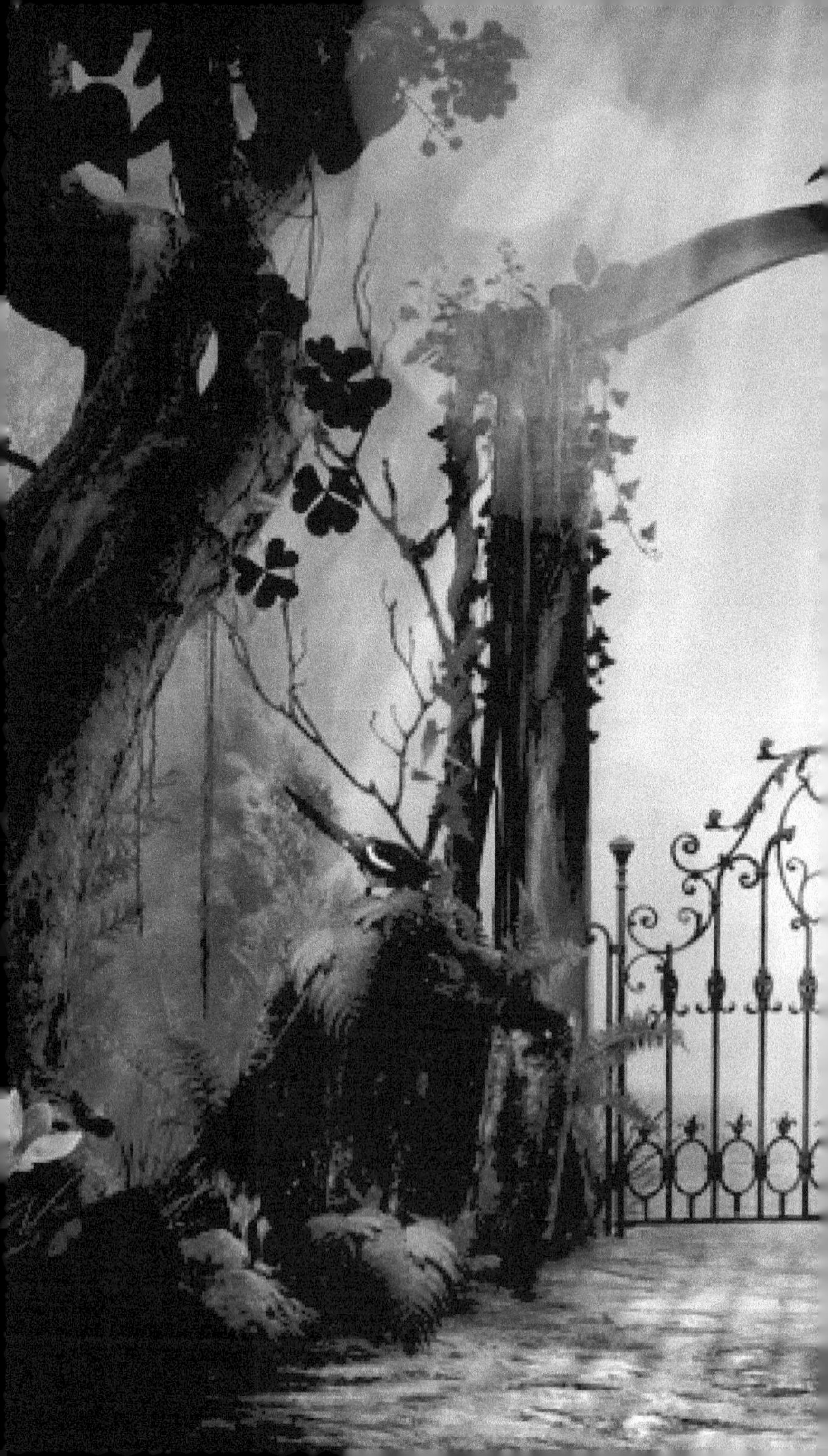

ADRIANNA

10

Another day, another rose.

I don't know why, but I'm compelled to bring them inside. There are three now. I've managed to prop them up in a mug with some water, but I need to come up with something better… and fast. The earth magic radiating inside of me is eager to nourish the hell out of them.

Stepping out into the hallway again, I heave a sigh of relief when it's empty. With my gray cloak draped over my shoulders, I'm ready to get back into classes. I'm certain the drama constantly surrounding me isn't done yet, but I can pretend for a while.

Thoughts of my mother rush to my mind again, but I tamp them down. If I don't think about it, I don't have to do anything about it. That's what I'm going with—for now, at least. Out of sight, out of mind.

I glance around to make sure there's nothing else left here with the rose, but I come up just as empty as before. I can handle a rose waiting for me out here instead of any of the guys who are forever getting under my skin.

Last night with Cassian was a disaster. A mistake.

I can only hope to keep control of myself for longer this time. The fact that he hightailed it out of there so fast is a relief. I think. At least I didn't have to summon the strength to kick him out.

Flora's door swings open, pulling me from my thoughts, and I force a smile to my face. It's not that I'm sad or unhappy, but my resting bitch face is more than happy to make me look that way if I don't make an effort to at least pretend to know how to smile.

"Everything okay yesterday?" she asks as Arlo steps out of her room after her, and I nod. Her eyes narrow as we head for the stairs, and her hand falls to my arm. "What don't I know?"

"So much." I scoff. There's so much, it's ridiculous. The concern on her face is instant, and before I can think better of it, I place my hand over hers as we head downstairs. "If you have time to schedule in some of *The Office* soon, I'll catch you up to speed."

"You're on," she replies with a grin, and my gut twists.

I need to decide how much sharing I'm open to, but

it might be good for me to get some of it off my chest. Especially to someone who hasn't been a total ass to me since I got here.

As if sensing my thoughts, one of them appears on the pathway as we step outside of the fae building.

Auburn hair shimmers in the sunlight and black ink flashes across any exposed skin that you can see. His gaze snaps to mine instantly and I sigh, despite the desire to take a moment and openly stare at him.

"Are dining hall escorts becoming a thing now, Kryll?" I cock my head at him, my eyebrows raised, and he simply shrugs in response.

"It's possible," he offers, and I shake my head in disbelief, moving to walk around him.

"I'm good, but thanks." I'm not thankful, not even a little bit, but the urge to dole out sarcasm is too strong.

Before I can completely escape him, his hand falls to my arm, just as Flora's had done a moment ago. I glare down at the connection, eager to use my magic, but instead, I sink my teeth into my bottom lip and tilt my gaze to his.

If I keep reacting with anger every time someone comes near me, I'm going to look like the troublemaker, and I'm still adamant that's not the case. I solve everything with actions, not words, but that doesn't always look good from the spectator's point of view.

"In what way do you mean *you're good*? Because if

you mean *you're good*, as in 'you can walk your sweet ass to the right table without prompt,' then I'm going to possibly high-five you like a good girl. However, if you mean *you're good*, as in 'you're going to sit elsewhere,' then we're going to have a problem."

Blinking at him, I consider my options. Where I sit is truly not a big deal in the grand scheme of things. I've seen some of the bigger picture that surrounds me now, and I can acknowledge the error of my ways when it comes to worrying over shit that really doesn't matter. If sitting with them gives me a little reprieve, then I'll take it.

I'm here to be a leader, to own my birthright. Part of that means sometimes being civil to others even though you want to throttle them. They may see it as me falling in line, taking their command, but more fool them because that's far from the truth.

"I'll meet you there, Kryll. At the table I'm summoned to," I state, my tone placid as I pull my arm from his grasp. He nods, a smirk touching the corner of his mouth, before he strolls off without a backward glance.

Hmm.

I remain frozen in place until Flora nudges me with her arm. Shaking my head, I fall into step with her and Arlo and follow after the shifter that has left me puzzled.

There was no further manhandling, no dizziness from being transported against my will, no anything. He listened, took me at my word, and now, I get to escort myself. The fact leaves me more lightheaded than the quick transport would have.

I remain quiet as we head into the academy building; only the mutters and clattering of the other students in the dining hall pull me from my thoughts. My gaze drifts toward the table in question as I head toward the food. Four sets of eyes peer in my direction, and although a part of me wants to turn and hide from their stares, I opt to look right back at them without faltering.

Hoping to appear as though I'm refusing to waver under their presence, I take the opportunity to see them properly.

Kryll, the surprisingly relenting shifter, has his blue cloak swept to one side. His muscles bulge beneath the black t-shirt molded to him beneath it as black swirls mark his skin. The cut of his jaw is tighter than it was earlier by the fae building. I don't know whether it's a public show of the harsher side to him, but that just seems ridiculous. Whatever side he shows the campus is exactly what he shows me, right?

Raiden sits beside him, his face now turned away from me. His back is ramrod straight, making the vampire's red cloak hang effortlessly off his shoulders. His dark hair is styled to perfection, and even with only a slight view of his side profile, I can see that his nostrils are flared and his lips are pressed into a firm line. I don't know what has him so pissed off, but he's irritated for sure. His inability to hide his emotions is almost amusing sometimes.

The purple-cloaked mage across from Kryll smirks at me as my eyes dance over him. He may have gotten a little heavy on Saturday, the conversation taking a different route than usual, but his charm and playfulness still lurk beneath the surface. Does he know about Cassian and me? What would he say about that? It's not that I didn't want to fuck him; I just didn't want the undertone of commitment that came with it. His blond hair and bright blue eyes draw me in, giving me a chance to forget the chaos as his aura of calmness and carefree vibes leave me intrigued.

Lastly, my gaze draws to my newly named nemesis. Cassian. The green cloak over his shoulders irritates the hell out of me. It has the ability to make his eyes shine brighter while making him look fiercer and I sort of hate him for it. The cords in his neck are tense, his eyes narrowed as he glares in my direction, waiting for my next move, and it almost makes me want to go back on my word with Kryll just to piss him off. He's as harsh on the inside as he exudes on the outside. I haven't seen a different version of him, despite the fact that he's now touched me more than once. I need to lose the claim to him, which means losing a duel. The thought of losing pains me, but if I want to put an end to this, then that's what I have to do.

"Let's go, Addi," Arlo calls out, pulling me from my appraisal of the four assholes consuming my thoughts.

Whirling around to Arlo, I find Flora and him a few steps ahead, selecting their food. I hurry to join them, opting for eggs and bacon, hoping the high protein will help in today's combat class.

With my tray loaded, I turn to my friend, feeling slightly guilty over how quiet I've been so far today. Despite that fact, I still consider her safety. "Are you guys going to sit at the fae table? I don't want to keep drawing you into this drama," I admit, nodding toward the table I've been summoned to.

Flora shakes her head. "Girl, you're my friend. Drama or not, I'm not leaving you to fend for yourself with those asshats."

Arlo smirks at her as she flicks her hair over her shoulder and leads the way. I stare with wide eyes as she takes off, slightly impressed with the boost of confidence she's exuding compared to usual, before I quickly remember to move with her.

Nearing the table, I eye the spot I usually take to the far left near Raiden, but after this morning's discussion with Kryll, I find myself swooping to the right and taking the seat directly beside him. No one speaks, enhancing the sound of the wood scraping across the floor as Flora and Arlo adjust their seats, too, sitting directly across from me.

"That's not your spot." The grunt comes from the tense vampire on the other side of Kryll. I don't bother to turn in his direction as I focus on the food in front of me.

"I wasn't advised I had a spot. I was *advised* to sit at this table," I grumble factually, earning myself a heavy sigh from the asshole that also pulled me out of Kenner's compound.

"You're more trouble than you're worth."

I smile wide, leaning forward so I can see him around Kryll's large frame. "Thank you."

Raiden rolls his eyes and turns his attention to his food before I go back to ignoring everyone at the table and do the same. I can feel eyes on me the entire time, shifting from one guy to another, but I try my best to block them out.

When I'm close to being done, Kryll leans into my side. "Are you ready for combat class?"

"As ready as I'll ever be. Why?" I ask with a frown, confused as to why he would ask that.

"No reason," he replies with a shrug, making me turn my full attention to him.

When he doesn't instantly expound, I give him a pointed look, which seems to do the trick.

"My brother may have mentioned he's dialing it up a notch," he explains before his eyes narrow. "Why are you grinning at that?"

Rolling my lips, I dip my head. "I don't know what you're talking about." It's coy as fuck, but I'm not going to sit here and get excited over the fact that we're going to be increasing our combat training. What can I say? I like it.

"Why is this bitch still at my table?" The shrill voice grinds on my brain as I instinctively turn toward the drama now drenching the table.

"Vallie, do us all a favor and fuck off. I've watched her beat the shit out of you enough times to know you're out of your league," Raiden grunts, and I gape at him in surprise. He doesn't even lift his gaze as he grumbles at her, which only seems to agitate her more.

Pressing her palms flat against the table, she leans closer to him. "Raidy baby, don't forget who I am."

I'm not entirely sure what that means, but it's no surprise to hear a vampire lording their social stature over someone else. I just hadn't really considered that they would do it with one another as well as other origins.

"How could anyone forget? Your lineage is the only thing keeping you alive. Now. Fuck. Off."

My eyes widen further as Vallie stands tall, folding her arms over her chest in a huff.

"I'm telling my daddy."

I bite back a snicker at her childish tantrum as Raiden finally lifts his head and shrugs. "He won't come for me."

Her smile widens, pleased that she has his attention, as

she wags her finger. "No, but he'll come for her."

My chest tightens, but I refuse to let her get under my skin.

"He already tried that, and I'm still here," I retort, making her bare her teeth with a sneer as her gaze settles on mine.

"Honey, he was just getting started."

THE REIGN OF BLOOD

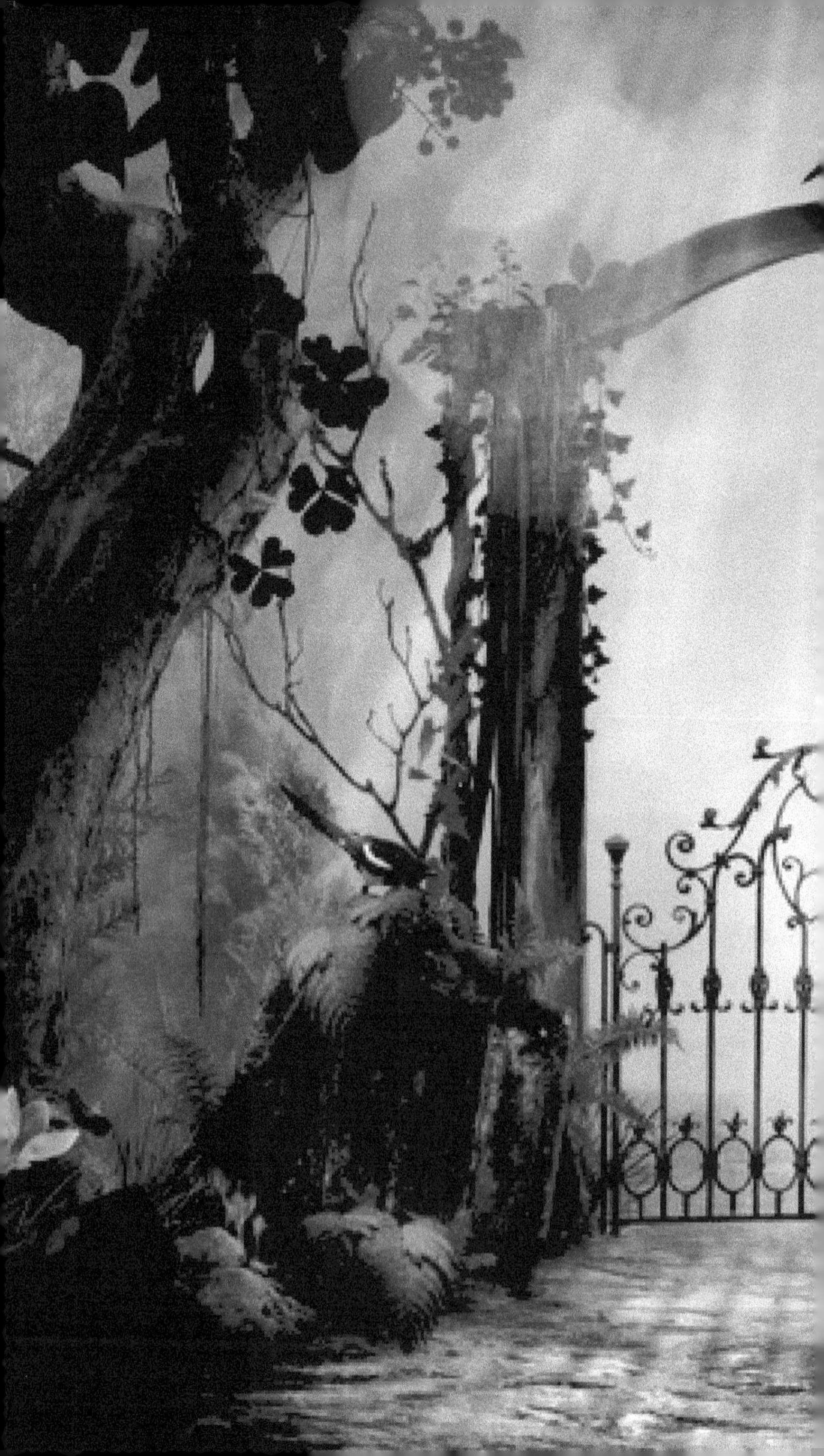

ADRIANNA

11

Professor Tora claps his hands, gathering everyone's attention as a circle forms around him. Those eager to participate stand closer, fingers twitching with excitement and anticipation, while those nervous about what they're about to go through edge closer to the back.

Kryll mentioned earlier that combat class was about to get more intense, and although the professor hasn't said a single word yet, I can tell it's true from the sparkle in his eyes. It's a glint reserved for chaos, destruction, and war. A glint that will make us push harder, bite back the pain, and come out of the other side stronger. If at all.

I like it.

A shiver runs down my spine as Professor Tora's gaze sweeps over where I stand. I have no idea what's about to come, but the exhilaration thrumming through my veins is exactly what I need.

No bullshit girl drama, no guys trying to wreak havoc on my soul, no secrets spilling over the walls I've worked so hard to build. It's just me and my body.

"Good morning, class. I hope you're ready for me to put you through your paces," he says with a grin.

Flora laces her fingers together nervously at my side as she tries to shuffle back a step, but Arlo's right there, making it impossible for her to disappear into the crowd.

Sass is her thing, mind power another. Combat, however, seems far off her list.

I tilt my face to look at her. Her pupils are dilated with worry, her teeth nip at her bottom lip with concern, and her gaze darts anywhere but at the professor. The guy beside her, a human, is bouncing on the balls of his feet, hands curled into fists as if he's ready to pummel someone right here and now.

They're a stark contrast beside one another. My chest tightens. It's hard. No two people are alike. We're all unique. Made with different strengths, weaknesses, and beliefs. What we may excel at, someone else may fail miserably, while they may rise to a challenge that is your greatest weakness, balancing the scales.

The whole reason we're all here is to find the new heir. Shit, it's in the damn title. *Heir Academy.* Are they going to factor in what strengths and weaknesses people have, or do you *have* to be able to battle with every fiber of your being? Do you have to be more victorious than anyone else, or are we given chances to learn and improve? On the flip side, is someone so eagerly bloodthirsty, like the guy standing beside Flora, considered a risk because there's more to controlling an entire kingdom than war?

Shaking my head, I pull myself from my thoughts and turn back to Tora. None of that matters. Not when I'm determined to be who my birthright declared I would be the moment I was born.

"Today, we're going to have you take to the fighting rings. Death or submission."

Gasps echo around me, starting from Flora as fear gets the better of her. The word *death* will do that, and that's likely why Professor Tora said it. It will either make you sink to your knees in panic or make you rise above the terror threatening to consume you.

Tora points toward the mats set up behind him in the grass. They don't live up to the name he just gave them. There's no fear in a blue mat surrounded by soil, but the damage that can take place on one, and the blood that can coat it once someone is done, is a lot closer to his description.

"Names will be called at random. There's no option to change so don't bother asking. Origins weren't taken into consideration. This isn't about pitting you against like-for-like peers; it's about the surprise of battle, the ability to adjust, and the desire to survive."

"Fuck, Kryll, you said he was upping the game, not setting us up to stop breathing altogether," Brody murmurs, and the hairs on the back of my neck stand on end. The need to turn and look is real. I didn't know they were so close.

"You don't know Beau like I do. This is going to be light in comparison to how far he will go," Kryll replies, and I can almost see his smile in my mind. The awe in his tone paints the perfect picture.

I wonder if I sound that whimsical when I mention Nora. Not that I would, nor would I be discussing something so deadly... I don't think.

"What are the rules?" Vallie asks, smirking from across the circle. Her eyes fix on mine, a promise of chaos burning just for me, but I ignore her as Tora replies.

"There are none. You simply stop when someone submits or one of you dies."

Vallie's lips tug up at the corners as she winks at me.

Bitch.

Professor Tora starts tapping away on his device at the same time Flora nudges me. Glancing at her from the corner of my eye, I can see her worries floating more to the surface.

"How do you do it, Addi? How do you stand so tall and

proud, like none of this fazes you? And don't say because it doesn't, I can already tell that, but I've definitely got at least five people looking my way, seeing me as an easy target."

My gaze darts around the circle, skimming over every single person.

She's wrong.

There are at least twelve, but I don't mention that because I don't think it will help her right now

"Stand tall," I murmur, not turning my gaze to her, just peeking out of the corner of my eye. She does as I say immediately, her body as stiff as a rod. "Now relax your shoulders... more... more... that's it." I rub my lips together, still watching the blond-haired vampire a few yards away who continues to stare at her like she's his next meal. I would love to say it in the hot as fuck way and tell my girl to go get some, but the sinister blaze in his eyes tells a different story entirely.

"I don't think it's making a difference," she breathes, audibly gulping.

"Inch your feet apart so they're the same width as your shoulders." She takes the order and moves subtly, nodding when she feels in position. "Now, loosen your hands. Keep them at your sides. Don't hold your fingers straight, but don't ball them into fists, either. Let them sit slightly curled as if you could slam your knuckles into someone's face at any given moment."

A small snort vibrates from her, as if the idea of it is ridiculous, but she quickly tamps it down, understanding the seriousness of the situation.

"What now?"

Peering around the group once again, at least five of the twelve people are staring down a new prey. It's not enough, but it will do. "Now, relax your jaw, stop averting your gaze, and stare right back at those motherfuckers. The more you let them think you're the prey, the more they'll treat you like it."

"But I *am* the prey, Addi." The desperation is clear in her voice, forcing me to give her my full attention.

"If that was true, which I don't believe it is, then they don't need to know that fact. You're as strong as you believe yourself to be. If you make a mistake, so be it. If you fail and fuck everything up, so be it. If you have to submit, so be it. You get your ass back up, strengthen your resilience, and persevere."

She nods softly, the tremble that was running through her moments ago simmering down as she smiles. "Thanks, Addi."

I offer her a smile back before turning toward Tora. I want to be ready for the moment he says my name.

"Why would you do that?"

I stiffen at the curious tone on my other side. My body

stiffens, but I quickly make myself relax before I turn to stare at the irritating vampire that drives me insane.

"What do you want, Raiden?" I sigh, cocking a brow at him.

"I want to know why you would do that." He peers past me to where Flora stands.

"You're going to have to be more specific."

He rolls his eyes like I'm the inconvenience in this situation, but to my surprise, he doesn't just wash his hands of me and saunter off. Instead, he inches closer. "Why would you hype her up like that? Make her feel strong? Why not let her know who you are and make sure she knows she is beneath you?"

My head rears back at his words as my eyebrows pinch together in confusion.

What the fuck?

"Why would I do any of those things?" I mutter, shocked that his head would even go there.

He shrugs, standing tall as he looks toward where Vallie and her friends are standing. Her gaze is narrowed on me, much to my enjoyment, but I'm too focused on waiting for Raiden's response to truly care.

"That's what a vampire would do." Tension builds in my head as I frown deeper. "A vampire's status is everything. We're not a team. We're all out to fight our own battles. Sometimes, they may be among each other."

That is some backward shit if I've ever heard it.

I shake my head. "We're at an academy to find a new heir for the kingdom, Raiden. That means someone who is going to not only take care of themselves, the wars, the battles, and the castle itself, but someone who is also going to take care of the people who make this kingdom what it is. Every origin, no questions asked. You're only as strong as your weakest link, and the fact that The Council acts exactly like what you just described explains why it's not currently working. I want a better life for the people of Floodborn Kingdom. I'm only going to be my best if they are theirs too, and as a leader, it is my responsibility to ensure everyone is given the time and knowledge to achieve that."

My chest falls harder than I prefer as I stop my rant. His eyes search mine, for what, I don't know. I feel like I just revealed a piece of myself and I want to take it back. Thankfully, Professor Tora takes that moment to start reeling off names.

"Franklin and George. Arlo and Flora." My gaze whips to theirs and I see a sense of relief flash through them. At least Arlo will go easy on her, but we may need to figure out how to get her up to snuff with her fighting. I'm not expecting her to be a warrior overnight, but we need to see what abilities she has. "Vallie and Raiden," Tora calls out next, and the audible huff of frustration from beside me is undeniable. He doesn't glance my way as he saunters off, but I could swear I could hear him chanting, "Don't kill her, don't kill her, don't kill her."

"Imagine if it was me and you, Dagger. I could show you a good time," Brody murmurs as he fills the spot Raiden just vacated. I roll my eyes at his cheesiness, but a part of me is glad it's back after our talk over the weekend.

"You would either die or submit, so you're right, it does sound like a good time." I smile teasingly as I turn to look at him. His blue eyes dance with mischief as his lips part, but once again, I'm saved by the professor.

"Brody and Addi."

Or not.

Gaping at the grinning mage beside me, my feet carry me toward the setup Tora pointed out for us. We come to a stop, and my facial expression hasn't changed an inch, and neither has his.

Fucker.

"What was that about a good time, Dagger?" he says with a smirk, wagging his eyebrows at me.

"Do you want to practice tapping the mat now, so you've got the hang of it before I send you to the brink of death?" I retort, and his head falls backward as he laughs. Irritation threatens to claw up my spine, but when his eyes reach mine, I don't get the sense that he's mocking me. If anything, he looks excited.

"There's no going back once we step foot on the mat," he states, and I nod, watching the grin fall from his face. He waves his hand, offering for me to lead the way.

Clearing my throat, I take a deep breath, shutting off my mind from the rest of the world before I take the initial step. The second I do, he follows after me. I'm wrapped in gray sportswear, while his purple is like a beacon, edging me closer.

"I know you're a girl, but I'm going to fight you like you're a ten-foot tall man with a dick bigger than my right arm."

I shake my head at him, completely distracted by his declaration, and he uses the opportunity to his advantage, charging at me before I can piece a single action together. We crash to the ground, a grunt breaking past my lips as I hit the mat. His weight on top of me is distracting, a reminder of the last time we were in a similar situation, and irritation claws at me.

Fucking focus, Adrianna.

I clench my eyes closed, taking a deep breath as my body warms and my vision clears. My body is no longer in control; my mind is.

He wrestles to grab my arms and pin them at my sides, his legs bolting mine to the ground. But before he can get a good grasp on my wrist, I jab at the delicate spot at his side. It does nothing more than make him grunt, but I repeat the process on the other side, and that earns me a glare.

"Feisty, Addi. I like it," he rasps, pressing his knees into the ground so he can adjust his feet, spreading my legs wide with the move.

Fucker.

I aim for his stomach with one hand, meeting rock-hard muscles, while my other fist swings toward his face. The crack from the contact vibrates between us as he leans to the side, and I press the opening, shifting my weight to slip out from under him.

Rushing to my feet, I circle to face him, knees bent, arms tucked in close, and my eyes darting over him from head to toe.

"Did you really have to hit me in the face? It's my best asset," he grumbles, rubbing at the reddening mark on his face.

"Oops," I whisper, batting my eyelashes at him.

He shakes his head, trying to smother the grin on his face as he charges at me once again. I sidestep him this time, knocking at his leg as he passes, but no sooner does he hit the deck is he back on his feet, circling me again.

"You're not too bad at this, Dagger," he assesses, nipping at his bottom lip as he stares me down.

"I'd say the same for you, but… it would be a lie."

It's my turn to charge at him, arms low as I aim for his stomach. He lets me get close, but as I connect with him, his arms wrap around my waist, putting him in control of our fall to the ground. He's quick to shuffle around, fighting to get on top, but I push back with every ounce of strength I have.

The second I have the upper hand, he sweeps it away from me, taking me to the ground again before we repeat the process. Not once does he hit me. He just guides control, and it almost makes me feel bad for aiming for his face.

Almost.

"Are you two fucking or fighting? I can't tell." The question comes from Professor Tora, earning a few chuckles, but I don't pay him any attention as I zero in further on my target.

Sweat clings to me, and loose tendrils of hair float around my face as I hit the ground beneath Brody once again.

"Submit, Dagger, and this will all be over."

I scoff. "Like fuck am I doing that." He's right, though. This needs to come to an end, and quickly. Especially if people are watching.

This time, when I twist to gain leverage, I wrap my arms around his neck, locking behind his arm and holding him in position. As we turn, I roll us completely over so he's still technically on top, but his back is to my chest, and he can't move.

"Sorry, Brody. It's not personal. If anything, you're one of the few people here I almost don't hate, but winning is winning, and you're in my way," I whisper in his ear, tightening my hold with all my strength.

His legs flail, but it's pointless. I've done this move too many times on men far bigger than him. I sense the moment defeat kicks in, and a split second later, it's followed by the sweet tapping of his hand on the mat.

One.

Two.

Three.

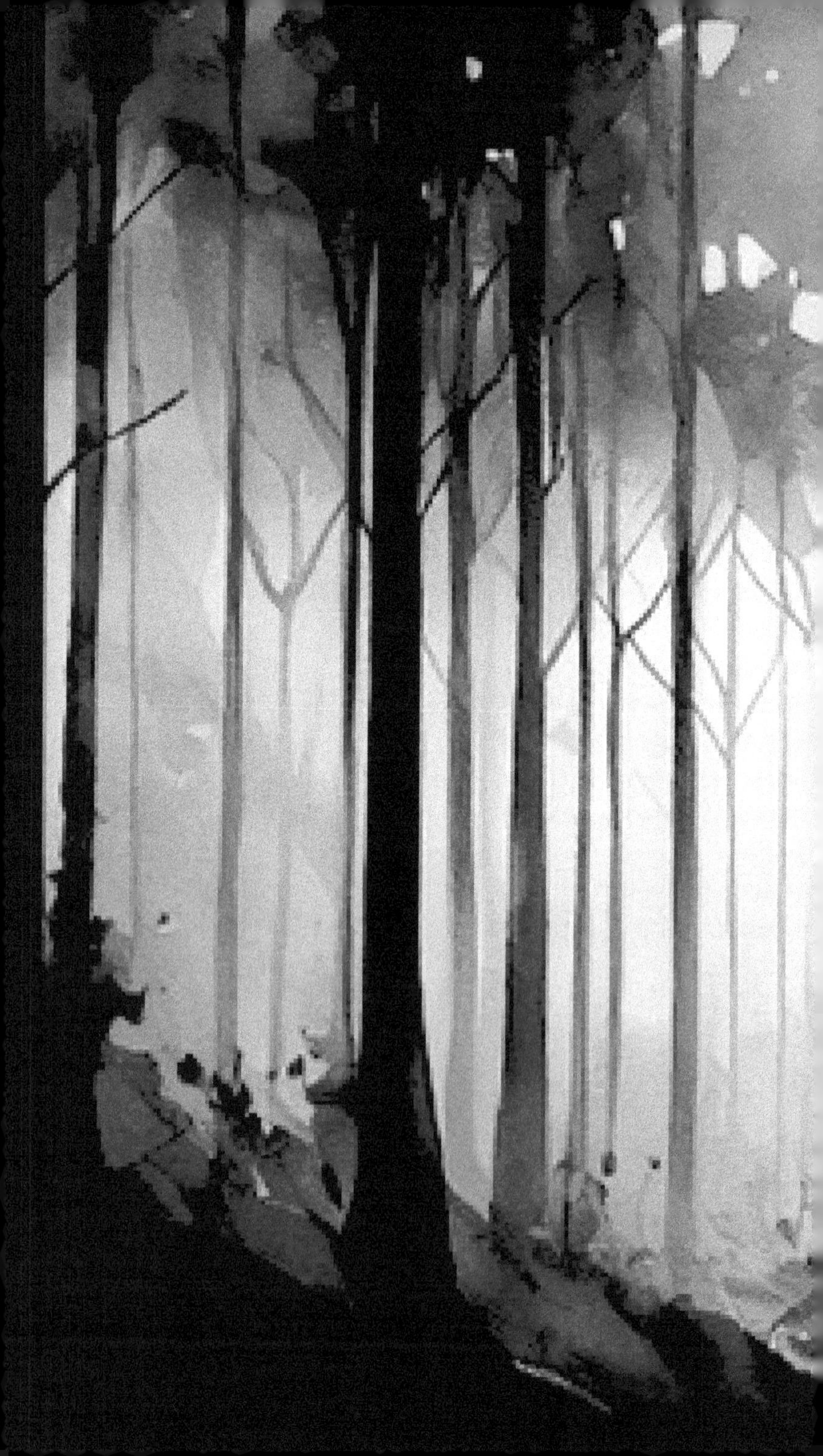

BRODY

12

She beat me.

She actually fucking beat me.

I can't even pretend that I let it happen. That shit was all her.

Stretching my neck, I try to ease the dull ache that remains. I refuse to use my magic. I refuse to admit that she really did me over that much.

Damn.

No longer in my sportswear, I fasten my purple cloak around my shoulders and head outside. I need to get to the next class, but I'm still locked on the fact that she took me down without using any of her magic—not an ounce. I thought I was playing it safe with her by keeping it solely about combat and not about our abilities.

I was expecting everyone else to be gone by the time

I reached the pathway to head back to the main academy building, but as I round the corner, I come to a stop at the sight of Raiden, Cassian, and Kryll waiting.

Fuck.

They're not going to let me live this down.

The smirk on Kryll's face says as much, but it's Cass who speaks first.

"Are you okay?"

"I don't want to talk about it," I grumble, wiping a hand down my face, and he smirks.

"I thought your brain was going to explode from how tight she had you in that hold," Raiden states, and I roll my eyes at him.

"She has the grip of death, and there's nothing I could do about it. Are we done here?" I cock a brow at them, and thankfully, they start to walk.

"We watched her fight Leticia, remember? We know she's got skills," Cassian grunts without glancing my way, and I sigh.

"Well, I can confirm those skills are far superior to what I anticipated," I admit, and Kryll all-out laughs this time, earning himself a death glare that he pays no mind to. "If it's so funny, then tell your brother you want to go up against her next time."

"Maybe I will," he retorts with a wink. Fucker. "The real question is, how hard did your dick get with all that rolling around on the mat?"

Raiden scoffs at Kryll's question, and I narrow my eyes but keep my gaze fixed on the academy building ahead. "You don't want my honest answer to that."

"Oh, I think we do," Cassian chimes in, intrigued, and I shake my head.

"Man, I tapped out because I was on the cusp of creaming my pants."

They laugh, loud and brash, and I can't help but join in a little.

That girl is something else entirely, and I'm caught in her web. I know exactly when it happened, and I know even more so when I fucked it up.

My curiosity toward her truly started when she helped the human and took the heat of Vallie's wrath. She didn't have to do that, but she did it anyway. I fucked it up on Saturday when I came on too heavy. I've never fucking done that.

Ever.

Yet here I am, fucking it all up.

"Maybe next time you can fight with your actual fists and not your dick," Raiden mutters with a grin, earning another round of chuckles as I shake my head.

"Honestly, I would love to see each of you go up against her. You wouldn't fare any better," I promise, my dick stirring to life once again at the mere thought of it.

I really could do with finishing myself off before our next class so I can focus, but there's no time for that.

Entering the building, we follow the hallways toward the classroom. When we reach the doorway, everyone else is already seated. Including the girl of the hour. I've never been happier to have to sit in alphabetical order, especially when it puts me next to her sweet ass.

Her blond hair is fixed and neat again, braided to her head in a swirl that makes me want to untangle it one inch at a time. The gray cloak draped around her shoulders makes her big eyes even brighter as she peers out of the corner of her eye in my direction. She quickly darts away, but I don't miss the curl to her lips as she does.

Oh, she thinks she's got the upper hand now, huh?

Sauntering toward her, I drop into my seat, splaying my thighs as I drape my arm around the back of her chair.

"Hey, Dagger, have you been up to much this morning?" I ask with a grin as she struggles to hide the growing smirk on her face.

"Not much. Just took down some measly mage, but otherwise, it's been pretty quiet." Her gaze settles on mine, the challenge clear.

"Measly mage? You're bullshitting me. I heard it was some hot god of a mage who let you win."

Her jaw drops as her eyes search mine, and I hope like hell she can sense the humor.

"That hot god of a mage definitely didn't let me win. He fucking wishes he did, but he's not that lucky."

I nod, my grin splitting my face so wide my cheekbones start to ache. "Hot god of a mage, huh?" I wag my brows as she gapes at me.

"I was just repeating your words," she grumbles, folding her arms over her chest as she turns her attention back to the front of the room.

"You can't take them back now, Dagger," I push, leaning closer.

"Whatever you say, Brody."

"No. No. No. It's 'hot god of a mage' from now on," I insist, and she smirks.

"It's not."

"You're going to hurt my feelings." I pout, and she turns to look at me with her eyebrows raised.

"Like I already hurt your pride?"

Oh, she's sassy today. I like it.

"My pride might have been hurt, but my dick was—"

"Are you done, Mr. Orenda, or are we all going to have to hear about your genitals?" the professor asks, interrupting me, and the class falls into a fit of giggles. It seems I'm on top form with amusing everyone today.

I part my lips, ready to give the all-clear to get on with class, my genitals can wait, but a drill siren rings out, halting me.

"It looks like you're saved by the bell, Mr. Orenda. Everyone, please proceed to your homerooms. It seems the dean has an announcement to make."

THE REIGN OF BLOOD

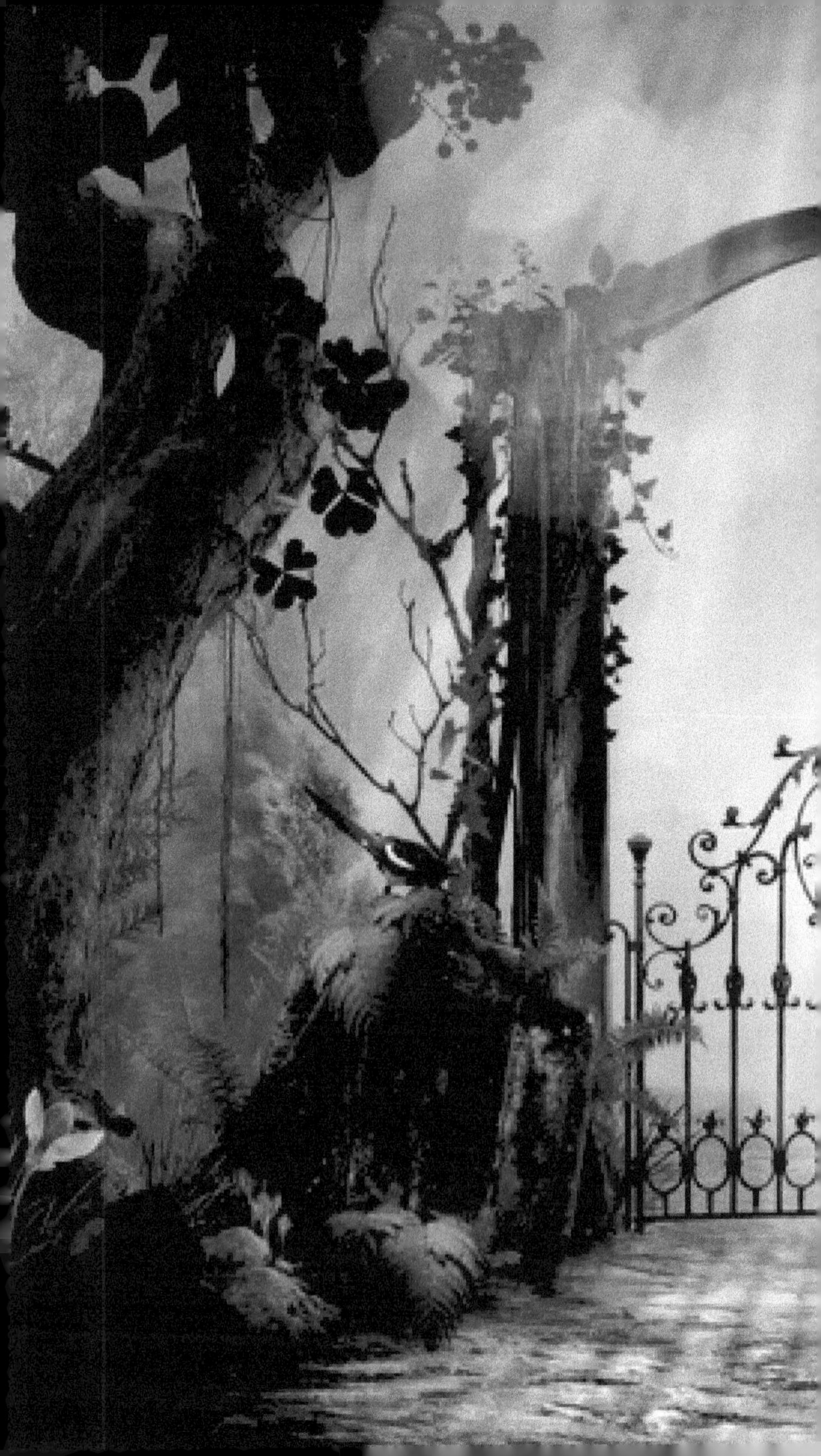

ADRIANNA

13

"What's going on?" Flora murmurs as she steps up beside me, and we follow everyone out of the classroom.

"I have no idea," I admit with a shrug.

I say that, but my stomach is churning, clenched so tight it makes me want to drop to my knees. Something isn't okay, and fuck only knows it's going to end up having something to do with me.

Today has felt less eventful than I envisioned it would be. Yes, Vallie has made her usual appearance, and I had the pleasure of dropping Brody to the mat and hearing the sweet sound of him submitting, but that stuff feels naturally par for the course at this stage.

The dean, however, has me concerned.

I've lasted this long without Cassian, Raiden, Kryll, or

Brody telling someone my big secret, which still doesn't make sense to me, but that doesn't mean someone else hasn't.

Taking a deep breath, I try to keep my body calm and relaxed, but nobody would notice otherwise since they're all bundled up in small groups murmuring over what it could be. Maybe it's something to do with the trials or the ball coming up. Maybe I'm just overreacting.

Hopefully, that's the case.

Stepping into our homeroom, I notice the projector is set up again, just like the last time the dean had some news to share with everyone. I take my seat, my spine stiff as I sit tall in my chair. A beat passes before I'm flanked by Brody and Kryll, who take their spots on either side of me. Raiden peers over his shoulder at me for a brief moment before he faces the front. I can't tell what that look was, and a part of me doesn't want to find out.

"What do you think it is, Dagger?" Brody asks, raising an eyebrow at me, and I shrug.

"Nothing is predictable at this place," I mumble, lacing my fingers together in my lap as he smirks.

"Maybe they want us to go another round in combat class at lunchtime so I can even the score," he replies, his smirk turning wicked as his eyes darken.

"Of course, that's where your head goes." I shake my head at him, which makes him snicker under his breath, and as I turn to face the front, I spot Kryll grinning from the corner of my eye too.

Assholes.

Before he can serenade me with any more of his quick-witted charm, colors flicker across the projector, and a moment later, Dean Bozzelli appears before us. The canary-yellow blazer and fitted skirt she has chosen for the day make my eyes squint. It doesn't help that she's standing outside and the sun is making her glow.

"I think she just burned my retinas," Brody mutters, squeezing his eyes closed. I roll my lips together, trying to pretend like that wasn't funny.

"Good morning, students of Heir Academy," she begins, the smile on her face not quite meeting her eyes as she brushes invisible lint from her jacket. "I truly apologize for pulling you from your usual schedule, but I have just come from a meeting with The Council where I learned some information that I feel is important for everyone."

The room grows quiet as my pulse starts to ring in my ears. My gut twists, and as much as I pray this has nothing to do with me, I really think it has *everything* to do with little old me.

"I've been informed by a very reliable source that there is someone among us—someone who has been hiding in plain sight."

Fuck. Fuck. Fuck.

Brody's hand clamps down on my left thigh, pinning me in place. My nostrils flare in anticipation, but I don't turn to him. I keep my gaze locked on the projector.

The words are coming. I know they are, but I can't let myself appear fazed by any of it. This is just like preparing for war, for battle, for carnage. I have to make myself void of any reaction that they'll so desperately be seeking. The reality is, I'm not ashamed of who I am.

"A member of the previous royal family is present on campus."

My hands ball into fists, my nails pressing painfully into my palms, and I refuse to even blink as I wait for the seconds to tick by. Murmurs pick up around me again, but I can't piece them together. I'm too tense, too locked in on Bozzelli.

"My students, I tell you now, just as I informed The Council… Queen Reagan has been seen on the grounds."

Gasps ring out as I fight not to frown at the dean. Queen Reagan… my mother? Has she been here?

How?

I'm too nervous to breathe a sigh of relief at the mention of my mother and not me. It still doesn't make sense why she would come here.

For me? I can't see them letting her go, which means they've brought her here for a purpose. But what? And if that was the case, is she captive, or is she able to roam freely?

Fuck.

It's consuming me again.

Sighing, I wipe a hand down my face, trying to ease the tension that continues to build inside of me, but it does little to nothing.

"I know this may be of great concern to many, but I assure you, we have swept the grounds four times now, and her presence no longer lingers. However, the matter of why she was here remains unknown, but rest assured we are going to get to the bottom of it."

"It doesn't make any sense for her to be here," a girl states from the row behind me. My brain wants me to turn and look, see what color her cloak is, but I can't. Any movement could bring unwanted attention.

"Shut up, Leona," someone else hisses, making my veins tingle with irritation as I silently plead for Bozzelli to just spit it out.

"She wasn't here for something, she was here for some*one*, and we have solid information in regards to who that is likely to be." It's like her eyes settle on mine, even though she's not actually here. "She was here for her daughter."

"Daughter? That's not possible," Arlo blurts from behind me, making my heart clench as I prepare myself for the truth to fill the air, consume my lungs, and claim me.

"Her daughter successfully enrolled into the academy,

under false information, but she is here nonetheless."

"Who? Who is it?" Vallie yells, slapping her palms down on the table as others holler in agreement with her.

"Please use extreme caution in your interactions with Adrianna Reagan, also known as Miss Addi Reed."

THE REIGN OF BLOOD

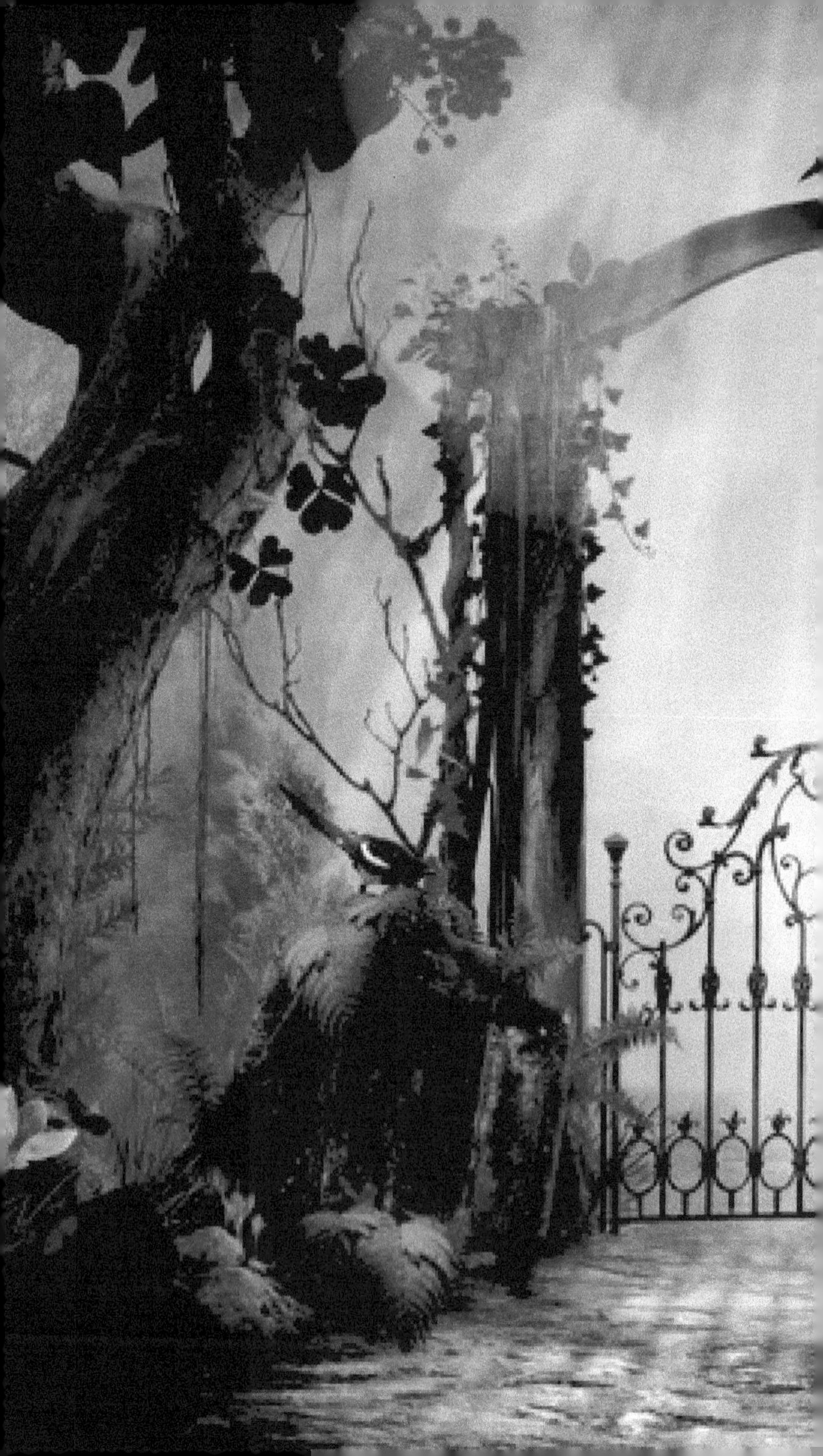

ADRIANNA

14

The bell rings out, calling the class to an end. With all the strength I can muster, I stand, turning for the door without glancing at anyone. My movements are steady, unhurried, and focused. The hairs on the back of my neck rise. Again. No sooner do they calm are they back at high attention.

Everyone seems to give me a wide berth as I slip between the desks and out into the hallway. They might not be in my personal space, but that doesn't stop their eyes from tracking my every move.

After Bozzelli exposed my secret to the academy, all eyes landed on me and they haven't turned away since. Not when we were dismissed from homeroom and sent back to our scheduled class, not a single beat during said class, and now it feels even more prominent.

The class professor was no better. Every time he adjusted the glasses on the tip of his nose, his gaze locked on mine. I didn't look away. I held my ground. For what, I don't really know, but I did it anyway. The last thing I need right now is to appear weak.

I'm acutely aware of every single piece of attention aimed my way. My magic is going haywire inside me, frazzling my focus with its need to reach out and protect me, but it's not necessary.

I've got this.

I knew this was coming; it just happened sooner than expected. To be honest, after this weekend, I was expecting it to happen before classes began. At least I got to experience combat class before every eye in the academy was turned my way.

Some of the stares seem to be in awe, while others give the vibe that they want to rip my throat out. I'd like to assume it's still the vampires and wolves that have already been giving me shit, but it's more than that. The knowledge of my presence isn't going down too well.

No one has said anything to me yet—*yet* being the keyword—but I'm alert and prepared for when the moment comes.

Brody has tried to speak to me a few times, but I've ignored him. I really can't be distracted by any of them right now when I need to be as vigilant as possible.

Stepping outside, I let the warmth from the sun soak into my bones, restoring life to me as my eyes lock with Flora. Someone else I've avoided since the information dropped. Now it's lunchtime and I don't think I can hide from the situation anymore.

A flutter of panic clenches in my chest as I step toward her. I shouldn't care, but I do. As if I'm not moving quick enough for her, she marches toward me, Arlo hot on her heels. With a whoosh of her cloak, she stops at my side, links her arm through mine, and takes off toward the dining hall.

Everyone else tends to stick to the halls, but I guess she knew I would head out here first and take the long way around.

"I'm just saying I think we should sit with those guys today. Out of choice. They may work as a buffer for you," she states as Arlo appears on my other side.

"What?" I ask with a frown, turning to glance at her, and she shakes her head.

"Sorry, I started that conversation in my head. I think we should sit with Cassian, Raiden, Kryll, and Brody. They'll be like a protective shield around you," she explains, but it does nothing to make my frown disappear.

"Protective? They're not going to protect me."

"I'm not saying they will, but people tend to steer clear of them so it's another layer of defense. People fear them.

That might stop people approaching altogether," she adds, eyebrows raised as she nods along with herself.

She seems certain about it, but that doesn't mean it will turn out that way.

Reentering the academy building, the food from the dining hall lures us closer. The second we step inside, the room falls silent. I pause in my tracks, glancing around the room and all of the eyes taking me in. It seems the moment of reprieve I was just basking in is gone again.

"Keep moving. They're not allowed to get under your skin," Flora whispers before tugging me toward the line for food.

As noise starts to register around us again, I take a moment to look at her. Concern crinkles her nose and worry dances in her eyes, but otherwise, there's nothing out of the ordinary.

"You're not mad," I state, making her eyebrows pinch in confusion.

"About what?"

I give her a pointed look that has no effect until Arlo nudges her.

"She means the fact that she's a princess and didn't tell us," he mock-whispers, tossing a wink my way. I almost roll my eyes at him, but Flora whacks him in the stomach with the back of her hand instead, and that seems good enough.

"Why would I be mad?" she asks, turning her attention back to me, and I shrug.

"I don't know. I lied to you." It sounds lame when I say it like that, especially with the way she's looking at me.

"For good reason," she blurts, her voice louder than necessary. She quickly presses her hand over her mouth, but it does nothing to hide the familiar pink blush taking over her cheeks.

I smile at her. *Really* smile at her. "Thanks, Flora," I breathe, something settling inside of me. It may be safe to say that I'm not in this alone. I have one friend at my side, at least. Maybe two if Arlo counts as well.

"Do I get a thanks?" he asks, as if sensing his name in my thoughts. This time, he definitely earns an eye roll, but I say it anyway.

"Thanks, Arlo."

He places his hand on his chest, fluttering his eyelashes as he sways. "The fucking princess just thanked me."

"You're insufferable," I grumble, turning away from him as he snickers.

"And don't you forget it."

How could we?

Moving farther along the line, Flora steps in closer. "How did Bozzelli find out, and why does everyone seem to be gaping at you except the four guys I think we should sit with?"

That's such an observational question right there. Damn.

Sighing, I glance at her. "I think she found out the same way they found out… through Cassian's father." There's no use denying it. It's not like that part really is a secret. Who he has in his grasp, however, seems important, especially since it's my mother—the same woman who was apparently seen on campus. Or was that a lie? A way for them to announce my presence without mentioning Kenner at all.

"I hate him," Flora declares, making my eyebrows rise as I reach across the serving tables to grab my food.

"Do you know him?"

"No, but that's not the point," she retorts, making me grin.

Loaded with our food, we turn for the table I've dreaded ever since Cassian demanded it. I lead the way, ready to turn away if I get the slightest inkling that something has changed. Brody and Cassian are seated next to each other as usual, but across the table, with their backs to us, are Raiden and Kryll. Instead of sitting right next to each other, there's a spot free between them.

It seems odd, but I don't think too much of it as I place my tray down beside Kryll just like I did this morning.

"We shifted around for you to sit between us," Raiden explains, not lifting his gaze from his food as Kryll smirks up at me.

"I'd rather not," I bite before I consider whether it's worth it or not.

"I'd rather eat my lunch in peace without your presence causing a scene," Cassian interjects, glaring at me, and I scoff.

Fuck this.

"Then I can sit elsewhere. I'm here because *you* demanded it, remember?" I cock a brow at him in challenge as I reach for my tray, but Kryll stops me from lifting it off the table.

"Sit down, Princess." My eyes narrow at him. He's never called me that before. I don't need him to start now. He must sense the irritation because he quickly continues. "Come on, Addi. Park your ass. I won't bite, I swear it."

It's not really him I'm worried about, and he knows it.

Breaking our stare-off, I peer at Flora, who is sitting beside Arlo. She nods for me to take the seat, and with great reluctance, I do.

The second I sit down, Raiden is up on his feet, lightning fast. The flurry of commotion quickly settles when Raiden pins a guy to the ground behind me. He's wearing a red cloak, confirming his origin as he snarls and snaps up at me.

"Fuck off, Sean," Raiden growls, slamming him into the floor before standing tall and dusting his clothes off.

"Did you not hear who she is?" the guy retorts, making me frown.

Confused, I glance at everyone else at the table, and it's Brody who offers an explanation.

"He was about to go for your throat."

My eyebrows rise in surprise. Well then.

"I heard perfectly well," Raiden states, drawing my attention to the two vampires.

"Then we take her out," Sean yells, rushing to his feet before jabbing a finger in my direction.

"Says who?" Raiden challenges, leaving me even more shocked than the fact that he attacked this guy to stop him from getting to me.

"Says history," Sean spits, a deathly glare aimed my way.

As much as it kind of makes my insides flutter that he jumped to my defense, I can handle myself, and if I want any chance of surviving this place now that my secret is out, then I need to remind them of that fact with more than just the bullshit that Vallie throws my way.

Standing, I stare down the vampire intent on putting an end to me. "What's your issue?" It's not demanding or defensive. If anything, I sound bored. I like it.

"You're the daughter of the king who brought our kingdom to its knees," he snarls, eyes wild as he takes a step toward me. Raiden lifts a hand to stop him, but I wave him off. To my surprise, he drops his hand without a word, and I narrow my eyes at the assailant who has done nothing but enlarge the target on my head.

"Do you mean the king who was never given the chance to help raise the kingdom from its pain and misery?"

He scoffs, shaking his head at me dismissively. "It was too late."

"What do you remember of it?" I ask, tilting my head to take him in.

His jaw ticks and his nostrils flare. "What?"

"Are you speaking from experience or from words spoken to you by your elders?" I push. Most of what we see and believe is what is told to us, which isn't always factual. Besides, we're also the product of our surroundings. If this guy was raised around vampires who hate King Reagan and anything associated with him, then the chances of him following suit are incredibly high.

"That's irrelevant," he mutters. It's my turn to shake my head as I take a step toward him. His hands flex at his sides, eager to reach out and grab me, but he doesn't.

"Is it? We're here, trying to find an heir to the kingdom because The Council isn't working. Are we going to officially call for the demise of each of The Council members too? I'm not standing here using my heritage to demand I take the throne. I'm here to prove that I deserve it."

My words hang heavy around me as my chest heaves. I can feel eyes staring at me from every direction and goosebumps rise along my skin, enhancing the tingling sensation of the hairs on the back of my neck.

"It's a wasted effort," he snaps, and I shrug.

"So you say, but one thing that does run through my blood is unwavering determination. I'm not going to give up here just because my presence makes you unhappy."

The cords of his neck throb, the only indication that he's going to attack, but before I can make a show of putting him in his fucking place, I'm swept up off the floor and turned away from my target.

"Get him the fuck out of here. Now," Raiden growls, his chest rumbling against my back.

"That sounds like a good idea." Everything stills at the sound of Dean Bozzelli's voice echoing through the dining hall. Raiden slowly lowers me to my feet, giving me a split second to lock eyes with the leader of the academy before she speaks again. "That's quite enough from you, Miss Reagan. My office. Now."

THE REIGN OF BLOOD

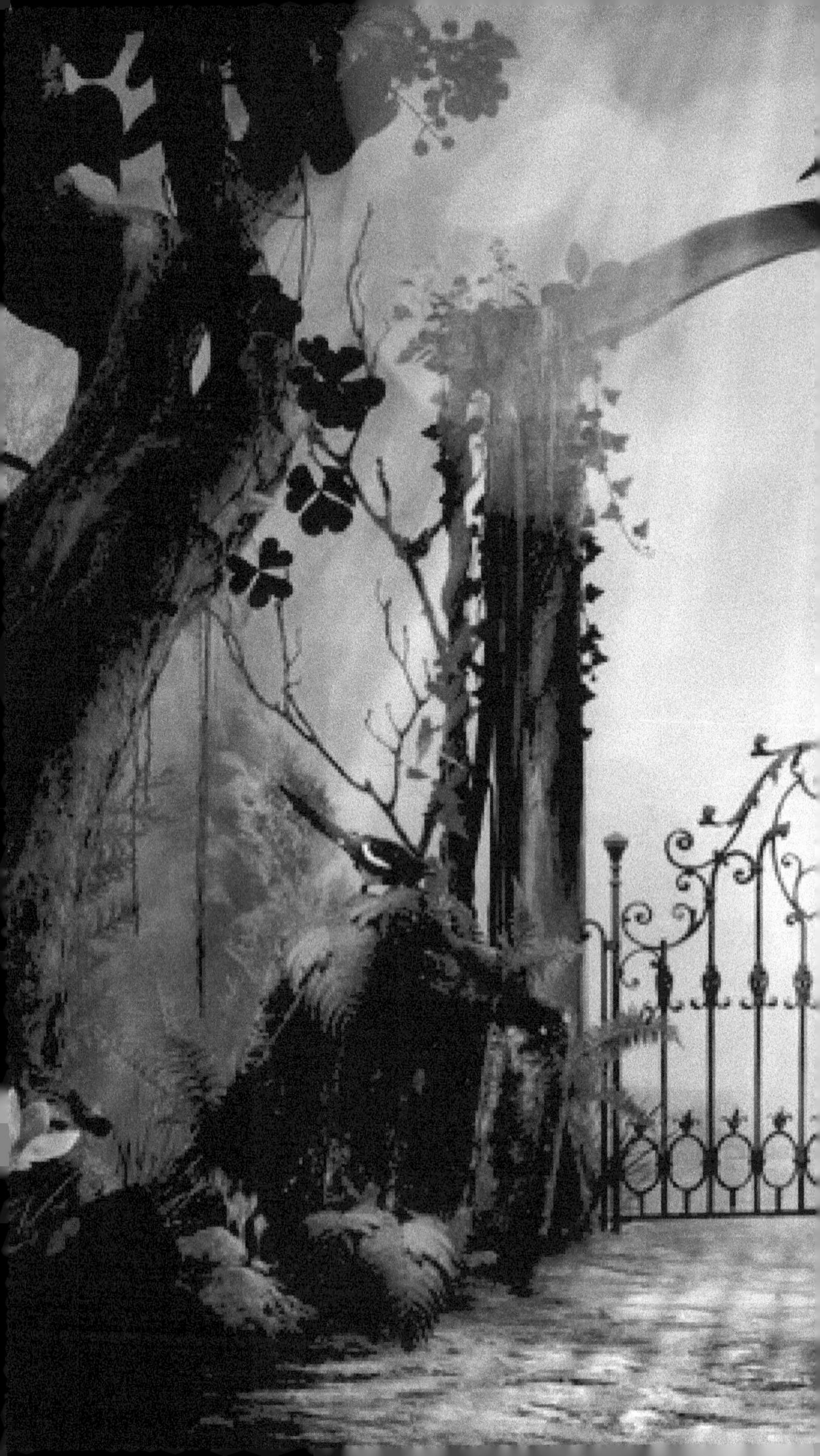

ADRIANNA

15

The door clicks shut behind me, declaring my summoning like the hammer of a gavel in front of The Council. Only, there isn't a single member of the leading body here, just Bozzelli. She didn't like me before, and she certainly doesn't like me now.

She saunters around her desk, never actually taking her eyes off me, as if I'm a convict and she's not safe, but the glimmer in her eyes tells me she believes she holds all the power. She's a mind fuck. I hate it.

"Take a seat." Her voice is cold as she points toward the seat across from her.

"I'm good standing, but thanks," I reply with a shrug, and she shakes her head in disgust.

"You're not a princess inside these four walls, Adrianna. You'll follow my order. Now, sit." Venom pours from her, confirming her opinion of me and my roots as a member of the Reagan line.

Pursing my lips, I recall the lessons my father would teach me in moments like this, and despite my better judgment, I do as she says. His words seemed strong and full of wisdom.

Allow them to guide you, even if their intentions are steeped in things you don't wish to hear or know. I'll teach you how to walk back from the edge of despair with control of the situation firmly in your grasp.

Sometimes, we have to relinquish a bit of power so we can understand their wants, needs, and desires.

The stories I've had to endure, the endless boredom, it's exhausting, but it's what always gave me the information I needed to make the right decisions.

Except for that one time. In that instance, there was no opportunity to find strength within the kingdom or to rely on my friends and allies. They were all gone in the blink of an eye.

I shake my head subtly, focusing on the present rather than taking one too many steps down memory lane. Instead, I focus on Bozzelli. Her canary-yellow suit is even brighter in person. I didn't think that was possible, but I almost consider a pair of sunglasses in here to shield myself from the glare.

She looks down her nose at me as she taps her finger

on the desk. "How do you feel now that your plan has been unraveled?"

"My plan?" I ask, frowning at her.

"Don't play coy with me. I'm no fool."

"I really don't know what plan you're alluding to. Why don't you enlighten me?" I offer with a raised eyebrow, which earns me a sneer as she leans forward and laces her fingers together on the desk.

"Your plan to ruin the academy and everything it stands for," she snaps, face reddening with anger.

I shake my head, lips set in a thin line. "I must admit, I don't recall that one."

"Why else would you be here?" Disbelief ripples from her.

"To win."

A bark of laughter rumbles from her as she shakes her head at me. "You're never going to win."

I should have known she would say that. I don't let her words get to me, though. Instead, I shrug. "I like my odds."

"Which are what?"

"Part of my plan," I retort, smiling wide as her lips curl in disgust.

Leaning back in her chair, she unlaces her fingers to grip the arms, digging her nails into the leather as her eyes burn into me.

"You think you're smart." I don't utter a word; I just let

my smile grow. "But I don't think it's fair for you to attend the academy as a more powerful student than your peers," she adds, making my stomach turn to stone. What does that mean? Is she going to kick me out? She can't. Not on these grounds, surely.

"I didn't realize fairness was a part of this. Each origin here has different abilities, some even have none. Yet they still show up, filled with determination and motivation. Why am I any different?"

"Because you deceived us," she snarls.

"No, I wanted to prove who I am and what I'm capable of without titles or prejudice. I want to prove that the kingdom can be in the hands of the fae again."

"That will never happen." Despite the anger and fury in her words, her grin spreads from ear to ear.

I've walked into something here. I know I have. I just don't know what. The longer I sit here without her getting to the point is another second of my agitation increasing. I can't act rashly or she'll use that against me, but I don't really know what the rules are and I need to toe the line the best I can, which means not attacking the venomous bitch despite the burning desire to do so.

"I can tell you're barely containing yourself, so why don't you spit it out and save us both the time and effort," I grind out, making the anger radiating from her rise.

"I'm your superior. You will respect me."

"It's really cliché for me to say, but respect is earned, and technically, you're not my superior, not in the way you would like. That's my father, the king, remember?" I shouldn't goad her, not when I don't even believe what I'm saying, but she pisses me off. Besides, the pinch of her lips is worth it.

The gleam in her eyes, however, isn't.

She doesn't take her eyes off me as she opens the desk drawer to her right. A glimmer of something purple, as deep as amethyst, flashes in her hand as she turns it over.

"Since I can't kick you out or contain you, I'll have to restrain you."

Her words hang heavy in the room, twisting my stomach into knots as uncertainty wars inside of me. I don't like that I can't predict her at all. It makes me uneasy.

"How?" I ask, despite not wanting to know, but like my father said, information is key. Bozzelli turns the golf ball sized gem in her hand and I watch the way it absorbs the light, making it look regal and elegant, but something tells me it's anything but. "What is that?" I push, but she continues to give me the silent treatment.

Without a word, she stands, slowly prowling around her desk until she's beside me. Her proximity is off-putting, but when I go to stand, I find it impossible.

"Why can't I move?" I bite, my body completely rigid. I can't even wiggle my damn toes.

"Because I haven't deemed it so," she breathes, making my eyes narrow as I try to twist my face to her, but again, I feel only restraint. The only thing I can seem to do is move my damn mouth and my eyes.

My teeth grind together as she yanks at my cloak, pulling it aside before tugging at the neckline of my black t-shirt to reveal the top of my back.

"What are you doing?"

My heart races, panic clawing at my skin as I try to act as unfazed as possible, but it's harder than I care to admit.

"This will hopefully only hurt… a lot," she muses with a chuckle before something slices into my skin.

I wince. The hiss from my lips is impossible to deny as she pierces my skin at the top of my spine. Pain vibrates through me, even when she takes a step back. As she comes into view, I notice the gem is no longer in her hands.

Is that the weight I can feel pressed against my flesh?

What the fuck has she done to me?

Leaning against the desk, she grins at me, pride erupting from every fiber of her being. "If anything, I'm doing you a favor."

"What have you done?" I ask, my head feeling light and fuzzy as a sense of dread clings to me.

"I've weakened you."

"Stop giving me bullshit answers. What have you done?" I snarl, eyes narrowed so tight they're almost closed.

"I've limited the magic you can access."

She did what?

That's bullshit. I haven't even been abusing my magic. I've spent a solid ninety-eight percent of my time here so far pretending I could only access earth magic.

"You can't do that."

"I just have," she retorts with a devilish smirk consuming her face.

"This is torture."

"You're welcome."

"You won't get away with this," I promise, the weight on my back becoming heavier the more aware of it I become.

"Oh, but I will, and I am. No one will challenge me, not when it's for the safety of our people. Besides, The Council has agreed."

"The Council isn't supposed to be in charge of the academy as we try to find the heir," I snipe, and she shrugs.

"The Council are still our leaders until someone is deemed the heir. Until then, you'll do well to fall in line."

She waves her hand dismissively as she saunters around her desk once more, and the restraints confining me to the seat ease. I'm up on my feet in a flash, eager to ruin her, but I can't.

I fucking can't.

The glimmer in her eyes begs me to. She wants to paint

me as the bad guy. Going for her will only make me out to be the villain.

Fuck.

Hands clenched at my sides, I take a deep breath, which does nothing to quash the anger burning through me.

"Is there anything else you need?" I grind out, eager to get as far away from her as possible.

With a shake of her head, she waves a hand toward the door.

"For now, no, but I'm watching you, Adrianna. For the good of this kingdom, I'm watching you."

THE REIGN OF BLOOD

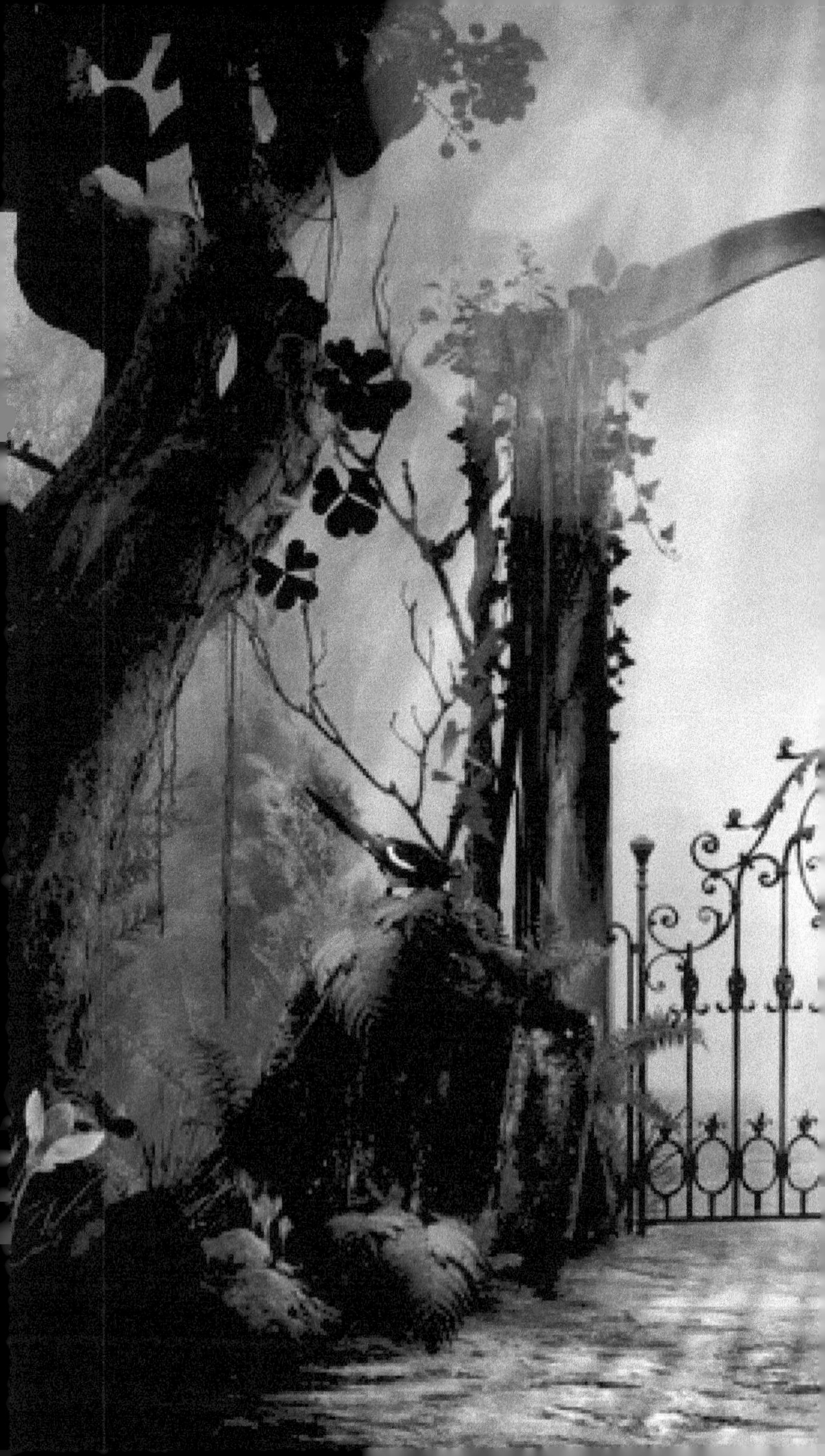

ADRIANNA

16

The door slams behind me, echoing just as it did on my way in, but this time it burns through my veins. The weight of the gem cutting into my back is unbearable. I need to get the hell out of here, and fast.

I take one step and immediately collide with a firm wall. I have no chance of keeping my balance. My arms flail, making the pain in my back worse, but I don't hit the floor as I expect. Hands grip my arms, halting me mid-air before I'm slowly brought back to my feet.

Blinking up at my obstacle and subsequent savior, I'm surprised to find Raiden. His black hair is slightly out of position compared to his usually perfect strands. His jaw is so tight I'm unsure whether it might snap, and his eyes are narrowed on mine.

He stares down at me, and with every passing moment,

his eyebrows knit further together. His fingers flex on my arms and I'm locked in his grasp.

"What did she do?" he rasps, and I shake my head in confusion. Too much has just happened. I can't think straight. "What did she do?" he repeats, pulling me closer to his chest.

"Why are you here, Raiden?" I ask, trying to breathe through the sudden tightening in my chest. After Bozzelli, I can't deal with his shit as well. Exhaustion clings to me from head to toe. I won't be able to give him my best fight right now. That's probably why he's here, to catch me at my most vulnerable.

"I'm here because I could tell she was going to do something ridiculous. I just don't know *what* unless you tell me." I cock a brow at him, my vision blurring slightly as I try to understand. "I tried to get in there, but the door was sealed shut. Otherwise, we wouldn't be having this conversation right now because I would have stopped it from happening."

"Stopped it from happening," I repeat, the words heavy on my tongue. None of it makes sense.

"I tried."

"To come in," I clarify, and he shrugs.

That doesn't align with my previous idea of his motivations. That would mean he wouldn't want me to be weakened and vulnerable. It doesn't make sense.

"Why?" I shake my head, trying to clear the fog, but it does nothing to aid me in my time of need.

"Don't deflect from the actual situation, Adrianna. What did she do?" His tone is firmer this time, and his grip on my arms tightens so much that I'm certain bruises are forming.

Shaking my head, the weight of the gem increases. "I need air," I rasp, and after he searches my eyes for what feels like an eternity, he nods. His hold on my arms loosens and I manage to head toward the door with him a step behind me the entire way.

Without him so close, I manage to think a little clearer, but whatever she actually did is wreaking havoc on my body, magic, and soul.

The fresh air hits me as soon as I step outside. My hands fall to my knees as I lean forward, attempting to stop myself from completely keeling over. Taking a few deep breaths in through my nose, slowly exhaling past my lips, I'm acutely aware that I have an audience in Raiden as he watches my every move.

There's no chance I'm going to my next class. Or any of them for the rest of the day. Not like this. Not with the new target branded against my back. If the vampire attacking me at lunch is anything to go by, then whatever I thought I was handling before has exponentially increased.

"You're bleeding."

I slowly tilt my head to glance up at Raiden, whose gaze is now focused on my back.

"What?"

He doesn't speak. Instead, he grabs the collar of my gray cloak, yanking it from my body and discarding it at our feet. Before I can give him a piece of my mind, his fingers skim over the neckline of my t-shirt, and a moment later, I feel the whoosh of air against my delicate skin.

I wince, managing to bite back the whimper threatening to burst from my lips.

"That bitch," he breathes, disbelief and shock laced in his words.

Standing, his hand falls from my skin, and I fold my arms across my chest nervously as I turn to face him. The fury that he emits is overwhelming, and it takes everything in me not to soak it in and act on it myself.

I've already talked myself out of something foolish, but the look on his face tells me the same can't be said for him. His gaze repeatedly swings between me and the door behind me, as if he's considering going back in there.

I don't need that on my conscience.

"What is it?" I ask, rolling my lips together, hoping like hell to distract him from whatever he's thinking.

"It's a kiss of amethyst," he replies, his gaze settling on me.

A kiss of amethyst? I don't recall that in anything my

father taught me. It sounds like something very *Bozzelli,* that's for sure.

"I'm assuming you've not heard of it." He would assume correctly. I don't say that, though; I just nod. He sighs. "It's used to weaken someone's magic. It's basically a torture device that acts like a kiss of death. You look pale."

I turn away like that will change his assessment of my appearance.

I feel pale. I feel ill. I feel awful.

Clearing my throat, I band my arms tight around my waist. "Lunch is nearly over. You should go."

He frowns. "Go where?" I shrug. That part really isn't my problem. "Come on."

It's my turn to look at him in confusion. He takes a step back, waving for me to follow him, and I shake my head. I really need to stop doing that. It's not helping at all.

"I'm not going to class. Not like this," I admit, and he rolls his eyes.

"I didn't say you were."

"Then where is it you think we're going?"

He reaches down and grabs my cloak off the ground, patting away any debris clinging to it. "I would carry you, but it looks like you really would puke this time," he states, and my stomach clenches at the mere thought of it.

"Thanks," I mutter, unsure if I'm thanking him for

considering my current state before acting on his primal need to caveman me or sarcastically appreciating his assessment of me.

"Standing around here isn't going to do you any good. Let's go," he repeats.

Nipping at my bottom lip, I consider my options. I'm definitely not going to classes—I couldn't stand the looks from everyone at the moment—but the thought of being alone right now isn't intriguing either.

Fuck.

Taking a step toward him, his shoulders relax a little, and we fall into step.

"Where are we going?" I ask as he drapes my cloak around me.

"To see how much it's affected your magic."

THE REIGN OF BLOOD

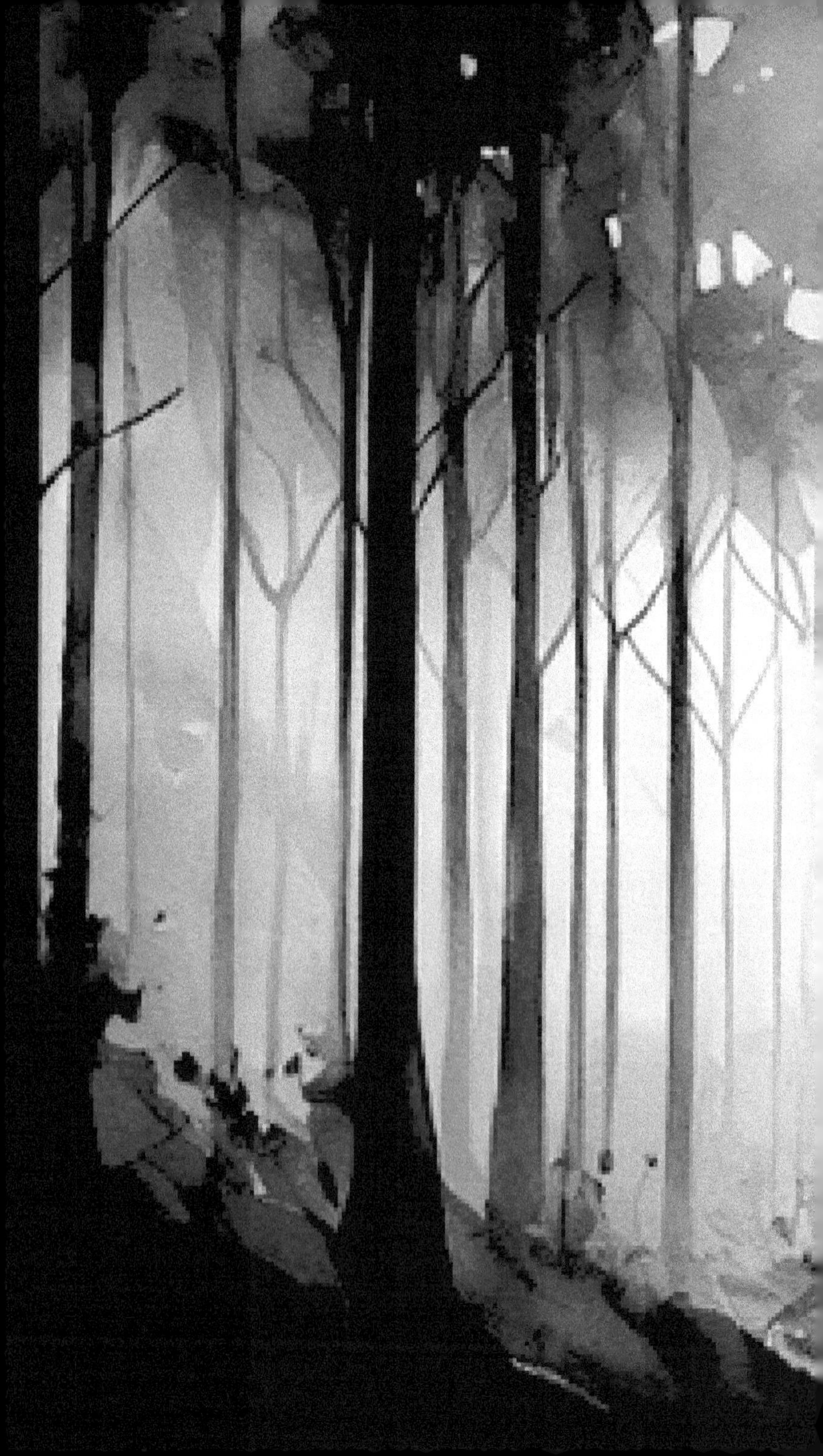

RAIDEN

17

A kiss of amethyst.
A fucking kiss of amethyst.
What is this shit?

She's a goddamn princess. Bozzelli should be worshiping the ground she walks on, not torturing her. And make no mistake, that's exactly what it is: torture. Why would something like that even exist on academy grounds?

Truthfully, this kind of thing shouldn't be a surprise. Shady moves are classic for The Council and everyone in their grasp. Shit, the revelations about Kenner holding the damn queen on the compound should say enough. Especially when Cassian confirmed they knew all along. The capabilities of those in charge here will be off the scales, and there's nothing we can do about it.

I want to go back there and tear Bozzelli to shreds,

but that would have the opposite effect than what I would desire.

Fuck.

We're here to find the perfect heir of our kingdom, not this.

Peering at Adrianna, I can't seem to shift the tightness building in my chest. Her skin is pale, her shoulders slumped, and her steps short and sluggish. She's a shell of her usual self. I bet if I said something to piss her off right now, I wouldn't get her usual snark I desire so much. I'd be lucky if she even waved me off, but my bet would be on no response at all.

She probably needs to get in bed and rest, but my grandmother used to always go on high alert when I was unwell. If I were as white as a sheet, she would be at my side the entire time, but instead of tucking me under the covers, she would have me out in the garden, playing, exerting energy, and remaining present.

"You can sleep when you've shown me how strong you are," she would say, and now I find myself in her shoes, eager to watch this fae girl prove her strength, despite the obvious.

The pathway becomes shaded as we slowly walk along the trail. The trees loom tall above us, and when I glance toward Adrianna, her eyebrows are pinched. Thankfully, she speaks before I can question it.

"Why do I always end up here with one of you?"

Glancing around, I realize we're in the spot where I first saw her, where she first unleashed that wicked tongue and put me in my place despite my efforts. The fallen tree lingers to our right, and I head toward it, eager for her to sit down.

"It's clearly our special place," I muse, and she scoffs. "Just don't get too sentimental over it," I add, aware my harsh front is slipping.

"Why would I?" she questions, cocking a brow at me.

I clear my throat, peering at her before fixing my gaze straight ahead. "Girls are strange with semantics like that. Don't give me that look, I'm just stating the facts," I add when she starts to glare.

Thankfully, she softens it with an eye roll, and I relish in the spark of her usual self rising to the surface, even if it is only for a split second.

She sits with a sigh, her head slumped forward as her eyelids close.

Taking off my red cloak, I drape it over the stump and take a seat beside her. Despite my eagerness to keep her present, I give her a few minutes to relax and come down from the walk.

I still can't wrap my head around seeing her like this. Maybe I should get the others, but a part of me wants to keep her all to myself. She doesn't need more people falling over themselves when she's not at her full capacity. Not that I know what any of this means for me.

She's the enemy, a fae, a fae *princess*, but a fae all the same.

I should hate her, now more than ever, just like Sean said when he tried to attack her earlier, but I can't. I was drawn to her before, but now? This is something else entirely.

A groan slips from her lips as she leans back, rolling her neck in an attempt to rid her limbs of the ache.

"Okay, let's focus on your magic so you're not consumed with the pain," I murmur, rising to stand before her. She looks up at me through her lashes as though she wants to punch me in the dick. She's struggling. If I can see it, she is most definitely feeling it. Distraction. That's what she needs. "So, you pretended to rock the earth magic for a while, and I've seen you use your air abilities, but you're going to have to rank all of your royal skills for me so we can figure it out."

"I'm not telling you any of that," she grunts, wiping a hand down her face.

My nose scrunches in confusion. "Why?"

"Giving you my abilities in order of my skill level only serves to reveal my vulnerabilities," she states, leaving me to gape at her.

"No, it doesn't."

"How so?" She looks at me like I'm insane, and I shake my head.

"You have access to all five magics a fae can harness. There's nothing vulnerable about that." She raises her eyebrows but still doesn't offer the information. "How about you don't tell me that then, but you rank yourself out of ten when compared to your usual abilities."

She purses her lips, considering her options as she always does before giving me a subtle nod. Her jaw ticks and a vein pulses at her temple when she pushes up onto her feet. I almost retract my offer to help her. She's not up to it, but life isn't fair and neither is this. She has to push through whether she likes it or not.

I open my mouth to encourage her when her gaze whips to mine. "Please just stop talking. I'm trying, and I don't need you dictating to me what should be done," she snaps, the warning clear in her eyes.

Snarky as fuck. I like it.

"Whatever you say," I reply, lifting my hands in surrender.

It's not lost on me that she interprets every action as a negative, but I don't correct her. Not if it fuels that fire burning deep inside of her.

Closing her eyes, she takes a deep breath. Nothing happens for a beat until the discreet sound of something stretching comes from below me. I look down to see vines protruding from the ground, inching toward my feet.

I take a step back, wagging my finger at her. "Not again," I grumble, earning a small smirk from her. I haven't forgotten the last time she did that when I was sitting at the table with the guys. I was ready to chase after her when she got up and sauntered off, but found myself rooted to the spot.

"But it's fun," she grumbles, giving me puppy-dog eyes, and I shake my head at her.

"How does it feel compared to usual?" I ask, continuing to dodge the vines until she finally relents and allows them to slip back into the ground.

Her lips twist as she thinks before she turns her back to me and moves toward one of the small flower beds lining the small wooded area. She crouches down, stroking her finger over the pink petal, and I watch as it brightens under her touch.

"Honestly, it's maybe like a seven. Usually, I would be able to keep the vines silent, but they probably heard the stretching noise at the damn academy," she grumbles, dancing her fingers over the surrounding flowers before rising back to her feet.

"Seven? We can work with that."

She hums in agreement, but disappointment dances in her eyes as she looks at me. "Maybe take a step back for this one," she murmurs, making me frown.

"Why?"

"You don't have to. I'm just being polite," she breathes as her eyelids fall closed again.

Without warning, the wind picks up around us, and I instantly realize she's focusing on her air magic. She's right. I definitely should take a step back for this one. I've been on the wrong end of her force before. I'd rather not experience it again.

The trees bow from force, and a few leaves fall to the ground, but the pinch between her eyebrows tells me she's not happy. When the magic stops, the breeze comes to a halt and her eyes open, the disappointment in them is stronger than before.

"Four," she croaks before clearing her throat and turning away from me once again.

This is bullshit. Absolute bullshit, but what pounds in my head more is the confusion over the fact that I want to make this better for her. I'm not a helper. I don't aid those who need it. I'm selfish, and I like it that way.

Clearing my throat, I pull myself from my thoughts. "Next."

"I need a minute," she grumbles, hands on her hips as she looks down at the ground. Her back is still to me, and that only makes the confusion inside me go haywire.

"You haven't got a minute," I grunt, and she whips her face to me with a glare.

"I'll have what I fucking well need."

"And if someone is attacking you, what are you going to do then?" I fire back, arms wide as I take a step toward her.

"The only person here who could attack me right now is you."

"That's not what I'm talking about and you know it." I shake my head, taking another step toward her. "Do you think Bozzelli is going to go easy on you now that she's weakened your abilities?"

Silence greets me as her gaze continues to darken. I'm very aware I'm fucking this all up right now, but I can't seem to stop myself. My instinctual reaction is to push everyone away, especially when they're getting under my skin as much as she is.

I shouldn't be out here helping her. I shouldn't be doing any of this.

She needs to rest, and I need some space. Something has shifted in my head and I can't think straight.

"If you can't get on with it, then let's call it quits," I bark, challenging her, and her nostrils flare with anger and irritation.

Good.

She stomps toward me, gaze fixed on mine in a way I've never seen before. It lasts for a solid five seconds before her face falls slack and horror dances in her eyes.

She takes a step back, and another. Despite my need to put distance between us, I inch toward her.

"What's going on?"

She shakes her head, turning away from me as she rushes toward the pathway as quickly as she can. It's barely a power walk. She's so weak. Keeping up with her isn't a hard task. Meeting her on the path, I reach for her arm but walk around her instead of tugging her to face me. I'm not sure if she'd tumble to the ground if I handled her too harshly right now.

"Talk to me, Adrianna," I grind out, noting the pain in her eyes isn't subsiding.

She slams her eyes shut, blocking me off, but she doesn't try to shake herself free from my grasp.

"I think I'm broken," she rasps, and I'm certain her chin wobbles slightly, but it lasts only a split second, not long enough for me to confirm or not.

"You can't be broken, Adrianna. You're incredible." I don't know where the words come from, but I wish they would return to their source.

"You're full of shit," she grumbles, and even though a part of me agrees with that statement, I find myself stating the complete opposite.

"No, I'm not."

She shakes her head, finally stepping out of my hold, and I let her go. "I was a lowly fae a few weeks ago. *Now*

I'm incredible. That's the biggest bullshit I've heard in a long time," she points out, and all I can do is shrug.

"I didn't see your worth then," I offer, the truth spilling from my lips once again, and I don't like it.

"You mean you didn't know I was of royal blood. Is that it?"

"Maybe."

It's not true. It's so far from the fucking truth, but it seems I'm on a mission of self-destruction.

"At least you're honest," she mutters, and I sink my teeth into my bottom lip, refusing to correct her.

She yawns as her eyes fall to the ground, a sigh parting her lips a moment later, and I feel it in my bones.

"You need to rest."

"Maybe."

Wetting my lips, I consider my options. They're limited, and as much as a part of me wants to take off and be selfish like usual, I can't. "Can you handle me moving you?" My question lingers in the air. There's something going on with her that she doesn't want to discuss with me, and right now, I don't want to hear it. Even if it's the key to me being the heir of the Floodborn Kingdom, I don't want it. "I'm going to take your silence as a yes," I state when she gives me nothing.

My hands fall to her waist and she tucks herself in against my chest. I feel her tense in anticipation before I take off. I try to make it as fast and smooth as possible, and a moment later, we're outside her bedroom door.

I make sure she's steady on her feet before I take a step back.

Glancing at her door handle, I point to the item resting there. "There's a rose."

"There always is." She turns to take it, running her fingertips over the petals.

"Always?"

"I'm collecting them. This is rose number four," she explains, her words having a whimsical undertone.

"You're keeping them?"

"They call to my magic; of course, I am," she retorts as if it were obvious, and I nod.

She looks up at me with a sleepy edge to her gaze and I reach up to stroke my thumb across her cheek.

"What are you doing?" she asks, and I shake my head.

"I don't know." My gaze flickers between her eyes and her pouty lips.

We're still close, chest to chest, with our breaths mingling between us. My heart rattles inside me, a feeling I'm not all that familiar with unless it stems from adrenaline, but this is different.

I inch closer, despite my head screaming for me to turn away and run. She doesn't move, so I eliminate another. And another. And another. Until the heat of her lips is pressed against mine.

Warmth dances between us as I bask in her energy.

It's everything.

It's too much.

It's intoxicating.

Overwhelmed, I disconnect, taking a huge step back. So far, my back almost presses against the wall behind me as I blink at her.

I nod, and she nods too.

I don't know what the hell is happening, but it seems I've forgotten how to function.

Clearing my throat, I take a side step toward the staircase.

"I'll be seeing you," I blurt, instantly regretting it as a small smile curls the corner of her lips.

"I'll be seeing you too."

THE REIGN OF BLOOD

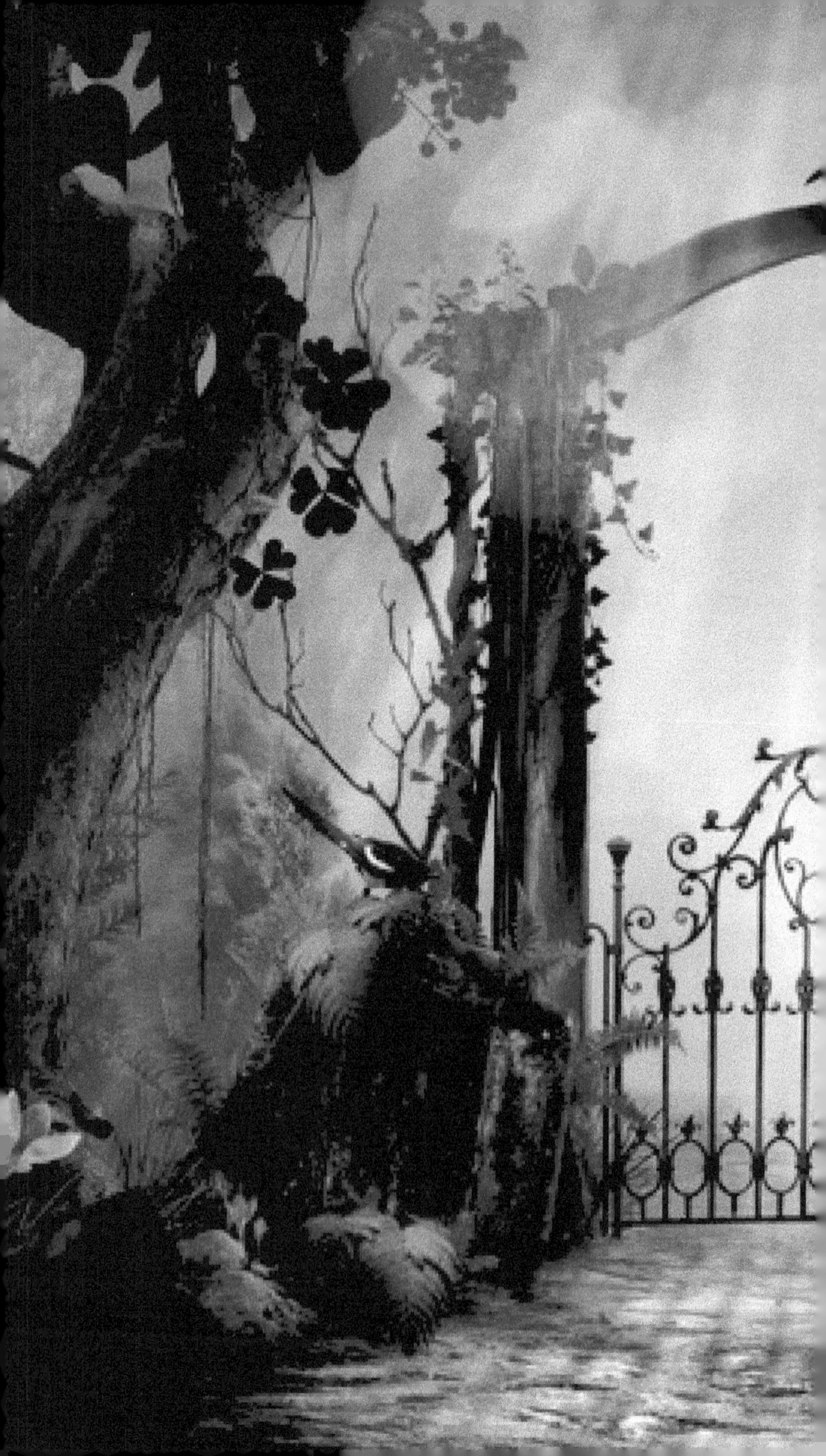

ADRIANNA

18

Panic flutters in my chest, horror consuming my bones as the wolf makes Nora cry out in agony.

My magic bubbles to the surface, desperate to save my sister. It rips from every fiber of my body, my own cry mingling with Nora's. My vision blurs, a bright light consuming every inch of the space around me before everything goes black.

I bolt awake, heart racing as I swipe the cold sweat from my brow. It does nothing to ease the ache weighing on my limbs.

With a heavy sigh, I swing my legs over the side of the bed as my breath slowly evens out.

It seems the infamous nightmare that loves to haunt me is here to stay for a while. Again. It has been a while, I suppose I should have known it would rear its ugly head eventually. The dull ache in my back is a stark reminder of another horror in my life that I wish was nothing more than a nightmare, but it's definitely real.

Yesterday was a mess, and that's putting it lightly because I truly can't find the right words to describe it all, but I need to get over it now. The moment Raiden left, I crashed. Which is probably why my stomach is practically turning in on itself.

I need to eat.

Peering at the time, I raise a brow at it, and two seconds later, my morning alarm goes off. I can never decide if I feel triumphant for beating the damn thing or heartbroken that I just robbed myself of a few extra minutes of sleep.

Either way, my day has begun and I need to muster the strength to face whatever is set to come my way.

Yesterday, just before Raiden brought me home, I had the horrible realization that my mind magic was non-existent. It's my weakest ability, which is probably why it's Nora's strongest. On a normal day, I might be a five out of ten, but yesterday was a huge zero.

Nada.

Holding my hand out in front of me, I focus on my center, summoning the heat particles in the room. Embers flicker in my palm before a small ball of fire erupts. It's still there, at least. But again, what would be an eight out of ten is struggling at a five.

I don't know whether it's the lack of food in my stomach or the kiss of amethyst, but it feels like it's draining me more. Maybe if I set off early enough, I can connect with the water in the fountain on the way to the academy. Then I can rate my water magic and figure out where I'm at.

If Raiden asks anything today, I need to brush over it. He doesn't need to know any more than he already does. A part of me expects him to give me his usual cold treatment. He started acting strange yesterday, getting growly for no particular reason. Yet he brought me here and kissed me.

Fucking kissed me.

And I didn't stop him.

I'm not sure which part confuses me more.

Shaking my head, I push that all to the back of my mind. I need to get dressed and eat, then I might be able to start thinking clearly.

I opt to conserve my energy, which means no cute air magic this morning to aid me getting ready. Fixing my cloak around my neck, I step toward the door when the telltale sound of my cell phone vibrating echoes around the room.

Glaring at the offending drawer where it's contained, I consider my options. I clearly take too long to decide because it stops a few moments later. Inching closer to the door, I pause a second later when it starts going off again.

Fuck.

Panic sets in and I scramble to get it, the tightness in my chest growing stronger as Nora's name flashes across the screen.

"Is everything okay?" I rush, not bothering with the pleasantries of a greeting.

"You're asking *me* that?"

I frown at the confusion in her voice. "Nora?"

"Video call. Now," she grumbles, and I accept without question, worry still getting the better of me. Her face comes into view, and when I don't see any imminent danger, relief calms me, just a little.

The pointed look on her face, however, doesn't give me the all clear just yet. "Addi, it's all over the news."

"Nora, I've just had the hardest sleep of my life and I'm starving, so you're going to have to be a bit more specific than that. But first, can you just confirm that you're not in any danger so my heart can calm down?"

She rolls her eyes at me like I'm being dramatic. She hasn't seen anything dramatic. Not yet.

"No danger. For now at least," she states, doing nothing to settle my heart.

"What does that mean?"

"It means you're supposed to let me explain what I was calling for before you keep interrupting," she sasses with a cock of her brow.

It's my turn to roll my eyes. "Sorry, what is so

important?"

She rubs her lips together nervously, taking a deep breath that makes her chest heave heavily. "Everyone knows who you are." She braces for impact, as if the words are going to cause a backlash that will travel through the cell phone.

"Oh."

"It's been broadcasted to the entire kingdom," she adds, still waiting for me to detonate, but after yesterday, it's no real shock that everyone is aware now.

"How bad is it?"

Her eyebrows rise, like she's assessing my reaction. "I don't know, Dad made me turn it off," she admits, turning her gaze off screen to presumably glare at the man in question.

"Because the media is a bunch of crap and I wanted to hear from my daughter."

There he is.

Hearing both of them fills my body with the dose of love I didn't know I needed. It's a stark reminder of what I'm doing all of this for. It makes me sit taller, focus, and want to fight past everything. Especially this damn amethyst.

"Hi, Dad," I breathe, and a moment later his face appears beside Nora's.

"Hi, Addi. What's going on?" He pushes his glasses up

the bridge of his nose. It's a sophisticated look he's always going for. There's no prescription in the lenses, but it's a part of his aura so we let him rock it. The wrinkles at the corner of his eyes stand out as his face stretches into a smile.

"What have the media said?" I ask, smiling despite the worry that exudes from both of them.

"That doesn't matter. I want to know what's been going on with you, how all of this has come about."

Because trouble follows me at every turn. Because it's nothing like the farm here. Because I'm dealing with more than I thought was possible.

How do I know how much to tell him without knowing how much has been released?

"I've been okay, Dad," I offer as I swipe their faces to the corner of my screen so I can access the Internet app.

"Don't try that business with me. I could sense it in your voice the last time we spoke," his retorts, giving me his usual inquisitive look. The one I'm a sucker for.

Quickly skimming my eyes over the news, I'm surprised there isn't an actual picture of me published, but the information I'm looking for is displayed bold and strong.

Queen Reagan.

Fuck.

I may as well tell him everything. I don't like to keep

secrets from them anyway, but the facts of last Friday have been a lot for me to grasp, too.

"Everything was okay until last Friday," I admit, and it feels like the truth. "Yeah, I was dealing with shit from other students on campus, but Friday was when everything escalated to another level."

"What happened last Friday?" he questions, remaining calm with me.

Taking a deep breath, I tap back on their image so they fill the screen again. "I went to the Kenner compound."

The despair on my father's face confirms everything. The vein at his temple throbs, just like the one at mine does. That's exactly where I get it from.

"Why the… why would you go there?"

"Because I have a… friend that's a wolf, and they invited me to a moon party. I wasn't aware I would be walking the territory of the men who attacked us," I add, lips pursed as Nora gasps. Her hand lifts to cover her mouth and I instantly wish I was there to hug her, but instead, I focus on the conversation to keep my mind occupied. "You should have told me who it was, Dad."

Silence drapes over us as he wraps an arm around Nora to soothe her. A defeated sigh falls from his lips as he adjusts his glasses and offers me a thin smile. "It seems I should have. I'm sorry for that, it was a failed attempt at protecting you."

Why does this man always accept his faults and apologize for them without any kind of defensiveness? I wouldn't. Hands down, I would explain my reasoning until he heard sense, but not him.

"What happened at the compound?" he asks, keeping the conversation on track.

"Kenner realized who I was because of my ears," I murmur, the scars burning at the memory of it happening and the reminder that Kenner declared it his handiwork.

"Asshole," Nora snarls, lips pinched, and I snicker despite the circumstances.

"Nora," my father scolds, and she gives him her innocent look that gets her out of trouble ninety-nine percent of the time.

"What? He is," she insists, and I can't help but nod in agreement.

"He is. He boasted about it before he brought out a special guest." My chest tightens at the reminder, worsening with the knowledge that I have to say it out loud and confirm the existence of the person mentioned in the news.

My father must sense the discomfort rising in me. "It's okay, Addi. Just say it. They're only words."

It eases my concern a little, but doubles my irritation as her name falls to my tongue. "Queen Reagan confirmed who I was in front of the Kenner pack."

"Mom." Nora's eyes instantly fill with unshed tears as her fingers tremble.

This, I can't console her for, not even if I was there. "No, Queen Reagan," I reiterate, making her glare at me.

"Same thing."

"Not in my eyes."

My father's gaze drops to the floor. Our thoughts on his wife have always been different. I think it's because I was older, more aware, not completely in the know, but Nora doesn't remember her at all. She just has a whimsical idea of what living as a princess would have been like.

"What happened next?" he finally asks, breaking the stare off between Nora and me.

"Another friend of mine got me out of there. The weekend was fine, and yesterday started off well too, until Bozzelli made an announcement to the academy."

Fury immediately burns in my father's eyes as he tries to scan me for any harm. "If anyone—"

I wave him off. "I can handle all of that. We knew people would come for me, that's what we've trained for. I just don't think we anticipated the likes of special gem devices being used to alter my strength."

"Special gem devices?" Nora repeats, concern dancing in her eyes, despite our frustration with one another mere moments ago.

"Not a kiss of amethyst," my father murmurs, shaking

his head in disbelief.

"That's probably another thing you should have taught me about, Dad," I state, trying to keep my voice as calm as possible as I confirm that the wicked kiss of amethyst is, indeed, buried into my flesh.

"Another mishap on my part, but in my defense, I had banished them. I didn't think there was anything to discuss about them, but I can help you, Addi."

"How?"

"Give me a few days," he breathes, and I nod. "What are you going to do now?" he asks, keeping me focused on the situation.

"What is the media saying?" I ask, and he shrugs while Nora answers.

"A bit of everything. There's almost a slight buzz of excitement around you, but others are…"

"Others are what?" I nudge when she doesn't finish her sentence. She looks to my father for guidance, who turns a soft smile my way.

"They're not so impressed."

"That's okay. We knew they wouldn't be."

"Yeah." Concern vibrates from Nora, like she's not convinced things are as okay as I'm saying. Maybe they're not, but admitting it to myself will only make it more real, and I'm more about manifesting strength than weakness.

She twists her hands in her lap as her eyebrows pinch

together.

"What aren't you telling me?" I ask, my adrenaline kicking up a notch as I search their gazes.

"They're on the hunt now," she admits, not making any sense.

"What for?" I push, and she rolls her eyes but refuses to meet my gaze.

"More like who for."

"Who?"

Her eyes latch on to mine, and I know with absolute certainty that I'm not going to like what comes out of her mouth next.

"They're on the hunt for Dad and me."

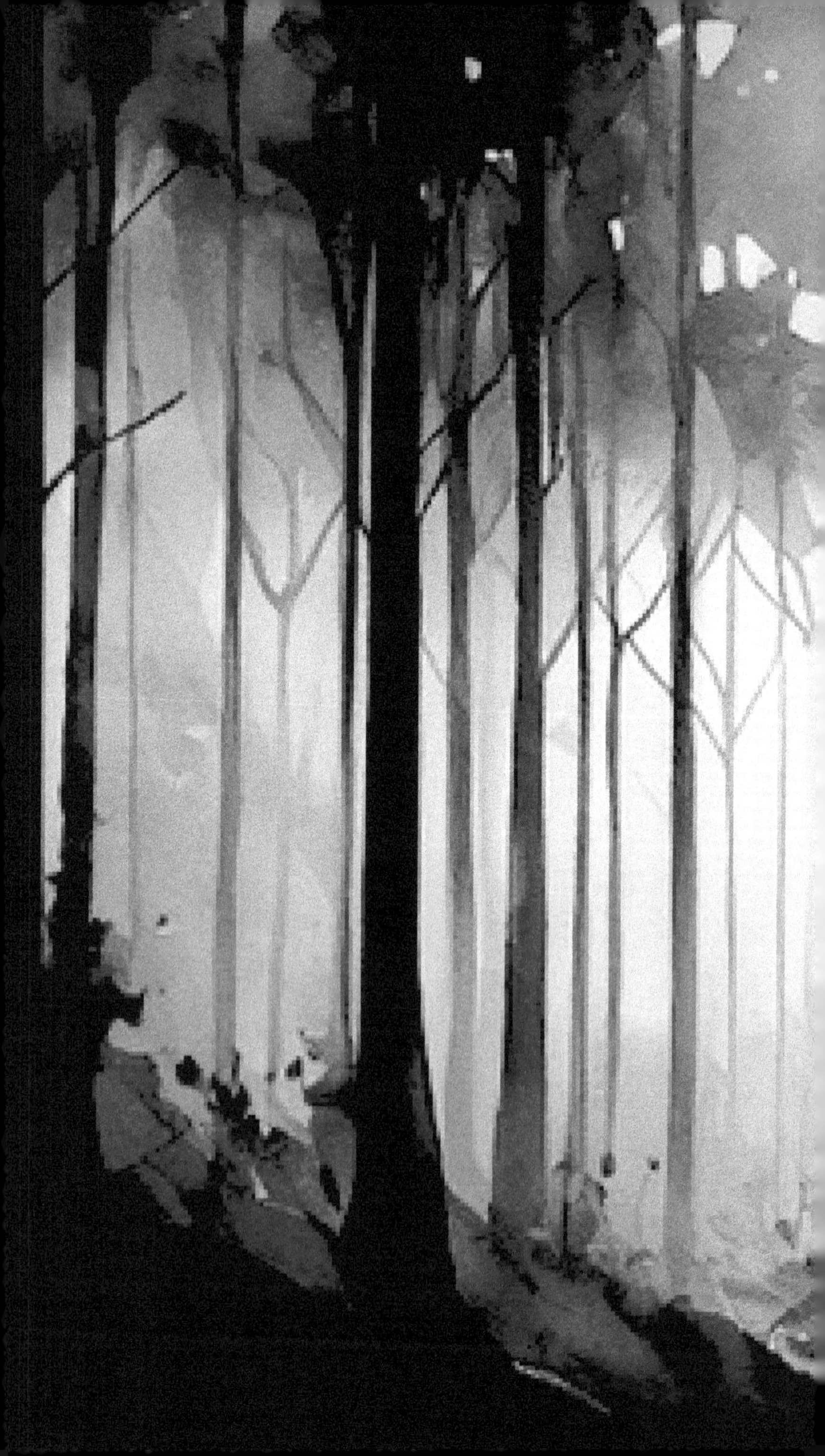

KRYLL

19

"What the fuck is going on with you?" Cassian grunts, staring at an almost frantic Raiden as he paces back and forth in front of his coffee table. I agree with the question, maybe not as harshly worded, but something definitely isn't right.

He's completely unkept, his hair sticking up in every direction as if he's raked his fingers through it a thousand times, and his creased pajama bottoms hang at his waist. He's usually the most kept, ironed, and put-together guy you've ever met, but the person standing before me is far from any of those things.

Are those bags under his eyes?

"I messaged you all to get here because I need your help, not your grunts and snarls," he retorts, planting his hands on his hips as he glares at the three of us.

Yeah, I'm at a complete loss with him now.

"Where were you yesterday?" Brody asks, slumping on the sofa to my right.

"On protective duty," Raiden retorts, making me frown.

"What does that mean?" I ask, earning the deathly glare again as his lips purse and his jaw ticks.

"Were none of you there when Bozzelli called Adrianna in the dining hall?" Distaste dances across his features as my frown continues to deepen.

"Where did you go after that?" Brody asks, recalling the fact that the vampire before us disappeared and never came back.

"To check on her."

"Why?" Cassian grunts, folding his arms over his chest.

"Have you met Bozzelli?" Raiden retorts, like that should explain it.

"She's harsh as fuck, but what does that have to do with anything?" Brody questions, lacing his fingers behind the back of his head as he gets comfortable.

Raiden glances over the three of us like we've grown a second head or something. "You didn't think something might happen to Adrianna when she was called. You know, after the news of her heritage was spread around the academy like a scandal."

"I mean, it *is* a scandal," Cassian snaps, and Raiden is in front of him in a split second.

"*You're* a fucking scandal."

This isn't heading in the best direction. Before I can try to simmer them both down, Brody beats me to it.

"Did something happen to her?"

Raiden spins to face him, completely forgetting about Cassian behind him. "Did something happen to her? Of course it did!" he bites, making my spine stiffen as Brody quickly stands from the sofa. His calm demeanor quickly shifts to one etched with concern.

"What?"

"Thanks, Brody. *This* is the level of concern we're supposed to be at," Raiden remarks, glaring at Cassian and me.

"Get to the point," Cassian grunts, stepping up to my side as he waits for the details. He's trying to play it off, but I can sense the undertone of worry. Even if it's only a smidge. "And can you make it quick? I'm starving. I'm only here because Kryll said your absence yesterday was a concern."

"So is the state of him and the text he sent," I add. I would be concerned about anyone under the circumstances.

His message was about as cryptic as he's being now. It's exhausting.

"Have you heard of the kiss of amethyst?" he asks, and

I shake my head along with Cassian. "Uneducated fucks," he grumbles, and I raise my hands in surrender. I don't need him to start over with the lack of knowledge we have. That's only going to stir up Cassian, too, and I can't handle them both like this.

"I have," Brody interjects, pulling Raiden's attention toward him. "It's a purple gem, shines like it's the prettiest damn thing in the world, but it has the ability to weaken anyone's magic. I thought it was banished years ago?"

"They were. Guess who now has one embedded into her back?"

My spine stiffens as I watch the horror dance over Brody's face.

"No," he mutters with a gasp as Raiden nods, a sneer on his lips.

"Yes."

"It's a torture device," Brody insists, raking his fingers through his hair, and Raiden nods eagerly.

"That's exactly what I said."

"Can't we just get it out?" I blurt, and Brody shakes his head slowly.

"It's not as simple as that. Not without an impossible magic and what I can only imagine is a lot of pain. Definitely more pain than the feeling of it being attached," he explains, making my chest tighten and my spine ache from how stiff it is.

"What do we do then?" I ask, feeling the need to come up with a solution to this situation. I can't believe I hadn't considered Bozzelli would do something like this. But more than that, I can't believe Raiden did.

"We decide," the vampire declares, slapping his hands against his thighs as he looks at each of us.

"On what?" I ask, despite secretly knowing I don't *want* to know where this is going.

"On claiming her or not." He says it with such a finality that it leaves me frozen in place.

"What the fuck are you talking about?" Cassian grunts, the cords in his neck tightening with every breath he takes.

"I haven't slept," Raiden states, starting to list off his points on his fingertips.

"Okay," Cassian bites back, and I'm intrigued to understand how this guy got from A to Z by somehow passing every other letter in the alphabet, too.

"I haven't stopped worrying."

"Okay."

"I kissed her."

"*You* kissed Addi?" Brody reconfirms, and Raiden nods.

"Adrianna? Yes."

"Okay," Cassian grinds out before Brody can interject. There's a glimmer of excitement in his eyes that tells me he's happy to agree with whatever Raiden suggests at this stage.

"I am not comfortable with any of these feelings," Raiden continues, swirling his hands around, and Cassian scoffs.

"You're telling me." I press my lips together to bite back the smile, but it quickly vanishes at Raiden's worry.

"But I'm even more uncomfortable with her out of my sight. It feels like my skin is crawling."

Well, damn.

"I'm not claiming her," Cassian declares, taking a step back.

"I thought you already had?" I interject, cocking my brow at him, and he sticks his middle finger up at me.

"Technically, she claimed me," he corrects, his eyes continuing to darken.

"Not by choice," Brody chimes in, earning a glare from the grumpy wolf.

"We're not asking for specifics right now."

"It feels like now is the time for specifics," I add, amused at the way they're acting in the midst of all this.

"Do you even like her?" Cassian bites, turning his wrath my way.

"What does that have to do with the situation?" I push back, instantly regretting opening my mouth. I'd rather not be put under the spotlight right now.

"It has everything to do with the situation."

"I'm quite certain it doesn't. Besides, you guys are

too amusing to distract from. Please, proceed," I repeat, my fingers starting to tingle with their gazes all turned my way. No, thank you.

"I vote we claim her," Brody announces, lifting his hand in the air while bouncing on the balls of his feet.

"Thank you!" Raiden hollers, swinging his arm around his friend's shoulder as they find some kind of solace in agreeing with each other.

"I don't," Cassian barks, and it's no real surprise.

"That leaves it to Kryll," Raiden states, making all eyes aim back at me.

Fuck.

"So your opinion *does* matter in this situation. Would you look at that?" Cassian points out with a raised eyebrow.

"Don't get smug. It's unbecoming," I grumble, folding my arms over my chest.

"Unbecoming? Fuck off. Place a vote so we can go and eat."

"I'm not placing any vote." I'm standing my ground on this shit right now. There's no way.

"That's how this works. We vote. On everything. Now isn't any different."

"Thanks for reminding me," I mutter, squeezing the back of my neck to try to ease the rising tension, but it does nothing to calm me down.

I need to get out of here. With all their opinions and

thoughts consuming the room, I can't breathe.

Turning, I don't make it one step before there's a hand on my arm, halting me in place. It's Cassian. I know it without looking. He's the only one who would dare to touch me without warning, irritating the animal inside of me.

"Where are you going?" he grinds out, and I shake out of his hold to glance at all three of them.

"Away from the drama you guys are swimming in. I've had a shower already this morning. I don't feel like getting wet again."

"That doesn't make any sense," Brody says, rubbing at his chin in confusion.

"Neither does any of this crap," I retort, and he rolls his eyes at me.

"You have to vote, Kryll," he states, keeping his tone soft and calm, but it doesn't change my mind.

"No, I don't."

"I'm not waiting around for your decision. I need to go and check that she's okay," Raiden suddenly declares, shaking his head in frustration as he stomps off toward his bedroom.

"She's fine."

He comes to a stop, slowly turning on the spot to face me with a weird look in his eyes. "How do you know that?"

Ah, fuck.

There's no point denying it—not when they'll be able to see right through me. "I flew past her window on the way here."

"The fae building is in the complete opposite direction of the vampire building."

I shrug. "I needed to stretch my wings."

"So you do care. Vote yes," Raiden murmurs, his eyes wide with hope.

I take a step back. "I think you're forgetting who and what I am."

The three of them frown at me. "Be specific," Cassian says with a sigh, his irritation at the situation clear. But it's almost as if he wants me to vote yes even though it will go against him.

They're giving me a damn headache.

"Now you want specifics," I mutter, shaking my head in annoyance.

"Don't be a dick."

"Then don't force me to tie myself to someone. I'm a shifter. That's not what we do," I growl, my emotions rushing to the surface before I can harness them.

"So you *don't* want to claim her," Brody interjects, confusion written all over his face.

You and me both, my friend. You and me both.

"I never said that."

"Then what *are* you saying?" Raiden pushes, and I

can't contain the agitation any longer.

"I'm saying nothing right now." I turn for the door again, and thankfully, no one tries to stop me this time.

Relief floods my veins as the door opens, and I step through the threshold.

"Leaving isn't going to help," Cassian states, but I don't bother to turn back to them to see how pissed they are.

"It's going to help me immensely."

THE REIGN OF BLOOD

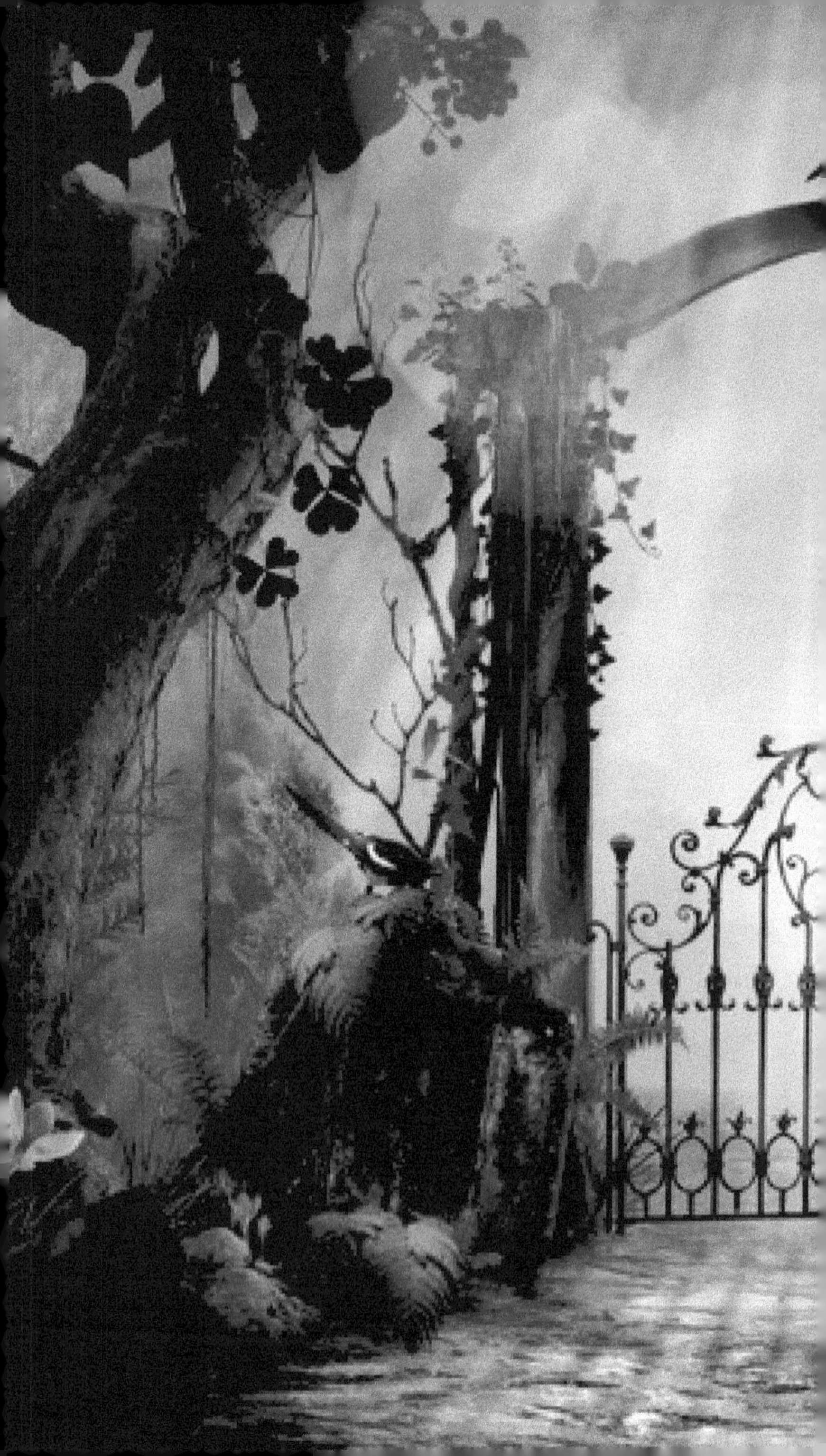

ADRIANNA

20

"Hey, are you okay? I saw you take off this morning and I was a little worried."

I pause my chewing to peer up at Flora, whose eyes dance with the same concern she speaks of. "I wasn't purposely being nosey. I just saw you through my bedroom window," she adds, and Arlo rolls his eyes beside her.

Finishing off the food in my mouth, I clear my throat. "I'm fine. I was just starving."

She takes the seat across from me, Arlo taking his usual spot too. It feels weird sitting at this table when the assholes who continue to dominate my life aren't here. I considered sitting elsewhere, but yet again, in the grand scheme of things, where I eat my food isn't at the top of my priority list. I have enough drama. That won't be added to it.

I'm sure they'll make their appearance soon enough, though. The dining hall is starting to pick up.

"I didn't see you for dinner last night," Flora says, cutting into her pancakes, and I nod.

"Yeah, I slept through it."

"Slept?" Arlo quizzes, brows knitted in confusion as he peers at me.

"I was exhausted," I answer with a shrug, which only seems to intensify both of their stares.

"Does it have something to do with Bozzelli?"

I pause, fork halfway to my mouth as I look her straight in the eye.

"What makes you say that?" The words aren't much more than a whisper. I feel like I can't breathe.

She shrugs, but I can sense the worry in her tense shoulders. "She summoned you, and this is the first time I've seen you since."

I consider that fact, recalling the moment the dean stormed in and ordered me to her office. There was no Professor Fairbourne this time. There was no buffer. But more than that, I realize I never actually got to have my lunch yesterday, so it's been practically twenty-four hours since I last ate. No wonder my stomach feels like a bottomless pit this morning. I can't stop eating. I won't tell either of them that this is my second plate of food.

"You don't have to answer, I just—"

I wave her off, interrupting her unnecessary backtracking. "Oh, it definitely has something to do with her. I just can't stop shoveling this food into my mouth," I admit, repeating the motion with the fork loaded with egg and bacon.

"A girl after my own heart," Arlo sings, hand on his chest, making me grin.

"A girl nowhere *near* your heart."

In slow motion, the three of us turn to see Raiden glaring down at Arlo like he's about to rearrange his face. We definitely don't need any additional issues today, so he can calm himself down real quick.

Brody taps the irritated vampire on the shoulder before taking his seat across the table from me. The rest of them move in silence, and a second later, I have Raiden on my left, Kryll on my right, and Cassian still giving me the silent treatment.

Excellent.

I frown at their lack of food trays, but not even ten seconds go by before plates are placed in front of them, piled high with food. I roll my eyes at the servers, who saunter off just as quickly as they came.

Of course they get their food served to them.

"Are you excited for ball prep this morning, Dagger?" Brody asks with a grin before he takes a bite of his breakfast.

I shake my head. "Nope." The *P* pops with way more sass than I expect, but I like it.

"Why?" His eyes narrow as he searches mine, but I turn my attention to Raiden. It's like he knows exactly what I'm asking without me saying a word because he nods a moment later.

"The fact that you know what I'm dealing with should be answer enough," I respond, earning a confused look from Flora.

"You're right, it is, but ball prep isn't physical. It's all slow dances." He wiggles his eyebrows suggestively at me and I roll my eyes again. "Perfect. Has she been this grouchy the entire time?" he asks, peering at Flora beside him, who grins.

"She's hungry. When a girl is hungry, she turns hangry real quick."

"Hangry?"

"I'm not hangry," I grumble, shoveling more food into my mouth as she snickers.

"You definitely are," Kryll interjects, and I turn a deathly glare in his direction.

"Nobody asked you."

He raises his hands in defense before turning his attention back to his plate. He doesn't look at any of the guys, just his plate or me, when he's giving me hell. What's that about? Come to think of it, Cassian seems stabbier than usual with the fork in his hand too. And Raiden… damn, I'm sure if he could move any closer to me, he'd be in my lap.

There's definitely a weird vibe between them, but that's probably to my advantage. Hopefully, they can use that to ignore me—well, everyone except Brody, who is grinning across the table at me.

I can still sense Flora and Arlo staring at me in confusion since they have no idea what I meant when I answered Brody. I make a mental note to explain it to them later. For now, I need all of the food I can get.

The weight of the gem doesn't feel as intrusive today as it did yesterday, but its presence is still there. Trying to put it to the back of my mind, I finish my food and down my water, ready to get on with the day.

As I push my chair back and stand, something collides with my back, knocking me forward. I brace my hands on the table to break my fall, wincing at the pain emitting from where the amethyst is buried deep beneath my skin.

Turning to see what the hell is going on, I catch a set of fists pounding into the table beside me before I can connect them to their owner.

"I challenge you to a duel."

Fuck. Me.

Sighing, I finally meet her gaze, and I have no clue who she is. Her brown hair is tied in a low ponytail and she's about three inches taller than me. Obviously, she's a wolf; the call for a duel signifies it, but the green cloak she unties and lets float to the floor confirms it.

"Who the fuck is this bitch?" I bite out, in no fucking mood to be dealing with any of this.

"I'm your worst fucking nightmare," she snarls, making me laugh as I turn to face her, but the second I do, she takes a step back, moving around the table so she's standing at the end closest to Cassian.

"Haven't you seen the company I keep? It doesn't get worse than this," I state, waving a hand at Brody, Kryll, Raiden, and Cassian.

Brody scoffs in shock, completely offended, while I spot the corner of Kryll's mouth curling up in amusement. Cassian, however, is glaring the bitch down while Raiden gives him the death stare.

I glance at Flora, who is watching with wide eyes as the drama unfolds in front of her, while I'm certain Arlo is going to pull out a bucket of popcorn at any moment. I wonder if their lives were this manic back home.

Shaking my head, I focus on the obstacle appearing before me.

"This isn't a joke to me. I want a duel. Now. I declare it," the wolf spits, hands clenched at her sides as she heaves each breath through her nose.

Smiling, I let my shoulders relax. "Of course you do.

Where do you want me to lie down, or can I tap out while standing up?" I ask, more than ready to lose the title of Cassian's... what even am I?

"Like fuck will you tap out," Cassian snarls, eyes narrowing on me, and I smirk.

"Don't give me any of your shit right now. If you can't see, I'm dealing with enough already." I wag my finger at him before turning my attention to my new little challenger. "Where do you want me?"

"Right here, right now." A wicked smirk takes over her face as she sizes me up, thinking of all the ways she can break me down.

Sighing, I nod in agreement, ready to get this over with. She takes a few steps back, inching past Cassian to where there's a little more space, and I follow after her. But when I get within an inch of Cassian, he grabs my wrist and pulls me against him.

"You're not throwing this challenge."

"Watch me," I bite, keeping my eyes fixed on the girl before me as a crowd begins to gather and murmurs become full-blown conversations at my expense. Again. At least I won't have to worry about this the next time a duel is called. Maybe next time, I can be a spectator instead.

His grip on my wrist tightens. "Not if I give you something you want in exchange."

"What could you possibly have that I would want?"

He whispers into my ear, making me pause as my heart races insanely fast in my chest.

Fuck. Fuck. Fuck. Fuck. Fuck.

Tugging my arm from his hold, he thankfully lets me go. I take measured steps toward the challenger as I consider his words, drowning in the offer as I try to decide my next move.

Dammit.

Why does he have to do that? I had a clear path out of his life. Why doesn't he want me to take it? I don't understand. I don't have time to figure it out as another wolf climbs up onto the table next to me.

"Let the duel begin," she yells, a round of cheers echoing through the dining room.

The challenger charges at me without a single moment to waste. I can't decide what to do until she's too close, and I find myself knocked off my feet and hurtling toward the ground. My back slams harshly against the floor, burning up my spine and aggravating the amethyst, wreaking havoc on my magic.

She bares her teeth at me as she snarls, raising her fist, but before she can reach her intended target, my face, I land my own punch at the side of her neck, making her lose her balance.

"Bitch," she spits, cupping the reddening area, but I don't wait around for her to react as I roll us. Bucking my hips and bracing my shoulders, I effortlessly switch us around so I'm hovering over her.

She may have a height advantage over me, but she definitely doesn't have the muscle I do.

The crowd boos around us, unhappy I'm showing some kind of advantage, and it's truly unfortunate for them, because I'm taking this bitch down whether they like it or not.

"I'll kill you," she growls, punching me in the side of the head, but my weight over her doesn't shift as I rear my arm right back and connect with her face a second later.

Blood instantly coats my knuckles, sprouting from her nose, but that doesn't stop me from raising it again. Ready to repeat the motion, I frown when a hand locks around my waist, holding me in place and preventing me from hitting out again.

"What the fuck?" I grumble, glancing over my shoulder to see Raiden.

"What's the answer now?" he asks, making me frown. My chest falls and rises rapidly as I try to contain the adrenaline running through my veins.

"What do you mean?"

"She's not dead, and she can't tap out, but she sure as shit is knocked out cold."

I turn, looking down at the girl once again to find her completely out of it. Shit. He's right.

"This is bullshit," someone from the crowd hollers, and a few murmur their agreement as Cassian slowly stands from the table, stepping closer to us with his hands casually tucked into his pockets.

"I declare Adrianna Reagan the winner."

"I'd rather you didn't," I grumble under my breath as Raiden pulls me from the injured girl.

My body tenses as if he's going to take off speeding through the corridors, but to my surprise, he keeps a slow pace until I'm at the entryway, where he places me down on my feet.

"What did he say to make you change your mind?" he asks, lifting my chin up so I meet his gaze, but I shake my head.

"It doesn't matter." I try to take a step back, but he follows straight after me.

"It does, Adrianna. I want to hear you say it," he breathes, running his thumb over my bottom lip.

I can't think with him this close, nevermind breathe, yet the words part from my mouth anyway.

"He offered information on my mother."

THE REIGN OF BLOOD

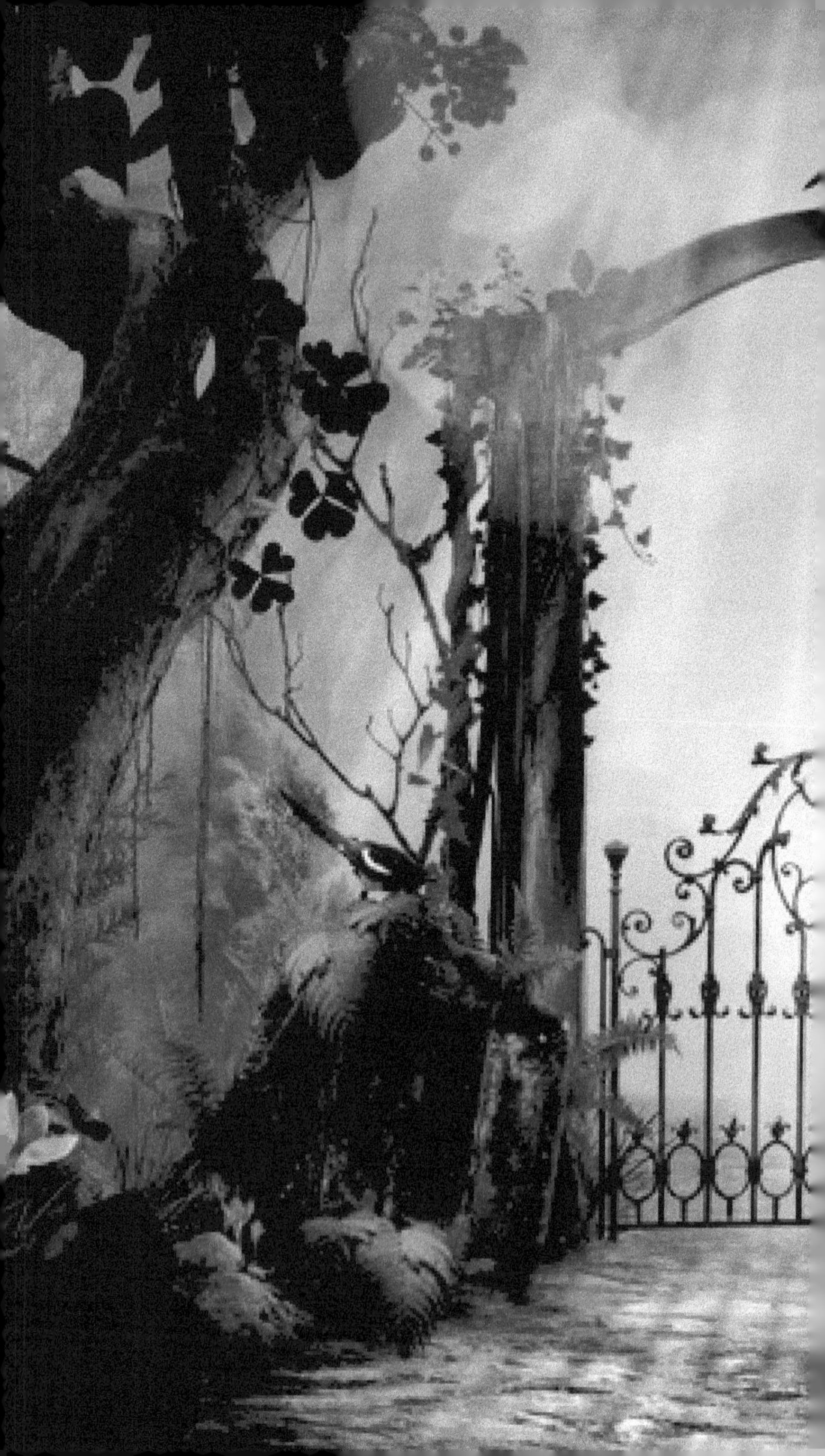

Adrianna

21

Information on my mother? What the fuck do I want that for? I don't know. Clearly, there's a part of me that subconsciously clings to some kind of remnant of her in my mind, but I'm trying not to think about it. Not when I'm already distracted. All of my father's focus training has gone out the window since I got here. I've barely been able to cling to any of it and everything has become an easy distraction. I'm not faring well, and I know my father would be helpless to get me on track.

Maybe it would be different if he were here, but that's not always going to be the case. I know I'm strong, resilient, and determined, but that doesn't mean I don't have my weaknesses, and it seems like I've found them.

Men. Boys. Assholes.

How can I even be a leader with this mindset? I'll never

earn my crown with self-doubt.

Sighing, I pinch the bridge of my nose and try to recenter my focus and attention. My head throbs from the punch the wolf landed, and I recall Cassian's words the last time I endured a duel: only the wolf you are fighting over can heal you. Like hell am I asking him to help me with this. The last time we spoke, we fucked, and then he stormed out. Did we really do much talking? Either way, I'd rather manage the pain than inflict further torment on myself.

"Good morning. If you can pair up with the partner I called out for you last week, we're going to get straight into the swing of things," the professor announces as he waltzes into the room. His black cloak flurries behind him, he's moving that fast, paying no one any mind, and a split second later, my view is blocked by the familiar blond hair and purple cloak that is Brody.

My partner.

Great.

It could be worse, but he's a handful, and we haven't really spoken since our chat in the forest. All of these men, with all of these unfinished or stilted conversations, are worsening my headache and driving it straight into a migraine.

"Did I mention how hot it was watching you take that girl down?" he states, rocking back on his heels as he runs his tongue over his bottom lip.

"You didn't, actually."

"Well, I am now. H.O.T. Hot. Hot, little Dagger. Hot. Hot. Hot."

My cheeks heat as I wave him off. "You can stop now."

"I'd rather I didn't," he retorts with a wink, and I shake my head.

"I'm sure."

"Has anyone here danced the waltz before?"

My eyes widen, recalling the last time we were in this class and Brody mentioned that he knew it a little. Before I can make sure he keeps his damn mouth shut, he waves to the professor. "I have."

"Excellent. Can you please show everyone how the male position should embrace the female position," he orders while I glare at the mage before me, who doesn't seem to notice.

I'm going to kill him.

He steps in closer, so close our shoes almost touch. His hand splays across the bottom of my back, making my spine stiffen and my nerve endings stand at attention. He doesn't miss a beat, lacing his fingers with mine as our breaths mingle together.

Definitely going to kill him.

"Would you like to lead her around the room for everyone to see?" the professor asks.

"No," I blurt at the same time he hollers "Yes!" in agreement.

"It's okay, Dagger. I've got you," he promises before his feet begin to move.

With one hand on his chest and the other engulfed in his, I cling on for dear life as he takes the lead, literally waltzing me around the room effortlessly. I stumble over his feet a few times, but he doesn't falter, and when we're back in our original spot, he catches me off guard, grabbing my waist and dipping me low.

The professor claps as I quickly rush to stand back on two feet, my cheeks heating even more as I pat at his chest. He thankfully takes a step back, but the embers of desire are undeniable in his eyes as he peers at me.

"It's cute when you get flustered," he states, making me frown as I fold my arms over my chest.

"I'm not flustered," I grumble, acutely aware that there's still an audience watching us.

"Of course you're not." He winks again. *Fucking winks.*

"That's marvelous, Brody. What a performance, may I ask you to come and aid me around the room so we can help everyone get into the swing of things? Addi, you, however, require some more practice. Please consider watching the videos online as I recommended in the last lesson."

A few snickers ring out as I avert my gaze. I haven't

watched a single one, and that's probably not helping, but in my defense, there's been a lot going on since our last class.

"I don't want to be apart from you," Brody says, stroking a finger down my cheek as I roll my eyes and push him back a step. He knows exactly how to get under my skin.

The second he's gone, another shadow casts over me.

Kryll.

"Where's Flora?" I ask, peering around him.

"Arlo somehow convinced me to swap partners."

"Arlo convinced you?" I clarify, eyebrows raised, and he smirks, rolling his eyes at me.

"I actually know Arlo's father. He has a business relationship with my father, and he's an alright guy. He's also hot for his stepsister, so I can't help but watch them stumble around each other in amusement."

"He does?"

"Of course that's what you took from that," he mumbles, his grin spreading wider.

"Everybody, start practicing. Brody and I will give pointers on our walk-through," the professor declares, and Kryll instantly reaches for my waist and hand, just as Brody had done a moment ago.

"Don't you think—"

"Shut up and dance with me, Princess."

My eyes narrow on him. "Stop calling me that," I grumble as we slowly begin to move.

"Why?"

"Because that's not who I am anymore."

His head rears back as he frowns down at me. "You think I'm calling you princess because you *were* a princess?"

I gape at him, at a loss for words for a split second before I shake my head. "I don't know. It sounds weird now that you're saying it out loud," I admit, and he snickers.

"That's because it's weird as fuck."

"Excuse me, that's my—"

"Fuck off, Delia," Kryll grunts, turning to the girl standing beside us with her hands planted on her hips. With her eyes narrowed, she storms off toward the professor, leaving Kryll to shrug and continue to try and lead me through this damn dance.

"You're causing a stir," I state, glancing down at our feet as I try to follow the steps.

"Is it me, or is it you?" he retorts, forcing me to glance back up at him.

"At the rate everything is going, it'll work out to be me, I'm sure." He smirks. "It's not funny," I snap, lips pursed, which only makes his face light up more.

"I never said it was." No one should look this good when they're making fun of me. It should be illegal.

"That ridiculous grin on your face says otherwise," I

mutter, and he shrugs again.

"I'm sure it does."

Shaking my head, I focus on the dance for a few moments, my head spinning from our interaction. It's always like this. He's a mystery, and it's half of the reason I'm distracted.

"You're an enigma," I blurt, tilting my head up to his as we manage to take five steps before I stumble.

"You're one to talk."

"Please, that's crap and you know it," I retort, making him shake his head.

"Maybe. I'm a shifter; getting close to people like this isn't in my comfort zone," he admits.

Intrigued, I tilt my head to the side as I assess him. "And how does that make you feel?"

"Uncomfortable as fuck," he grumbles, glancing off into the distance for a second.

"Stepping out of your comfort zone will do that to you," I admit with a snicker of my own, and he rolls his eyes before settling his gaze on me.

"It's not so bad when it's you and not some whiny brat," he explains, nodding to where Delia is still complaining to the professor.

"You're welcome."

"I wasn't thanking you," he quickly retorts, and I smile up at him sweetly.

"That's not what I heard."

"Of course it isn't." This time, we complete seven steps before we restart. This is going to take me forever to get the hang of. "Did you attend any of the fancy balls when you were the princess?" he asks, startling me.

Clearing my throat, I shake my head. "No. I was too young for any of this."

"But not too young to feel the wrath of the wolves when the downfall came," he states, making my heart race as his gaze shifts to my clipped ears for a split second.

"Funny how that works, isn't it?" I breathe, my heart racing.

"Is there anything you can do about the amethyst? Brody mentioned that it wasn't likely." I blink at him, close to whiplash from the different conversations as we attempt to move.

"I have no idea," I admit, hating the fear that creeps over me at the thought of it being there permanently.

"Does it hurt?" I can't decide if that's concern in his gaze or not.

"Yesterday, like a bitch. Today, I know it's there, but the bite of the pain doesn't linger the same." It's the truth. It's weird how I keep doing that, offering people information they don't necessarily need. I guess it doesn't hurt to share some things with people. It alleviates the pain in my chest for sure.

"It's crazy how strong you are."

His words make me freeze, halting the dance again before I clear my throat and try again.

"You don't know me enough to make that assessment."

He shrugs. "I know enough."

"You do?"

"I'm a shifter, remember? We don't get close to people. Which means we can make judgments and assessments early on." He states it so matter of factly, there's no room for me to argue.

"Noted." Eager to move the conversation away from me, I consider him for a moment, and a question comes to mind. "Are you here to be the heir or a support system?"

His eyebrows raise. "That's a change of subject."

It's my turn to shrug. "I mean, you asked me about glamorous balls when I was a princess. I feel like it's fair game," I reply, and he smirks, glancing away again before looking down at our feet.

"Maybe." A few minutes pass as we focus on the steps, making it to fifteen before I stumble, and I'm certain he's not going to give me an answer until his eyes suddenly latch on to mine. "Right now, I'm just here. I haven't decided in what capacity yet."

"You're telling me the four of you haven't had discussions about this?" I retort, caught by surprise.

"No, we've had a lot of discussions, but adding

pressure to a situation and forcing an outcome isn't really my style."

"Your style is elusive as fuck," I blurt, and he chuckles. "Thanks."

"It wasn't a compliment."

"That's not what I heard," he states, throwing my own words back at me.

My lips part, no response ready, when Brody appears to my left.

"I'm here; give me back my girl."

"I'm not your girl," I retort, wagging a finger at him, and he rolls his eyes.

"If you say so."

"I *do* say so." This guy is insufferable.

"Okay then, if we're being politically correct, you're *our* girl."

"I'm no one's girl," I bite out, taking a step back from Kryll as my hands ball into fists at my sides.

"You sound like a shifter," he states as Brody continues to stare at me with desire dancing in his baby blues.

"Is that a bad thing?" I ask, flicking my gaze between the two of them. I don't even know why the words left my lips. I don't care, but they're out there now.

"Maybe, maybe not," Kryll whispers, confusion glazing over his eyes as he takes a step back, running a hand through his red hair. Without another word, he turns and darts toward Delia.

"Don't worry, Dagger, he's coming around. He's just going to need a little time."

I frown, glancing at Brody. "Coming around to what?"

"You. Him. Us."

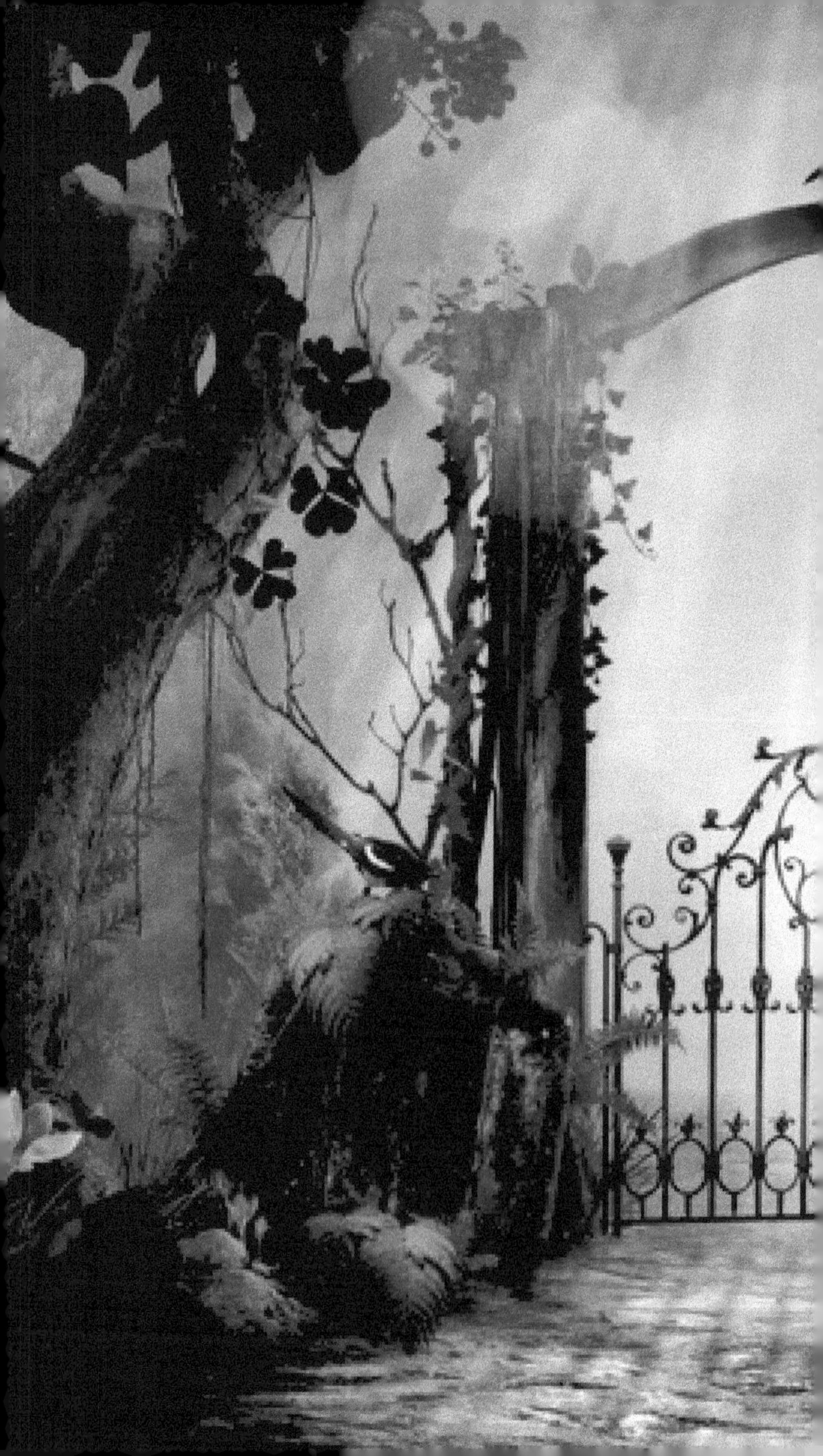

ADRIANNA

22

I march up the stairs of the fae building with a small sense of relief clinging to me. Flora and Arlo are a step behind me, but they leave me to my thoughts as they murmur among themselves. I don't know how, but I've made it to the end of the day with no further issues. Voicing it out loud is off limits, though. It would only jinx my chances of the evening going in the same direction.

That's just how my luck works at the minute it seems, and I'm not about to put the odds against me any more than they already are.

My mind lingers on the dance class this morning. As much as I don't want to admit it, it's been the highlight of my day. Kryll seemed… off. I don't know if that's exactly the right word to describe him, but it's the best I've got right now. There seems to be something going on with him, but I don't know him well enough to make that full assessment.

Brody, on the other hand, is back to full form. Flirty winks, biting at his bottom lip as he stares at me, mingling with the occasional brush of his hand against my thigh or arm has me strung tighter than I care to admit.

"Is that a rose?" Flora asks, pulling me from my thoughts as we reach our floor. Looking down the hall to where she's pointing, there's a stunning red rose resting against my door.

"Another one," I murmur, the sight of it warming my chest, but I quickly try to rid myself of the sensation.

"Another?" Flora asks, eyebrows raised in question.

"I've had a few."

"A few?"

"Is there a parrot in here?" Arlo blurts, leaning against Flora's door with a grin on his face.

With a pointed look, she whacks him in the chest.

"Shush you."

He holds his hands up in surrender, but the amusement doesn't leave his features.

Peering back at the rose, I sigh.

"I really need to find a real vase for them."

"Maybe they have one down at the dining hall," Flora offers, and I hum in agreement.

"Maybe. I was kind of hoping to get some sand and…"

My words trail off as my lips purse.

"You want to make one?" Flora asks, and I nod.

"But maybe something from the dining hall will do." I smile at her, mind made up as I move toward my room.

As I reach for the rose, the thornless stem in my grasp, she speaks. "I think the mages have sand."

Looking back at them, I find Arlo nodding along with her.

"They do."

"What would they have sand for?" I ask, confused, as I mindlessly run my fingertip over the petals.

"For their magic. Sand is a widely used item for chants and potions," Arlo answers with a shrug.

"Oh, that makes sense, I guess." How had I not thought of that?

"You could ask a mage," Flora offers, a smile starting to form on her face.

"What mage is going to willingly hand me sand? Me, the certified villain among us all," I grumble, aware I'm the bad guy to most people on campus.

"I know of one," she states, eyebrows rising as her smile continues to spread.

Brody.

That's who she's referring to.

"Maybe," I breathe, avoiding her gaze.

"There's no maybe about it," she pushes, and I shake

my head.

"The kitchen feels safer." My eyes latch onto hers to find a solid pointed look in place.

"But it won't make your magic happy."

Fuck. She's right there.

"It won't." The truth slips from my lips, leaving me feeling vulnerable and exposed, but that's not how she reacts to them. Frowning, I point a finger at her. "Are you saying that because you can see inside my head or because you understand the feeling?" My gut tells me I already know the answer, but I'm programmed to clarify.

"I understand the feeling," she answers, her smile softening. "With my mind magic, the hardest thing I've had to learn is how to scratch the itch even when it's not possible."

"It's weird when you say that," Arlo muses, folding his arms over his chest as he gets comfortable against the door.

"Why?"

"The thought of scratching your itch with mind magic makes me think of you actually scratching your brain."

I shudder at the thought, and now that he's said it, I'm never going to unsee it.

"Thanks, Arlo," I grumble, making Flora snicker.

"It's easier for you," she states, pointing at Arlo. "You're a water fae. If your magic flares to life inside of you, desperate to escape, you can connect with the water and ease the sensation. Whereas dealing with mind magic isn't as simple as that. Most people aren't too happy about me using my magic on them. Especially not to alleviate the fizzle of magic consuming me."

That makes sense. I haven't really considered it like that before. Since I have access to all the magic blessed upon the fae, I can exert it in any way and the fizzle she's talking about dissolves. Mainly because the royal blood that runs through my body is a stronger power than others, so if we use that magic, it generally eases everything. My chest tightens at the reminder that I can't access my mind magic at all right now, but I opt to answer as though that's not the case.

"That's true. I don't have the same struggles with mind magic as my sister does."

"Is it true? That royal fae have a stronger and weaker ability among them all?"

I nod. "Yes," I confirm, acutely aware of the fact that I'm talking about my sister, and revealing her strength, but I can't seem to stop. "Her strength is unreal. Actually, when she's struggling to 'scratch the itch', as you put it, she has an orb. I'll find out how we can get our hands on one, but it's really good for her when she feels like she can't expel her magic," I rattle off, a warmth growing in my chest with the fact that I can be of use.

"That would be amazing, thanks, Addi."

"No problem. Now, I better take care of this rose," I mutter, looking down at the crimson petals. I need to go before I continue talking about things that I shouldn't.

Smiling, I step into my room and let the door click shut behind me. The second I do, my chest swirls, irritation zapping through my veins. The possibility of sand has my fire magic ablaze.

Pressing my lips together, I lean back against the door and peer at the roses I'm continuing to acquire.

I guess it wouldn't be too bad if I paid a visit to the mage building.

THE REIGN OF BLOOD

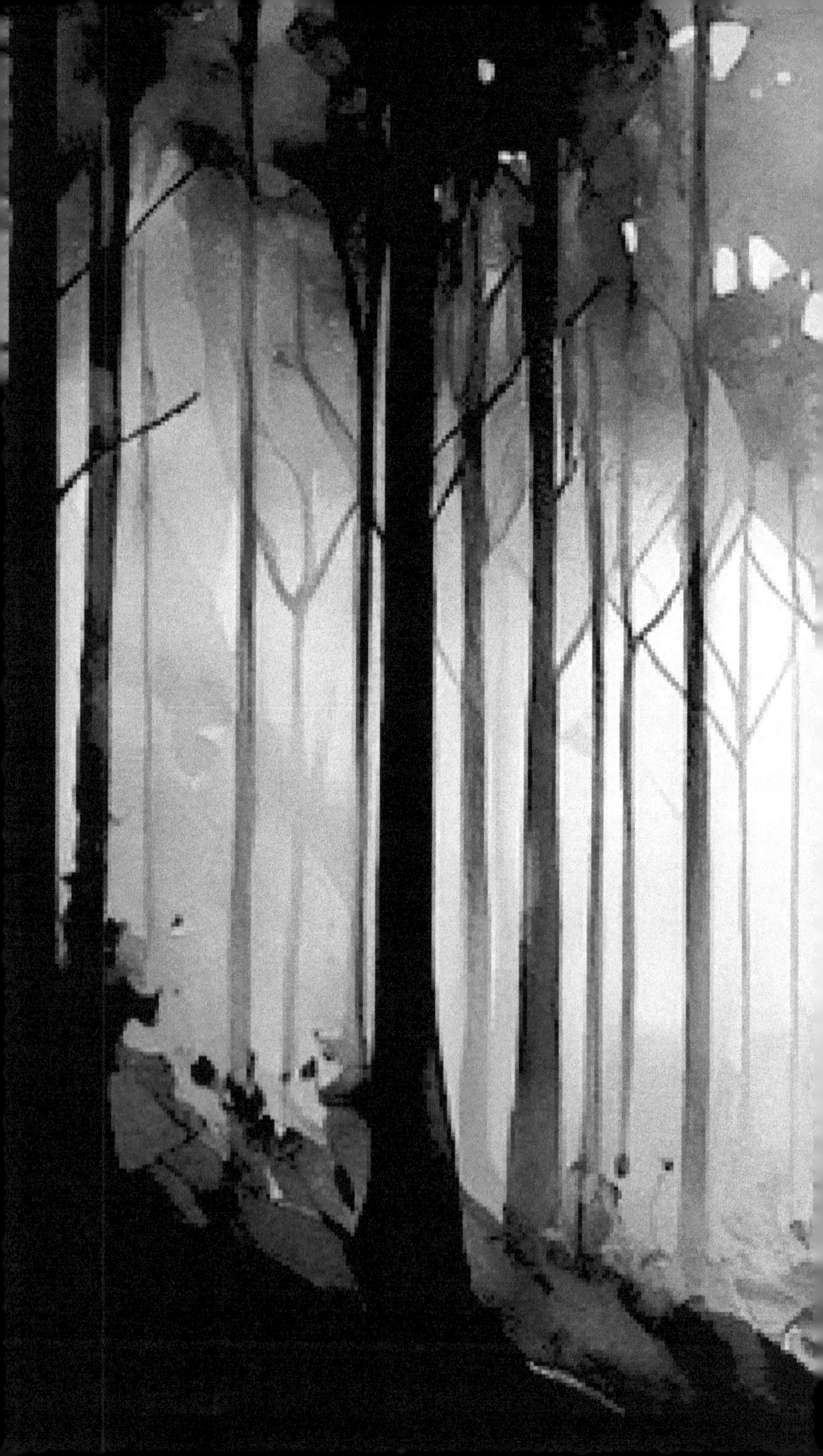

BRODY

23

Someone kill me now. Slay me dead. I'm done with this man's lecture.

"Are you even listening, Brody?" My father's condescending tone grows tiresome through my cell phone.

"No."

He sighs, his irritation palpable even though he's not standing in front of me. It makes no difference with this man. He's a member of The Council, and that doesn't change when he's at home or speaking with people outside of that capacity. He's business, through and through. No exceptions.

"I think we're done," he mutters, and I scoff.

"I already thought we were."

Another sigh. Another gold star on my chart for being an upstanding son.

"You know, Brody, one day you'll wish you had listened to the wealth of knowledge I have to offer."

A wealth of knowledge. Fuck off. I can picture him now, bushy eyebrows gathered as his lips mush together, disappointment oozing from him. His so-called *wealth of knowledge* has made him nothing but predictable. Which is why I know exactly what to say and do to make him fuck off.

"And maybe one day you will actually hear me when I speak. The apple doesn't fall too far from the tree."

I can envision his nostrils flaring as he heaves yet another sigh. "I'm not discussing this with you again, Brody. It's final. It's irrelevant what you think or feel. Some decisions are greater than you. That's life."

My chest squeezes in the grasp of an unrelenting vice as anger thrums through my bones. "But—"

"Enough. I have to go. I have another call."

"Of course you do," I snap, but the call is already over.

Discarding my cell phone on the bed beside me, I brace my elbows on my knees and shield my face in my hands as I take a few pointless deep breaths. My head pounds as I feel my pulse throbbing with my increased heart rate. Despite how familiar I am with this man, he still affects me in every way I despise.

His ability to get under my skin is a trait I know I got directly from him, and I hate to admit that I truly dislike being on the other end of it.

Not that I'll learn my lesson. I never do.

Sighing, I sit tall, rubbing my palms over my thighs before focusing on the window. The late afternoon sun peeks through the glass, cascading over my room with a kiss of bliss that I wish I could absorb.

It helps to soothe me. The sun is always a beacon for my calmness and joy, especially after I've had the pleasure of speaking with my father.

"You can't go in there. I said you can't go in there!"

I frown at the shouting coming from the other side of my bedroom door before a knock pounds against it. What's going on now? It's probably some idiot complaining to me about how another mage is being unfair, like it even matters to me.

Pushing to my feet, I cut the distance between me and the drama awaiting in the hallway.

"Are you dumb? I said—"

The mage slams her lips shut when I swing the door open to find her pointing and yelling in the face of my favorite little fae.

Adrianna Reagan.

"I'm sorry, Brody. This girl won't listen," Clara grumbles, offering me a sympathetic smile before turning her wrath back to Addi. "You," she starts, pointing in her face. "Don't get to come in here and—" She's muted once more, but this time it's not from my appearance; it's from Addi's hand wrapped around her throat as she slams her into the wall beside my door.

"I quite specifically warned you not to aim that finger in my face again, or you would face the consequences," Addi hisses, nostrils flaring with agitation before she flips her gaze my way. "Hi."

It's soft, delicate, sweet even.

"Hey," I breathe, completely caught up in the way the sun lights up her hair, making the small smile on her lips even more alluring.

"I was hoping to ask for a favor," she states, ignoring the mage in her grasp.

Favor? Yes, please. Put this woman in my debt and seal it with the wax of King Reagan himself.

"Of course, come in." I take a step back, swinging my arm out wide for her to follow me, but before she moves a single inch, she looks back at Clara.

"Did you hear that?" she asks, cocking her brow as Clara's face scrunches in discomfort.

"Fuck you," the mage spits out, wincing a beat later when Addi tightens her grip.

As hot as this is, and it's fucking smoking, I'm intrigued by the favor she wants. "Let the poor mage go, Addi. She's not worth your time," I murmur, extending my hand in her direction.

Her glare at Clara stretches out for a few more beats before she looks down at my hand that awaits the warmth of hers. She purses her lips, considering the offer, then releases her hold on Clara's throat and places her hand in mine.

I pull her inside without wasting a single second, and she drops her hand from mine as soon as the door shuts. She saunters into the center of my room, slowly spinning as she casts her eyes over every inch of the space.

Trying to envision it from her perspective, I trail behind her gaze.

Soft gray walls are barely visible behind cluttered shelves and cabinets, which also frame the window straight ahead. They're all filled to the brim with books, ingredients, and everything in between. You name it, I probably have it. I see being a mage as an art form. One that requires access to items some people haven't even heard of.

My bed is central on the wall to my right, a nightstand on either side, with a doorway in the corner leading to my private bathroom. A desk sits against the wall by the door, the wood matching the cabinets, while the drapes and sheets are an olive green, lightening the room despite so many dark fixtures.

"What brings me the pleasure of a favor from the sweet dagger in my life?" I ask once her gaze settles on mine. Her blonde hair is braided in a crown on her head, but a loose tendril still dangles around her face. She busies herself, attempting to tuck the loose curl behind her ear as she seeks the words.

"I was wondering if you have any sand."

"Sand?" I clarify, and she nods, clearing her throat as her lips rub together.

"That's not what I was expecting at all," I admit, running my eyes over her, and she grins.

"Surprise." Her sass brings out a smile of my own.

"What do you need it for?"

Her eyebrows pinch together as she folds her arms over her chest.

"Does it matter? It's just sand."

"Color me intrigued."

"Color you a pain in my ass," she snaps back, irritation fluttering over her skin as my gaze narrows on hers.

"I'd be a real pain in your ass if you let me."

"You did not just say that," she says with a snicker, waving me off, and I shrug.

"I did."

She shakes her head at me, glancing away, and I'm certain there's the slightest tinge of pink to her cheeks, but it disappears too quickly for me to be sure.

"I want to make a glass vase."

My eyebrows pinch in confusion. "Wait; you want sand to make a glass vase? For what?" She seems to be one-thousand percent hitting me with surprises today.

"What goes in a vase, Brody?" She gives me a well-deserved pointed look, and I roll my eyes back at her.

"Flowers, obviously, but I'm intrigued by the flowers that may need a vase. The questions I have are endless."

Like, where the fuck is she getting flowers from? Are they from someone specifically, or is she gathering them herself?

"Can you help me or not?" she asks, cocking her brow at me, and I nod.

"Of course." Sauntering over to the cabinet to my left, I crouch down to look through the small drawers. I know it's in here somewhere, but knowing exactly *where* is a different thing entirely.

In the fourth drawer, the familiar grains of sand in a glass jar come into view.

"Is this enough?" I lift it up for her to see, watching as excitement dances in her eyes,

"It's perfect."

Standing, I offer her the jar, and she snatches it out of my hands, cradling it like a baby.

"So, are you going to make it yourself?" I ask, not wanting the moment to end yet.

"I hope so," she murmurs, eyes still transfixed on the jar in her grasp, but the glazing over her eyes makes me frown.

"You hope so?" She's a royal. She should be able to use whatever magic she pleases.

"Kiss of amethyst, remember?"

Her eyes meet mine, her pain evident before she swiftly blinks it away.

"You've got this. One hundred percent," I insist, stepping closer to squeeze her arm in comfort. She offers me a soft smile, like my words of encouragement aren't quite enough to fill her with positivity. "Can I watch?"

It's her turn to frown. "Watch?"

"Yeah, like, watch you make the vase." Why the fuck do I sound nervous?

"Why?"

Clearing my throat, I move my hand from her arm to rub at the back of my neck. "Magic fascinates me," I admit, and it's true, it does, but not as much as she does. That's the secret factor here.

Her lips purse as she thinks, and it takes everything in me to keep my mouth shut while she comes to a decision.

"Where?" she finally asks, and I can't contain the grin on my face.

"Here's fine," I insist, pointing to the center of the room. "Do you want a table or anything?"

She frowns at the center of the floor where I'm pointing to before looking at me with real uncertainty dancing in her orbs. "But what if my magic—"

"Don't worry about it. I'm a mage, remember? I can combat any issues we might have," I insist, not really sure if that's where she was going with her worry, but when she nods, I hope I've hit the nail on the head.

"A table isn't necessary, but something that won't burn when I'm done with it would be handy," she breathes as she drops to the floor, crossing her legs as she unclips the lid on the jar.

I grab what she needs and place it in front of her. She doesn't look, though; she's too engrossed in the sand to pay any attention to anything else.

Stepping back, I lean against the wall, watching her every move as she scoops out a handful of sand. I'm mesmerized as her hands start to move, red and orange hues dancing between her palms as she uses her magic. It's the most beautiful thing I've ever seen.

Her eyelids are at half-mast, and her hands move on their own as she brings the sand to life. All too quickly, she places the newly made glass down on the heat-resistant plate I put before her and smiles down at her masterpiece.

At first, it looks like a simple vase, but as I peer closer, I notice the intricate design etched into the glass throughout. It's like small, thin vines intertwine up the sides, embedded in the glass.

"What's that old film my mom used to make me watch?" I murmur, and she blinks at me, her eyebrows pinching together.

"How am I supposed to know that?"

I wave her off. "Obviously, you don't, but I'm sure you will. Where the guy was dead, but he helped her make something with the clay. I can't really remember much about it."

"I don't know what you're talking about."

"You do, for sure you do. I think he was a ghost. Wait, is that what it was called?"

Her nose scrunches. "That sounds weird."

"It was, but she loved it," I reply with a snicker, the memories flooding me, but I stop the thoughts before the heartache sets in.

"Loved it?"

"Hmm." I glance away, running my fingers through my hair as I turn my attention back to her.

She runs her tongue over her bottom lip as she turns back to the vase. "How is this similar?"

Before I can think better of it, I drop to the floor, planting my legs on either side of hers before intertwining our fingers. "In the movie, they molded the clay together. A song was playing in the background, making it all cute and shit." I run her hands over the vase, my heart hammering at our close proximity as her back presses against my chest.

She sighs, the weight of it vibrating through her body and resonating in my own. The sweet floral scent of her hair intoxicates me as she shuffles slightly, getting comfortable enveloped in my limbs. Before I can think better of it, I inch closer, running my lips over her neck. She shivers, tilting her head, encouraging me to press a kiss to the same spot.

Her back arches, inviting me further in as I bring our hands to her waist. Still intertwined, I run my thumb along her stomach, hating the t-shirt that sits between us. My mouth has a mind of its own, trailing pathways in every direction as her head tilts to the side, offering me more access.

Fuck.

Releasing one of her hands, I tug at the back of her cloak, searching for the fastening before it cascades around her waist. The outline of the kiss of amethyst is visible through her t-shirt and I can't stop myself from revealing the delicate purple gem.

Her skin is raw and sore around the edges where it's clawed at her flesh. Running my finger around the edge, she stiffens. "I might not be able to remove it, but I can soothe the broken skin," I explain, quickly muttering the chant quietly. She softens, her tension easing as her head lolls forward.

"Thank you."

"Anytime," I promise, pressing a kiss just above the offensive object digging into her flesh.

She tugs her hand from mine and I immediately feel the loss. Before I can heave a sigh of disappointment, her hand is on my cheek, fingers splayed as she peers deep into my eyes. She shifts so we're facing each other, and my hands immediately fall to her waist.

There's uncertainty in her eyes, uncertainty over me, I'm sure. So, I hold my position, waiting for her to be the one to make the move. I want this more than anything, my cock bulging against the cotton of my boxers, desperately seeking her, but this has to be her decision because we both know she's aware of what I desire.

Her.

She inches closer, our breaths mingling together as I hold her gaze, watching her pupils dilate just before she lets her eyelids fall closed and her lips press against mine.

The feel of her fingers against my face as she claims my mouth is all-consuming, and I'm moving before I can even think about it. Standing with my hands fixed on her waist, I hoist her into the air while our lips remain connected.

I take the three necessary steps to my bed before lowering as gently as possible. Her hands stroke down my neck and latch onto my shoulders as her legs wrap around my hips.

Fuck.

Crushing my lips further against hers, she moans against my tongue as I taste every inch of her I can get my lips on.

I need to feel her skin against mine.

Now.

Blindly searching for the hem of her t-shirt, I grip it tightly with both hands, but before I can tug at it, she pushes against my chest, parting our lips.

"Don't you fucking dare tear my clothes when I have to walk home. I'd rather not do the walk of shame naked," she grumbles, making me cock a brow.

"Walk of shame? Is that what this is?" I ask, following her order and pulling her t-shirt over her head instead of shredding it like I want. I toss it aside, reveling in the pretty pink bra covering her chest.

"No, but you know what I mean," she mutters, slipping her hands beneath her pants, and I shift, undressing along with her. In a flash, we're both naked, chests heaving as we stare at each other. "Are you going to take care of—"

I eliminate the distance between us, diving face-first between her legs and effectively bringing her sass to an abrupt halt. As I run my tongue through her folds, her back arches off the bed and her hands clench the sheets beneath her.

Fucking her outside was one thing. Watching her leave her mark on my personal belongings is something else entirely. I need more of it. I rake my teeth over her clit, loving the gasps that part her lips as I tease one finger at her entrance.

"Please, Brody," she whispers with a gasp, making my lips curl against her skin.

"That's it, Dagger. Beg me." Thrusting two fingers into her core, I don't get more pleading like I want, but the cry of pleasure that echoes around my room is even better. "I want you to come all over my sheets. I want the scent of your essence all over my room. Then, when I wake up in the morning, you're going to be all I can think about, all I can smell, and all I can envision from this moment right here. It's going to be too much for me to bear. So much so that I'm going to have to slip into my shower and fuck my palm so hard and fast it's going to be over too quickly. But it'll be worth it. Won't it, Addi?" It's not a question. Not really.

She nods, eyes wide as she looks at me, and I twirl my fingers in her pussy, watching her pulse flutter at her throat before I lap at her clit again. She writhes beneath me like it's exactly where she was meant to be, and I'm going to prove to her that it is.

"Please. Please. Please," she chants, like the perfect harmony to fit the way I play her body.

Adding a third finger, I thrust deep inside her, feeling her core clench around me as I sink my teeth into the sensitive flesh around her clit. Like an orchestra reaching its crescendo, she hits her peak, cries of ecstasy parting her lips as she climaxes.

I lap at every drop, making sure to wring every ounce from her. Her tense muscles turn to puddles beneath me as she tries to catch her breath. Trailing soft kisses over her pussy, around her belly button, and between the valley between her breast, I find my way to her mouth.

She doesn't shy away from the taste of herself on my tongue.

No.

Her kisses deepen, making my cock harder than ever.

Reaching for the top drawer of my nightstand, I pull a condom out, tearing at the wrapper and sheathing my needy cock with quick precision.

"I want my sheets wetter, Dagger. Do you think you can do that?" I ask, lining my cock up with her entrance as she shuffles up onto her elbows, peering down at the already damp material.

"Take me like this, and I will," she purrs, running her tongue over her lip as she shifts to her front, tilting her ass up in the air. Her back is arched perfectly, and I run my hand down her spine before stroking the globes of her ass.

She presses her shoulders into the mattress, reaching her hands underneath her chest to pinch her nipples.

"Fuck, you're a damn tease," I grunt, desperate for her, and she grins, eyes closed as she consumes every fiber of me.

Eager to turn that smile into a face of raw pleasure, I realign my cock with her core and thrust inside. Her heat intoxicates me as I pause, unsure whether I'll last more than five seconds if I don't give myself a moment to catch my breath.

One of her hands shifts, clinging to the sheets beneath her again, bracing for impact, and I let everything else in the world fall away as I give her a reason to hold on.

Retreating, I slam my cock deeper inside her. Harder, faster, it's everything.

The slap of skin on skin echoes around us and my hold on her hips tightens. I hope there are bruises for her to see tomorrow, to remind her.

Her legs tremble beneath me as I slam into her again and again, chasing the euphoria I know she brings. Reaching a hand around to her pussy, I pinch and nip at her clit, making her groans of pleasure grow louder until she's a panting mess.

The telltale signs of her core contracting around me tell me I'm close to feeling her climax. I need it more than I need my own.

It takes everything in me to keep my pace and not lose myself to my own needs until her cries reach new heights.

"Fuck, Brody. Fuck."

Doubling down, with the feel of her release dripping between us, I tumble over the jagged edge with her. My vision darkens, my orgasm ripping through my body as I fall forward, rugged thrusts prolonging the taste of ecstasy between us.

Holy fucking shit.

Perspiration clings to us as we try to catch our breaths, and one thing is for certain.

I thought being a fuckboy was fun, but learning every inch of her body is even better.

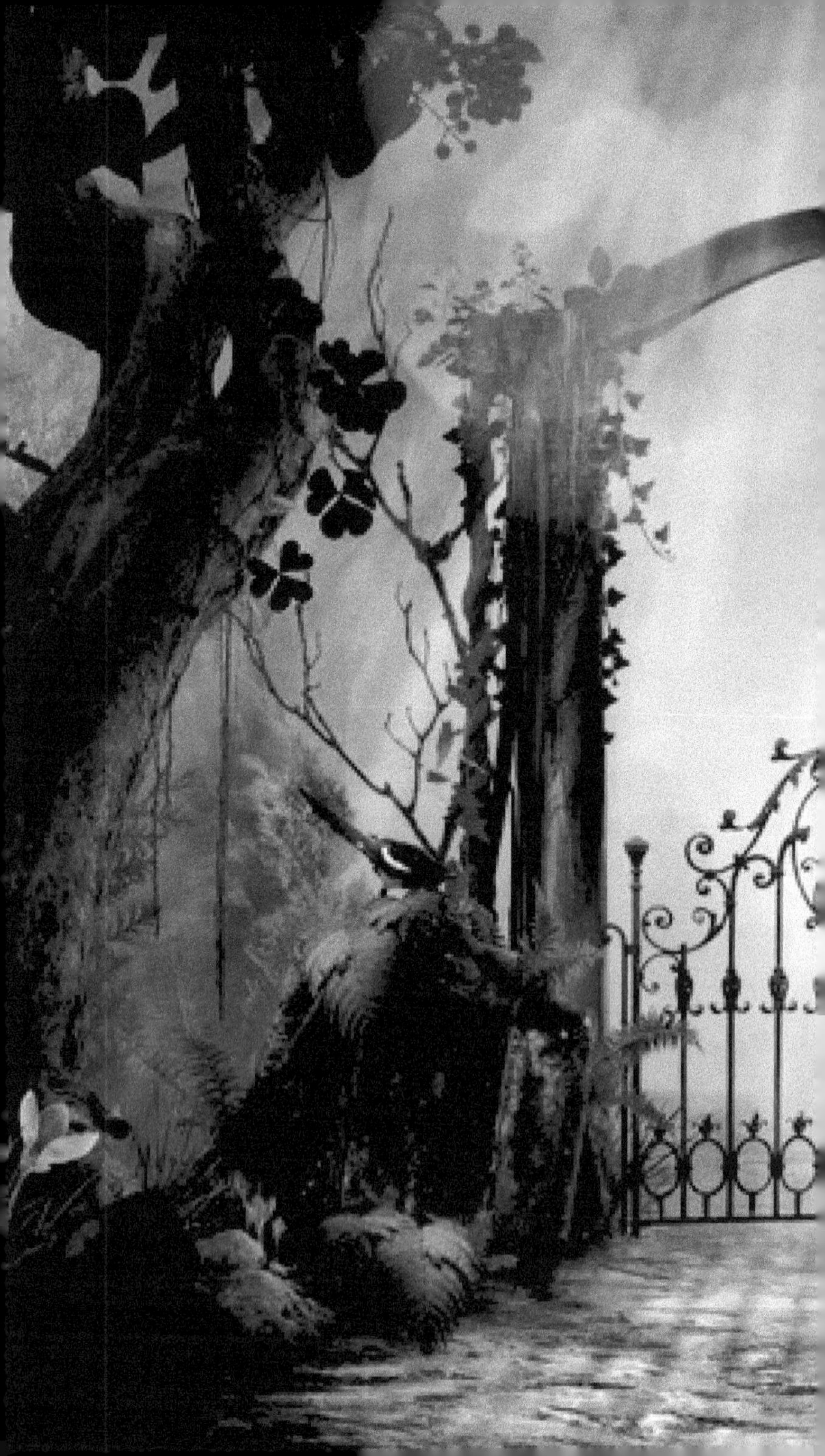

ADRIANNA

24

Two days. It's been two days, and I can still feel the remnants of Brody between my thighs.

Fuck.

That's not what I'd gone over there for—not even a little bit—it just happened, just like the last time and just like every time Cassian has claimed me. So much for not focusing on them and giving all of my attention to being the next heir.

It seems I'm a liar when it comes to them, and I can't even blame them for everything. I'm just as accountable.

My mind is consumed with it all as I sit here staring at the eight roses that now fill my handmade vase, and I can't help but wonder who they're coming from. Shaking my head, I rise from my bed and try to put it to the back of my mind. It doesn't matter, really; it means nothing, all of it. Brody, Cassian, Raiden, Kryll, and mystery rose guy. I have to be focused on the future, even though I keep trying and failing.

Perseverance is my best friend; I hope I'll eventually reach the end goal. My spine tingles and I'm certain I won't be able to avoid them like I intend.

Stepping toward my window, I plant my hands on the ledge as I peer out at the world. I can see a few groups of people heading toward the main academy building for dinner, and I'll be joining them in a few minutes when I head over with Flora.

My guard is still up, anticipation clinging to me, but no one has tried to attack me in the past few days. Which feels like a positive, even though the wide berth I continue to get is noticeable. I like it, but in the grand scheme of things, it's the opposite of what I need, especially if I want to be the new heir to the kingdom.

If I want to lead, I need to show the students on campus, as well as the rest of the kingdom, that I can. It's going to take them a minute to warm up to that, if at all, but regardless, I'm here to prove that mistakes can be made and recovery can be a reality at the hands of the fae. I'm here to earn their trust because that's what is vital when it really boils down to the core.

Glancing at the time, I slip my boots on before reaching for my cloak. The plan is to eat, then head back to Flora's for some girl time. Which is the code word for watching *The Office* again, but sans Arlo, whom I've learned spends the entire time speaking the words over the show because he's watched it so many times.

Checking myself in the mirror, I pat a few loose curls down and tighten the pins holding my hair in place. Ready for food, I've taken a single step toward the door when my cell phone vibrates. My eyebrows rise as I glance around the room. Has Nora got a visual on me or something? It seems every time I take a step toward the door lately, the damn thing goes off.

I slide my nightstand drawer open, expecting to see her name flashing across the screen, but to my surprise, it's my father.

"Hey, is everything okay?" I ask, more panicked with him on the other end of the cell phone than if it was Nora.

"Everything's fine, Addi. How is everything there?" he asks, concern etched into every syllable.

"Okay," I answer, taking a seat at the foot of my bed as the initial anxiety subsides.

"Just okay?" he asks, and it feels like the gem at my back burns more, reminding me it's there.

"Nothing else has really happened since Bozzelli gave me the kiss of amethyst," I admit, hearing him sigh through the line. Not at me, but with disappointment at the situation. I've heard it many times, enough to decipher between the two. When the former king of the kingdom is trying to teach you everything at such a young age, you get a lot of heavy sighs of exasperation, and the one he just let loose definitely wasn't it.

"That's what I'm calling for. I'm sorry, it would have been sooner, but I didn't want Nora to be here," he explains, making my eyebrows pinch.

"Why? Where is she?"

It's a stupid question, really. All either of us ever does is protect her, even if it *is* against her will.

"I just don't want her to worry more over you than she already is, and she's in the meadow with Talia. I can see her from the top window, don't worry," he adds, and I exhale slowly.

Talia is the girl from the neighboring farm and Josh's younger sister. The stupid guy Nora often likes to remind me of. They've always been friendly, playing while I trained, so I know she's in good company.

"I guess that makes sense," I reply, relating to not wanting her to worry, and he flusters through the line.

"Hey, I make sense all of the time. You're saying that like I don't," he grumbles, and I grin.

"Whatever you say, old man."

"Old man? I'll give you *old man*," he threatens with a scoff, and I snicker. "I miss you," he breathes, and my smile becomes weighted with the same feeling.

"I miss you too."

We knew we would have to be apart, but this is the longest I've ever gone without seeing my father and Nora, and it's harder than I thought it would be. Not that I would tell them that. It would only inflict more worry on them.

"How was it?" he asks, his voice low and nervous, making me frown.

"How was what?"

"Seeing her." Understanding instantly washes over me and my heart clenches.

I try to swallow past the lump lodged in my throat, but it's useless. "Unexpected," I rasp, clearing my throat.

"I can imagine it was."

"Honestly, I would have expected to see you there before her," I admit, taking a deep breath to ease the rising tension.

"I'm sure."

Silence hangs in the air, and in that seemingly-eternal moment, my father holds all the control. He's always been like this, giving me the silence and space to think about how I feel so I can express it in its truest form.

"I'm torn over it all," I admit.

"What do you mean?" he asks, keeping his question light and open as I try to decipher what has my chest twisted in a knot.

"I don't feel compelled to go and save her, and I don't

know if that makes me a bad person or not." I exhale the biggest breath, realizing the weight of what's been riding my shoulders.

He clears his throat and I imagine him wiping a hand down his face. "She doesn't need saving, Addi."

"She doesn't?" My body stiffens, another frown marking my forehead.

"She chose to be there. She chose to be with them."

"Oh."

I don't know how that makes me feel, either. She chose to be there instead of with her family? It's times like this that I hate the fact that we haven't spoken more freely about her. But in the same breath, why bother when she chose something else anyway?

I'm aware she's always been connected to the downfall of the kingdom, but as much as I hate her, I've never dared to find out the truth.

"Did you know she was there the entire time?" I ask. It's the deepest question I've ever asked about her, and I instantly hate it.

"I guessed, but I was never certain. When we ran, I didn't look. There was no need. If she wanted to be with us, she would have run too."

My eyebrows knit in confusion, but I refuse to delve deeper when it comes to her. My mind refuses, shutting me off. Instead, I'm focusing on something else entirely. "So it doesn't make me a bad heir to not worry about the safety of someone in the kingdom?"

"Oh, Addi. No. Far from it. Being a leader isn't all sunshine and roses. There's always something ugly around the corner, things we don't want to face or have to handle, along with bad decisions we don't want to make for the greater good. But the fact that you question that, the fact that you consider the kingdom as well as yourself, is what makes you a worthy heir."

My chest tingles with the praise from my father, easing the self-doubt threatening to creep in.

"Thanks, Dad." A knock on the door interrupts our call. "Sorry, Dad. My friend is here. We're going for dinner," I explain, and his voice chirps up.

"Of course, I won't keep you. I just wanted to mention the kiss of amethyst," he states as I open the door to see Flora on the other side. She smiles but instantly panics when she sees I'm on a call. I smile back, holding a finger up for her to give me a second, and she nods.

"What about it?" I ask, averting my gaze from Flora as my father speaks. My teeth sink into my bottom lip as I listen, unsure of what he's telling me. "Are you sure?"

"I'm positive, Addi. I banned it, remember? I know enough."

I nod even though he can't see me. "Thank you."

"You're welcome. Now, you go, try and have fun. I

love you."

"I love you too," I breathe, ending the call.

I look down at the device, still a little bewildered by the entire conversation, when Flora clears her throat, pulling me from my head.

"Are you ready to go, or do you need a minute?" she asks, and I hurry to put my cell phone away before I step out into the hall with her.

"I'm absolutely starving, let's go."

THE REIGN OF BLOOD

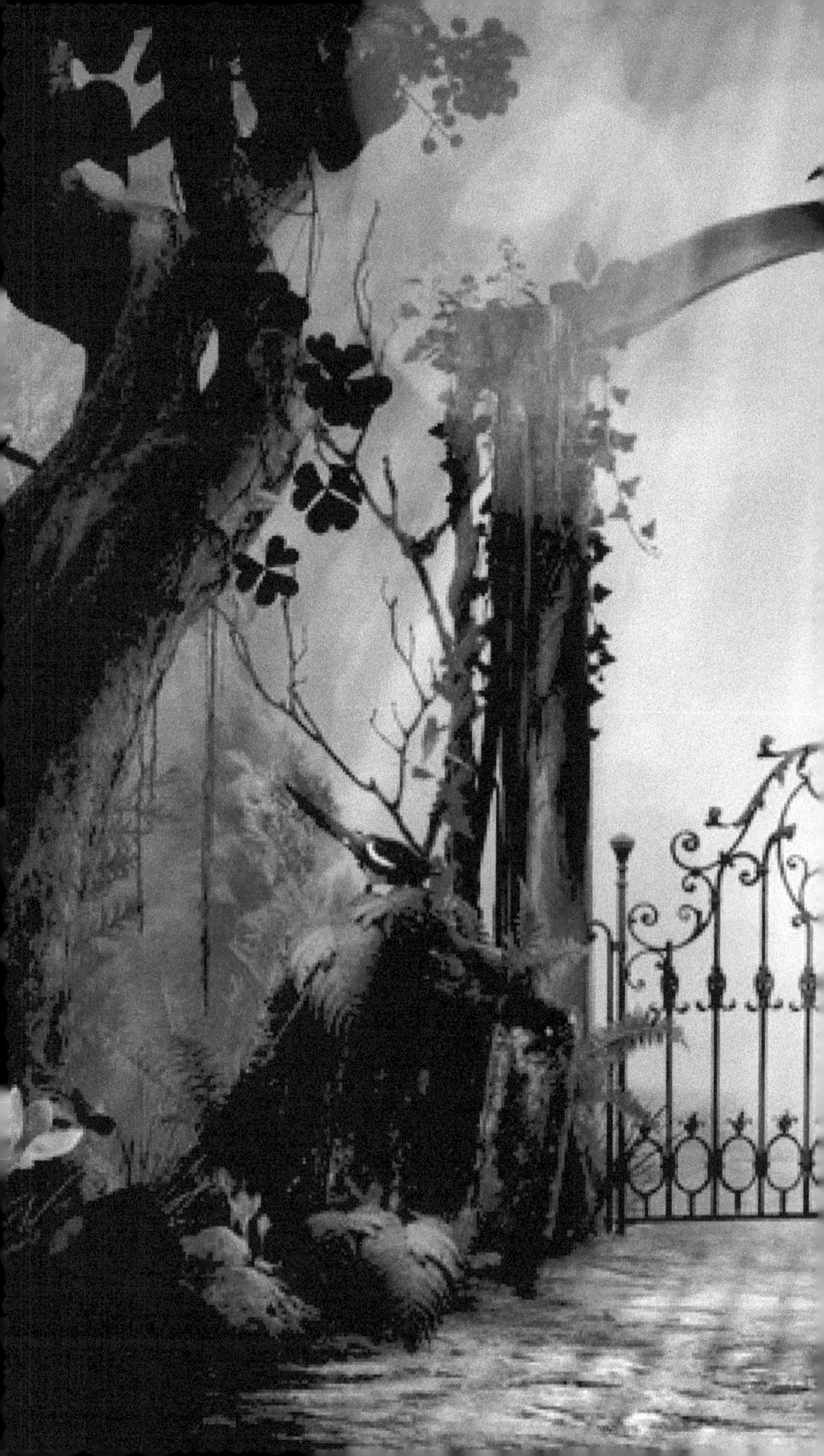

ADRIANNA

25

A cold sweat drips down my back and fear clings to every inch of me as I bolt upright in a blind panic. I can't catch my breath, and it only worsens when I can't place where I am.

The room is nothing like mine. It's warm, cozy, and smells like… strawberries.

My terror subsides when a flash of bright red hair catches my attention, and I sag in relief when I realize it's Flora beside me. The relief is short-lived when she blinks up at me, eyebrows gathered with uncertainty.

"Are you okay?" she rasps, tiredness clinging to every word.

"I'm fine," I croak, rubbing mindlessly at my chest as I will the terror detonating inside of me to pass.

She shuffles to sit up, leaning back against the

headboard as I subtly inch away from her. I don't need her too close right now. I feel on edge and unpredictable. I already feel unsafe and tangled in unfamiliar surroundings, and I know the smallest thing could set me off.

"Are you sure? I don't mean to pry, but you were…" Her words trail off as she glances down at the sheets, trying to find the right words. When they don't come, she exhales softly and turns on the lamp at her nightstand.

My eyes burn from the intrusion, but it works to calm the demons inside of me.

"What was I doing, Flora?" I dare to ask, my chest tightening with more fear as she offers me a soft smile.

"You were crying."

I rear back as if she's slapped me in the face, jaw slacking as I lift my hand to my cheek, pressing against it to find the skin drenched in tears. Embarrassment curls through me and I avert my gaze.

"I get nightmares. I'm sorry, I didn't mean to wake you," I explain, swinging my legs over the side of the bed before pushing to my feet. My muscles clench, aching with the tension taking hold of me as I turn to face her.

"Don't apologize," she says with a shake of your head. "Is there anything I can do to help?"

I fall in sync, shaking my head back at her. "What time is it?"

She peers at the clock beside her bed. "Five."

Five is late enough for me not to have to go back to sleep, at least.

Pointing over my shoulder, I take a backward step toward the door. "I should probably have a shower. Clear my head," I ramble, still feeling lightheaded and disoriented, but I need to move. She's kind and caring, but I don't want someone to witness this right now.

"Of course, if that's what you need."

I offer her a tight smile. "It is. Thanks, Flora." My hand wraps around her door handle as she yawns.

"No worries," she manages with her mouth stretched wide. "Oh, and don't forget we're going shopping on Friday. Ball preparations. I'm holding you to it." She gives me a pointed look, despite her tired eyes, and my smile morphs into a real grin.

"How could I forget? You wrote it on my hand, remember?" I retort, waving the ink on my skin at her.

"Just making sure. Besides, it made you smile."

I pause. The ricocheting of my heart in my chest calms as I soak in her naturally sweet nature. "You're a good friend, Flora."

"I know. You're welcome." She waves me off, turning the light off and slipping beneath the sheets again as I close the door behind me.

I need to be a good friend, too. She's on another level, though, so reaching her standards isn't going to be so easy.

Heading for the communal bathroom, I don't even bother to get a fresh change of clothes. Instead, I step into the first stall, flick the water on, and move straight under the spray. Clothes and all. It's ice cold at first, but I breathe through it. The shock to my system works wonders, and as it warms, it takes some of the stress along with it.

I peel out of my clothes, letting them flop to the floor until the beating hot water laps at my bare skin. Inching my face under the shower head, I let the memory of last night come back to mind, helping ground me as I release the last of the pent-up worry inside of me.

We had dinner in peace. No guys, not even Arlo. It was just the two of us. No interruptions and no drama. It was perfect. As soon as we were done eating too many slices of pizza, we headed back to Flora's room, where we proceeded to watch episode after episode of *The Office*. Mention of the ball preparations came up, which is how I've now been roped into dress shopping, but I'm sure it will be fun.

The idea of getting off campus, even if just for a hot minute, feels exciting. Especially since it's nowhere near the Kenner compound.

Then, I must have fallen asleep again. Wiping a hand down my face, I lean my head back and catch my breath. The nightmare feels jagged. I can't recall it fully, but I can still feel the remnants of it coating my skin. Even with the shower pounding down on me, it doesn't eradicate it altogether, but it does make me present and alert.

It's not enough, though. I need to get rid of the energy coursing through me.

With my mind made up, I rush through the mundane task of washing my body and hair. Once all of the suds are gone, I switch off the water and peek behind the curtain. Certain the coast is clear, I reach for a towel from the barely stocked shelves. Draping it around my chest, I can't help but wonder if other origins get the luxury of fuller and thicker material because every time I shower I feel like these become more threadbare than the last.

With a sigh, I grab my wet clothes and rush back to my room, the concern over my towel long forgotten in the grand scheme of things. It's no surprise that I don't run into anyone at this time of the morning, but I still hurry to lock my bedroom behind me.

Taking a moment to absorb the familiar surroundings, I mentally call out three things I can see.

My bed. The window. The roses.

Taking a deep breath, I catch their scent. There's not much to hear at this time, though, so I save that for when I get outside. That's what I need. Fresh air, the wind whipping at my face, and my feet pounding on the ground beneath me.

With my mind made up, I set my sights on the academy-issued sportswear hanging in my closet. Channeling deep into my core, I connect with my air magic and let a warm breeze finish drying me off as I let my towel cascade to the floor. It takes a little more effort to use the same power to dry my hair completely, and by the time I'm done, I'm practically panting.

Fuck.

Maybe I don't need to get my heart rate going with a run. Simply doing magic, which I have practiced and harnessed for so long, will do the trick now that I'm controlled by this damn gem.

Shaking my head, I try to rid the negativity from me, but it's futile. Instead, I slip from my bedroom, tiptoe down the staircase, and step outside into the early morning air. I take the deepest breath since I first woke, letting the chill in the air ground me to the present as the sound of birds chirping in the distance rounds out my senses.

This is exactly what I needed. The sun is barely breaking the horizon, offering a small glimmer of natural light to the grounds.

Slowly making my way down the pathway that leads to the fountain, I go through the motions of some stretches. I wouldn't always, but since I already exhausted myself using my magic, I decide it's better to ease myself into this.

Focused, I reach the fountain and jog, hoping the exercise will ward off the cool air and warm my limbs.

I follow my usual path, sticking close to the edge of the academy. Maybe jogging at this time should become a regular thing. There's not a single soul in sight.

The peace and tranquility this offers me outweigh the little sleep I would lose. That's what I think now, at least. Tomorrow morning could be something completely different.

I watch in awe as the sun continues to rise, painting the academy in an array of pinks, oranges, and yellows. It's enchanting, the way it dances over the flowers, spreading their petals wide as the trees preen under its glow.

Reaching the peak of the hill, I slow my pace and take controlled steps as I begin the decline. The edge of the all-too-familiar forest comes into view and my gaze instantly darts to the fallen tree in the distance as I breathe through my steps, keeping my heart rate calm.

It's clear the gem doesn't have an effect on physical exertion. Its sole purpose is to contain my magic, and that's exactly what it's doing.

Movement pulls my eyes to the right of the walkway, at the edge of the tree line, but I don't immediately see anything. I slow, eyes darting over every inch of the forest, until I catch sight of the shuffling again.

Is that a—

I don't get a chance to think before my thoughts are confirmed.

A chestnut-brown wolf appears from between some shrubs, prowling toward me with calculated steps, and I freeze. My hands ball at my sides as I force the tension in my veins to ease. I need to be ready to act, to defend myself, which means being as calm as possible.

The wolf continues to approach me, its eyes giving nothing away, even as it steps up right beside me. Their fur brushes against my leg for a split second as they circle me, making my eyes widen at how soft it is. It's hard not to stretch out my fingers and feel the softness again, reminding myself that it's not just an animal; there's a person beneath it, too.

As if sensing my thoughts, the wolf moves to stand in front of me, and with a single blink of my eyes, they shift before me. My adoration for the animal quickly disappears when I realize it's the most infuriating one of them all.

"What are you doing out here so early?" he grunts, irritating me instantly.

"That's none of your business, Cassian." I fold my arms over my chest. I'm in no mood to deal with his shit right now. How does he shift and still have clothes on? What's that about?

"Anyone could attack you."

"It feels like someone already is," I mutter, cocking a brow at him, which earns me an eye roll. Yeah, I'm definitely not getting an answer to his whole clothing situation right now.

"Don't be dumb, Addi."

"Don't be you, Cassian," I remark, my chest tightening as if that statement was one step too far, but if he thinks the same, he doesn't show it.

Wanting to put some space between us, I proceed past him, keeping my arms locked around my waist as I head through the forest. I can sense him a step behind me the entire way, not saying a word, which somehow has the ability to get even more under my skin.

"You can leave now," I holler over my shoulder as we reach the clearing on the other side of the forest. The fountain is a few yards away and we're both heading back to different origin buildings, so there's definitely no reason for him to talk himself into staying.

"I'll go when I'm ready," he grunts, making my lips purse in agitation.

Whatever.

Upping my pace, I reach the fountain, acutely aware that he's still behind me at the same time Professor Fairbourne comes into view. The sight of him after nothing at all the past week makes me halt in my tracks.

"Where have you been?" I blurt, like I have a right to know.

A pained crinkle flickers around his pinched eyes as he swipes at his chin. "I'll get to that," he mutters, peering at me for a split second before turning his attention to Cassian. "Are you harassing fae?" he bites, jaw ticking as he looks down his nose at the wolf, and I snicker.

"Not plural, just this one," I state, pointing at myself, which does nothing to ease the tension rolling off the professor.

"Is that true?" he pushes, taking a step toward Cassian, who shakes his head at him.

"Watch your tongue, old man. My wolf is hungry."

My eyebrows rise in surprise at his threat, but Fairbourne doesn't seem to pay much mind to it.

"You'll do well to stay away from her."

"Will I?" Cassian inches toward him, shoulders broad, back as straight as an arrow, and the desire to fight emitting from every part of him.

"I think that's enough from you two," I mutter, moving to stand between them. I have no idea what's actually going on but it's way too early in the morning to be dealing with this. It seems like one problem I have just evolves into another. At least they're keeping me distracted from the issues that woke me in a fit of panic.

Turning my attention to the professor, I fold my arms over my chest, giving my back to Cassian in hopes that he will just go away. "For a professor who is supposed to take care of the fae, you've been pretty useless the past week."

He clears his throat, glancing at the ground for a second

before returning his eyes to mine. "About that," he starts, but tilts around me to point a finger at Cassian. "You've been summoned."

"By who?"

"By your father."

"Since when?" Cassian snaps, the news catching him off guard.

"It's the reason I'm out here. I was going to speak with you later today, Addi, but for now, my orders are to bring the Kenner boy."

Cassian sneers at the label he brands him with, but instead of giving him another mouthful of threats, he grinds his teeth, nostrils flaring. "Why would they send you and not my own origin advisor?"

"Because I just left a meeting with Bozzelli. It was quicker for it to be me."

"Where?"

"Bozzelli's office."

"Of course." Cassian takes two steps before turning back to glance at me. His jaw tightens as his fingers flex at his sides. "Can I trust him with you?"

I frown. What kind of question even is that? "I'll be fine."

I can sense that he doesn't like that answer, his right eye twitching ever so slightly, but after a few beats, he takes me at my word and saunters off.

Silence descends over Fairbourne and me. I let it hang there, waiting for him to explain.

"I apologize for my lack of presence this week. Truthfully, I was being questioned."

My head rears back. "For what?"

"For any involvement in you being here," he admits, making my pulse quicken and confusion deepen.

"You didn't know I was here until I was here. I don't even recall you from my childhood," I state, noting the slight flicker of disappointment, but it's the truth. All I remember is the pain that came with leaving everything behind. Anything else is hidden away.

I always thought that was the wrong way around. How the pain should be hidden and the joy should be at the forefront of my mind. Until one day, I realized it is the pain that fuels me, the pain that gives me purpose, and the pain that gives me the drive to succeed.

"I know that, but everyone knows I was at your father's side all those years ago, so they had to be sure."

I run my eyes over him, looking for any obvious signs of discomfort or pain. "Are you okay?"

"I'm fine," he murmurs, wincing through the fake smile on his lips. His hand lifts but quickly falls, as if he was going to reach for something but stopped himself.

"Why are you wincing?"

"No reason." The cords in his neck are pulled tight,

and a sickly feeling settles in my stomach.

"Turn around."

He shakes his head. "No."

"Professor, turn around," I repeat, his sheepishness only confirming where my thoughts are leading.

He sighs, defeated, as he slowly turns. There's a raise to his t-shirt at the top of his spine and a few droplets of blood stain the fabric, concealing what lies beneath.

"You got a kiss of amethyst, too?" I breathe, and he whips around to face me with horror dancing in his eyes.

"They did this to you?"

"They did," I admit, watching the horror deepen to terror as he takes a step toward me, but I instinctively take one back.

"Sorry, it's not personal, I just…"

"It's okay," he murmurs, tucking his hands into his pockets. "I can help you," he offers, and I give him a tight smile.

"My father already has, but thank you."

Next time I speak to my father, I'm going to mention this guy just to be sure what he says adds up.

"I'm sorry I wasn't there when you needed me, Adrianna. I won't let it happen again," he promises, and I nod, not planning on counting on him for anything.

"It's out of our control. Don't worry about it. What we should be considering is the fact that Kenner is back on campus again. How does he keep getting away with that?" I ask, hoping to shift the conversation away from me to a topic I would still like details on.

Fairbourne scoffs. "Because this place is just as fucked as the rest of the kingdom."

THE REIGN OF BLOOD

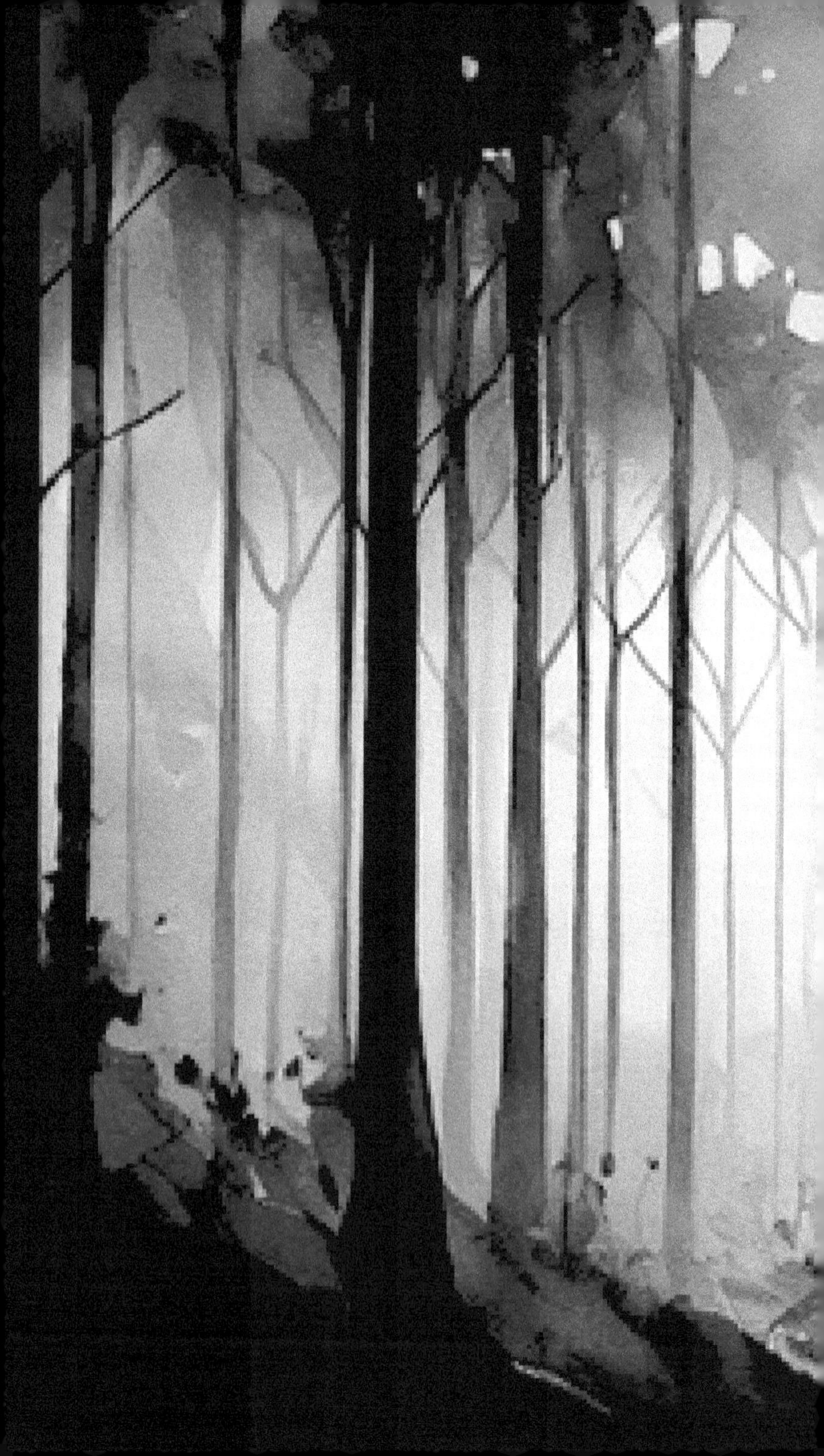

CASSIAN
26

Fucking Fairbourne.

Fucking Addi.

My fucking father.

My brain can't deal with any of it. I was hoping to start the morning off strong, giving my wolf a moment to stretch and enjoy a calm and peaceful environment before the day began, but all that seemed to do was bring more drama.

I should have stayed inside. Instead, I'm marching across campus toward Bozzelli's office to face my father, who has been incessantly calling and messaging. I was hoping he would take the hint that I didn't want to talk with him, but I should have known it would only push him to pursue more drastic measures.

Hindsight is a bitch.

So is Fairbourne.

Who the fuck disappears for a week when one of his origin members needed him? He's lucky I didn't slam my fist into his face; professor or not. Maybe if he had been present, he could have prevented the amethyst from being lodged into Addi's back. Not that it matters to me. Or it shouldn't, at least.

Warning me away from Addi only makes my distaste for him grow. I don't take orders from anyone, not even her, so why would I take his? Fool.

The *her* in question, the thorn in my fucking side that I can't shake, needs some sense knocked into her… and fast. What the hell was she thinking running across campus alone when so many people are gunning for her? Is she that delusional? Surely not.

Maybe she is. Maybe she thinks she's so invincible that she can't be knocked off her feet. I know I haven't seen it happen every time she fights off a wolf, or Vallie for that matter, but that doesn't mean life is smooth sailing like that. Fuck, my father can get on campus. Imagine if it had been him she bumped into. His wolf wouldn't brush against her in a friendly, heart-warming way.

He'd slaughter her.

Dead.

It'd be too late to regret the lack of safety then.

She's lucky he only sliced her ears the last time she met

him. Now, I can imagine him being even more ruthless.

My gut clenches, an indescribable ache that settles inside of me every time I think about the fact that it was indeed my father who harmed her like that. I don't want to admit it to myself, but I'm fairly certain that's the reason why I can't bring myself to see him.

I want to kill him with my bare hands for laying a single finger on her, and whatever he did to her sister… the pain I saw in her eyes at the mention of it makes me want to double down my efforts so she never gets that look again.

Entering the main academy building, I shut down my thoughts and focus on clearing everything from my mind until the only thing I'm focused on is my father's presence. Bozzelli's office comes into view far too quickly. The door is ajar, and just as Fairbourne mentioned, my father awaits me inside.

At least he wasn't just saying it to get me away from Addi.

Stepping into the office, my father's gaze shifts from the large, arched window behind him to me.

"You took your time," he grunts, and I shrug.

"Did I?"

"I watched you. You could have used your speed."

He's right, I could have, but I wasn't ready to hurry this along. I'm not ready to deal with him now, either.

Taking the seat across the desk from him, I get

comfortable, slumping back a little as my knees spread and my foot starts tapping. Quickly halting the action, I ball my hands into fists, purposely digging my nails into my palms to keep myself in check.

"Why are you here?" I ask when he doesn't proceed.

His gaze narrows on me as he leans against the desk. "Because you've been ignoring me."

No shit.

"You were supposed to take that as me not wanting to speak with you. You're not supposed to show up here and force it just to suit your needs," I grumble, and he smirks.

"If I want to speak with you, I will."

"Of course you will," I say with a sigh, and his eyes darken.

"Watch your tone with me," he warns, wagging his finger at me.

"What do you want?" I ask, trying to get to the point of all of this.

"I'll get to that when I'm ready," he snaps, making my nails dig deeper into my flesh.

It's all mind games with this man. I knew it when I was under his control, but now, from the outside looking in, it's even clearer.

The first time Raiden called upon me to help get control over some frenzied vampires, I went, did what was needed, and went back to the compound drenched in blood. The four of us had made a pact to have each other's backs and always support one another no matter what, and I was sticking to it.

My father didn't like that. That was the first time I knew my core values and ethics didn't align with his. Which meant I didn't align with the pack.

The questioning I got was off the scales. I didn't have anything to hide, though. I told him where I'd been, what I'd done, and why I'd done it. The fury that brought out in him was one I'd rarely had the opportunity to experience. He trashed my room, destroyed everything I valued, including a picture of my mother, and tried to make me swear that I'd never aid the vampires again.

I refused.

It was the beginning of our demise.

The second I was no longer a puppet dancing to the will of his fingertips, his mind games went up a notch. I'm certain there are wolves here under his order, watching me and reporting back. I wouldn't be surprised if the girl who challenged Addi to a duel yesterday did so because he ordered it, but I'll never have proof.

This man is too good at covering his tracks.

I look at him now, contemplating everything he's ever said to me. Was it all a lie? Was there any ounce of truth to a single word?

Did my mother truly die in a freak accident, or was it

at the hands of this man? Is she even dead? Deep down, I hope she isn't. I hope she's as far away from him as possible, living some serene life like she deserves.

Feeling my mental fortitude tumble, I take a deep breath and focus back on the conversation. I can't get distracted when he's so intent on asserting his dominance.

"I have classes to get to, you know," I grumble, relaxing my hands and bracing them on the arms of the chair instead. The wood serves as a stronger element against my tight grip, but the depth of my hold doesn't make the pain any less.

"I'm aware," he bites, running his tongue over his teeth as he glares at me. "I've been informed that your little princess defeated someone else in a duel."

Like fuck.

"She did."

"Hmm. I don't think waiting until next month for someone else to attempt it is going to work for the good of the pack." He leans back, eyebrow raised, as he waits for my response.

What the fuck does that mean?

"I'm not a part of any pack," I remind him, and he sneers, pupils turning black as his glare deepens.

"You're a part of mine."

"You exiled me, remember?"

He's so quick to forget. It probably doesn't help that I

keep giving in to him.

"You need to see the error of your ways," he states, and it takes everything in me to bite back the scoff threatening my tongue.

"The only errors I see are sitting across from me."

It's the truth, but that doesn't make him appreciate my assessment.

"I made you, son. I can take it all away just as quickly."

I'm sure that's what he thinks, but I have connections and power, too. Legitimate ones. There's only so long this man can creep around in the shadows, causing mayhem, before it catches up with him.

"What's the point of your visit, Kenner?" I ask with a sigh, ignoring his warning.

"It's Alpha to you," he corrects, and I shrug.

"I said what I said."

His hands ball into fists, slamming down on the desk between us with rage as his wild eyes meet mine. "I want you and your little fae princess to make an appearance at the compound."

"I can't imagine why we would do that," I answer, hating the mention of Addi on his tongue, but I can't show it. That will only serve to work in his favor.

"Because I fucking said so," he snaps.

I shake my head. "That's not enough, especially after the last visit. Wouldn't you agree?" I give him a pointed look, but it goes right over his head as he smirks, his gaze drifting, clearly remembering the performance he put on last time. I bet he got off on the power trip that gave him for sure.

"You will be there," he repeats, nostrils flaring, and I'm certain he's going to slam his fists again, but to my surprise, he manages to keep it under control. For now.

"For what purpose?" I ask, still not seeing how he thinks this is going to go his way.

"I want you to bring that little bitch, and I want her to fight a selection of wolves who I believe would serve you better."

I'm on the verge of splitting the arms of the chair in half as I try to contain my rage. He's calling her everything but her name to degrade her and get a reaction out of me.

Fucker. He won't get it. Especially not when he wants us there so she can take on an army of fucking wolves.

"That will be a no."

"Why? Because Bozzelli used one of my amethysts to contain the little whore?" he asks, a grin spreading across his face.

Anger bubbles inside me. It takes every fiber of my strength to keep my heart rate even and my claws hidden. Of course he had something to do with that too.

"You're still not selling it to me," I mutter, trying to act bored, but it's too fucking hard.

"If she wins, I'll leave you be. If she loses, you never go near her again. It's as simple as that."

My brows knit in confusion. "Why?"

"Because some half-breed like her doesn't belong in power," he snarls, fists hitting the desk once more.

"Half-breed?"

What the fuck does that mean?

"She has no ears, she's no true fae, she's no true anything. She'll never take the place as heir of the kingdom." It's not a thought or an opinion. It's a promise.

He forgets the part where he was the one to mark her like that, which pisses me off even more, but I refrain from offering even a single ounce of acknowledgement that he's getting to me.

Sighing, I lean forward, bracing my elbows on my knees as I stare at him. "I still don't see her fighting these people for you to leave *me* alone. There's no incentive for her," I point out, even though I know there's nothing that would make her fall under his spell like this. She can be foolish, but she's not *that* foolish.

"Her incentive? She can have the ultimate prize if she defeats the five wolves I've selected."

Five? That's not as high as I expected, but he doesn't specify if they're all women or not, which means they're definitely men because he loves to play games like that. But it's the mention of an incentive that he believes she will fight for that has me intrigued.

"Which is what?" I ask, watching as his smile spreads from ear to ear.

His eyes shimmer like he thinks he's doing me a favor, and his entire demeanor relaxes as though I'm right where he wants me.

"The queen, of course."

THE REIGN OF BLOOD

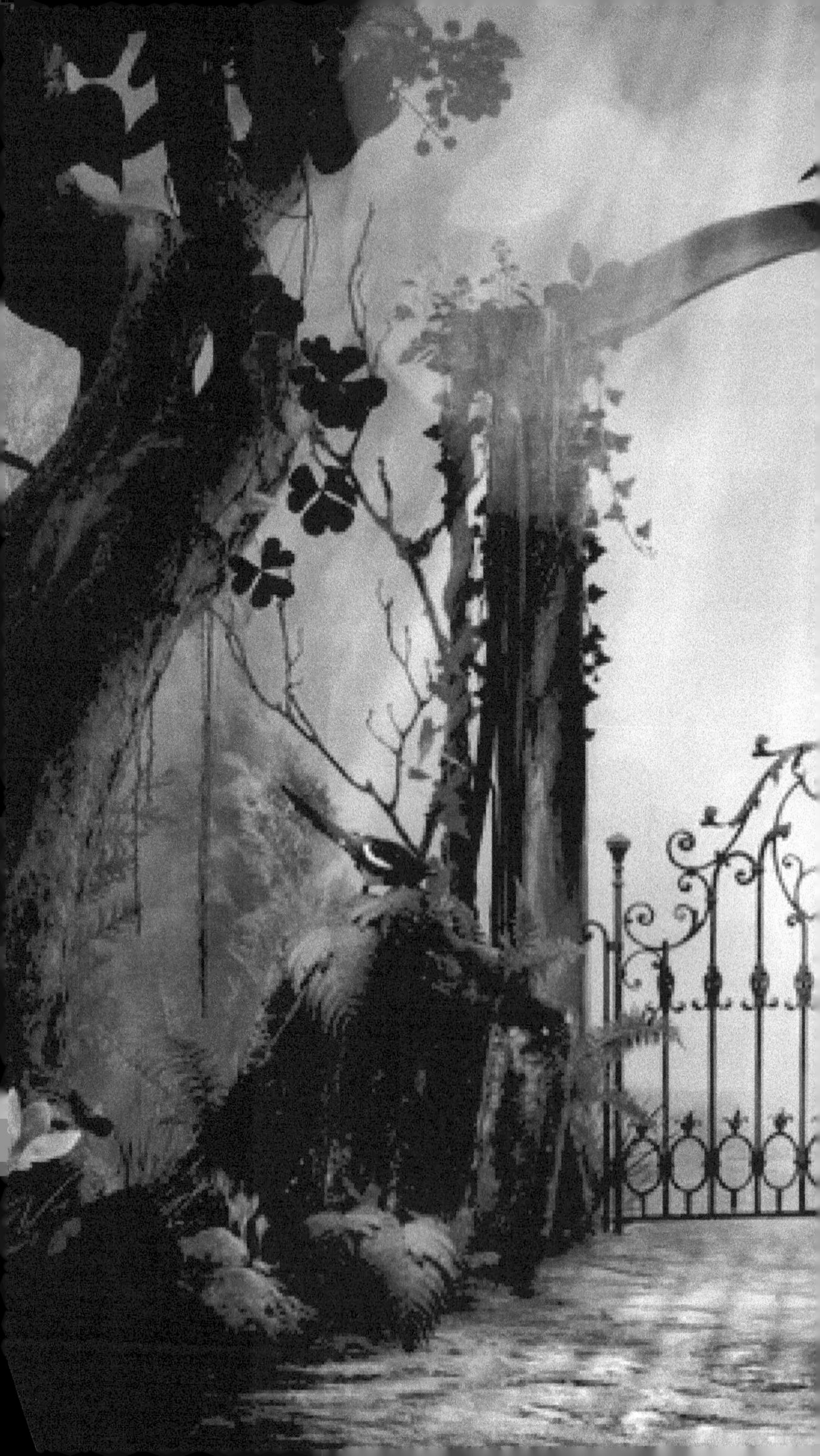

ADRIANNA

27

I sense the concern coming from Flora as she sits across from me in her usual spot, but I opt to focus on my breakfast instead of trying to explain the cluster fuck that has been this morning. I can't believe I'm thinking this, but I'd rather get our classes started for the day. There's no combat on the schedule, which is a bummer, but I'll take whatever distraction I can get.

Speaking of distractions, three out of the four men hell-bent on causing destruction in my life take their seats at the table. Brody is across from me. Raiden and Kryll get comfortable on either side of me. Arlo and Flora smirk like all of this is amusing. If they only knew the stress these fuckers really put me through.

"Where's Cassian? I was expecting him to be here already," Brody asks, looking at Raiden and Kryll. Like clockwork, a member of staff brings their food over not even ten seconds later.

Raiden rolls his eyes at Brody. "Probably moping."

I frown. They actually don't know where he is. Which means I have the pleasure of delivering the news. Fun.

Running my tongue over my bottom lip, I clear my throat. "Uh, his father summoned him."

All eyes whip to me. Flora and Arlo included.

"How would you know that?" Raiden asks, his eyebrows gathering with doubt.

"Because I was there when Professor Fairbourne told him." I take a fork full of food as he purses his lips at me, while Brody grins from ear to ear, wagging his eyebrows.

"Why would you be there? Was it because—"

"Ew, please, don't say anymore," I grumble, making everyone chuckle. "And I was there because he was giving me a hard time about the fact that I went for a run," I admit, and Flora gasps.

"You went for a run?" I can sense the same shock I got from Cassian oozing from her. "You said you were going to shower."

"And I did. It just wasn't enough, so I decided to go for a run as well."

Flora's eyes widen further. "What the hell kind of nightmare—"

"Flora. Stop," I interject, my heart racing at the mention

of it in front of everyone.

"Nightmare?" Kryll murmurs, but I shake my head, focusing on my plate.

"Nope. We're not talking about this. We're talking about Cassian," I grumble, trying to refocus the conversation on something that doesn't leave me quite so vulnerable.

"Why are you talking about me?" His gravelly voice makes me shiver as he catches me by surprise.

"Because you're an asshole," I retort, refusing to lift my head.

Silence stretches out around us when he doesn't deny it, and I use the moment to eat as much food as possible because I get the feeling today is only going to continue to go downhill.

"We need to talk," he states, as if sensing my thoughts, and I force myself to look up at him. Much to my dismay, it's me he's looking at.

His jaw is tight, lips set in a thin line, and eyes swirling with a storm of emotions that I can't decipher. It looks like someone had a fun visit with their father. I shouldn't care, yet my stomach clenches with concern for him.

"We did enough of that this morning," I retort instead, shaking my head at him as I catch amusement dancing in Flora's eyes. I need to put distance between us, not encourage him to be in my proximity more, and that's exactly what the look in her eyes is suggesting.

"I barely said two words," he barks back, and I shrug.

"And it was two too many."

I yelp in surprise when my chair drags across the floor at the hands of the asshole wolf. He turns me to face him as he braces his hands on his knees, getting down to my level and right in my face.

"Are you walking, or am I carrying you?"

This fucker.

"You wouldn't," I bite, hands clenched in my lap as he takes my warning as an opening.

In the blink of an eye, I'm hoisted over his shoulder, my stomach clenching from the impact of his tight muscles before he starts sauntering through the dining hall with ease. "Put me the fuck down," I growl, irritated and embarrassed that I can sense people looking at us, but he proceeds to ignore the hell out of me. "Everyone is looking!" I push, my irritation growing to new heights.

"I can speed walk if you like?" It's not an offer. It's a threat. One that makes my stomach churn.

"Nope, an audience is better than the nausea," I snarl at him, accepting my fate as he leads us outside and away from the crowd.

He lowers me to my feet, holding my body tightly against his so we are pressed chest to chest. My hands fall to his chest, feeling the warm pitter-patter of his heart before he releases me. Remembering myself, I take a step back, clearing my throat as I try to remind myself how agitated I am with him.

"What's so important we have to talk right now?" I ask, folding my arms over my chest in hopes of putting a defensive layer between us.

"My father."

"Is an asshole."

"That's putting it lightly," he grumbles, swiping a hand down his face.

"You're telling me," I retort, pointing at my ears.

His jaw ticks as he looks away. His gaze settles on one of the picnic benches set up outside and he strides toward it, taking a seat. It's clear the conversation isn't over, no matter how much I would like it to be. So, with a heavy sigh, I take the spot beside him.

I get comfortable with the silence. It's not me that needs to get something off their chest. It stretches out for what feels like an eternity as his gaze remains unfocused, staring off into the distance.

"He wants me to take you to the compound."

"No," I snap back quickly, and he nods.

"I know."

Trying to take a deep breath to calm my racing heart, I shake my head in disbelief. "Why?"

"Because he doesn't like that you're my alpha."

"I'm not your alpha." He cocks a brow at me in

challenge and I avert my gaze. I'm not a wolf or a shifter of any kind, so I'm not his alpha. Not in the way his father would assume, anyway. The nickname he seems to throw at me, though, is out of my control. "He said that?" I ask, needing to understand what the leader of the Kenner pack thinks.

"No, but he doesn't like the fact that you keep winning the duels."

"I mean, there have been two, and I would have thrown them both, but—" His hand claps down over my mouth, effectively cutting off the rest of my words.

"Don't piss me off and finish that sentence." His voice is low, but the rumble of irritation is evident enough to know that I'm toeing the line with him. Gulping, I keep my mouth shut. "Have you finished with that train of thought?" he asks, and only after I nod does he remove his hand, taking his heat along with him.

"You're nothing but mind games," I mutter, and he scoffs.

"If you think these are mind games, you have no clue what else awaits you out there," he mutters, leaning back against the table as he looks at me. "He wants you to face five wolves of his selection. If you lose, I have to stay away from you."

My heart races, and my chest clenches. "That sounds like a win to me," I quickly sass, even though deep down I don't believe that to be true.

Cassian gives me a deathly glare. "Sass may suit you, Addi, but sarcasm doesn't." My eyes narrow on him and his shit statements, but he pays no interest as he continues. "If you win, he will leave me alone and offer you what he believes to be the most luxurious prize that was ever offered."

I scoff. There's no chance in hell this man has anything of interest to offer me. Despite knowing it already, I still ask. "Which is?"

"Your mother."

My head rears back. That's not what I was expecting him to say at all. Not even a little bit. She was completely gone from my mind.

"I don't want her," I blurt, glancing away, and I could swear I hear him snicker, but when I turn back to him, his face is as stoic as ever.

"I didn't think you did."

"No, my father was adamant that if she is there, she chose to be," I admit, watching his nose crinkle in confusion.

"What does that mean?"

"Fuck if I know, but it's not a prize I'm interested in winning," I reconfirm, and he nods in understanding.

Another bout of silence graces us, but this one seems to hold less hostility and more… understanding.

"Does it leave you as intrigued as it does me?" he asks, spiking my pulse as my lips rub together.

"The whole thing calls to my curiosity, but it's a path I don't think I'm ready to take." It's the truth, a vulnerable part of me, and I don't know if I've shared too much.

"I understand that. I also know that even if you won, which he wouldn't allow, he wouldn't deliver on his promise anyway."

My eyebrows rise. At least he can admit that.

"What will happen when I say no?" I murmur, refusing to look at him as I await his answer.

"Don't worry about it," he breathes, which spikes more uncertainty than him telling me it would be a death sentence.

"Cassian," I push, turning to him with a pointed look.

"To you, I don't know, but I wouldn't rule out the fact that he's got an ax to grind, and it's aimed at your head."

I gulp. I can sense there's something he's not saying, something that relates to him. "And to you?"

Silence again. But there's nothing comforting or calm about this one. Not with the way his eyes darken and he looks at me with a void expression. It's more unsettling than hearing his wrath.

"He'll take great pleasure in asserting his dominance and make an example out of me for the entire kingdom to see."

THE REIGN OF BLOOD

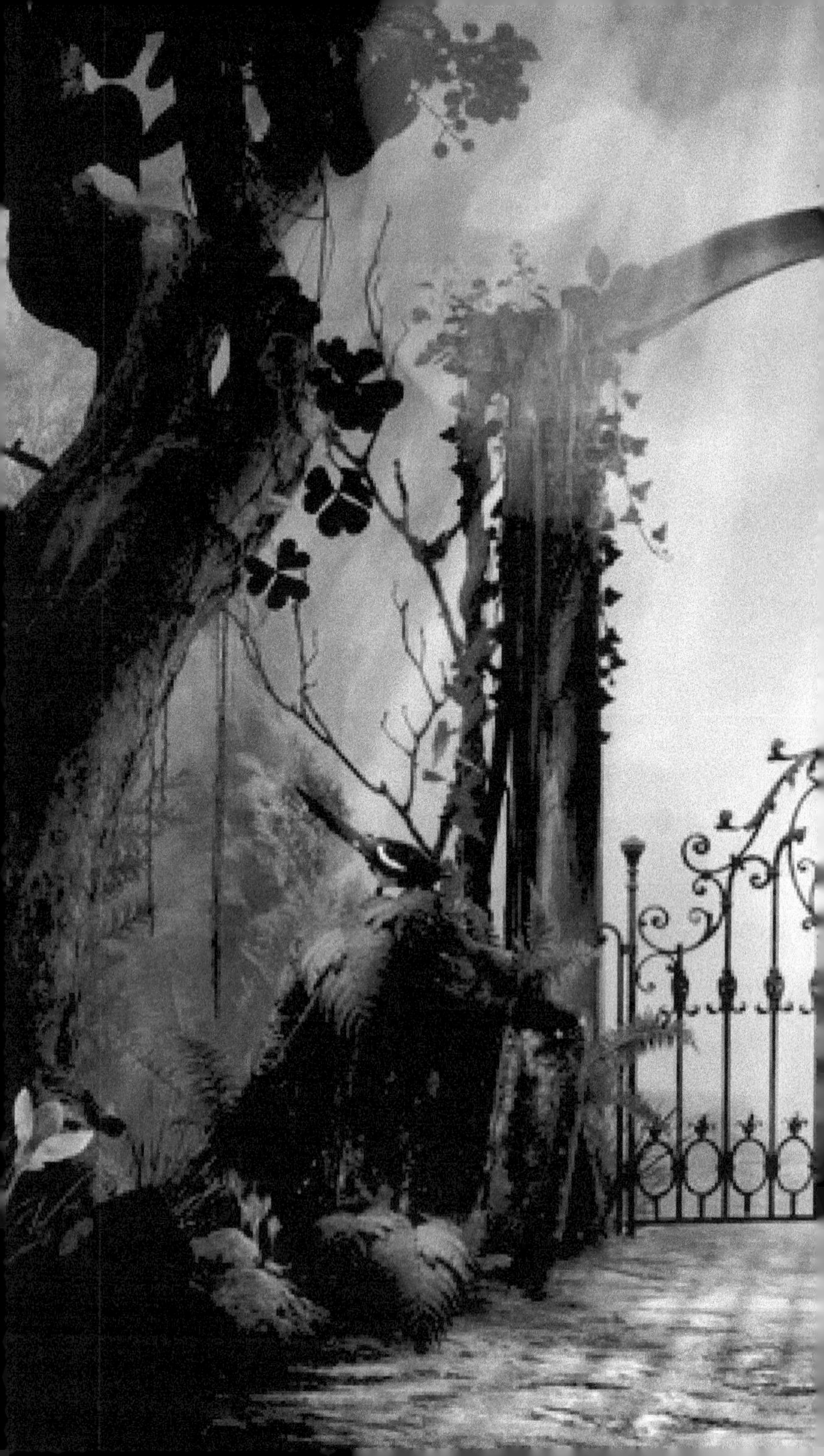

ADRIANNA

28

"Girl, you are seriously collecting these," Flora mutters in disbelief, twirling the rose in her hand. The petals dance with the spin of her fingers, enchanting me with their beauty. "How many do you have now?" she asks, peering over it to meet my gaze.

"Ten."

"Ten!" Her eyes widen as I nod, confirming the number of roses currently filling my vase.

"Aren't any starting to wilt?" Arlo asks from behind her, frowning down at the flower as if its mere existence confuses him.

I cock a brow and he rolls his eyes at me as Flora speaks. "You're keeping them alive," she assesses correctly.

Taking the rose from her hand, I smile and rush back

inside to add it to the vase with the others. "They're pretty," I offer in explanation before shutting my bedroom door behind me.

"You're such an earth fae," she remarks, making me roll my eyes as Arlo scoffs.

"She's an *everything* fae."

Flora turns to him with a stern look on her face as she plants her hands on her hips. "I said you could come if you were quiet. You're not being all that quiet, and actually, she's a *royal* fae, not an everything fae," she states, and he makes the motion of zipping his mouth shut and tossing away the key.

I bite back the smirk threatening to spread across my face, but neither of them notice as we head downstairs, making it outside without running into anyone. Part of me wishes we did. Part of me wishes an issue would arise so I didn't have to be subjected to the pain I know today will bring.

Shopping.

Not just any shopping, *dress* shopping.

Kill me now.

Heading straight down the path, we bypass the fountain and head toward the main gate. It feels strange seeing it loom ahead as I make my first official trip off campus. Every other time I've left, it's been at the hands of someone's magic. Walking out like this somehow fills me with more nerves than the alternative.

Guards stand on either side of the wrought-iron gate, glaring at us as we approach.

"We're heading into the City of Harrows. Preparations for the ball," Arlo explains, smiling at them, but all he gets in return are four disgruntled looks.

"And what makes you think we're going to let three little faes come and go as they please?" the closest one remarks, making me glare at him.

"Is there a problem?" I ask, stepping up to Arlo's side, and I notice one of the guards on the other side of the gate shrink back at my appearance.

"No problem at all, your royal… I mean… uh…" He stutters and stumbles over his words, making my cheeks heat with the acknowledgment. I wave him off as quickly as I can and he wastes no time ensuring the gates open.

"She's no royal to me," the first guy grunts, and I pay him no mind. I don't expect anyone to treat me any differently, I just wish the fae weren't treated so terribly to begin with.

"Thank you," I murmur to the helpful guy as I pass, and he nods.

"Anytime."

"What's your name?" I ask, pausing in place with Flora and Arlo right behind me.

"Jeffries."

"Thank you, Jeffries," I repeat, making a mental note to remember his name.

It's another to add to my list of allies, along with Flora and Arlo, which is embarrassingly much shorter than my foe list.

"Do you get that a lot?" Flora asks once we're out of sight, linking her arm through mine, and I shake my head.

"Never. Well, not that I remember anyway," I explain, taking the cobbled walkway down under the arch that leads into the main center of the City of Harrows.

A shiver runs down my spine at its familiarity and I take a deep breath—one, to clear the tension that had started to rise inside me at the first guard's remark and two, to smell the telltale scent of fresh oranges nearby.

There's a hop in my step as we make our way down the narrowed streets before we come to the larger arch that leads into the square itself. It feels like forever ago that I last caught a glimpse of the fountain that takes up the left side of the square, and the merchant's stalls selling fruits and fabrics are exactly where they always are. The reality is, it's been mere weeks.

It's not a lot of time at all, yet it feels like everything has changed since then, or is it just me?

Instinctively, I step away from Flora, wrapping my black cloak around my body protectively as I adjust the hood on my head. It feels too foreign to move around these cobbled streets any other way. If Flora or Arlo find it odd, neither of them say anything about it.

"We should eat first," Arlo states, scratching at his chin as Flora immediately begins shaking her head.

"That will make me bloated when trying on dresses, so eating can come second," she informs him.

"That's dramatic," he grumbles, tucking his hands into his pockets.

"It's the truth," I add, hating to admit it because the thought of food instead of shopping sounds far superior.

Flora leads the way, approaching a cute boutique, and I follow after her. My eyes widen when I take in the space. It's nowhere near as small as it appears to be from the outside. There are rows and rows of dresses spaciously laid out for us to search through—so much so that I don't even know where to begin.

"May I help you, ladies?" the assistant asks, smiling softly at us.

Pointed ears.

She's a fae.

My shoulders sag and the worry that weighed heavily on me eases. I feel like that's all I do anymore; ease one weight to replace it with another. It's exhausting.

"I think I know what I'm looking for, but my friend here looks like she might bolt," Flora muses, winking at me.

I give her a fake, harsh look before turning to the assistant. "She's correct," I admit, and the assistant's smile grows wider.

"I can help with that," she insists, turning toward the far right corner of the room, waving for me to follow after her. Her brown hair swishes from side to side with every step, her walk confident and strong for a fae.

I like her already.

I didn't know there was such a thing as too many choices, but here I am, staring at them as I move through the store.

"Head on in there," she states, waving for me to step into a large changing room with a huge mirror on the wall. Once I'm positioned where she wants me, I turn to her and she nods. "Now, what are your three favorite colors? Actually, two, I already know you're going to say black."

I gape at her, speechless, but there's no denying that she's right.

Clearing my throat, I consider her question. "Yellow and deep purple."

"Nice choices; the yellow would work perfectly with your complexion, too. Do you have any preference on sleeve and skirt length?" she adds, tilting her head at me.

"Long skirt, the sleeves are open," I reply instantly, and she darts back into the main area without another word. The long skirt will make it harder to move around, but it will allow me to conceal my weapons. I hope it's not necessary, but with my luck so far, I'd rather be safe than sorry. At least my arms aren't likely to be as restricted, so I can defend myself.

I shake my head. Slightly irritated that my thoughts go straight to protection mode, but it's ingrained into me at this point.

"Okay, I have a long black option with long sleeves and no back, a deep purple choice with a long skirt and a strapless, sweetheart neckline, or a yellow spaghetti-strap bodice dress with a long layered skirt. Try them on, see what you think, and we'll go from there, alright?"

My eyes widen with everything she rattles off, but I nod along all the same. She hangs them to my right before closing the curtain for me to try them on. Gulping, my gaze rakes over each of them as I try to decide where to begin.

Opting to simply go from left to right, I start with the black option, shaking off my cloak and piling my clothes on the chair by the mirror. It's made of silk, the material unbelievably soft against my skin, but I'm not overly fond of the neckline sitting across my shoulders, and the long sleeves feel a little restricting.

Hanging it back up, I turn my attention to the purple option. It's noticeably heavier than the black one, and the skirt is puffy with tulle and so many layers. The neckline is cute, though, but it's not going to serve its purpose for me.

I turn my attention to the yellow option, the layered tulle lighter and floaty. Stepping into the skirt, I pull it over my hips, where the bodice sits snugly against my torso. I secure the fastening the best I can at my back before adjusting the thin straps on my shoulders.

It's perfect.

It's not too heavy, there are no additional restrictions in comparison to the others, and the color really does suit my complexion.

"How's it going in there?" the assistant asks, and I realize I'm smiling at myself in the mirror.

"The yellow one. I'm going for the yellow one," I declare, my smile spreading wider across my cheeks.

"Perfect, leave the others in there and bring the yellow dress to the front when you're ready," she replies before I hear her talking with Flora.

Quickly changing, I drape my black cloak around my shoulders once I'm done. Dress in hand, I pull back the curtain and head toward where Flora is already waiting.

"Have you found one?" I ask, and she beams from ear to ear.

"I did. Have you?" She nods at the dress in my hand and I nod.

"What have you gone for?"

"It's a surprise."

I raise my eyebrows at her, but the joy on her face tells

me all I need to know. "Surprises are good," I breathe, and she bounces on the balls of her feet.

"Right?"

I'm not sure if she's going to explode with excitement, but the store assistant appears, taking the dress from my grasp before anything insane happens.

She boxes the dress, layers of tissue paper and all, before sliding it into a bag and offering me the straps. Before I take it from her grasp, I offer her my money, but she shakes her head.

"Ah, this has already been paid for," she admits, cheeks pink.

"It has? By who?" I ask in confusion. If it's Flora, I'm going to tell her there's no way in hell I'm accepting that.

The assistant clears her throat, avoiding my gaze. "The owner."

"Why would the owner do that?" I rear back in surprise, glancing around as if they were going to appear out of nowhere with an explanation.

"Because... long live the kingdom of the fae."

My cheeks heat as I stare at her, my jaw slack as I fail to find anything to say.

"Say thank you, Addi," Flora murmurs beside me, pulling me from my blank mind, and I nod.

"Thank you," I breathe, and the assistant grins, winking at Flora and me in quick succession.

"Always. Friends of the kingdom are friends of ours."

Taking the bag, I follow Flora toward the door, but I'm not aware of anything as my mind swirls with disbelief.

"Now, can we eat?" Arlo asks, bringing me back to the present as we step outside. I adjust my hood around my face again, shielding myself from bystanders.

"Yes," I answer immediately, my stomach grumbling at the thought of food.

"Where shall we go?" Flora asks, spinning on the spot as if a place will just pop up for us.

Nipping at my bottom lip, an idea comes to mind. "I know a quiet spot not far from here. It's not the prettiest of places, but the food is amazing," I offer, and Arlo claps his hands together excitedly.

"Lead the way, oh wise one," he insists, shooing me along.

I chuckle along with Flora as we take off through the narrow passageways again.

It only takes a few minutes until the familiar sign hangs in front of us.

"You weren't lying, Addi. It's not the prettiest," Arlo muses, frowning up at the place while Flora waves him off.

Heading inside, the familiar scent of garlic fills the air, making my stomach grumble again. "If I knew I'd been serving royalty all this time, I would have upped my prices," Pearl states, stepping toward me with a grin teasing the corner of her mouth.

"No, you wouldn't have, but I bet you would have had me washing the dishes," I retort, making her head fall back as she laughs all the way from her belly.

"That's my girl. Same as always?" she offers, waving for me to choose where I want to sit. "Oh, you're not alone," she adds, eyebrows raised in surprise at the sight of Flora and Arlo moving with me.

"They'll want to look at the menu," I answer, trying to remain calm about this entire conversation. I've spent years slipping in here alone. A time or two with my father and sister, but that's always been rare. Anyone else other than those two people would startle anyone who knows me.

"I'll get the menus; you get comfortable," Pearl answers as I take my favorite spot in the far left of the restaurant. From here, I can see the entire room without anyone really being able to see me.

"Do you come here a lot?" Flora asks, and I shake my head.

"Not really."

"But enough to know that woman and not need to order because she knows what you're going to get?" she retorts, giving me a pointed look.

"I'm a creature of habit. Stick around long enough and you'll see my choice of food doesn't sway all that much,"

I admit, and Arlo grins.

"That's true. Your breakfast of choice most days is scrambled eggs and bacon."

"It's a good choice," I insist with a shrug, and Flora snickers.

"On one hand, you're a complete mystery; on the other, you're simple and predictable."

"How's that for keeping you on your toes?" I retort with a grin, and she shakes her head at me.

"Here are the menus for you to take a look at," Pearl states, placing the worn leather before Arlo and Flora, who murmur their thanks. "Addi," she adds, turning to me. "I have a call for you."

"A call for me?" I repeat, confusion dancing through my veins.

She nods, pointing toward where the phone stands beside the coffee machine. Panicked, it takes everything in me to keep my steps measured and calm as I approach it like an explosion about to go off.

Bringing the device to my ear, I take a deep breath. "Hello?"

"Do you go everywhere without your cell phone?"

I look around, eyes wide with fear. "Where are you?" I rasp, chest tightening.

"Come find me."

THE REIGN OF BLOOD

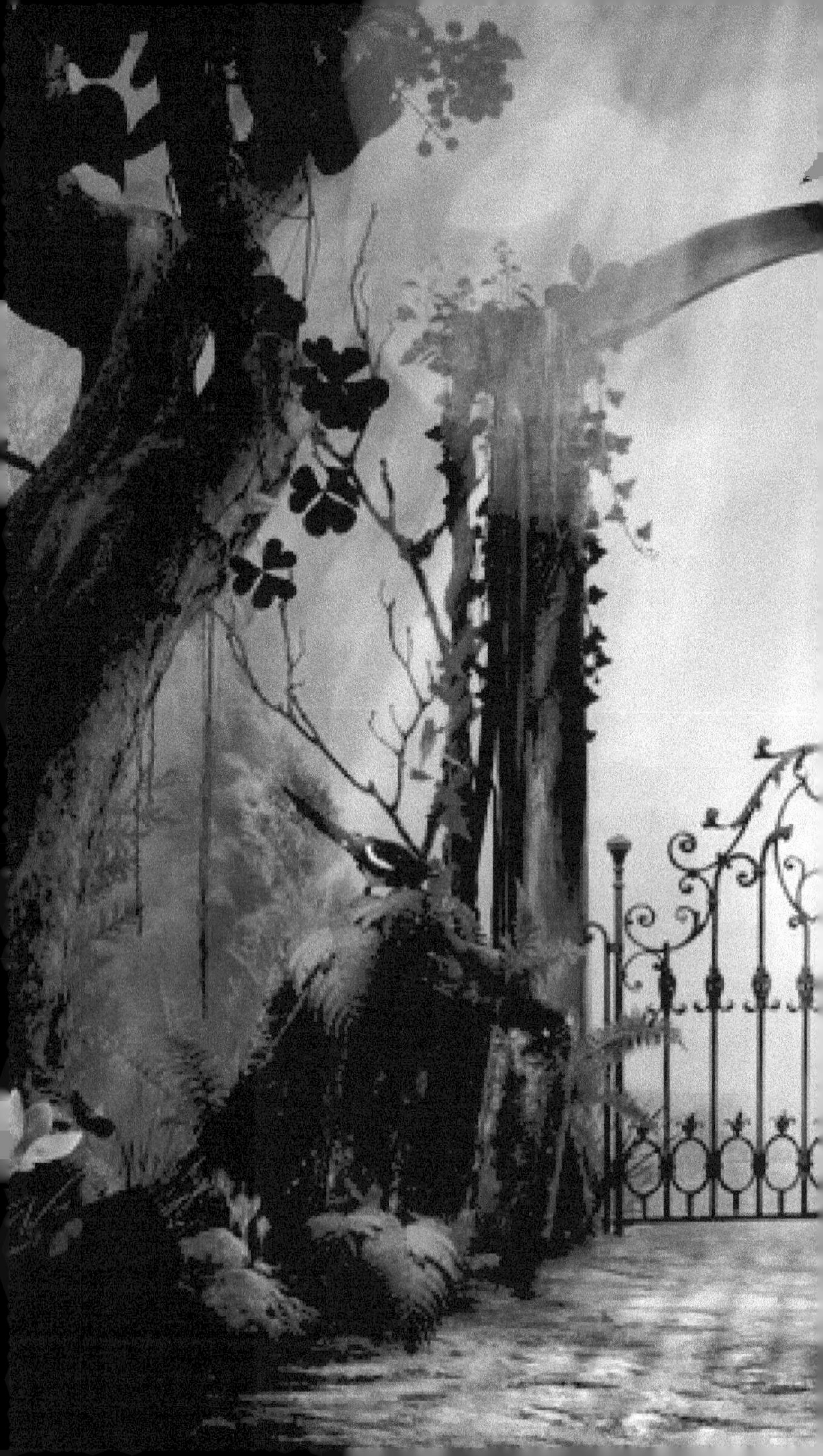

ADRIANNA

29

The call cuts off just as quickly as it began, the tone echoing in my ears as my mind goes on high alert. Sweeping my gaze around the restaurant once more, I don't catch anything out of the ordinary. I need to leave right now.

Discarding the phone, I take a few steps toward Flora and Arlo, but the moment I have their attention, I start backpedaling toward the door. "I need to go."

"Go where?" Flora asks, confused. Her gaze runs over me from head to toe, searching for an answer to my sudden urgency, but she won't find it.

"Just…if you're not here by the time I get back, I'll assume you've gone back to the academy," I answer, nodding, more to myself than them. I press my shoulder against the door, the little chime echoing out as Flora calls my name.

"Addi, wait!"

I give her a soft smile, hoping like hell she'll understand eventually, but there's no time for that now. Slipping through the door, I pause a moment to take a single deep breath as the fresh air hits me.

My heart races as every single one of my senses hones in on where I should go first. Where to look. Wiping a hand down my face, an idea comes to mind, and before I can second guess myself, I take off.

Fixing my hood, I make sure to hide my face, keeping my head down as I hurry through the cobbled streets. The narrow passageways extend into wider spaces, busy with people, and I try my best to keep pressed against the wall.

When I reach the square, the crowds become thicker. Shouldering past a few people, I hear grumbles of complaints, but I don't pay any attention to them. My mind is focused and I won't be distracted.

Eventually, cobbled ground leads to well-trodden paths, and the high walls protecting the City of Harrows dwindle down, leading to a smattering of trees. I know the nook I'm looking for—straight ahead, beside an oak tree and a bramble bush.

Dirt kicks up around me as I hurry my steps, looking over my shoulder a few times to make sure I'm alone. I can see the tendrils of magic twinkling off the bramble leaves and I don't waste any time slipping through the net.

A squeal bursts around me the second I'm through the veil and I drop to my knees, falling into open arms. I cling to the blanket in her lap as her hands press into my back, holding me as close as possible from this angle.

Each breath fills my lungs further, and with each second, I feel whole. With every inhale, each cell in my body becomes more in tune with hers. That is until I peer up and meet her gaze. Her round face, button nose, and her infectious smile come into full view.

"Fuck, Nora. Don't do that."

"Language, Addi."

I peer over my shoulder to where my father is standing, an eyebrow raised at the cuss falling from my lips.

"Don't give me that, Dad. I was scared," I retort, still unable to control my heart rate as it threatens to burst from my chest. Glancing around, the telltale surroundings come into view. The trees are lush and green, the flowers in full bloom, and the yellow dirt path that leads around the outskirts of the City of Harrows toward home.

This is our secret passage. My father's magic at its finest, offering us some kind of solace among the madness that has haunted us for as long as I can remember.

A smile ghosts over his lips as he takes a step toward us. "It's good to see you."

I rise, slipping into his open arms as we meet in the

middle. "It's good to see you both too. What are you doing out here?" I ask, squeezing him once more for good luck before I refocus the majority of my attention on Nora.

My sister avoids my gaze as my father clears his throat. "You mentioned your plans to Nora last night, and once she gets an idea in her head…" His words trail off.

"There's no letting go," I finish, shaking my head in disbelief at my sister.

"Never mind giving me one of those pointed looks you're so familiar with. Get back over here. I miss you so much," she orders, waving her hand for me to take. My fingers lace with hers effortlessly, as they always do.

"I miss you too," I breathe, crouching beside her.

"So, did you pick a dress?" she asks, eyes lighting up with excitement as I nod.

"I did."

She looks around me, disappointment growing in her eyes before she gives me her award-winning pointed look. "You left it at the restaurant, didn't you?"

Ah, fuck.

"You know I did. You had me all twisted in knots," I grumble, and she gasps.

"Don't blame me." My knowing stare intensifies, and five seconds later, she relents. "Fine, blame me, I don't care. I get to see you, and that's all I care about."

My heart warms as her hand clenches mine.

"You look good, Addi. Healthy," my father states, and I peer up at him with the strain on my face that I know I carry in my heart right now.

"I don't feel it," I admit, earning me a soft smile from him.

Clearing his throat, he scrubs at his neck. "Can I see it?"

I instantly know what he's referring to. Releasing Nora's hand, I stand and turn, adjusting my cloak to reveal the kiss of amethyst embedded in my flesh. He runs his thumb over it, making me shiver at the contact, but it doesn't hurt to touch anymore.

"Did you try what I said?" My pulse quickens as I nod. "And?"

I don't want to discuss it out loud. Not here, not anywhere, but ideally not in front of Nora.

"And Professor Fairbourne has one as well," I answer instead, looking over my shoulder at him as the color continues to drain from his face.

"I shouldn't be so surprised," he murmurs, his gaze falling to the ground as he shakes his head in disappointment.

"We're good people, Dad. It shocks us because this isn't how we would act," Nora states, the truth shining through in every word as I nod in agreement.

"I couldn't have said it better myself," I muse, winking at her and watching her smile grow with pride. A bubble of doubt knots in my stomach as I consider the bigger picture and my father's words from the last time we spoke.

Would we do something like that?

The conversation drifts away from the heavy topics as Nora informs me of all the gossip in the small town we live in. Josh has a girlfriend. *Good for him.* His family's crops aren't growing, and they may need to sell. *Not so good for him.* Otherwise, it's hearsay or gossip through the media, but nonetheless, I sit and absorb every word from her mouth.

I've missed this, missed *her*. Her aura and mere presence are enough to chase away all of my worries. All too quickly, though, the sun starts to lower and her stomach grumbles for the second time in ten minutes.

"I should go," I mutter, hating the way her face instantly loses some of its light.

"Can't you stay a little while longer?" Nora protests as I squeeze her hand and sigh.

"I have to make it back through the city, get my dress, and then head to the academy. I don't want to outlast the sun. The City of Harrows is safe for no one once night falls."

It's the truth, and we all know it.

"Fine," she grumbles, tugging at my hand so I can wrap her in another hug.

Damn. I don't ever want to let go, but right now, our

separation will only make us stronger while I'm at Heir Academy. All of this will be worth it one day, just not today, but that's okay; it's part of the plan.

"I love you, Nora," I breathe into her hair, holding her just a little tighter, and she mirrors my grip.

"I love you too, Addi."

Reluctantly, I lean back, and my father takes me into his arms again, rocking me from side to side like he always did when I was a child.

"Please be safe; with everything going on right now, we know it's dangerous for you guys."

"We know, don't worry. The veil is in place, and it serves its purpose," my father promises, and I nod.

"Before you leave… Fairbourne… can I trust him?"

My father stares deep into my eyes before he presses a hand to his chest, right over his heart. "With your life."

My father doesn't say those three words very often, so I know them to be true. I nod again, a stronger sense of hope and determination swooping through my body. "Let me watch you guys go."

They offer me a smile before my father grabs the handles on Nora's wheelchair and starts down the trail. Once they reach the bend in the distance, they glance back, offering me one more wave before they disappear from sight, taking a piece of my heart with them.

I take a moment to stare at the empty spot they occupied

seconds ago, but they don't return. I need to get a move on anyway. With a sigh, I turn, ready to step through the veil once more, when I startle at the shadow casting over me from the last guest in the world I would expect right now.

"That was a cute family reunion."

"What the fuck, Raiden?"

THE REIGN OF BLOOD

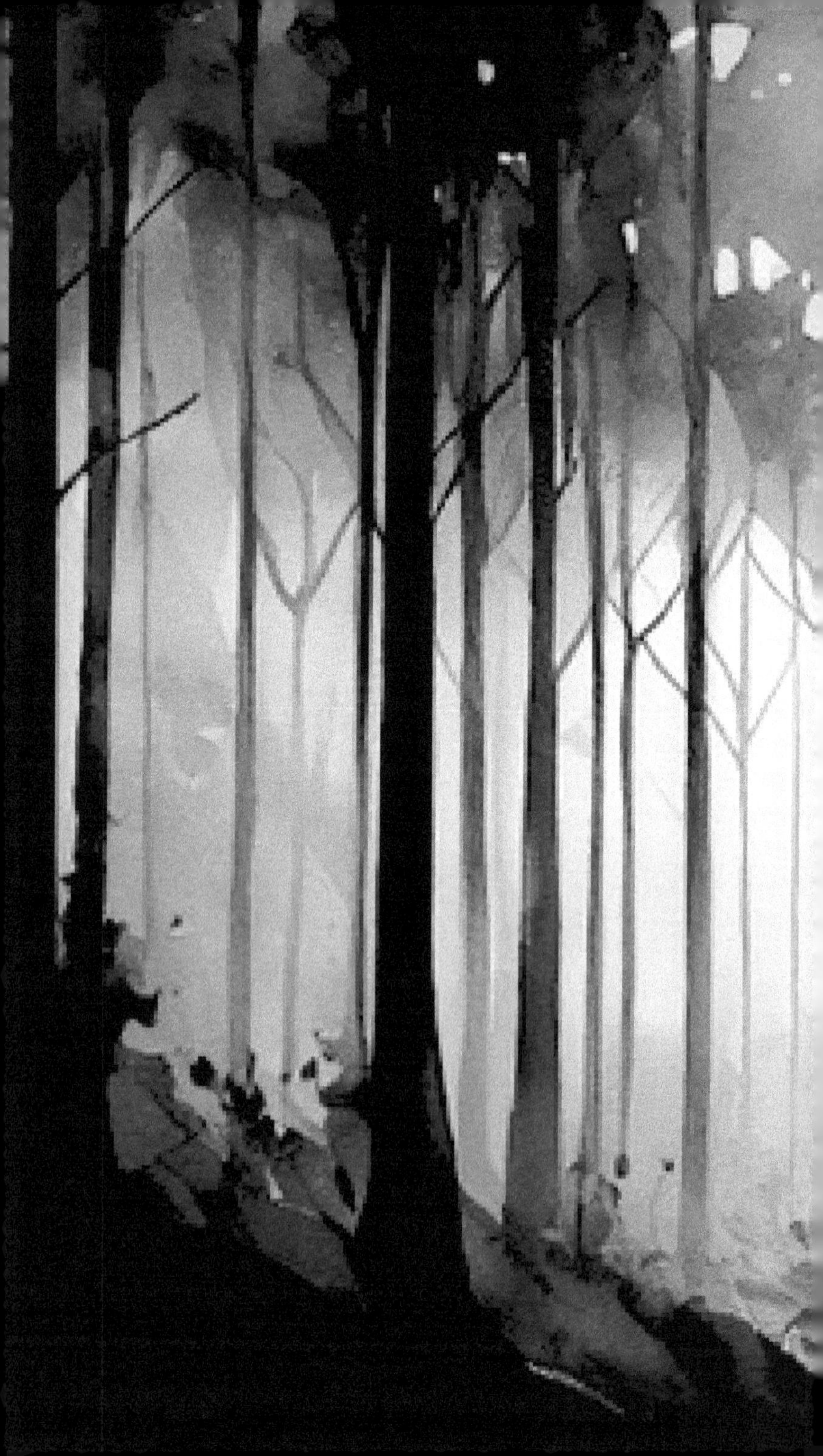

RAIDEN

30

My gaze bores into hers, an array of emotions flickering over her features. Emerald green eyes delve deep into mine, trying to search for fuck knows what, and there's the smallest crinkle on her nose, confirmation that despite her harsh tone, she's panicked.

Reaching out, I capture a loose blond curl between my finger and thumb. The softness reminds me of the summer days when I was a child, running my grandma ragged in the back garden as the sun beat down on us.

"What are you doing here, Raiden?" she repeats, her nostrils flaring as her hands ball into fists at her sides.

"The same thing as you," I reply with a shrug, making her eyebrows rise.

"I can't imagine so," she snaps, folding her arms over

her chest with her fingers still curled as if she might take a swing at me at any moment.

"You came here, so I came here."

It's as simple as that. I expect it to ease the tension seeping from her limbs, but it only seems to make her stand taller before me.

"Wait, have you been following me?" Her brows touch her hairline now, eyes still flicking over mine like the truth will be revealed if she manages to stare long enough.

"You're saying it as if it's a bad thing."

"It is a bad thing," she retorts, pointing her finger at me, and I shrug again.

"Not from my perspective."

"And what perspective is that?" She juts her chin up, glaring at me with a new level of wrath.

It's not a difficult concept to grasp. I'm surprised she can't see it already. "You're a target. I have a vested interest in keeping you alive. That interest won't last long if you're dead now, will it?" I grumble when she doesn't magically seem to garner an understanding of the situation.

She scoffs, shaking her head at me. "You're unbelievable," she mutters under her breath.

"That doesn't sound like a thank you," I state, slightly turned on by the way her lips thin and her eyes darken.

"You won't be getting one," she declares before turning toward the small veil that's nestled between the oak tree and shrub behind us. It's nicely hidden, that's for sure. I would never have known it was there if I didn't witness her stepping through it with my own eyes.

"Where are you going?" I ask, hot on her tail. I've been following her since the moment she stepped off campus grounds. I've spent the entire time hiding in the shadows, so it's refreshing to not have to focus on that now.

Watching her with her family is like seeing an entirely different side to the cryptic woman who consumes my every breath. At Heir Academy, she has an ice princess vibe about her. All standoffish and harsh, but it seems beneath all of that, she has the ability to melt into a puddle at the sight of her loved ones.

What an odd feeling that must be. It was strange to see. It's like they all actually care for one another. There is no backstabbing, no personal gain, nothing.

Just a man and his two daughters.

Not even a king with his princesses.

It is just a wholesome family.

I don't know how I feel about that. I hate her, yet I'm drawn to her. It's exhausting, but I can't seem to stay away, no matter how hard I try.

"Where are you going?" I repeat when she proceeds to ignore me.

"None of your business," she hollers over her shoulder, adjusting the hood on her cloak so it shields her face from sight. She did it earlier, too. It's a natural move that looks as though she's done it one thousand times.

"If it's to the restaurant, I already made sure Flora took your bag," I state, and she pauses in her tracks, whirling around to face me with another pinch of anger knitting her brows together.

"You did what?"

"A simple 'thank you' would suffice."

"For who?" she gasps, exasperated, as she throws her arms out wide.

"For me." Another flare of her nostrils, another dose of irritation, another shade darker to her green pools. "Your sister looks like you," I acknowledge, which somehow has the opposite effect of what I'm going for.

"Don't talk about my sister." The snarl is harsh, raw, and real. I like it.

"Why?" I can't stop myself from pushing her further, amused as her lips set in a thin line.

"I'm not doing this with you," she grinds out, taking a step back, and I shake my head.

"You're not doing much with me, and it's driving me insane." The truth parts my lips against my will, but I can't take the words back now.

A sickly sweet smile draws across her face, the venom already on the tip of her tongue. "I'm a lowly fae, remember? The trash. That's how you put it, isn't it?" She plants a hand on her hip, waiting for my response. I roll my eyes.

"You're dramatic, and we've already been over this," I state, as tired as I feel revisiting this conversation. I wish we could put it behind us already, but something tells me a woman like Adrianna Reagan isn't going to forgive and forget my stupid comments as effortlessly as I would like.

"Go away, Raiden," she says with a sigh, turning away from me once more as she takes the first turn onto the city's cobbled streets.

"I'd rather we went to eat," I retort, keeping a step beside her, but I don't miss the telltale sound of her stomach grumbling as we start through the crowd of people trying to survive the mayhem around us. "See," I insist, stepping to her side so I can point at her. "Besides, Pearl is expecting you back," I add, making her stop dead in her tracks again. A few passersby grumble at the inconvenience, but if she notices, she doesn't acknowledge it.

"Why were you near Pearl?" she snaps, eyes frantically searching mine.

"Are we going there or not?" I ask, getting bored of this constant struggle against doing something as simple as eating.

"I don't want to go anywhere with you."

"So you keep mentioning, but she's waiting," I repeat, raising a brow at her, which has the opposite effect on her gaze as it narrows further.

"Have you done something to her?" Her head rears back a little, the panic in her eyes flickering with anger as she awaits my response.

"Why would you say that?"

"With the way you're saying that?" she grumbles, waving her hand at me.

Shrugging, I nod for us to carry on walking. "Then come and find out."

Her finger jabs against my chest. "If you've hurt a single hair on her head—"

I opt to cut her threat short, pulling her to my chest before I take off through the pathways. Her fingers cling to my t-shirt like her life depends on it, but a moment later, we're back outside Pearl's restaurant.

Stepping inside, the chime above the door announces our arrival as I slowly lower her to her feet. "Pearl, we're back," I holler, watching as Addi grips her stomach and brings her other hand to her mouth.

"Raiden, what on Earth have you done to her?"

I hold my hands up in surrender. "She gets motion-sick with the whole vampire speed."

I don't remember it being this bad last time, but I can't change it now.

"Ah, that makes sense. She had to have a weakness somewhere," Pearl states with a knowing grin as Addi gapes at her.

"Hey."

"It's not a weakness. It's almost endearing," I murmur, staring at the wicked fae that has me trapped under her spell.

"Endearing?" she repeats with a frown, and I shake my head.

"I said almost."

Her eyes turn to slits, but instead of giving me the sass I expect, she turns her attention to Pearl. "Did he hurt you?"

Pearl frowns, glancing between us. "Who?"

"Raiden."

Pearl's gaze settles on me, silence falling heavily over the room for a split second before she bursts into laughter. "He wouldn't dare." She wipes at the tears spilling from her eyes before clearing her throat. "I love that you two know each other. My two favorites."

"Wait, you know him?" She points an accusatory finger in my direction, making Pearl chuckle again.

"I don't call just anyone my favorite. Of course I do. Now I think about it, it's hilarious that you two have never been here at the same time before," she muses, waving for us to take a seat. "Now, sit. I'll get your food," she orders before sauntering off into the back.

I tilt my head, giving her the choice of where to sit, and I'm not surprised to see her head toward the same booth she took earlier. I've never sat there before, but as I lower into the booth now, I see why it appeals to her. It's an excellent vantage point for someone who is always on high alert. Someone who is a princess among men. Someone like her.

Silence descends, clinging to us as I stare at her while she tries to look anywhere but at me. I get comfortable. I can deal with the silent treatment if it means I can still be in her presence for a while. Actually, not talking feels like a better option. We won't piss each other off this way.

"Please don't mention my sister to anyone," she breathes after a while. Her voice is so soft I wonder if I made it up, but the way she peers up at me confirms the fear.

"Why would I?"

She shrugs. "I don't know. Just… don't."

My brows crinkle with confusion. "She's not a secret for you to keep, Adrianna."

She rears back again, disdain etched into her features. "No, she's my sister to protect at all costs. Do you know my face has been plastered all over the media?" she barks, irritation coming through thicker and thicker.

"Yes."

"Do you know the threats that are now connected to her and my father?"

"Yes."

"So you understand?" She looks at me as if that should

all make complete sense. And as much as it does in some aspects, in others, it's the complete opposite.

"Not entirely, no, but I guess that's because I'm a vampire, and we're far too self-centered to worry about others. Family included," I admit, glancing down at the table to avoid her intense stare from across the table.

"You worried about me today. That's why you followed me. It's like that feeling, only more intense," she states, and I shake my head in disbelief.

Nothing could be more intense than what I'm feeling lately, and it's all because of her.

Thankfully, before I have to worry about finding a response, Pearl appears at the table with two plates, both loaded with the exact same food. "My two favorite people both with their favorite dishes. It could be fate," she says with a wink, making Addi choke on thin air. "I'll go and grab some sodas," she adds before darting off as quickly as she appeared.

Steak, medium-rare, with cajun fries, a dollop of garlic butter, and sauteed vegetables.

Yes, please.

We eat in comfortable silence, enjoying the best food in the City of Harrows. Time passes, and with every minute that goes by, Addi's shoulders slowly relax. When they're no longer touching her ears with anger at my presence, I decide she might be calm enough for a conversation.

"So, yellow, huh?"

"What?" she barks, shoulders lifting but only a millimeter or two.

"Your dress."

"You saw my dress?" Her jaw falls slack.

"I had to peek," I offer, shrugging, but as she leans closer, elbows braced on the table between us, I know that's not enough of an answer for her.

"In the box or when I was in the shop?" Her tone is low, too soft, like a predator circling their prey with whimsical words to lure them in.

She's fucking good.

"In the box, of course. I'm not a stalker," I retort with a roll of my eyes, and she tilts her head at me.

"Are you sure?"

"You're a handful."

She scoffs. "A fact I don't believe has changed since we've met. It's not going to change any time in the future either, so you better run for the hills now," she threatens, but the warning only makes my body react to her more.

"I didn't say I didn't like it," I reply, watching as she shakes her head at me. Again.

"I don't think you should."

Matching her stance, I push. "Is that because you don't think *we* should—"

"You know I'm at the academy to be the next heir,

right?"

I frown at her interruption, but nod in acknowledgment. "I assumed."

"What are *you* at the academy for?" she asks, and my tongue peeks out, sweeping along my bottom lip before I answer.

"The same."

"So that puts us at an impasse, and I've worked too hard for anything to get in my way. Especially a vampire who treated me like dirt on the bottom of his shoe the first time I met him." Her chin tilts up, making her look down her nose at me a little.

"We've talked about this," I say calmly, knowing I am fighting an uphill battle with this woman.

"No, *you* have. You've made it abundantly clear that who I am and where I come from disgusts you. That is, until you found out I am royal, the single part of me that truly means nothing in comparison to everything else."

Her words are like a punch to the gut, confusing me and leaving me breathless all at once. How can that be the part of her that means nothing? To a vampire, that's all that would matter. But as much as she may think that, it's not that she's a royal that draws me in. It's the fact that she's a survivor.

This kingdom has done nothing but cause her pain and anguish from a young age, yet here she is, still fighting for herself, her people, and the kingdom.

That's a trait in a woman I've never seen.

Not until her.

"You're overreacting," I breathe, unable to express the thoughts in my head so she can hear them and understand.

"I'm a handful. That's what I do, remember? I'll make my own way home," she grumbles, and my defenses rise at her dismissal.

"Suit yourself," I grumble, folding my arms over my chest as I lean back in my seat.

"Don't bother following me," she hollers over her shoulder, and I scoff.

"You can't stop me."

Not now, not tomorrow, not ever.

I'm Raiden fucking Holloway. I get what I want, when I want, and if I want that to include her, it fucking will.

THE REIGN OF BLOOD

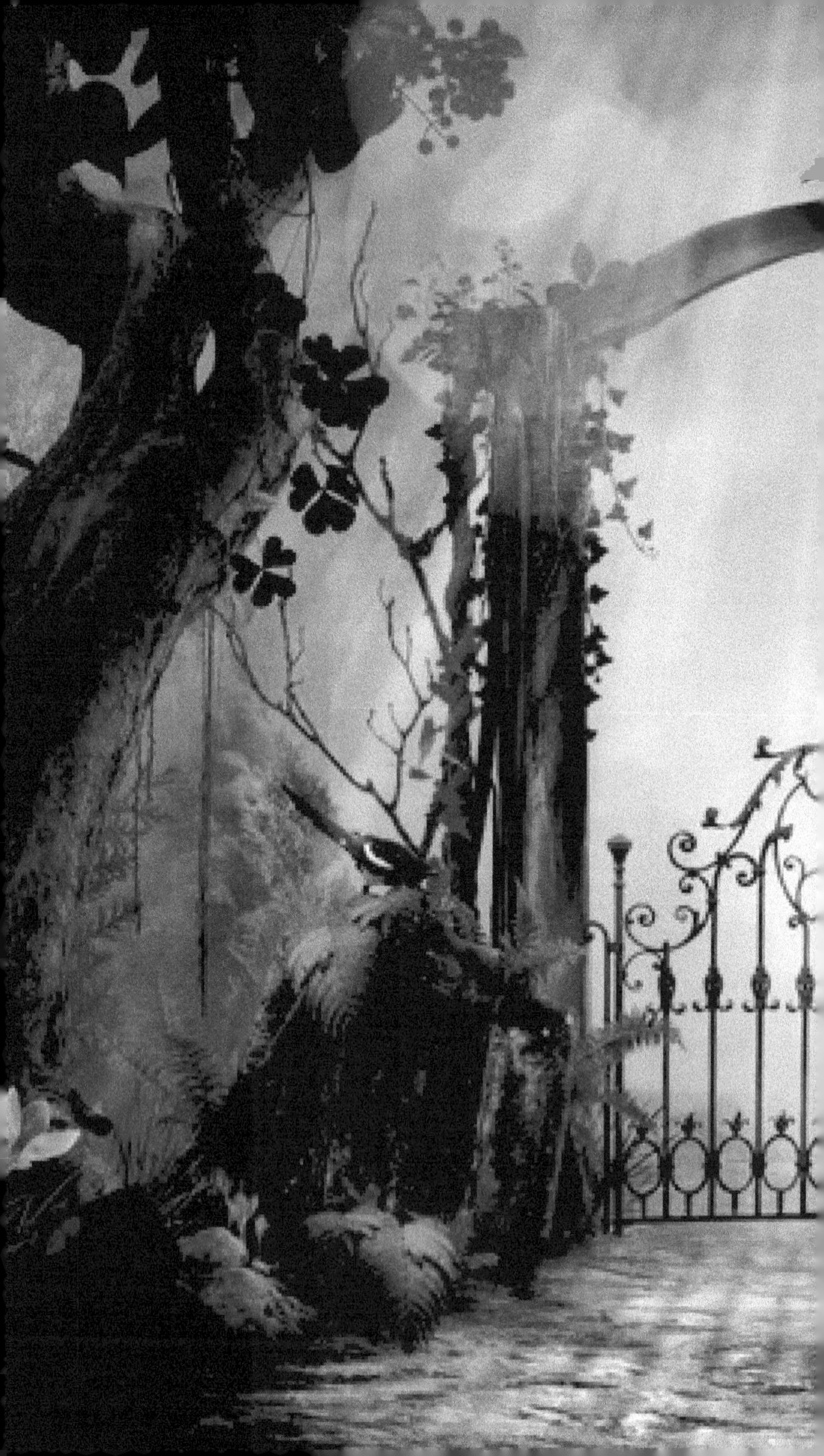

ADRIANNA

31

I adjust the straps on my dress, my mind elsewhere as Flora helps secure the fastening on the back. Apart from getting ready for hours, I've spent the day reeling over yesterday with Raiden.

He saw my sister *and* my father. No one has come barreling toward me demanding further details, so I can only assume he's kept his mouth shut. It's all I can hope for, but I don't like the idea of being indebted to him.

After I left the restaurant yesterday, he followed me back to the academy every step of the way, but this time I knew he was there. I just had the strength to pretend he wasn't, which felt like an achievement all on its own.

Flora meets my gaze in the mirror, pulling me from my thoughts as I run my hands over the tulle.

"Stop touching it. It's making you look nervous," she

states with a pointed look, and I roll my eyes.

"I *am* nervous."

"Do you want them to know that?"

I don't know who she means by *them*, but the answer is still the same. "Obviously not."

"Then stop," she retorts, taking a seat at the foot of her bed to put on her heels.

"Easy for you to say," I grumble, turning from side to side in the mirror as my hands touch my dress again, but I manage to stop myself, balling them into fists at my side.

"Not really. I'm about to spend the entire night with my mother fawning all over Arlo's father."

"Ew."

She looks at me with a soft smile. "Yeah, ew."

"Maybe you should talk to Arlo about—"

"Nope. No way," she interjects, jumping to her feet with her heels now secured.

"But—"

"No, Addi," she says with a sigh, giving me another pointed look, and I hold my hands up in surrender.

"Okay."

"Thank you," she breathes, exhaling as her shoulders relax.

"But I'm just saying if he doesn't realize how stunning you are in that dress tonight, then he's dumb. Like *dumb* dumb," I point out, and she rolls her eyes, but I don't miss the gleam of excitement.

Her dress is red, deep crimson, accentuating her auburn curls and making her skin look like porcelain. It swoops down between her breasts and clings to her body in what she explained as a mermaid style, revealing her curves before flaring out at her knees.

"Are you sure you don't want to wear the heels?" she asks for the fifth time, glancing to where I discarded them.

"I'm sure," I repeat, waving her off. I'm wearing my combat boots. No one can see them, and they offer me a little extra height anyway, so it doesn't make a difference. They're just safer if anything happens to go wrong.

"And do you really need that many daggers?"

It's my turn to give her a pointed look. "Yes."

My hands run over my thighs, feeling the outline beneath the material. There are twelve of them strapped perfectly in place. I was going to add two more until Flora told me I was going from overly cautious to insane.

"And you definitely want everyone to see the kiss of amethyst?" she asks, nodding toward where the purple gem glistens under the light.

"One thousand percent." It was one of the additional reasons I opted for this dress. It may make me look weakened to those around me and show the kingdom that I've been restrained, but it only serves to prove to everyone that I can and will rise above it.

"You're badass, Addi," she states, a mixture of awe and disbelief dancing in her words, and I grin.

"So are you. Now, let's go."

Flora grabs her bag, a shimmering gold to match her heels and jewelry, while I opt to go bagless. I don't need to carry anything; it's all on my body. A bag is just an inconvenience at this stage.

She glances at herself one more time in the mirror before opening the door to find Arlo standing on the other side, poised and ready to knock.

"Holy shit, Flora. You look beautiful," he gasps, failing to discreetly adjust himself beneath his pants. Not that I think Flora sees. She's too focused on gaping at him.

"You don't clean up too bad yourself," she mutters, cheeks blushing under his heated stare until he shrugs, breaking the moment.

"It comes naturally," he states, running his hands over the lapels of his jacket as he grins at us. The black suit frames his shoulders perfectly, and the pristine white shirt beneath makes his natural tan look even more golden.

"I'm sure it does," she muses, still gaping at him as he clears his throat.

"Ladies," he declares, offering his elbows out for us to link him. Flora doesn't waste a second while I wave him off, opting to take the lead as we head for the stairs.

There's a buzz in the building, a level of excitement in

the air that I don't exactly like the feel of, but I'm a part of the whole event whether I like it or not. The communal area is busy with fae who are giddy with excitement, and I'm certain there's already a couple making out in the far corner. I have to admit, it's nice to see them feel something other than the usual doom and gloom that lurks over their heads.

Tonight, they get to mingle and experience the wonders of a ball, as do I and the other origins. It might even be fun, but I'm not getting my hopes up.

Opening the front door, I get one foot outside before I freeze in place, blinking at the four assholes standing on the pathway.

"What in the fuck," I breathe, glancing from one to another, before Raiden steps forward, fixing his jacket as he gives me an irritated stare.

"I was here first," he starts, but Brody shoves at his arm.

"Yeah, but she's *my* dance partner, so that makes her my date," he insists, appearing in front of me with a white rose corsage.

"I don't recall that being in the rules," Kryll points out, amusement flashing in his eyes as Cassian sighs from the back of the group.

"Are we going or not? You're boring the fuck out of me."

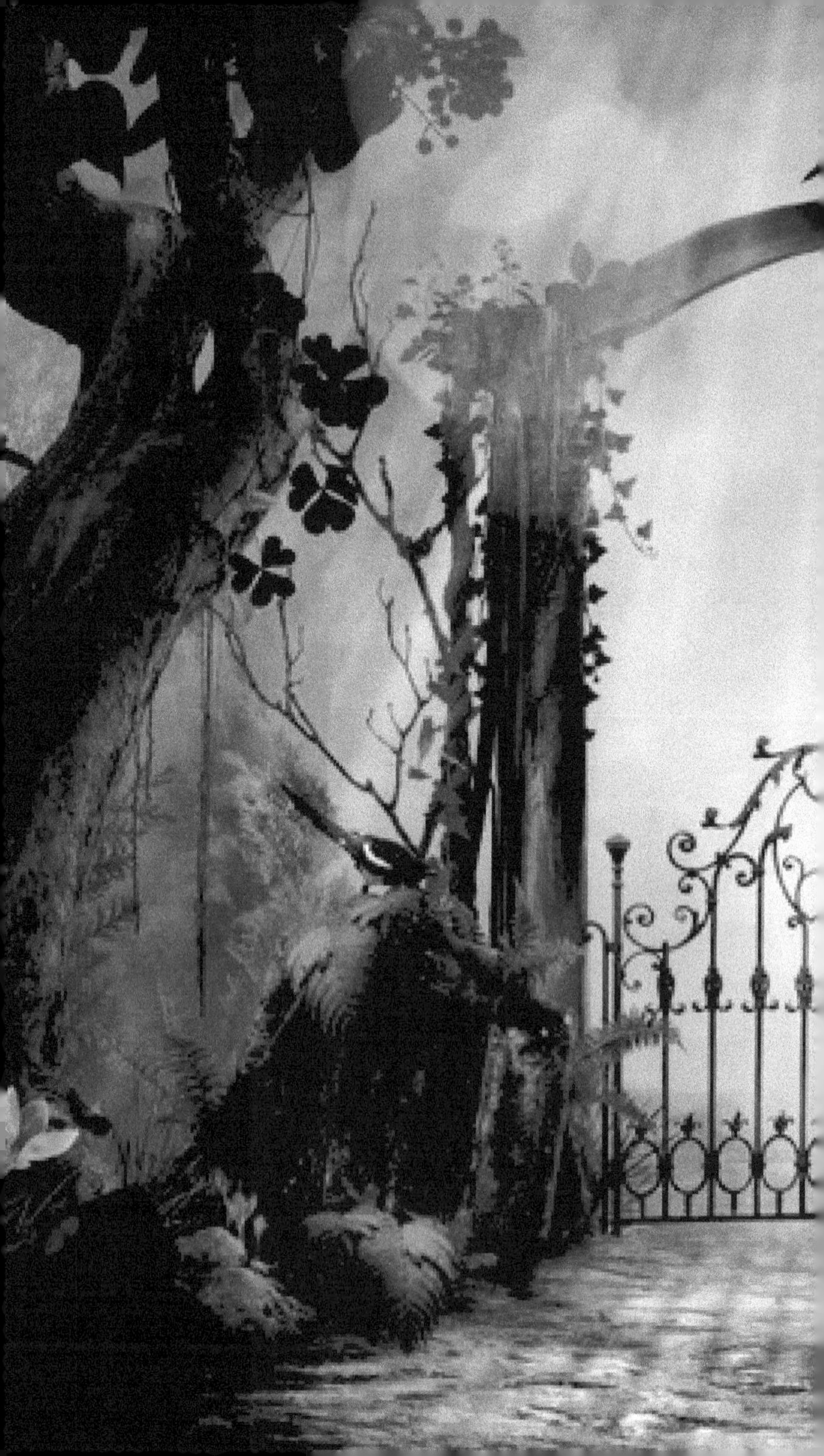

ADRIANNA
32

I can't tell whether it's Heaven or Hell, having the four of them standing before me. Hell, because I know they're going to come with drama and a headache. Heaven, because holy fucking shit, what is this level of hotness burning bright before me?

Where to start the discreet admiration?

Brody slips the corsage over my wrist as I admire the pale gray suit that molds to his body so epically that my core tightens. I've seen this man naked, I've felt him inside me, but damn, the muscles that are wrapped in expensive fabric are next level.

"Thank you," I murmur, watching the grin spread across his face, but his eyes don't meet mine; they're too busy running over my body from head to toe.

"Don't thank him. He's making up stupid rules that

don't count," Raiden grumbles, shoving his friend aside, and I hear Flora giggle from beside me. I give her a pointed look, but it does nothing but make her laugh louder.

She's in trouble later.

Bringing my attention back to the stalker vampire who seems to be everywhere I turn, I give myself a second to absorb his ridiculously chiseled and handsome looks. He's dressed head to toe in black—suit, shirt, shoes, tie—everything.

He looks like a mafia leader out of one of those movies I've seen. He has that same edge about him in real life. Maybe he is a part of something insane like that outside of the academy.

How would I find out?

Shaking my head, I look past him to where Kryll stands with a smirk teasing the corner of his lips. He's wearing a tailored navy suit that reveals how broad his shoulders really are. His shifter cloak has been hiding a lot of him, that's for sure.

Black ink curls up his throat and across his hands, leaving me to wonder how far they go. His white shirt is open at the top and there's no tie in sight, which only reconfirms the shifter that he is.

An irritated growl comes from the asshole at the back, drawing my attention his way as he folds his arms over his chest, glaring at me with an intensity that makes it hard for me to breathe.

His suit is almost an exact replica of Kryll's, but he's wearing a pale blue shirt with a navy tie and tan shoes. Even pissed off, he looks sinful in all of the right ways, which only serves to irritate me more. "Are we moving or not?" he snaps, pursing his lips as he turns for the fountain.

Brody rolls his eyes at him, offering me his arm, but I shake my head. Raiden does the same and I smirk as I sweep between them both, opting to walk alone.

"Such a loner. Are you sure you're not a shifter?" Kryll muses as I pass him, falling into step with me without offering me his arm.

"I know my ears are lacking, and my magic is somewhat contained, but it's all still there," I reply.

"Are those combat boots under there?" Brody hollers, and I peer over my shoulder with a grin.

"You shouldn't have expected anything different," Arlo adds, making Flora chuckle as she clings to his arm.

"How would you know what I should and shouldn't expect from her?" Raiden grunts, turning a deathly stare Arlo's way, forcing me to stop in my tracks.

"Leave him alone."

Dark eyes turn my way. "Have you fucked him?"

I rear back in horror, my chest clenching at the accusation on his tongue as anger builds inside of me. "I don't answer to you, but to save Arlo from your bullshit, no, I haven't," I snap, offering the man in question an apologetic look, but he shrugs with a grin as if it's not needed.

The energy around us is tainted with agitation, but I embrace it, letting it remind me where I am and what I'm walking into. Which I don't actually have a clue about. Other than the fact that there will be food and dancing, everything else is a mystery, but I know people from the outside world will be there, and that leaves me on edge.

We walk the rest of the way in silence, groups of other students joining us as we continue along the path. Everyone looks completely different without their academy-issued cloaks. I can't tell who is who. You can't differentiate an origin tonight, and I like it.

As we round the corner, the entrance to the main academy building comes into view, but it looks nothing like it usually does. Everything is so… grand. A red carpet has been roped off, leading in through the double doors, while photographers stand on either side, snapping pictures of everyone.

Fuck.

I hadn't considered the media would be here.

Nerves spike through my limbs until a hand lands at the base of my spine.

"Let's go, Princess. Two loners together can get through this madness, right?"

I peer up at Kryll, nipping at my bottom lip, and before I can think better of it, I nod.

His hand remains in place, a warmth I didn't know I needed as we near the masses. Students ahead of us stop and pose for pictures, enjoying the attention as I look for an alternative entrance, but I come up empty.

"Your brother doesn't have a secret access point so we can avoid all of this, does he?" I ask hopefully, looking at Kryll again, who gives me a grim smile.

"I wish."

Entering the ball suddenly seems like an even more ridiculous task as we wait for everyone to have their moment in the spotlight. Nausea burns in my throat as I step up to the rope, next in line.

"Do we have to stop?"

"We can try and just keep walking," Kryll offers, leaning closer to whisper in my ear, and I shiver.

"Or you could use your shifter speed to bypass it all," I offer at the same time someone calls out *next*.

Too late.

Fuck.

Plastering the best smile I can muster on my face, which feels more like a grimace, I let Kryll guide me along the red carpet. He keeps our pace calm and collected, even waving a time or two, but never drawing to a stop. We're three-quarters of the way through when my hope for a peaceful passing is shattered.

"Wait. That's the princess. It's Princess Adrianna!"

Murmurs increase quicker than we can make it to the door as the photographers rush to block my path. The red carpet disappears beneath their trampling feet, creating a wall of flashing lights as I remain stunned.

"Smile for us, Princess."

"What happened to your ears, Princess?"

"How are you finding the academy, Princess?"

"Princess Adrianna, where's your father? Your sister?"

Lights flash, igniting the panic in my veins as Kryll moves his hand from my back and wraps it around my waist, tugging me into his side, attempting to shield me from the chaos.

"That's enough of your incessant shit, don't you think?" Raiden declares, stepping in front of me to block me from view even more.

"She's the princess. The kingdom has a right to answers."

"The kingdom didn't give a shit about her for the past sixteen years, but now your questions need answers?" he retorts with a deadly scoff, making my eyes widen.

I don't want him to fight battles for me. That's not what this is, but the more I hide between him and Kryll, the weaker I'm going to look. I just need a damn second to adjust to it all and to remember everything my father taught me.

Clearing my throat, I look up at Kryll with a nervous smile. He frowns, but understanding flashes through his eyes. His hold on me slackens and he takes a step back. I place my hand on Raiden's arm, making his gaze snap to mine.

Thank you, I mouth before stepping around him.

"Princess."

"Princess Adrianna!"

"Princess!"

I wave my hand, halting their calls as I take a deep breath. "Good evening. I hope you are all having an enjoyable time so far," I breathe, my hands slightly trembling at my sides as I look directly into the video camera ahead. "I'll happily offer you a smile in a moment as you initially requested, but to address other matters that were brought to light first, my ears were damaged when I was small and forced to flee my home. My family is of no relevance to my attendance at the academy, and I don't believe their whereabouts are required." Clickers and shutters go off around me, making it hard to focus, but I picture that I'm on the mat in combat class, circling my prey. "You do have a right to answers, but I don't have them. Not with words, at least. I'm here as an attendee of the academy, just like everyone else. My answers will come in the form of action, which I believe is exactly what the kingdom needs."

Running my hands over my dress, I plant a hand on my hip, jut my chin up, and make myself smile like I mean it. Lights flash, and more questions are hollered, but I block them all out as I give them two whole seconds of this fake-ass shit before turning toward the doors.

I feel the tendrils of freedom surround me as I step into the corridor, relief flooding me until the shrill voice of the most irritating person on campus announces her presence.

"Why the hell are you walking in with her?"

Reluctantly, I turn to find Vallie pointing a blood-red nail in my direction. Her dress is black, and if she weren't such a bitch, I'd say she looked pretty, but she *is* a bitch, and I'm petty as fuck, so I refuse to admit it.

"Vallie, please do me a favor and fuck off," Raiden grunts from behind me, his hand falling to my waist, and my spine stiffens at the contact.

She cocks a perfectly arched brow over my shoulder. "Raidy baby, my daddy is here, and once he sees…" Her words trail off, making me frown, but I sense a shift in the man at my back before he steps around me.

"Move," he grunts, pointing at her, and a wicked smile spreads across her face as she peers back at me. "I apologize," he murmurs, glancing down at me, and I frown.

"For?"

He sighs heavily. "For this," he breathes before

stepping up to her side and entering the grand hall with her.

I stare after them, a mixture of disbelief, horror, and jealousy coursing through my veins.

"What just happened?"

"Vampires are… complicated," Brody states, stepping to my left as Kryll appears to my right.

"Oh, I thought you were going to say assholes," I joke, but the laughter doesn't come.

"That too," Cassian grunts, walking around us.

A soft hand strokes down my arm from behind and I turn to see Flora staring at me with concern etched into her eyes. "Are you okay?"

"I'll be okay," I answer, unsure what I'll actually be okay with, but I attempt to compartmentalize it all for now. I need to survive this shit. I can worry about everything in more depth later.

Moving into the grand hall, where music plays softly in the background, I try to take a deep breath and ease the weight on my shoulders.

"Name, please?"

I look at the attendant, startled, but quickly realize they're here to guide us to our seats. Thankfully, Flora answers for me and Arlo, collecting our table number before we saunter through the room.

Gold tables, gold chairs, gold drapes. Everything is so luxurious and over the top, but the white tablecloths, chair covers, and floral centerpieces manage to mellow it all out a little. Chatter is high as we walk through the room, the excitement and buzz back in the air.

As we make our way to the table, I focus again, no longer distracted by all the pretty gold things; I realize that even without our origin cloaks, we're still segregated.

Shifters with shifters.

Mages with mages.

Wolves with wolves.

Humans with humans.

Fae with fae.

Vampires sit with vampires, like Raiden, right beside Vallie, which makes my nostrils flare and anger rush to the surface, but I push it back.

"Here we are," Flora murmurs, pointing toward the table in front of us. A woman's face lights up at the sight of her, and she rushes to her feet.

"Flora!" She wraps her in her arms tightly as Arlo embraces the man beside her.

These must be their parents.

Even I have the fun of watching them now. Great.

"Princess Adrianna, it's an honor to meet you," Arlo's father says, tilting his head in a show of respect. I quickly wave my hand for him to stop.

"Just Addi is perfectly fine. It's lovely to meet you too," I reply, and he smiles at me as Flora's mother steps forward to stroke a hand down my arm.

"I've heard such wonderful things about you. It's lovely to meet you," she gushes, her smile so genuine it warms my soul. "Come, sit. Food will be served soon and then we get to dance," she exclaims excitedly.

Flora rolls her eyes at her mother, but I find it endearing. Taking my seat, I glance around the room, and I hate the fact that I instinctively pinpoint where Brody, Kryll, Cassian, and Raiden are.

What's even worse is when I locate each of them, their gazes are already set on me.

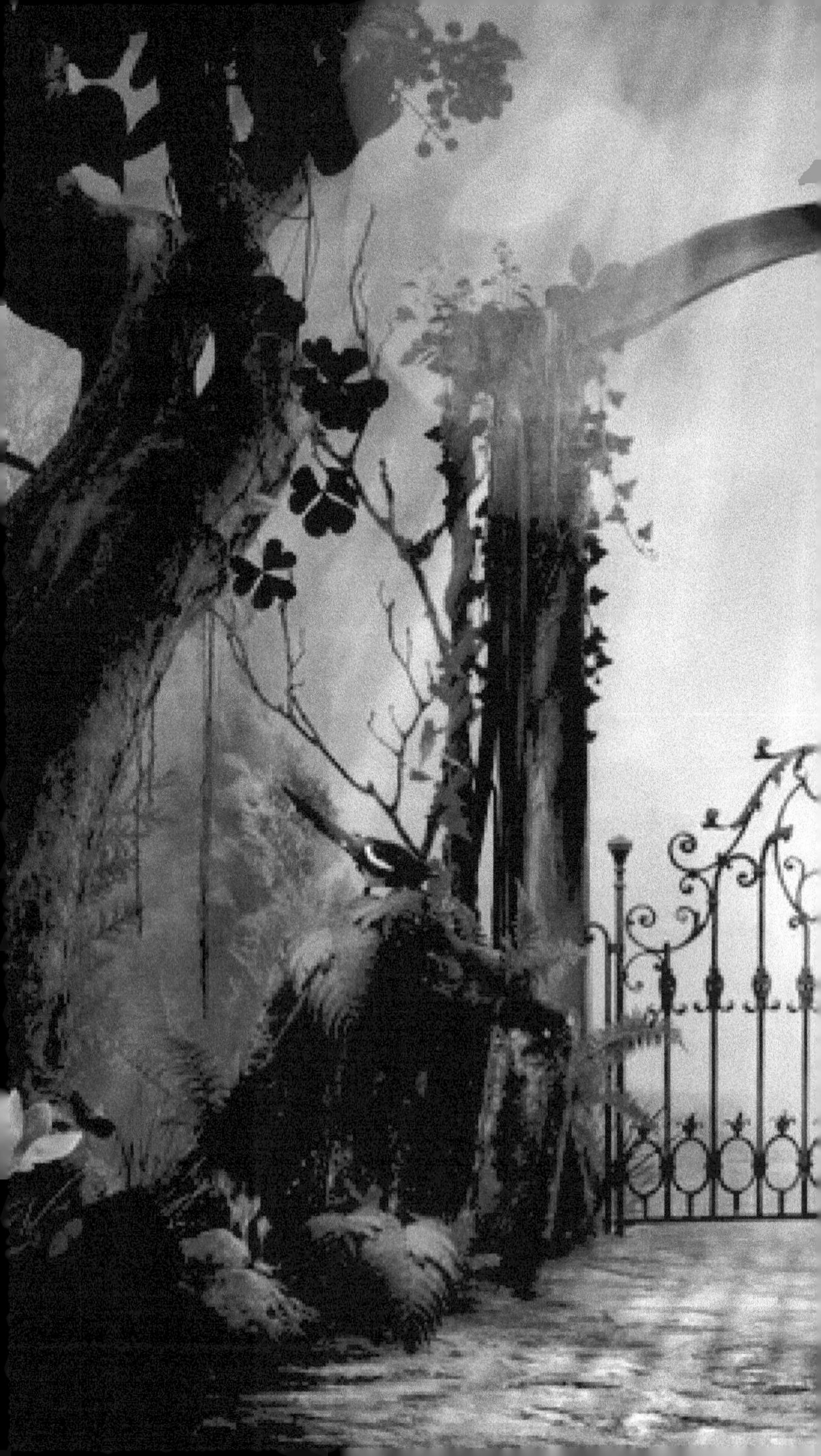

ADRIANNA
33

Surprisingly, the food is good and the conversation is entertaining. I don't know what I was expecting, but Flora and Arlo's parents have set me at ease, talking to me as Addi and not trying to pepper me with an inquisition about my heritage.

However, it hasn't stopped the gazes from many others around the room. Their stares penetrate my skin like a weapon, attacking me all at once as I try to keep my shoulders relaxed and my smile plastered in place.

I know the four of them can sense it, too. The tight smiles between my friends' parents and Flora's determination to remain perky and upbeat confirm it, and I've never appreciated them more.

I've learned far too much about my two friends, from their earliest stories to embarrassing blunders; like when

Flora decided to cut her own hair as a nine-year-old, resulting in a cropped cut that her mother has pictures of on hand to go along with the memory.

Swirling my glass of water, I take another sip as the music softens and someone taps their finger on a microphone. Turning my attention toward the small platform on the other side of the room, my muscles stiffen at the sight of Dean Bozzelli.

I haven't seen her since she forced this damn gem between my shoulder blades, and the sight of her makes its presence burn stronger against my flesh.

"Good evening, ladies and gentlemen. I hope you're all having a wonderful night," she begins, arms out wide as she smiles at the crowd, but I don't miss the fact that she doesn't waste her time looking toward the fae corner of the room.

Her neon choice for the night is a shade of green, so bright some may argue the fact that it's yellow. She wears it with pride, and it suits her. She's as insane as her clothing choice, but who am I to judge?

"Why is that outfit making my eyes bleed?" Arlo murmurs, making me snicker along with Flora.

"It's wonderful to host our first celebration. An important factor in the success of this academy is incorporating traditions that we cherish while embracing the wonder of the future." Her sickly sweet voice makes me want to vomit. "Before we enjoy the opening dance that has blessed so many balls before this one, I just want to take a moment to thank you all for being in attendance this evening, but more than that, trusting that your children are in safe hands."

I scoff.

"There's nothing safe about those hands," Flora mutters, lip curling in distaste, and I can't help but smirk at her remark.

"There is a leader among us, a long-awaited heir to the throne that we will crown, along with a solid council around them. We will bring strength to our kingdom, rise from the flood once more, and be reborn into greatness as the Floodborn Kingdom deserves."

I roll my eyes at her choice of words while others offer her a small round of applause.

"Somebody definitely wrote that for her," Arlo whispers with a chuckle, and I shake my head. We can't underestimate this woman's mind. She may seem foolish, but there's a depth to her that I don't think we've seen the end of yet.

"Please, enjoy a demonstration of the waltz from our fabulous students, have a wondrous evening, and we look forward to seeing more of you in the future."

The applause grows louder as some stand, and I'm most definitely ready for the floor to open right now and swallow me whole so I don't have to do this dance. Before I can even consider an escape, I feel a hand on my shoulder.

I know who it is before I turn and look, and the smolder that greets me is no surprise.

"Brody, do we really have to do this?" I complain, but he's already reaching for my hand and tugging me to my feet.

"You know we do."

I roll my eyes but tamper down my dramatics as he leads me toward the dance floor to join the other students. He doesn't let go of my hand, his grip firm but relaxed, and it spikes my veins. I can practically feel every groove of his fingertips branding me with each second that passes, and for some reason, I don't pull away.

He doesn't stop until we're at the very center of the hardwood dance floor. His hand falls to my back while the other shifts my hand in his, putting us in a perfectly poised position.

"Follow my lead?"

"It's the only way I'm going to survive this thing," I breathe as the music shifts around us.

"One... two... three," he whispers against my ear before he takes off.

All I can do is hold on and hope for the best. He moves with ease, a finesse I can't wrap my head around, as we glide across the floor with everyone else. I catch a glimpse of Flora laughing with Kryll as she makes a misstep. I see Cassian remain stoic and vibrating with irritation as he clumsily leads his partner.

I pause my staring there, turning my full attention back to Brody. Seeing them with other girls, even my friend, does something to my chest, and I don't like it.

"What are you thinking about, Dagger?"

I exhale, stumbling over my own feet, but he keeps us moving effortlessly.

"Nothing."

"That look in your eyes tells me a different story," he muses, suddenly spinning me out and tugging me back in before I can make sense of it all.

"That's not part of the dance," I grumble, making him chuckle.

"Maybe not, but you look hot when I do it."

I roll my eyes at him again, but his carefree warmth is exactly what I need.

"Mr. Orenda. Your father wishes to speak with you."

Brody comes to a halt, his attention steering to the man suddenly at our side. "My father can go fuck himself," he retorts with a scoff as I stand frozen in place.

"He assumed that may be your response. He also advised me to relay a message that can be delivered in private or for everyone to witness. Which would you prefer?" The man seems embarrassed by the words he has to repeat while Brody sighs, dropping his hands from my body.

"I won't be long," he murmurs, and I nod, eager to get the hell off the dance floor, but the second he turns to leave with the guy, another hand lands on my arm.

Whirling around, I startle when I find Kryll. Panic sets in, and I instantly search for Flora. He must sense my concern because he waves me off before pointing to where she's standing with Arlo.

"Dance with me."

Three words.

Simple. Small. Soft.

Yet they're laced with heat, promise, and desire.

Fuck.

Before I can think better of it, my hand slips into his and he pulls me in close. I have to tilt my head back a little further to look at him as he sways us from side to side. The song in the background changes and the waltz everyone is trying to follow drifts into a calmer tune.

"You've garnered quite an audience tonight," he states, peering around me. He slowly spins us, giving me the opportunity to note everyone looking in my direction, and I hum in agreement.

"So it seems."

"I don't know whether it's how beautiful you look in this dress or the amethyst you're displaying so carefree," he offers, threatening to turn my cheeks pink at his compliment, and I shake my head.

"I thought it might have something to do with the fact that I'm Satan's spawn."

He grins, a snicker falling from his lips as he peers down at me. "It could be that too. Or the fact that you're wearing combat boots with such a sweet dress," he adds, and I grin.

"Damn. I thought it was the outline of the daggers underneath all this tulle," I muse, watching his gaze shoot to my thighs, eyes darkening as he slowly raises them to meet mine, staring at me intently.

"Fuck. You're something else," he breathes, lifting a palm to my face. His hand is huge against my cheek, and I shiver at the way his thumb coasts over my skin.

The room falls still as he inches closer, and closer, and closer until there's nothing but a millimeter between us. We search deep into each other's eyes, for what, I'm not entirely sure, but a split second later, we must find it because we move in sync, eliminating the remaining distance between us.

Soft, full lips claim mine as I rise up on my tiptoes, palms pressed against his chest as I lose myself in his warm embrace.

My eyelids fall closed, separating me from everything around me apart from him. Goosebumps ghost over my skin as desire dances through my veins.

All too quickly, he retreats, his eyes almost black when I blink my lids open to see him.

"That was some of the most magical shit I've ever experienced in my life."

I chuckle at his proclamation, stepping in closer as a wave of dizziness washes over me. The kind that comes with euphoria.

"This is the bitch causing a stir, Daddy. I want her gone. And I want her gone now." The shrill sound of Vallie's voice interrupts our moment, making my blood boil even more than usual when I'm in her presence.

I turn to find her standing beside a man who is practically the male version of her. Same nose, same eyes, same chin. They've even got the same shade of hair, which doesn't feel like the most natural of colors, but that's irrelevant when they're both glaring at me with a fierceness that doesn't fill me with a sense of joy.

"So it's true. The Addi Reed causing issues for my daughter is none other than *the* Adrianna Reagan, former princess and heir," he declares, speaking loud enough over the music that the other students still dancing around us stop to watch the drama unfold.

Reluctantly, I step out of Kryll's embrace, turning to face the pair of them head-on as I sigh. "I'm quite sure your daughter causes her own issues."

His eyes narrow as Vallie clings to his arm, shaking him for good measure. "Daddy, she's trying to steal Raiden away from me. The deal promised—"

He waves his daughter off, keeping his eyes narrowed on mine. It's hilarious that he's even entertaining her with this bullshit right now when I was literally just kissing another guy. I've kissed Raiden for sure, and despite my sound mind, I'd do it again. I know it, but that's beside the point.

"That's enough, Vallie. The agreement with the Holloways still stands," he promises, patting his daughter's hand on his arm. I don't know what they're talking about, but I can't deny that I care. Kryll inches closer behind me, letting me know he's there, while I can't help but wonder where the vampire in question is. "None of this will end well for you, Miss Reagan," he adds, the promise just as clear as the threat as he jabs a finger in my direction.

"I'm not sure what you're referring to, sir," I bite out, trying to keep my composure instead of taking a swing at this man's smug face.

"A fae is never going to take that throne again. And as a member of The Council, I'll make sure of it," he snarls, his composed demeanor quickly disappearing. He quickly reaches for the cigar tucked into his blazer pocket, lighting the end like a seasoned pro as I smile at him.

"We should never say never, but enjoy your evening."

"I'm not done talking to you," he snaps, stumbling a step forward and revealing the liquor that clearly runs through his veins right now. I'm not getting involved with anyone in this state, especially not a man who wields his perceived superiority like a weapon. Not when he still holds some power on The Council. The consequences aren't worth it.

Pushing my shoulders back, I keep my smile intact. "I'm done talking to you. Your games are as childish as your daughter's and it's growing tiresome. There are more pressing matters in this kingdom to attend to other than if your daughter gets the man she longs for. Vampires are in a frenzied state, uncontainable and destructive, but instead of warning the people of our kingdom, the media fixates on me. A great distraction for you, I'm sure, but that is most definitely something you should have under control, especially as a vampire. But what would I know? I'm just a failed fae heir."

"You can't speak to my father like that!" Vallie yells, making sure we have everyone's attention now. Keeping myself calm and collected is getting old.

"I can, and I just did. One day, you're going to learn this world doesn't revolve around you and your needs. One day, the kingdom will need you in a greater capacity than what you are capable of offering in that moment, and you will fail, without a shadow of a doubt, and I will watch you fall, because we all know that you wouldn't take a fae's hand to help you rise again. Or would you? If the alternative was death?"

My pulse thunders in my ears as I take a step back, watching them both gape at me as I spin for the exit. I startle when I realize Kryll isn't alone anymore. Brody and Cassian are with him too, but still no vampire. Surely, if ever there was a reason for him to make an appearance, it would be the drama which, yet again, revolves around him.

Maybe then he could explain this so-called deal to me so I can politely put as much distance between us as possible.

I make it out into the hallway without interruption, my shoulders sagging with relief as the noise dissipates.

"That was the hottest shit I've ever seen in my life," Brody declares, draping his arm over my shoulder and drawing me to a stop.

"I'm sure it was because you need to get out more," Cassian grunts, peering at me through hooded eyes. I can't sense what's going on in his head, and it's clear there's no chance he's going to freely share.

"Do you want to leave?" Kryll suddenly asks, and I nod profusely.

He offers out his hand, palm faced up ready for mine, and before I can change my mind, I take it.

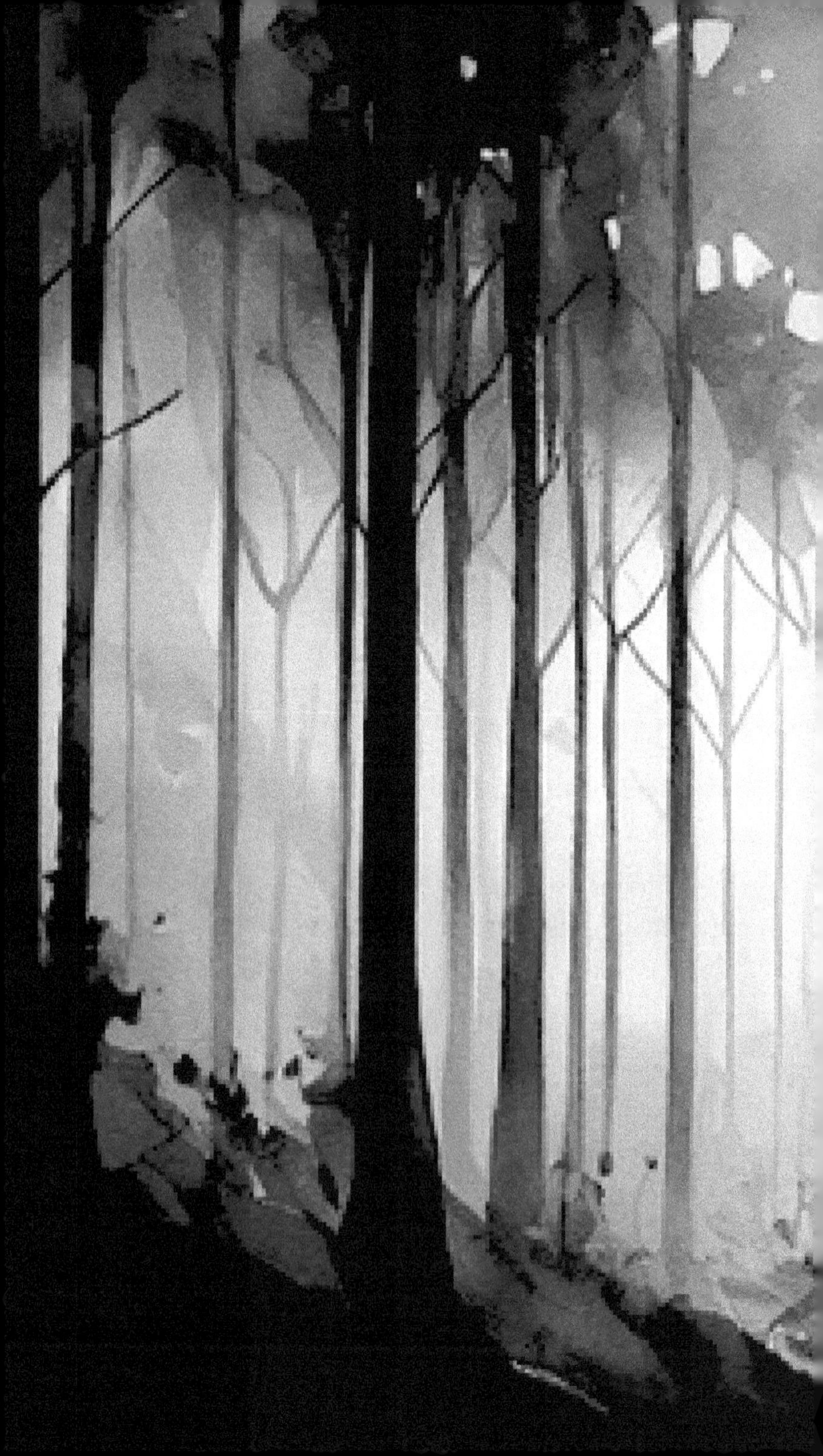

KRYLL

34

In a sea of hundreds of people, the beauty dressed in a soft yellow, with her hair braided in a crown around her head, holds me captive. I can't breathe when I'm watching her from across the room; having her hand in mine as we run down the hallway, giddy and crazy, is a level of euphoria I'm certain I've never experienced before.

Knowing there are combat boots on her feet, daggers at her thighs, and a destructive gem nestled into her flesh only reminds me of the strength she harnesses. She's not your typical woman, and she's far from what you envision a princess to be.

She's irrevocably Adrianna Reagan. No one else in this world has a chance of standing beside her. She outshines the damn sun. A fact I would be able to confirm if the moon wasn't shimmering in the night sky right now.

Her heat is undeniable, her fire ablaze for all to see, and I can't seem to bring myself to care if I get burned at her hands.

Our steps slow as we approach the exit, coming to a complete halt when we realize the media is still camped outside. I bet I can guess who they're waiting for.

Her.

The princess.

The way she addressed them earlier was awe-inspiring. She slaughtered them with her words while remaining all prim and proper, giving them no room to degrade or shame her in any way.

H.O.T.

She refused to hide under my arm or behind Raiden's back, and as much as I would have been happy for her to stay there, the fact that she stepped forward, unguarded, was the moment of no return.

My dick liked it. I liked it. My animal liked it.

Rubbing my lips together, I consider our options. "Are you up for some motion sickness?" I offer, pulling her deep green eyes to mine, and she nods.

"Please."

I don't wait for her to change her mind before I tug her against my chest, lifting her an inch off the floor before I take off. I move so fast that the media doesn't get a chance to acknowledge our existence. The world blurs around us. I rush as quickly as I can, considering my options as I near the fountain along the usual pathway, but before I can regret my decision, I hurry on past.

It's only an extra ten seconds—seconds I'm sure she'd rather not have to deal with—but I hope it will be worth it.

Coming to a stop, she clings to the lapels of my blazer, her eyes taking a second to focus on mine, and I can't deny that she's a little paler than she was a few moments ago.

"Thank you," she breathes, smoothing her hands down my blazer before taking a step back. Reluctantly, I let her go.

"You're welcome," I rasp, watching as she slowly spins on the spot, attempting to take in her new surroundings.

"Where are we?"

I press my finger to my lips as her gaze turns to me. "Shh, it's a secret."

She sighs, a sense of contentment seeping from her. "It's a very pretty secret."

I hum in agreement. "It's where my animal likes to be," I admit, revealing a piece of myself that I don't share with anyone else, but it feels necessary with her, like I'm compelled in some way. I just can't pinpoint why, or I don't want to accept the reality of it, either way, I'm not delving into it right now.

Moving to stand beside her, I follow her line of sight. The dark cave glows with trinkets that line the walls, illuminated by the moon that peers through the opening at the top. There's a king bed tucked in the far corner, but otherwise, everything else caters to my creature.

Thick, warm blankets are scattered all over the floor, but it's the view the opening offers that brings me back here time and time again. The City of Harrows glimmers in the distance, the kingdom's skyline gothic from this vantage point, with the castle glistening in the background. If you focus, you can also see the edge of Evermore to the left and the town tower of Foley Hill to the right.

"Do you like your creature?" she asks, peering up at me with a sense of inquisition that vibrates through my bones, leaving me eager to lay everything out for her to sift through.

"Yes." One word. That's all I can manage as I stare into her shimmering emerald eyes.

"Am I going to have to tiptoe around asking what you are? Or, more specifically, am I likely to get an answer, or would you prefer not to share?"

Her words hang in the air, leaving me speechless as my mind reels a mile a minute. "It's not a secret," I rasp, scratching at the back of my neck.

"But…"

How can she read me so well? Clearing my throat, I turn to look out at the kingdom beneath us. "I don't know. I guess I just naturally like to keep things to myself."

"That sounds exactly like something a shifter would say," she muses, pulling my gaze back to her as she grins.

"Exactly."

"I'm going to have to start observing your every move so I can try and piece it together," she decides, eyes lighting up with excitement as the challenge settles between us.

Turning to face her, my hands instinctively move to her waist. She tenses beneath my touch, but not in a way that screams she doesn't like it, more that she doesn't want to admit she wants it. Just like me.

"Is that so?"

"Uh-huh."

"What have you got so far?" I ask, inching closer, and her hands drift to my chest.

"You must be able to fly."

"How so?"

"You got us all the way up here for one, and for two, you crashed through my window." She gives me a pointed look to accompany her facts, and I grin.

"That I did. Anything else?"

Her fingers reach for my neck, trailing over the black markings that grace my skin. My teeth grind together as I try not to react to her touch like my creature desires. I can't stop my eyelids falling to half-mast as her fingers dip below the collar of my shirt.

"I feel like your tattoos represent something. I just can't

piece together what exactly," she admits, stirring my cock to life with the simple fact that she's even thought about it.

"That's correct," I reply hoarsely, and she grins from ear to ear. It feels like the first time I have had a chance to see her carefree and calm.

"Check me out. Two for two."

"Any guesses?" I ask, adjusting us so we're flush with one another, our chests touching with every breath, and she shakes her head.

"No. I don't want to make a fool out of myself until I'm certain."

Fuck, she's too fucking beautiful. "Do you want a hint?" I offer, dragging my thumb over her cheek, just as I did earlier on the dance floor, relishing the softness of her skin against my touch.

"That's cheating," she breathes, jaw slightly slack as she looks up at me with the most mesmerizing glint I've ever seen.

"I can't wrap my head around you," I admit, watching as her eyelashes flicker, subdued as she practically sways in my hold.

"Then don't."

I take the invitation without a moment's consideration. Crushing my lips to hers, our mouths mold to one another's. She's tantalizing, running her tongue over the seam of my lips, sending a shudder through my limbs as I cling to her more tightly.

Delving past her lips, her tongue slides along mine, practically bringing me to my knees, but my creature rises beneath the surface, rushing us across the room. Her back slams against the wall harder than I would like, but she doesn't react. If anything, she arches against me, needy for more.

My cock throbs, my creature snarling in my ears, but the desire is muted by the fear and panic, forcing me to jerk back a step. Then another. And another. Until I'm almost across the room.

"Shit, I'm sorry," I ramble, raking my fingers through my hair, tugging at the ends, desperately needing control to come back to me.

"Another hint?" she asks, eyebrow raised as her tongue sweeps over her bottom lip.

"Another way you loosen my grasp on my control," I retort, panting for breath as a smirk curls the corner of her mouth.

"That feels like a compliment."

"I don't know what it is," I admit, and it's the truth. I can't think straight right now, which only serves to leave me even more confused. Wiping a hand down my face, I try to at least harness my breathing, but even that feels like a struggle.

"Are you okay?" she asks, concern etched into each

word as I shake my head.

"No, but I don't think I ever have been," I reply with a snicker, but it rings dark through the air.

"Is there anything I can do to help?"

I shake my head again, at a complete loss.

Taking a deep breath, I inhale through my nose and exhale slowly through my mouth. After a couple of passes, my heart rate starts to calm down. When I focus my attention back on Addi, I startle.

"Why are you taking deep breaths?" I rasp, and a guilty look shifts over her face before she clears her throat and shrugs.

"I just thought it might help if you could subconsciously hear it in the air, too."

Well…fuck.

Turning toward the opening, I focus on the castle in the distance. I sense her moving, but I don't turn to see where she is as I focus on the cool air drifting around me.

"Are you doing that?"

"Yes."

I scoff, disbelief rippling through me. She's using her damn air magic to try and cool me down while I literally turn into a puddle before her instead of running for the hills as she should.

"I don't let people close for a reason," I admit, the words slipping from my lips before I can reconsider.

Sensing her getting closer, I catch sight of her out of the corner of my eye, tilting her head at me in confusion. "I'm trying to understand why." The way she says it feels like she doesn't understand any more than I do, yet I still find the words to answer her.

"Because the other side of me is always right beneath the surface, and I lose control really fast." My spine stiffens at the truth as my hands ball into fists.

"Sometimes losing control isn't all that bad," she muses, glancing out over the kingdom, and my heart clenches.

"Sometimes, it's not safe."

"Do you want to explain that?" she asks, shifting to face me.

My lips twist as I instinctively turn to face her. "I don't get close to anybody like this because the second my blood heats with my desire, my... my creature bubbles to the surface, and I'm scared of hurting someone."

My cheeks heat, embarrassment coursing through my veins as the admission takes over. Her hand lifts to my arm, squeezing in comfort as concern dances in her pretty eyes.

"Have you ever hurt someone?"

I shake my head, the word heavy on my tongue. "No."

"Then—"

I wave my hand, cutting her off as I stare deep into her

eyes. "I haven't hurt someone because I've never allowed myself to get close enough."

"I don't understand." She rubs her lips like she's trying to piece the jigsaw puzzle together, but she's a curved edge out of place, and the picture is distorted.

As pretty as her confusion is, instead of leaving her to twist around the words I'm not saying, I take a deep breath and blurt them out instead.

"I'm a virgin, Princess."

THE REIGN OF BLOOD

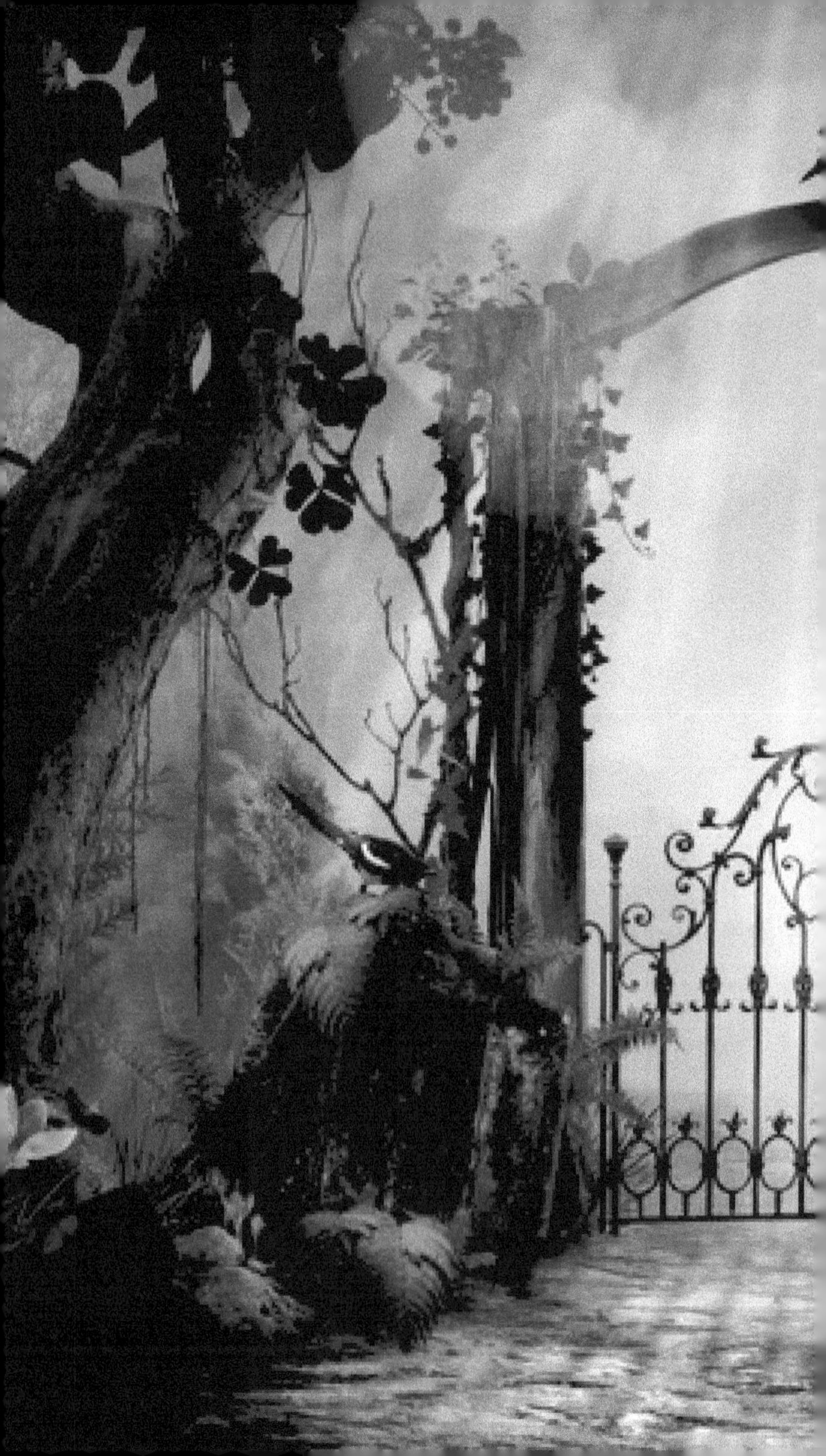

ADRIANNA

35

A virgin.

A fucking virgin.

Those words were spoken to me on Saturday, and they still have me reeling now, on Monday morning, when I should be focused on the classes I have today.

Fuck.

It takes everything I have to try and push it all to the back of my mind, and even then, I come up short.

I can recall the soft smile that accompanied the words before he tossed all the excuses at me to take me home. I didn't argue, even though I really fucking wanted to, but it wasn't about my wants and needs, it was all about him.

I wanted to peek beneath his unbuttoned shirt, I wanted to trace his ink with my tongue, and I wanted to touch him in a way he never had before, but I chickened out in fear of scaring him off. I'm a lot, too much, really, especially if you've never…

Fuck.

He offered me the most wistful kiss at my front door, where another red rose was waiting, before disappearing like a dream I'd made up.

I know shifters keep everyone at arm's length, but seeing it and feeling it myself for the first time threw me off kilter. I haven't seen him since, but I know he'll be at breakfast this morning. I'm just praying things aren't awkward.

A knock sounds from my bedroom door, pulling me from my thoughts. I quickly throw on my gray cloak, letting it fall around my shoulders before opening the door to reveal Flora on the other side.

Her eyes are a little glazed over, her gaze off to the side, and I frown. "Hey, are you okay?"

She startles at my presence, even though she just knocked, before shaking her head and clearing her thoughts. "Oh, yeah, sorry, this was leaning against your door," she murmurs, her voice softer than usual as she offers me a long-stemmed red rose.

"Huh, twelve," I muse, taking it from her grasp to quickly add it to the vase. They all stand tall and pretty, the petals delicate and soft.

"Aren't you creeped out?" she asks, frowning at them

until I step into the hallway and close the door behind me.

I shrug. "I was at first, but they're too pretty for me to stay mad," I admit, and she shakes her head. The color comes back to her face a little, but it still doesn't feel like she's her usual self. "Are you sure you're okay?"

She sighs, chin dipping to her chest. "Dammit, Addi, I just—"

"There you both are. Ready for food?" Arlo hollers from halfway up the staircase. He rubs his lips together nervously as he scans his eyes over Flora, who quickly tucks a loose tendril of hair behind her ear, nodding.

There's a weird vibe between them, one I can't decipher, but as we move closer to him, I can sense that he's the cause of her dismay this morning.

We head downstairs in a strange silence that I have no control over as I make eyes at Flora. The sadness that dances beneath her lashes is like a swift punch to the gut. Whatever is troubling her involves him, and she needs me to step up and be the same kind of friend to her as she is to me.

"We need a girls' night," I declare as we reach the bottom of the stairs, and Arlo takes off to open the front door for us.

"Hell yeah, we do," she says with a gasp of excitement, squeezing my arm as she tries to contain the buzz the offer has given her.

"I can organize the hell out of it or—"

"Please, I'd rather you didn't. I'll handle it. Your attendance will be exactly what I need. Are you free on Friday?" she asks, her voice a few octaves higher than moments ago, and it feels like it's at least giving her something to focus on.

"I'm free whenever you need me."

"Friday it is. It gives me time to prep," she explains, linking her arm through mine as we head along the pathway to the main academy.

"To prep?" I question, concern starting to make itself known as I peer at her, and Arlo scoffs.

"Oh, you have no idea what you've signed yourself up for." He grins, winking at Flora, which makes her cheeks stain pink.

"It'll be fun, I promise," she confirms, and I nod.

"I don't doubt it."

The silence that drapes over us for the rest of the walk is a lot more comfortable, even though there's a strange sort of distance between them. If she wants to tell me about it, she can, if not, then I'll be here for whatever else she needs. It's about time I repaid the favor.

Stepping into the dining hall, my gaze drifts to the table in the center of the room, where Cassian, Raiden, Brody, and Kryll are already seated. I join Flora and Arlo at the food station, opting for my usual eggs and bacon, before heading toward the four assholes that cause a stir inside of me one way or another.

I take my newly assigned seat between Raiden and Kryll, giving the vampire on my left the cold shoulder as Kryll turns to me with a soft, nervous smile.

"Hey, how are you?" I ask, feeling completely awkward as my tongue peeks out to sweep along my bottom lip. It does nothing to quench the dryness forming, and my throat tightens with every swallow.

"He's fine. Why do you ask?" Raiden interjects, answering for him, and I frown. Turning to him with a deathly glare and a finger pointed in his direction, I huff.

"I'm not talking to you."

Before I can whip my head back around, his eyebrows gather in confusion. "You just did."

Semantics. Asshole.

I roll my eyes and turn back to my plate, peering at Kryll out of the corner of my eye, who smirks as he shovels a fork full of food into his mouth.

"Why aren't you talking to me?" Raiden pushes, but I ignore him, tilting my face to Kryll again.

"Kryll," I start, ready to ask him again, but he cuts me off.

"I'm good, Princess," he breathes, his voice raspy like Saturday night, and I can't help but nip at my bottom lip to keep my mouth shut so I don't say anything stupid.

"Hey, I'm talking to you," Raiden calls out, tapping at my shoulder, but I don't turn to face him.

"And I'm talking to Kryll. Take the hint," I retort, making the vampire eager for my attention sigh in exasperation.

"Did I miss something?" Raiden quizzes, but I ignore him.

Brody snickers, winking at me from across the table before settling his gaze on Raiden. "You miss everything."

Flora blurts out a giggle and quickly claps a hand over her mouth as I decide to take a bite of my bacon so, again, I don't say anything stupid.

"Can we just fucking eat," Cassian snaps, nostrils flared as he narrows his eyes at us.

"Cassian is so sweet with his words," Brody says in a high-pitched voice, all whimsical and delicate.

"Fuck off, Brody," Cassian snarls, earning an eye roll from the mage, and I can't help but smirk at their constant back and forth.

We eat in silence, but I'm completely alight with Kryll's thigh pressed against mine. It's there on purpose; I know it is, but I feel too shy to turn and look at him for confirmation.

What the hell is he doing to me?

I thought he was the virgin, not me.

Taking my last bite of food, I stand, eager to put a little space between me and these guys. Cassian, because his constant growling is stressful yet hot at the same time.

Brody, because all I can think about when I look at him is how he fucked me in his room. Kryll, because all I want to do is see him naked and have a piece of him no one else has, which is the most selfish shit I've ever heard, nevermind thought. And Raiden, because he's the biggest asshole out of all of them and he doesn't even see it.

"Honestly, what the fuck did I do?" Raiden blurts, grabbing onto my wrist as I go to take a step away from the table. Glancing down at where his fingers wrap around my skin, I follow his arm all the way until my gaze settles on his.

The fact that he doesn't realize it all on his own only serves to irritate me. "You left me standing in the middle of the dance floor with an entire fucking audience while Vallie and her fucking father laid into me because of you, yet the topic of conversation was nowhere to be found," I snap, the anger that I've contained over the matter since Saturday night finally unleashing itself.

"I was—"

I wave him off, interrupting before he can give me any of his bullshit excuses. "I don't care. Whatever you say won't go back and change the fact that it happened, and I can't shake the irritation I feel toward you because of it," I admit, yanking my wrist from his grasp, which only makes his gaze grow darker.

"That's not fair."

"Life isn't fair, asshole. Get over it," I retort with a shrug, spinning away from the table.

Flora and Arlo stand alongside me, sauntering from the room without a backward glance as I try to ease the tightness in my chest and the spike in my heart rate.

"You guys give me life. It's too entertaining," Arlo says with a chuckle before earning a whack to the gut from Flora.

"Arlo, shut up," she whisper-yells, making me grin, and some of the tension radiating through me subsides.

There's a little pep in my step as I remember that we have combat class first thing this morning, which will be the perfect way for me to release all these pent-up feelings. My steps falter when we enter the field and find Professor Tora, Kryll's brother.

It's a good thing he doesn't have mind powers, so he can't see what I think about his brother. As if sensing my thoughts about the matter, his gaze spins my way, eyes locking on mine for a moment as he assesses me before turning back to the student he's in a conversation with.

What the fuck was that?

He can't read my thoughts, right?

"Everybody hurry up and gather round. Today is going to hit you in the face so hard and fast, you're going to end up with whiplash, so I'd like to get on with it sooner rather than later," Tora hollers, and I join the other students, forming a circle around him.

"I don't like the sound of this," Flora whispers, panic in her voice, and it startles me to realize not everyone is pumped and ready to go with whatever he throws at us.

Glancing around at the other students, I notice the same level of uncertainty and weariness.

It's me. I'm the odd one.

I sense somebody shifting up to my left side, and I'm not surprised in the slightest when I see it's Raiden. Rolling my eyes, I turn away from him, focusing on Professor Tora as he continues to explain the lesson for the day.

"Now that the ball is out of the way, I can focus more on the trials. Which means we're going to experience one today."

Holy shit.

My fingers flex at my sides as I refrain from bouncing on the balls of my feet. Gasps echo around me, worried murmurs ringing in my ears, but all I feel is adrenaline coursing through my veins with a glint of excitement.

"Practice trial number one is all about resources, coordination, and working with others to return safely," Tora explains, circling his gaze around the gathered students, making sure everyone understands the objective.

"Return from where?" Vallie asks, a level of exasperation parting her lips that only she can produce.

"Evermore."

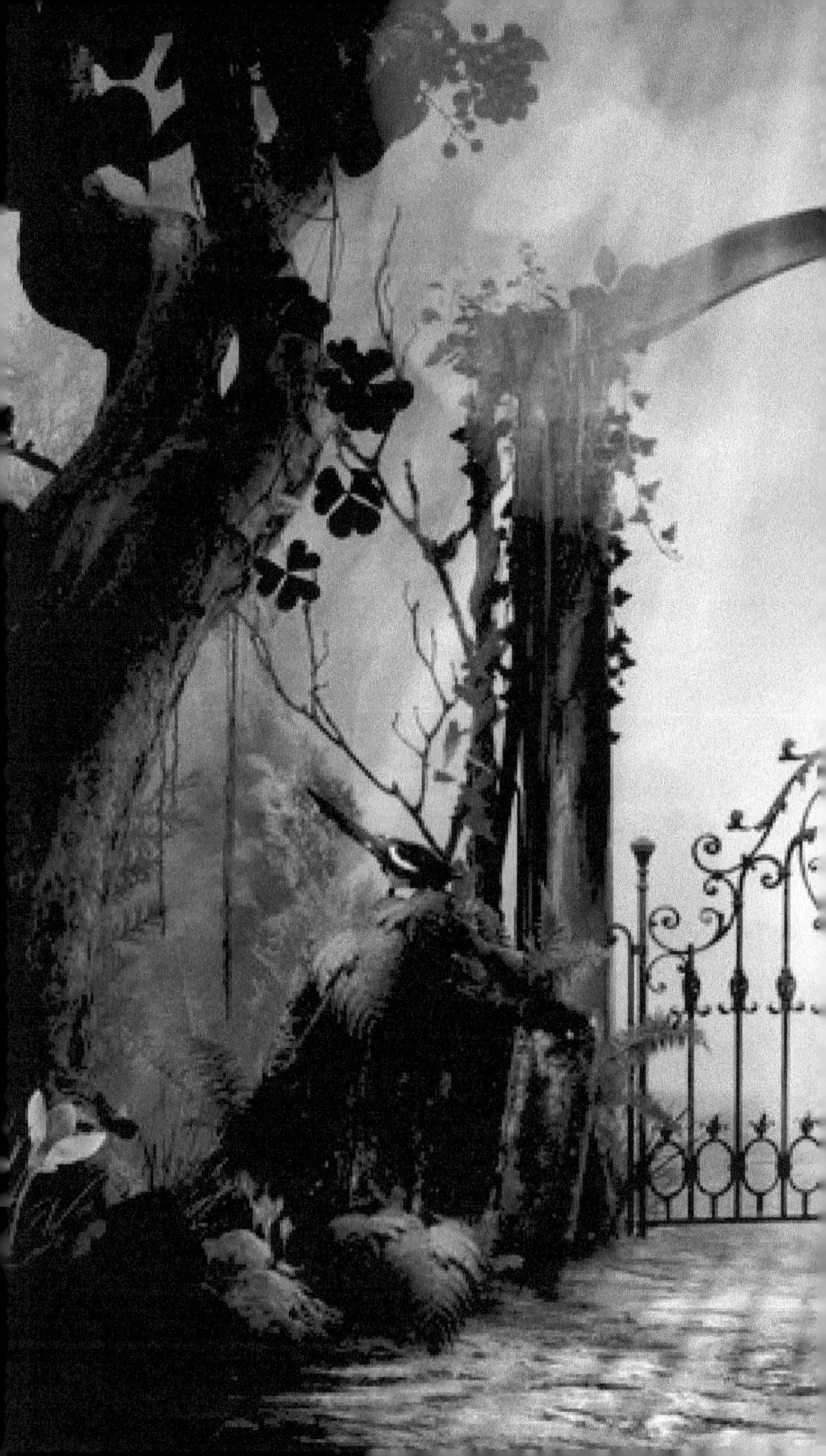

ADRIANNA

36

The word Evermore is barely past his lips before we're all moving. The ground shakes beneath us, disappearing into a bright abyss, before everything settles again. Only now, we're not on campus anymore.

It's bleak. The sun is barely visible through the tall, slim trees that surround us. They seem to go on for miles. There is nothing else in sight except the other students and Professor Tora, who is wearing a pleased smile.

"How did we move?" A human guy steps forward, arms folded over his chest as he bites back the anger thrumming from him.

"Mage magic. Problem?" Tora questions, eyebrow raised as he stares the student down. The guy takes a step back, mouth pressed into a thin line to hold back what was sure to be a snarky comment. "Now that we're here, let's get straight to the rules, shall we?" he asks, not waiting for an answer as he peers down at the device in his hands.

"Ready for a challenge, Dagger?" I glance at Brody, who peers down at me with a knowing look in his eyes.

"You know it," I quip, running my tongue over my bottom lip as I eagerly await Professor Tora's next words.

"I'm going to separate you into groups of five. Origins will be mixed and selected at random. You cannot and will not change from the groups you are in. It's a team effort. You must use your combined skills to find your way back to the academy before sundown. Any questions?"

"What if we don't make it back in time?" Arlo asks, arms folded over his chest as he cocks a brow at the professor.

"Then, hopefully, you make it home before the dining hall shuts."

"So if we don't make it back, we're stuck out here?" he confirms, and Tora shrugs.

"I mean, if you're still not home in forty-eight hours, I might send a search party, but I'm also going to be under the assumption that you might also be dead then," he retorts.

Well, fuck.

The murmurs of concern pick up again, but Professor Tora doesn't pay attention to them as he starts to read out names.

"Brody, Flora, Grant, Arlo, and Falon."

Flora heaves a sigh of relief at the mention of Arlo's name in the same group as hers, while Brody nudges me with his elbow. "Don't worry, Dagger, I'll protect your friends," he promises, pressing the softest kiss to my temple before sauntering off without a backward glance.

"Cassian, Edith, Otis, Danaka, and Poppy."

Cassian stomps off with a grunt, making me grin. At least he doesn't save his sunshine attitude just for me. He seems to shower everyone with the same level of harshness, which is almost comforting.

"Adrianna, Raiden, Vallie, George, and Kryll."

My eyebrows rise, disappointment consuming me as Kryll moves in a step.

"It looks like all your prayers have been answered," he muses, nodding toward the snarly vampire approaching with her lips pursed and her hands clenched at her sides.

"All of them. What a life," I mutter back, making him snicker as I sense someone at my side. I know by his scent that it's Raiden, but I refuse to turn and look at him.

"Don't fucking speak to me," Vallie grunts, pointing a finger at me, and I roll my eyes as the human from earlier steps toward us.

"George?" I ask, and he nods. "Addi. Are you ready for this?"

"I know who you are, fae bitch," he snaps, baring his

teeth at me, which is utter entertainment to Vallie, who laughs like a hyena while Kryll and Raiden instinctively step toward him, ready to defend whatever honor I have.

"Let you die if something attacks, got it," I muse with a wink before turning my attention back to Tora, but I can't see him. "Hey, where's your brother?"

Kryll frowns, glancing around, eyes sweeping the ground for the second time before he comes to the same conclusion as me. "That fucker," he mutters, shaking his head in disbelief.

"We better get moving then," Raiden grumbles, pressing his hand to the small of my back to move me forward, but I step out of his reach, folding my arms over my chest as I start to take the lead through the trees.

"I'm not following you," Vallie calls out, her shrill whine irritating me.

Rolling my eyes, I sigh. "Do what you please, Vallie. I don't care, but I'd like to make it back today."

"You can't let her speak to me like this, Raidy," she grumbles, the nickname getting under my skin, but it has nothing to do with me. They have a deal, that's what her father said, and I want nothing to do with it.

"Vallie, shut your fucking mouth before I do it for you," Raiden grunts, appearing at my side a second later. "Are we talking yet?"

I rub my lips together, desperate to hold back my grin

at the dismissal the annoying bitch just received. A part of me wants to let him back in with open arms, just for the hope of pissing her off, but I'm a stubborn bitch and he left me to deal with their shit. I'm not forgiving him so easily.

"Why don't you go and talk to Vallie, Raidy? She actually wants to spend time with you. I don't." I hate that it tastes like a lie on my tongue, and I refuse to acknowledge it.

His fingers curl around my arm lightning fast, tugging me into his side as he presses his lips against my ear. "You can be mad, Adrianna. You can be mad all you like but do not try to push me into her grasp. Those aren't the games I play."

"No? Do you just deal with the ones where you kiss me while you have some kind of agreement with her? The girl I despise more than any other? Unfortunately, *I* don't play *those* games. Find someone else who will," I snap back, annoyed that my irritation is on full display. "Now let go of me before I use my magic to do it, just like last time," I threaten, recalling when I threw him across his room.

He must recall it, too, because he releases my arm a moment later. The sigh that rumbles from his throat is enough to make the ground shake as he tries to bottle his anger. "Evermore is vampire territory, I lead the way. Keep up or fuck off," he grunts, his harshness not piercing my skin like it did the first time he snapped in front of me.

Raiden is complex as fuck. That's clear enough for anyone to see if you look hard enough. I don't think he's ever heard the word *no* because every time he doesn't get his way with me or I push back too hard, he has a little temper tantrum like this.

His tongue gets sharper, his words get harsher, and his entire demeanor turns more tense.

When he's ready to climb back down off his little mountain of superiority, then maybe we can address some things. I know I should probably hear him out, but I'm not ready to yet, not with others present, and especially not with him still looking down his nose at me.

"Exactly, Raidy should lead us. He was born to be a leader," Vallie praises, making me roll my eyes again as I catch a glimpse of Kryll out of the corner of my eye. He looks about as impressed as I feel, which is reassuring.

"Nobody likes an ass licker, Vallie. Use your vampire speed to do a perimeter check. I want to know how far we are from the edge of Evermore forest, then I can coordinate our way back from there," Raiden orders, and to my surprise, she nods without a single word, snarky or sickly sweet.

She takes off, and I heave a sigh of relief for the reprieve, even if it is only for a moment. Glancing over my shoulder, I notice George is still with us. Anger tightens his jaw and irritation dances in his eyes.

Part of me wants to console him, give him a pep talk or whatever, but that's a bit difficult when you know you're also the source of his rage.

All too quickly, Vallie's back, her hand on Raiden's arm as she rises up on her tiptoes to whisper in his ear.

"Adrianna Reagan, is that a hint of green I can see in you?" Kryll whispers, making my gaze whip to his as I glare, but he simply chuckles like I amuse him.

"I don't know what you're talking about," I lie, pursing my lips as I continue to stomp after the two vampires, who remain close for a few more moments before they come to a halt. Before either of them speak, Kryll moves in closer, lips ghosting over my ear.

"He wants to claim you, you know? Maybe you should go easy on him."

I rear back in shock and my jaw slacks as I process his words. That's not true. It can't be. Besides, that's not what I want… right?

Fuck. I can't think about anything other than getting out of here.

"Professor Tora put us on the farthest side of Evermore, that sneaky asshole," Raiden states, giving Kryll a pointed look like it's his fault. "Unfortunately for him, we're not going to waste our efforts getting out of here like he hoped. I know where we are, and I know the easiest way back to the academy; we just need to use our speed to get it over with quickly."

I blink at Raiden, surprised it could actually be this easy when the human scoffs from behind me. "Please, that's great and all, but not all of us have speed."

"Vallie will help you," Raiden answers immediately, waving him off as his gaze settles on me. "I'll help you."

"No, you won't," I retort, pointing at Kryll. "He'll help me, right?" I ask, turning to him with hope shimmering in my eyes. He glances between us before a glint of something I don't like the look of settles over him.

"Actually, it'll be better if Raiden helps you so I can focus on following since I have no idea where I am or where I'm going."

"You wouldn't do this to me," I breathe, my heartbeat kicking into action as my body grows tense. He shrugs—fucking *shrugs*—like it's no big deal while I gape at him in horror. "You're an ass."

"You'll forgive me, Princess. Remember what I said," he whispers so quietly against my ear, I'm certain the others can't hear him, even with their supernatural hearing. Standing tall, he nods at Raiden. "Let's go."

"You owe me for this," Vallie grumbles, stepping up to George, who glares at her.

"I don't owe you shit."

"Not you. Him," she clarifies, pointing her familiar red nail at Raiden.

He doesn't answer her, stepping up to me with his arms outstretched. I curl my arms around myself, trying to give myself an extra layer of defense between us. "You're going to want to wrap your arms around my neck, Adrianna. I'll be able to move quicker, which means this will all be over even faster," he promises, a wicked smirk tainting the corner of his lips.

"Fucker," I mutter under my breath as I do just that.

This position presses my chest against his, and he looks down at where we're touching as I balance on my tiptoes.

"Let's get a move on, Raidy," Vallie snaps, and it instinctively makes me press further into his hold.

He smirks knowingly, and it pisses me off even more.

"Yeah, Raidy, let's go," I rasp, and he grunts in my ear.

"Don't call me that."

"It's a cute nickname," I insist, and he pinches the globe of my ass, making me yelp.

"It's vile. *She's* vile. But that's a conversation for another time."

Before I can breathe a word in response, he takes off, leaving my stomach nestled between the trees. Clenching my eyes shut, I try to keep breathing, even as I press my cheek against his. I hate how vulnerable it makes me feel, being in his grasp like this, but despite my stubbornness and harsh exterior, the desire to pass this trial prevails.

I have no idea how much time passes, five minutes,

ten, an hour? But we come to a stop, and Raiden doesn't miss a beat before giving out orders. "We need to head west from here. Once you see the peak of the castle in the distance, you need to shift south. The academy won't be far from there."

"How long will that—" Vallie's question is cut short by the sound of puking, which makes my stomach churn as I dare to open my eyes. I quickly clench them shut again when I realize it's George spewing his guts from the movement. That could be me at any minute. The stench reaches my nose and nausea churns in my stomach. "What am I going to do about this?" she yells, referring to George, and my nose crinkles.

"Wait for him to be ready to go again. Keep at top speed and we'll be there in thirty minutes," Raiden answers, taking off before I can catch my breath. I'm secretly relieved to be away from the mess—both Vallie and the puke.

What I assume are the first ten minutes feel like the longest moments of my life. My stomach swirls like I'm on the most extreme roller coaster of my life, leaving my throat burning with acidity. But as we lead into the next ten minutes, everything slowly, extremely slowly, starts to calm down. The burning nausea in my gut eases to a dull ache, to the point where I even test opening my eyes.

Nope.

Bad idea.

Clinging tighter to Raiden, I feel his hands shift over my hips, pinning me impossibly close to his chest. "Ten more minutes, Adrianna," he mutters, his voice somehow audible over the wind whipping around us.

I spend the ten minutes reciting facts and tips my father gave me over the years. From slowing my words when speaking publicly to ensuring I don't become distracted. The latter is where my main focus is because, for some reason, I can't seem to put those words into action when I'm surrounded by one or all of the four guys plaguing my thoughts.

Plaguing is exactly the right word to describe it.

It's against my will and I don't want it.

Especially not with what Kryll whispered in my ear. Claim me? Who? The four of them? Fuck that. My mind is overwhelmed by the mere thought of all of their opposite personalities consuming me.

We come to a stop, my chest tight as my heart races, and it takes a second for me to gather the strength to release my hold on him. The echo of wings flapping in the distance sounds odd, and a moment later I hear Professor Tora's voice.

"Why do you always have to show off, Kryll?"

"I'm not."

"Just because you're able to—"

"Don't say it."

"Don't say what?"

"What I am," he grumbles, making my eyes pop open. It takes all of two seconds to find him among the small gathered group, and unfortunately, he's no different from when I last saw him.

Two ears, two eyes, a nose, and the most delicious ink covering his skin. Not a single hint of what else he is. He winks at me with a smirk, and I stick my tongue out at him, feeling childish and giddy.

We're back at the academy, by the water fountain that leads to the origin buildings instead of the usual space we go to for combat class.

Tora peers between us both, eyebrows knitted in confusion before he shakes his head and lets the matter go. "Well done, you're the second team back. I can't award you second place until the other two from your group make an appearance as well, though."

"That's bullshit," Raiden grunts, taking a step back from me to wager a look of disdain at the professor. "And who the fuck was first?" Professor Tora points behind us, and I turn to see Brody, Flora, Arlo, Falon, and Grant. "How?" Raiden grinds out in disbelief, hands on his hips as anger burns through him.

"It's okay, Raiden. Maybe next time you'll be on my team and it will all work out," Brody says with a smirk, making Flora giggle.

I'm relieved to see that her and Arlo are okay, and the gleam in Brody's eyes tells me he's taking full credit for it.

"What do we do now?" Kryll asks, and I glance at Professor Tora, awaiting the answer myself.

"You made it back. You get the rest of the day to do as you please."

My eyebrows rise in surprise. "Why was it easy?" I blurt, earning a curious look from Tora. "I mean, I didn't do much, but I feel like... I don't know," I breathe, cheeks heating with embarrassment.

Tora smirks. "Despite your differences, your team worked together. You used the strength of someone in your group. In this case, it was Raiden, with his vampire speed and familiarity with the area I dropped you in. Brody, however, guided his team by simply connecting to the remaining tendrils of mage magic that lingered in the air in the forest and using them to revert the spell, transporting the five of them back."

Holy shit. That sounds insane. I don't even know how he would have thought of that, but I'm not a mage, so I have no clue how it all would have worked anyway.

I nod in understanding as Brody clears his throat. "So we can go?"

"Oh, not your team. The winners have to stay here to greet the return of everyone."

"What? How is that even a bonus for winning? That feels like punishment," he grumbles in response as Kryll snickers at his friend.

Waving, I earn a pouty glare from Brody before I turn on my heels and get the hell out of there. Desperate to avoid any more confrontation with Raiden, which I know will come eventually, I keep my pace quick without running. I don't dare turn to glance over my shoulder as I hurry down the pathway, practically stumbling through the front door before shutting it behind me.

I take the stairs two at a time, tumbling to a halt when I reach the top to find Raiden standing beside my bedroom door. "I told you, Adrianna, I'm not a stalker. That would imply I follow you. That's pointless when I know exactly where you're going and I can get there before you."

"That definitely sounds like something a stalker would say," I retort, muscles bunched tight as I approach him, unable to predict his next move.

He rolls his eyes, and as I step up beside him, I waste no time opening my bedroom door and stepping over the threshold.

"I'm not done talking to you," he states, cocking a brow at me.

"Well, *I'm* done talking to *you*." I offer him my worst smile before swinging the door toward him. I'm ready to relish in the thunder of the frame rattling from the slam, but it doesn't come.

I watch in slow motion as he launches his hand out, crossing over the barrier of magic that seals my room, to stop the door from reaching its destination. "What the fuck? How are you doing that?" Panic trembles down my spine as I gape at him.

He takes a step forward, moving into my room effortlessly, and I instinctively take a step back.

"How the fuck are you in here right now? Brody's spell—"

He moves around me like this is his space and not mine, coming to a stop by my desk where the roses take up most of the space.

"Nice roses. How many do you have now? Twelve?"

The wicked grin that tilts the corner of his mouth leaves me gaping at him as I connect the dots together. "They're from you," I breathe, and he nods, triumph dancing in his eyes.

"You're welcome."

"Get the fuck out of my room, Raiden." I point a shaky hand toward the door, but he shakes his head at me.

"I don't think I will," he muses, plucking one of the roses from the vase and twirling it in his hand. I will the magic in the room to throw him out as I beg it to, but nothing happens. "I bet when Brody gave you the spell to protect your room, he didn't mention the loopholes." I gulp. He's right, and he knows it.

"What loopholes?" I rasp, unsure if the glint in his eyes is a tinge of darkness or desire.

"Blood magic, for one" he states, like that explains it all.

"I don't know what that means."

He eliminates the distance between us, offering the rose to me, and despite my desire for him to get the hell out, I reach for it.

"You don't have to invite me in and you can't throw me out because I sacrificed twelve droplets of my blood on these pretty little roses, and you walked them right into the protected space without any sway from me."

THE REIGN OF BLOOD

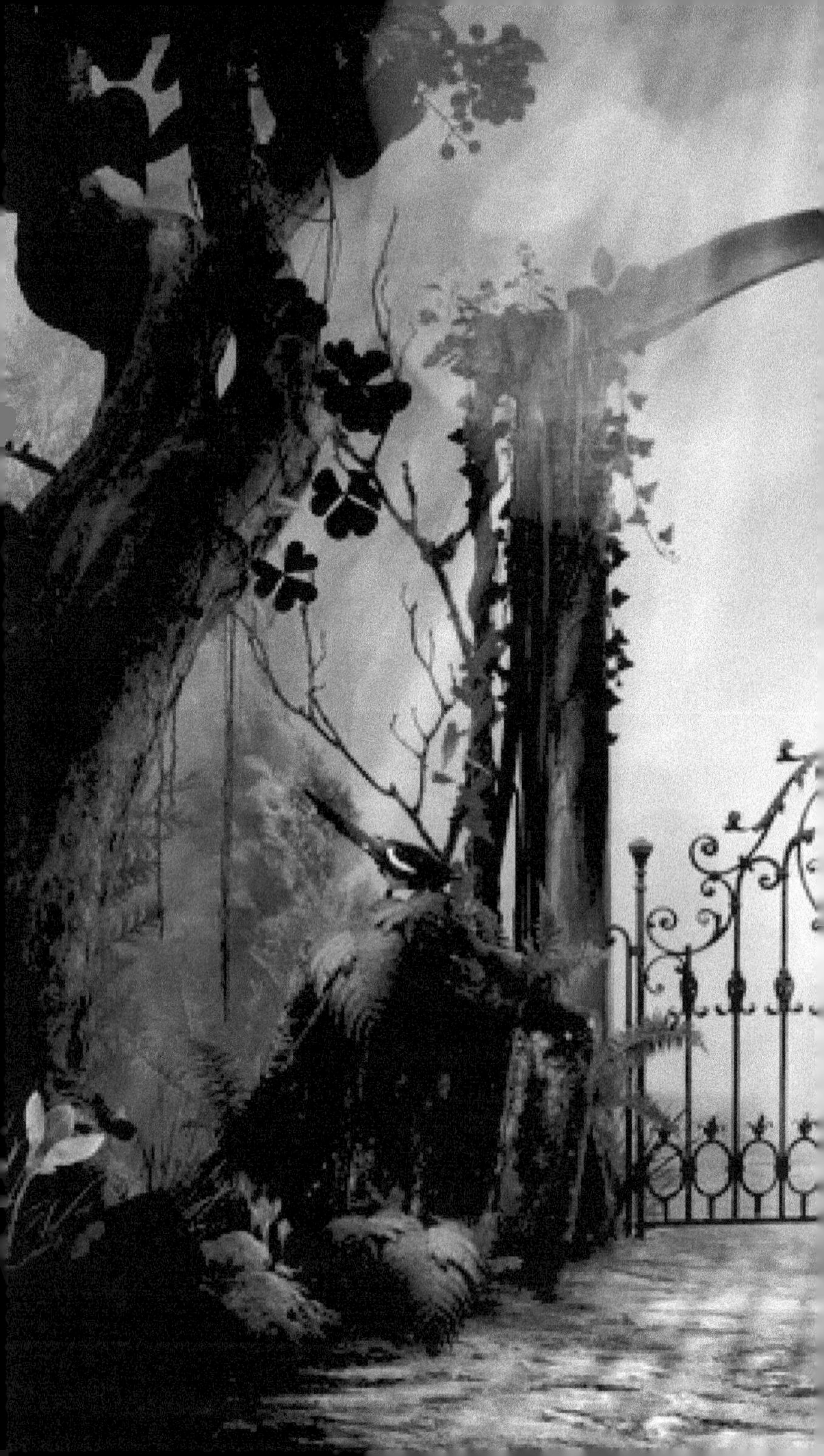

ADRIANNA

37

"You gave me flowers to break through the protective spell on my room." The words leave my mouth, rife with disbelief, as he grins at me.

"I did."

"Why?"

"So you can't hide from me. So I can be in here when I want to be and not just when you want me to be." he explains with a shrug like it really is that simple.

"But I wasn't hiding when you started giving them to me. That's just today. And technically, I'm not hiding, I just don't want to deal with you right now." I correct, adrenaline coursing through my body.

"I knew it would happen eventually."

I scoff. *This man. This fucking man.* "So you wanted

to break past my trust." I raise my eyebrow at him and he shrugs.

"I don't think I've ever had your trust to break it." Well, fuck. He has me there. "Now, we're going to talk about this like adults. Where would you like to sit?" He waves a hand around the room as I shake my head.

"We're not talking about anything. You're going to get the hell out of my room and leave me in peace."

He pulls the desk chair out, spinning it around on one leg before getting comfortable. The chair is backward, his arms folded over the back as he stares at me. It's the most out-of-character thing I've ever seen this guy do. He's prim, proper, and full of himself—always. And it doesn't usually look like this.

"Adrianna, I've got all day, straight into the night, and I'm more than happy to skip out on tomorrow if it means we get to the bottom of this. How long this takes falls in your hands."

This cannot be real right now. "You're an ass."

"No, I'm persistent, and you're just now learning the extent of it," he retorts with a shrug, and I turn away from him. I hate that I'm torn between slamming my fist into his jaw and claiming his full lips with my own.

I need him out of my space—quickly.

My gaze settles on the roses perched on the desk behind him. "Will you be kicked from the room if I throw out the roses?" He shakes his head, a teasing smile at the corner of his mouth. "How do I know if that's true?"

Without missing a beat, he stands, the vase in hand, and marches over to my bedroom window. He swings it open before holding the vase in my direction. "Throw them. Find out."

I blink at him, my chest clenching in pain for what will happen to the flowers if I toss them from my window. Rubbing my lips together, I take a deep breath, contain my rage, and remember one of my father's lessons.

Sometimes, you have to be submissive to get the information you want. Have patience.

Clearing my throat, I settle my gaze on his. "How about we get to the point you're here for? Then, you can get the fuck out," I grumble, stretching his smile out as he closes the window and settles the roses on the desk.

He retakes his position on the chair as he nods at the bed. "Get comfortable, Adrianna."

Pursing my lips, I narrow my eyes at him as I slowly take a seat at the bottom of my bed.

"Perfect. So why are you mad, Adrianna?" he asks, getting straight into it. His eyes are almost... gentle, his tone light, and his facial features relaxed—a complete contrast to the man who usually stands before me.

I tilt my head at him. "The Raiden I'm familiar with is rash, full of outbursts and rage... not this."

"I'm trying something new. Entertain me."

"I'd rather not."

He doesn't respond, not a single word, as he waits me out.

Just spit it out, Addi. The sooner you get it off your chest, the quicker he will leave.

"Fine, I'm mad that I was completely bombarded by Vallie and her dickhead father in front of everyone in attendance at the ball. Everyone except you, the very reason I was being bombarded in the first place. The last words you spoke to me were actually an apology for the fact that you entered the event with Vallie. You have a fucking talent of constantly showing up in my life, interjecting yourself when I don't need it. Yet when you were actually needed, you were nowhere to be seen." I sound petulant, but I don't care. I know my worth, and I'm not going to have some guy, hot vampire or not, giving me hot words and even hotter stares when they leave me in the shit when it actually matters.

"So you don't think I had to apologize for leaving with Vallie?" he asks, brows knitting in confusion, and I shrug.

"No."

"Bullshit."

"Raiden, my problem isn't with you entering the ball with her. It's that you left me stranded. Don't go off-topic," I grumble, and he shakes his head at me.

"It's not off-topic. I think it's completely relevant and total bullshit."

He's clearly not going to let this go. "How?"

"If you had to leave with a guy that wasn't Kryll, Brody, or Cassian, then I would be beyond furious," he grunts, his jaw ticking at the thought of it.

"Whatever I do with any guy, one of your friends or not, has nothing to do with you."

He scoffs. "Keep telling yourself that."

"You're delirious," I bite, hands balling into fists in my lap as I glare at him.

"No, I'm focused. You just haven't caught up yet."

"I don't plan to," I snap back, irritated with myself that my sass is revealing just how much he's getting under my skin.

Closing my eyes, I take a deep breath, trying to gather some self-control.

"I'm sorry I wasn't there."

My chest tightens at the sincerity in his voice, forcing me to look back at him again.

"It doesn't matter now. I already said that at breakfast. I'll get over it without your apology. It's just going to take a minute for me to realize it didn't matter." I lace my fingers together in my lap, attempting to offer a simple smile, but it just feels like my lips are set in a thin line.

"It did matter," he states, staring deep into my eyes as

I shake my head.

"It didn't."

"I was summoned by my mother."

"What?"

"I was summoned by my mother. That's why I wasn't there." He stares down at his hands for a moment before looking at me with a darkness in his eyes that I haven't seen before. "I was promised to Vallie when I was three years old. It's never been my choice, and I've never been given an option."

Wow. That's some heavy shit. Heavier than I can fully process right now, but I guess it all makes sense.

Patting my knees, I force my smile wider. "Okay. If you feel better for explaining now, you can leave."

He stands, disregarding the chair as he takes a step toward me. "I'm far from done, Adrianna."

I stand too, not liking his extreme height advantage while I'm still seated. "You're getting on my nerves," I grind out, desperate for him to leave.

"On your nerves or under your skin?"

Fucker. I shake my head. "You're unhinged."

"You're beautiful."

"Don't give me that shit," I grumble, inching toward the window when he takes a step toward me, eager to keep as much distance between us as possible, but he doesn't seem to get the memo.

"Is everything always a battle with you?"

"Maybe," I retort with a shrug, feeling the tingles of irritation curling up my spine.

"It's all you've known," he says soothingly as he takes another step toward me, and I quickly match him with a step back.

"Don't assess me."

"You don't want to know my assessment of you?" he asks with a cock of his brow, and I shake my head despite the curiosity creeping beneath the surface.

"Just leave, Raiden," I murmur, forcing myself to stand my ground as he takes another step toward me.

"No."

My chin tenses as he reaches out, his long fingers curling around my cheek. His breath ghosts over my skin as he stares deep into my eyes, penetrating my soul.

I can't think with him this close.

Pressing my palms against his chest, I do the only thing I can think of and push him away. He stumbles back a step, jaw ticking as he looks at me through his lashes. His nostrils flare, and a second later, he's charging toward me.

I brace for impact, acutely aware that I have nowhere to run, and my back collides with the wall, stealing my next breath.

His body touches mine, from head to toe, as he crowds my space, leaving nothing between us. Our chests rise and fall rapidly as we try to catch our breaths, but it's pointless. It's all pointless.

I don't know who moves first, but my concern for the matter quickly disappears as our mouths collide with force. Battling for control, I ball my fingers into his t-shirt as I attempt to draw him closer than he already is.

His tongue delves between my lips, taking everything from me as I battle to take a part of him too. With me tugging at his t-shirt, his hands move from the wall beside my head to my waist, clenching the material of my leggings so tightly it pulls against my skin.

Sinking my teeth into his bottom lip, I grin with triumph, feeling the upper hand within my grasp. However, he quickly regains control as he tugs hard and fast at my leggings, tearing them in two.

"Fuck," I gasp against his mouth, unable to catch my breath as he tilts my head back and kisses me deeper. I feel the cool air wrap around my legs, ghosting over my panties that shield my core as he turns his attention to my t-shirt.

The material snags from my body, along with my leggings, leaving me in my white bra and panty set, along with my sneakers and socks. Eager to even the score, I yank my mouth from his, attempting to catch my breath as I twist my hands further into his t-shirt before pulling as hard as I can. The telltale snag echoes through the air as I rip the red fabric from his flesh, revealing his toned abs and firm pecs.

Nobody should be able to make me this hot and mad at the same time.

"It's taking too long," he rasps, and before I can piece together what he means, he whips the rest of the clothes from his body, sneakers and all, before ridding me of anything attached to my skin.

Gaping at him, my chest and pussy exposed, I peer into his eyes with a sense of wonder I can't explain. We both stare at each other, unsure what the next move is, until I place my hand on his chest and he kicks into action.

I yelp as he hoists me up in the air, hands gripping my thighs as he leans me against the wall. If someone were to look up at my window right now, I'm certain they would be able to see his profile, but I don't care enough to move.

No words are spoken, no teasing or tantalizing touches, nothing. Just his cock at my core. His tongue sweeps over his bottom lip, mesmerizing me at the same time he lowers me onto his dick. He spreads me wide, taking his sweet time filling every inch of me.

My back arches off the wall, the moan from my lips low and feral as I cling to his shoulders, nails pressing into his flesh.

His jaw falls slack as he peers up at me, his long black eyelashes blinking as he shakes his head slowly. It's on the tip of my tongue to ask, but any hope of forming a question disappears as he slowly retreats from my pussy until only the tip of his cock remains before he slams deep inside of me again.

One thrust of his hips, followed by another, and everything merges into euphoria. My back arches to the point of pain as I try to grind against him, desperate and eager for every slam of his cock. Our movements turn savage, needy, and delirious as our bodies take over.

He takes. I give.

I take. He gives.

Sweat clings to every inch of my skin as the sound of his flesh slapping against mine fills the room.

The first tingles of my climax start in my toes, my muscles clenching as my jaw falls slack. I'm on the cusp of the greatest fall when he leans in closer, grazing his teeth over my throat while maintaining his unrelenting thrusts, and I see stars.

My cries ring so high, I no longer hear them as my pulse pounds in my ears while he fucks me through every drop of my orgasm. Just as my body starts to relent, his fingertips bite into my thighs, adjusting my position against the wall just a little before his movements become jagged and on the verge of violence.

"Fuck. Fuck. Fuck," he chants with every pounding of his cock before his head falls back and he finds his release.

The pulsing of his cock in my core makes my own

muscles spasm again, leaving me delirious as I cling to him, failing to catch my breath.

Slumping forward, he holds me in his arms, and a moment later, the press of the wall behind me disappears as he moves across the room, lowering me to the cool sheets on my bed. Blinking, I struggle to settle my gaze on him in my languid state as he brushes a loose curl back off my face.

"This makes you mine now," he breathes, making my back stiffen as I frown.

"It doesn't," I retort, trying and failing to push myself up onto my elbows.

I manage to focus my gaze just long enough to level my stare with his, to see him smirking at me with a whimsical glint in his dark eyes.

"Keep telling yourself that, but just a little secret between me and you," he breathes, peppering kisses all over my face. "When my mother summoned me, I told her I wasn't going to be a part of her deal with Vallie any longer because my sights were set on someone else."

My next breath lodges in my throat as I freeze. "No," I croak, making his grin spread wider.

"Yes," he replies, bopping my nose with the tip of his finger.

"No," I repeat, trying to get up, but he crowds my space, making it impossible to think, nevermind move.

"Yes, Adrianna. You're mine, and now everything my family has worked so hard for will unravel."

He can't put that on me.

"You take it back," I rasp, pressing at his chest, and he snickers.

"You love it, don't lie," he murmurs, dragging his nose over my throat.

"Raiden," I warn, but it falls flat.

"Adrianna."

"You'll be the death of me," I mutter with a helpless sigh, and he leans back just enough to catch my gaze.

"No, Adrianna, but *you* may quite literally be the death of *me* if they don't accept my withdrawal."

THE REIGN OF BLOOD

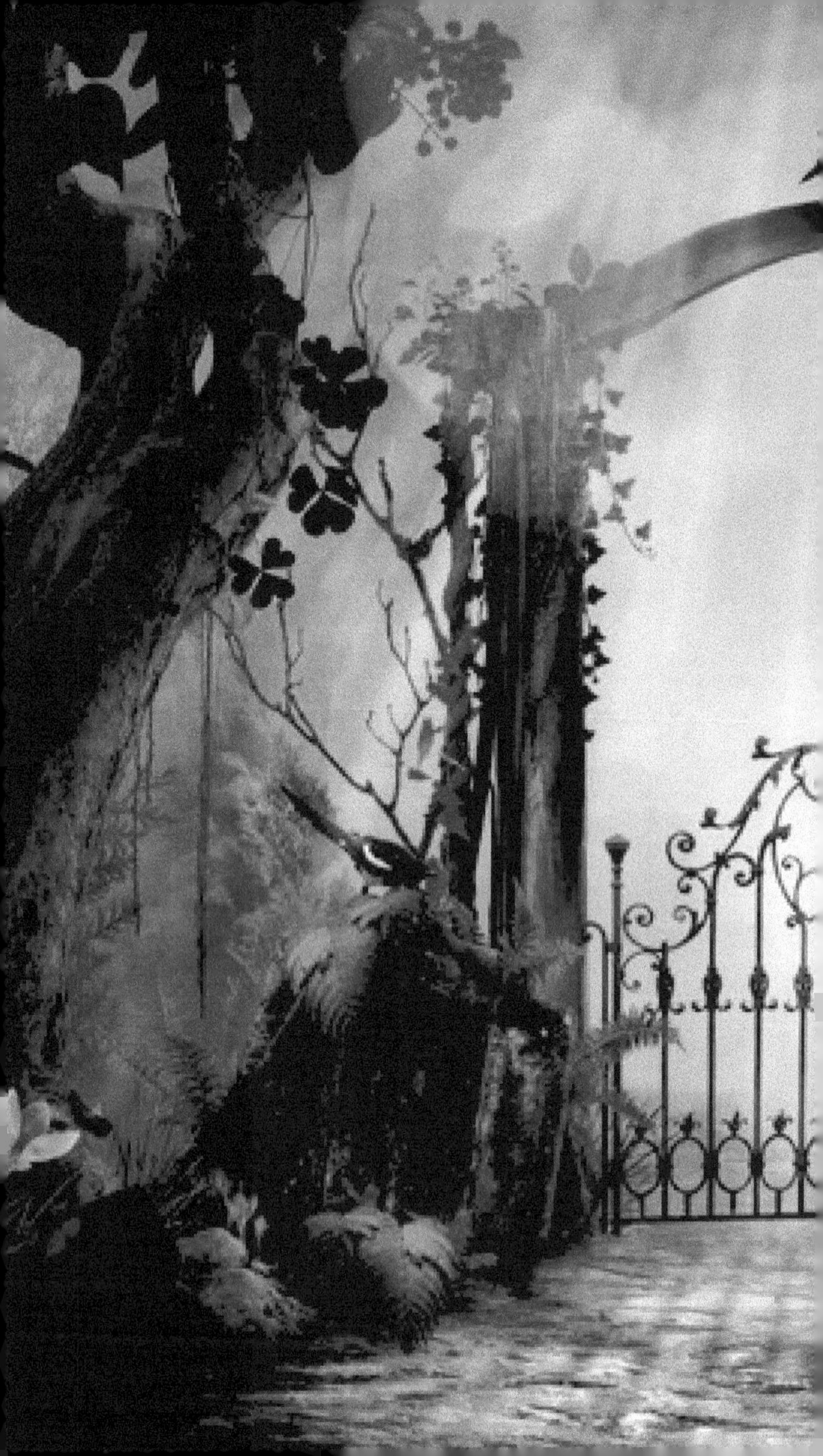

ADRIANNA

38

Sweat clings to my temples, gluing my t-shirt to my chest as my feet pound on the ground beneath me. The morning sun shines through the trees as I make my way back around to the fountain with just enough time to hurry back to the fae building, shower, and then head to breakfast before classes start for the day.

That's what my mind should be focused on, yet the tendrils of Raiden's words still burn through my thoughts. *You may quite literally be the death of me if they don't accept my withdrawal.*

Who fucking says that? Someone who believes it to be true. It's like I thought things couldn't get any worse, and yet he accepted the challenge to prove me wrong.

When I asked him to leave, he did. A little too willingly in the end, likely because he got what he wanted from me.

I can only hope that's what it is.

Shaking my head, I try to put that information away for later, but it plays on repeat in my mind as the fountain comes into view in the distance. As my steps begin to slow, the hairs on the back of my neck stand on end, the feel of eyes touching my skin has me on high alert.

Glancing back, I yelp, stumbling over my feet as I spot Raiden jogging behind me. His grin grows wide as he waves, making my eyes narrow before I take off running as fast as I can.

"Your ass is so hot from this angle," he hollers, and I stick my finger up at him over my shoulder as I grind my teeth and keep pushing. "The side boob from this angle too… fuck, chef's kiss," he insists, effortlessly moving to my side.

"Fuck off, Raiden," I snap, and he scoffs in disbelief.

"I'm keeping you safe."

"No. You're doing that stalker shit again," I retort, glaring at him, and he shrugs.

"You're welcome."

"I'm not thanking you."

"You should. There were two wolves planning to jump you at the fountain," he states as I slow beside the fountain in question. I shake my head, not believing his shit, as no one comes into view.

"No, there weren't."

"Round the other side, Adrianna," he murmurs, nodding for me to follow him.

My lips purse, my decline on the tip of my tongue, when I find Cassian standing over two girls sitting with their heads hung in shame.

Well, fuck.

Cassian doesn't pay me any attention. He keeps his voice low while speaking to the girls, and I gape in surprise. All I was trying to do was go for a run. Why can't I have a calm start to the day?

"You're welcome," Raiden murmurs, appearing right at my side a second later, and before I can respond, he presses his lips against my cheek. The spot warms at his touch, making my cheeks heat even further, and I take an instinctive step back.

I'm awake and out here at this time because of him and everything that happened last night, and here he is, still causing me drama in the morning.

Quickening my pace, I hurry to the fae building, refusing to look back over my shoulder for fear of seeing him follow me again. Thankfully, when I reach my level, he's not waiting by my door, so I hurry into the bathroom just like I had planned.

The door falls closed behind me as I brace my hands on the vanity. I peer at myself in the mirror as I try to catch my breath when the hinges creak. Anger vibrates through my veins as I catch another reflection in the mirror.

"You're pushing it, Raiden. Get. The. Fuck. Out," I snarl, my knuckles turning white as my grip tightens.

He purses his lips, considering his options, and I stand tall, whirling around with my finger aimed in his direction.

"Fine, but I'm waiting outside," he mutters, lifting his hands in surrender before I can say a word.

"As long as you're not in here, I don't care," I snap, chest heaving with every breath.

I need him to get the hell out right now before I start making stupid decisions again. True to his word, he slips back through the door, leaving me in the pits of silence, and I quickly move to turn the shower on, appreciating the melodic sound as I close the shower curtain and undress.

Maybe he isn't so willing to hear me out and back off. Maybe he isn't as done with me as I had hoped. I shake my head at myself, a tiny bud of excitement blossoming in my chest, and I don't like it.

Fuck.

Trying not to look over my shoulder with every passing moment, I go through the motions of washing my body and hair, increasing the temperature until it resembles the pits of Hell before I finally feel fresh and clean.

Reluctantly, I shut the shower off and step out into the main space, slightly surprised that he's still not in here. I spy my clothes in the far corner where I placed them earlier before I set off on my run and busy myself getting dressed as I conserve my magic to blow dry my hair.

I secure my hair in a braided crown, keeping it pinned to my head. It's a long process but it's worth it. I rake my eyes over myself in the mirror before I step out into the hallway.

"How are you dressed? I was waiting for the towel walk of shame," Raiden complains with his arms folded over his chest and a pout on his lips.

Rolling my eyes at him, I breeze past him without pausing as I wave him off.

"You can go now."

"I'd rather not," he replies, keeping a step behind me as I head for the stairs instead of my room.

"I'm heading to class."

"What about breakfast?"

"I can't deal with you right now," I grumble, shaking my head at him as I reach the bottom of the stairs, but no sooner do my feet hit the hardwood floor am I hauled in the air and tossed over his shoulder.

A few gasps ring in my ears, confirming we're not alone, but I can't see from this position, thanks to the asshole vampire lugging me around.

"If I don't get to eat you out in the shower like I wanted for breakfast, then you *have* to eat breakfast with me."

My cheeks heat and my thighs clench with desire.

"How does that make any sense?" I rasp, and he shrugs, jostling me on his shoulder.

"I never said it did."

"Can you put me down then?" I snap, willing to relent if he stops making a show out of me. "All of this tossing me over the shoulder and carrying me around like a rag doll is not doing my image any good," I add, frustration getting the better of me.

"You're right," he breathes, immediately lowering me to my feet before delicately kissing my temple. "Let's go."

I blink at him, stunned that he's actually listening. "Just like that?"

He takes my hand, and when I try to snag it back, he tightens his hold. "I'm a vampire, Adrianna; if I understand anything, it's maintaining an image."

THE REIGN OF BLOOD

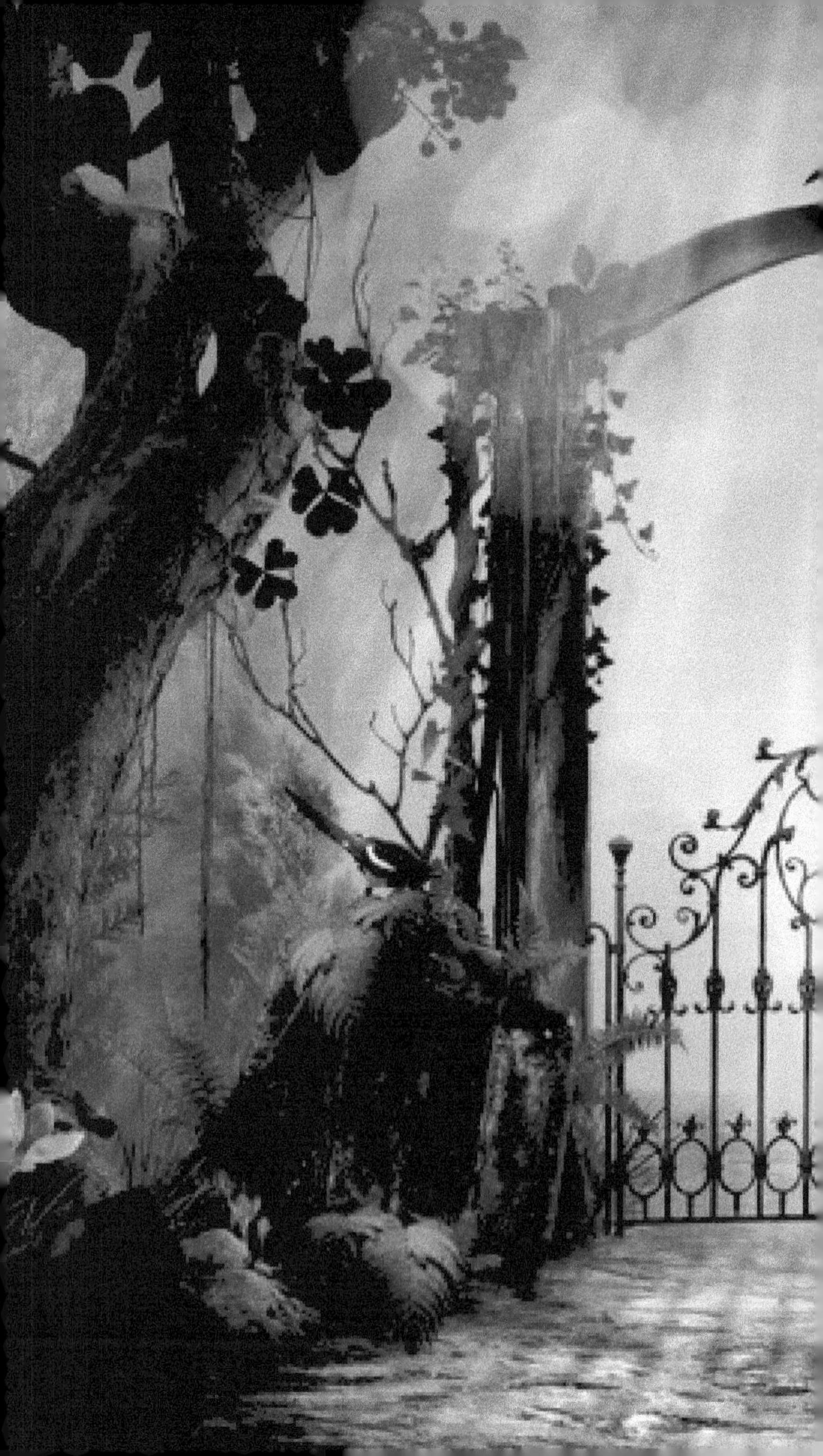

ADRIANNA

39

One class blurs into another and another, and thankfully, Raiden relents. A little. Much to Kryll's amusement. As I take my seat between the pair of them, my lunch tray in hand, I barely get my ass in my seat before they're both touching me.

I should push back, move, and get the space that my mind knows I need, but my body refuses, loving the warmth that surrounds me from both of them. Raiden's arm is around the back of my chair, laying claim to me for everyone to see, while Kryll's hand rests on my thigh, his thumb stroking back and forth discreetly.

Brody isn't missing out from across the table either, with his ankle pressed against mine, while Cassian excels at ignoring me like always. He's the whole reason I'm sitting here. I'm trapped in this web of desire because of him, forced at this table to suit his needs, yet he continues to ignore me.

Classic.

I should appreciate it. At least I can think in his presence.

"What has you glaring?" the wolf in question asks from across the table, eyes narrowed at me, and I shake my head.

"Nothing," I answer sharply, letting my cutlery clatter on my now-empty plate. Turning my attention to Flora, I nod to the exit. "Do you want to head to class?"

"Yes," she answers, rising to her feet with Arlo right at her side, and the second I stand, Raiden and Brody follow suit.

"I'm coming," the mage declares from across the table, making Raiden grumble.

"I was talking to my friend," I state slowly, pointing at Flora, and they both scoff.

"I can walk by your side, Adrianna, or do the whole stalker thing that you like so much," Raiden offers, causing my nostrils to flare with irritation.

More than that, I'm annoyed with myself for giving him the ability to wield such a threat over my head. Fucker. "Whatever," I grumble, rushing to Flora's side.

I link my arm through hers, the move feeling strange since it's usually the other way around, but she takes the hint and starts marching through the dining room. The chuckles that bubble from her throat make me give her the stink eye, but that only makes her laugh more, and she thankfully ups her pace.

Cutting through the grounds, I'm on edge, waiting for someone, Vallie specifically, to appear out of nowhere, jabbing her finger at me and causing more drama since Raiden hasn't been shy around me, but she's nowhere to be seen.

Something is coming from her, though. I know it. If what he said was true, if he's really backing out of their deal, she's going to have her sights set on me even more than before.

"Come in. Hurry. We're taking a little field trip, and the quicker you all gather, the quicker we can get there," the professor calls out from the door to his classroom, waving everyone inside.

"Field trip? Yes, please," Arlo says, rubbing his hands together as he slips into the room ahead of us. Flora rolls her eyes at him, but there's still something in her gaze that hasn't shifted since I first saw it.

Friday can't come soon enough, and hopefully she will be comfortable enough to confide in me, and I can pretend to have my shit together enough to be of help to her.

Filing into the room, no one takes their seats since we're not staying. Raiden, Brody, Kryll, and Cassian are right behind us. Smoldering gazes turn to irritated glares as I glance between them before turning my attention to the professor.

"We're going to spend the afternoon where you all really want to be. Can anyone tell me where that is?"

"The beach?" Grant hollers, high-fiving his friends, who chuckle at him.

"Nice try, but no," the professor replies with a sigh. "Anyone else?"

"The castle," I breathe, chest tightening at the thought as the professor nods in agreement.

"Exactly. Now, pair up. Don't make me do it for you," he grumbles, adjusting the glasses on the bridge of his nose.

Arlo instantly drapes an arm around Flora, tugging her into his side, leaving me to stare at the three guys looking at me.

Brody. Raiden. Kryll.

I twist my lips, my pulse quickening as I take in their intense looks, but before I can think better of it, I sidestep them all and brush my shoulder against Cassian.

"You're being my partner," I declare, not actually looking at him, and I feel his stare on the side of my face.

"I am?"

"You are," I repeat, not backing down. The fact that he doesn't immediately shove me away feels positive.

"Do I want to know why?" he asks, and I shake my head. "Amuse me," he pushes, and I know he won't relent until I do, so I give in quicker than I would like in order to get it over with.

"You're the only one that's going to give me a minute to breathe." I can feel my blood pressure rise, my face tingling with the sensation as he scoffs.

"Please, girls love the attention."

"Girls also like it when you're not a complete asshole one hundred percent of the time, but what would I know?" I retort, finally turning to him with my eyebrow raised in question.

He offers me a pointed look in return. "I thought you came here for peace?"

"Then shut the fuck up," I grumble, turning back to the professor.

"Okay, if we're all ready… perfect. We won't be using magic to transport us this afternoon. We have legs, and there's no reason we can't use them," he explains. "Besides, I feel you get the true effect of Floodborn Castle when you approach it from the City of Harrows on foot," he adds, his eyes glazing over with a wistful gleam.

Surprisingly, no one argues as we follow him out onto campus and toward the main gates. I chance a glance over my shoulder to see Brody and Kryll have paired up, leaving Raiden to be with… fucking Vallie.

I watch as she tries to grab his arm and he swiftly moves it out of her reach, making her pout, but he doesn't see it; his sights are set on me. He gives me a dark, pointed look as if to confirm that it's my fault he's having to deal with her, and I quickly turn back around, refusing to acknowledge any more drama from him today.

We take our time leaving the campus and entering the City of Harrows. Passersby stop and stare at us, the colors of our cloaks making us stand out, and the murmurs of the Heir Academy students being among them ripple through the city like an undercurrent.

Once we reach the other side of the city, a long, windy path comes into view and my steps falter. The professor was right. The view of the castle as we take the sloped path is breathtaking and completely overwhelming all at once.

Its jagged peaks, the long and thin windows, and the stained glass that decorates each window are spectacular.

I feel breathless as we approach the large, arched, black, wrought-iron doors of the castle, and it's not from the incline to get up here. No. It's the fear of what lies inside.

Will I remember any of it?

Do I want to remember any of it?

I won't know until I step through those doors, but I can't deny the panic that threatens to make me run in the opposite direction.

"I'm glad you're all still with me," the professor states, turning to face us. "When we step inside, I will offer a guided tour through a few parts of the ground floor and take you to see the royal suite upstairs. After that, you'll have some time to explore the halls yourselves, but I swear to you, if anything is damaged by any of you, I'll wipe the mess up with your damn head. Do you understand?"

Agreement parts everyone's lips as we nod in understanding before he takes a step back and opens the doors with a flourish.

Following the crowd inside, my heart thunders in my ears as I step over the threshold of the castle with a silent Cassian at my side. My gaze darts around the open entryway, trying to recognize anything, but I come up empty. Our footsteps echo off the floor as we follow the professor through the wide hallway until he moves into a room on the right.

My gut twists and a sense of disappointment washes over me as I try with everything that I am to remember something… anything.

"This is the kitchen. It looks like any kitchen really, likely on a much grander scale, of course, but otherwise, it services the castle just as any kitchen does," the professor explains, waving his arms around the dated space. Dark wood cabinets line the walls, with a matching small table tucked away in a small nook. Chrome fittings have started to rust since it has sat here unattended for so many years, and the windows along the far wall are so dusty you can barely see through them. "What sets this kitchen apart are the secret passageways that lead from this room. The entire castle is riddled with them. Can anyone spot an access point?"

Everyone's gazes dart around the room, looking for something. Everyone except the man beside me. "Show me."

I blink at Cassian, who raises a questioning brow at me, and I shake my head.

"I can't remember anything," I breathe, shuffling around the gathered students to try and get a better look as a few others do, but still, nothing stands out.

"Princess Adrianna?" the professor calls out, making the hairs on the back of my neck stand on end at the formal address, and I turn to face him with a forced smile.

"Just Addi is fine," I reply as calmly as I can. A few students curse slurs under their breath, but I try my best to ignore them.

"Can you show us one?"

Fuck.

How hadn't I considered that he would do that? Pressing my lips together, my eyes dance around the room. I can't come up empty-handed, I can't look weak right now, and I already feel vulnerable enough being inside these walls without any recollection.

Silently pleading with the castle before me, I beg for something to reveal itself.

My feet carry me toward the small table and chairs set up in the nook. My fingers run over the side panel of the wall instinctively, and it almost feels as if I've done that before. Inching closer, I feel a little wiggle room behind the board and press my palm firmly against it in the bottom right corner.

At my touch, the panel swings open on hinges, revealing a small passageway you would have to crawl through. Relief seeps from my shoulders as the professor claps, making me cringe.

I might not know where it leads, but I seem to be more in tune with the castle than I initially thought.

"Excellent, Addi. Let's continue to the ballroom, shall we?" The professor exclaims, pointing for everyone to step back out into the hallway.

"I thought you couldn't remember?" Cassian murmurs, appearing at my side, and I shrug.

"I couldn't."

"You're telling me that was a lucky guess."

"I'm not telling you anything because you wouldn't believe me anyway," I grumble, rolling my eyes at him as I follow the crowd.

The ballroom is very similar to the one at the academy,

large, grand, and luxurious, but it needs some tending to in order to restore it to its former glory.

From there, we swiftly move into the meeting room. Parchments are still stacked on the huge table in the center of the room. Chairs are scattered, not tucked in, with a few overturned. Crimson stains mark the wood at the head of the table where the king would sit, and my blood runs cold.

Nothing has been moved since it was last in use, which would mean it hasn't been touched since my father was here. My chest aches, it's clenched so tight. I instinctively take a step toward the blood stain, but a hand on my arm halts my movement. Peering over my shoulder, I frown at Cassian, who shakes his head.

"Don't hurt yourself by going there, Alpha," he rasps. I press my lips together, uncertainty tormenting me as I consider his words.

If I go down there and get a closer look, all I'm going to do is feel rage and anger over something that happened a long time ago. Going down there will reignite a fiery vengeance that doesn't need any more fuel as I tread a fine line of remaining a civilized fae. If I go down there, everything I've worked so hard to achieve will shatter.

He's right.

"Please get me out of here," I whisper, hating how vulnerable my voice sounds. If he notices, he doesn't say a word as he pulls me toward the door. I slump against the wall outside, my heart racing in my chest as I gather myself. "Thank you."

"Don't mention it."

I take a deep breath, standing tall again as I roll my shoulders back just as the professor steps back into the hallway.

"Let's take a look at the royal suite before you explore on your own, but remember my warning," he calls out, heading back to the front entryway where the grand double staircase leads to the second floor.

I run my hand over the banister as I head upstairs, no memory coming to mind, not even as we trek down the hallway to a set of double doors at the very end. My lips twist as I consider if it's worth stepping in there, knowing it was my father who occupied those four walls last. As the professor opens the doors, I calm a little when I realize it remains tidy and untouched. No remnants of a struggle or blood tainting the space.

"This will be the king or queen's bedroom when the time comes. Embrace it." His eyelids fall to half-mast as he takes a deep breath in through his nose, dropping his arms at his side. "We shall meet back at the main doors in one hour. Don't touch anything," he orders, dismissing everyone.

Stepping away from the room, I press myself against the wall, letting everyone else pass as I exhale slowly. "You can do as you please," I murmur to Cassian, who shrugs.

"I'm good."

I don't answer, looking at the other doors that line the far wall to my right. I come to a stop outside of one that hasn't been opened, and a human rolls their eyes at me. "That one doesn't seem to open," she grumbles, and I nod, but I can't help but run my hand over the wooden panels that decorate it.

There's something about it that just—

My hand grazes over the door handle, and an audible clicking echoes around us before it falls open.

"You just unraveled some magic right there," the girl whispers in awe. "Do you think… do you think that could have been your room?" she adds, eyes wide as I gape at her. It's only when Cassian steps between us, effectively dismissing her as he grips my chin and turns my face up to look at him that I remember to breathe.

"Do you want to go in or not?" he asks, searching my gaze for the answer my mouth can't find.

Running my tongue over my bottom lip, I nod subtly before pressing my hand against the door. My gaze darts around the room, a sense of familiarity vibrating through my bones as I step into the space, and Cassian is quick to follow after me, shutting the door behind us so no one can follow.

That girl was right. This was my room. Not just mine.

Nora's too.

My father has mentioned so many times before that our love for one another is rooted in the castle. Our friendship and bond wasn't strengthened because of our trauma; it was already there. All the rooms in the castle and we wouldn't sleep unless we were in the same one.

Moving into the center of the space, I cast my eyes over everything. It's like yin and yang. One half is smattered in pinks and purples, color popping everywhere, from the bed sheets to the children's colorings pinned to the wall. While the other half is bleaker. Blacks, whites, and grays. Pictures of soldiers and past monarchs are framed on the walls over gray bed sheets, and I know exactly whose side was whose.

I'm drawn toward Nora's bed, the pink floral-patterned sheets pristine despite how long it's been. Whatever magic was protecting this room was clearly working in more ways than one.

Running my fingers over the bedding, my heart feels like it's about to burst, and I all but collapse onto the bed, trying to catch my breath.

"Are you okay?" Cassian asks, but any snarky response I have for him is halted as my eyelids fall closed and a memory flutters to my mind.

Nora is laughing beside me, kicking her legs gleefully as my chest aches and a similar laugh explodes from my lips.

"I'm coming to get you."

"Quick, Nora. Under the covers," I order, trying to calm my laughter to help her tug the sheets back, but it's not as easy as I hope.

"I can hear two little flowers chuckling. Is it you?" The woman's voice is full of joy, playfulness, and... love. "Here I come in three... two... one..."

Just as soon as I tug the cover over our head, it's ripped away, and we squeal in delight. Delicate fingers tickle at our tummies, making us writhe beneath her, and I blink up to see the wide eyes of my mother.

Opening my eyes, I lurch from the bed, my heart galloping so wildly in my chest, I'm certain I may be sick.

"Addi?"

I find Cassian blinking at me in confusion, a hand outstretched toward me, but I'm so overcome with the emotions weighing heavy on my chest that I can't form a response.

Swiping at my cheeks, I'm not surprised to feel them wet, but it doesn't stop the embarrassment from consuming me.

"Alpha?" Cassian pushes, taking a step toward me, but I quickly move away from him, rushing to the window. There, I plant my hands on the ledge, my chin dropping to my chest as I try to calm the swell of pain and allow the sense of happiness to take over.

I take a deep breath, then another, and another, but they're short, sharp pants that do nothing to settle the storm inside of me.

"Addi, breathe," Cassian murmurs, stroking small circles at the base of my spine, and I shake my head.

"Can't," I croak, making the panic rise even more.

"You can," he insists, spinning me to face him. I'm helpless in his grasp as he reaches for my hands. Silently, he places one against his chest, right above his heart, while he circles the other around his throat.

I frown at him in confusion, unable to form a question, but I don't need to. I can feel the rhythm of his heart beating beneath my palm. My hand at his throat feels the rhythm of his breathing as his pulse pitter patters against my skin.

"Let's get you out of here," he murmurs after a while, and I nod in agreement. "Do you want to walk, or do you want me to make it quick?"

"Quick," I rasp, unable to fix my eyes on a single thing in the room now.

At my request, he rushes us outside. Glancing around at the open space, I take a more clearing deep breath as his hands remain at my waist.

"I used the back door to avoid the gathering crowd," he murmurs, spiking my heart rate as I take a look at where we are—where we *really* are.

The tree line in the distance garners my attention immediately as my throat bobs and a pained cry parts my lips.

"What's wrong?" Cassian asks, grabbing my chin to force my face to his, and my eyes widen in panic.

"It was here. It was here," I chant, barely louder than a whisper, as terror floods my veins.

"What was?"

I shake my head, covering my ears, unable to answer, but the moment his eyes flick to my ears, I know he knows.

"Fuck," he grunts, pressing me to his chest again before he takes off. We don't go far. He stops by the front doors of the castle, pressing his forehead to mine as he sighs. "I'm sorry, I didn't know."

"I know," I murmur, my breath becoming jagged again, and he strokes a hand down my back.

"Just breathe, Addi," he says soothingly, just as he did upstairs, but the overwhelming bubble of emotion subsides.

"I'm okay," I breathe, and he leans back to peer into my eyes.

"Are you sure?"

I nod, my mind in a state of chaos with everything, but I know one thing to be certain more than anything. Turning my attention to Cassian, I exhale slowly as I try to find the words. "I want to see my mother."

"You want me to call my father?" he asks, brows

furrowing in a mixture of surprise and confusion.

"No," I breathe, shaking my head, and understanding flickers in his eyes.

"Incognito?"

"Yes."

He stares at me. Like *really* stares at me before he nods. "I can make it happen."

"When?"

"Tonight."

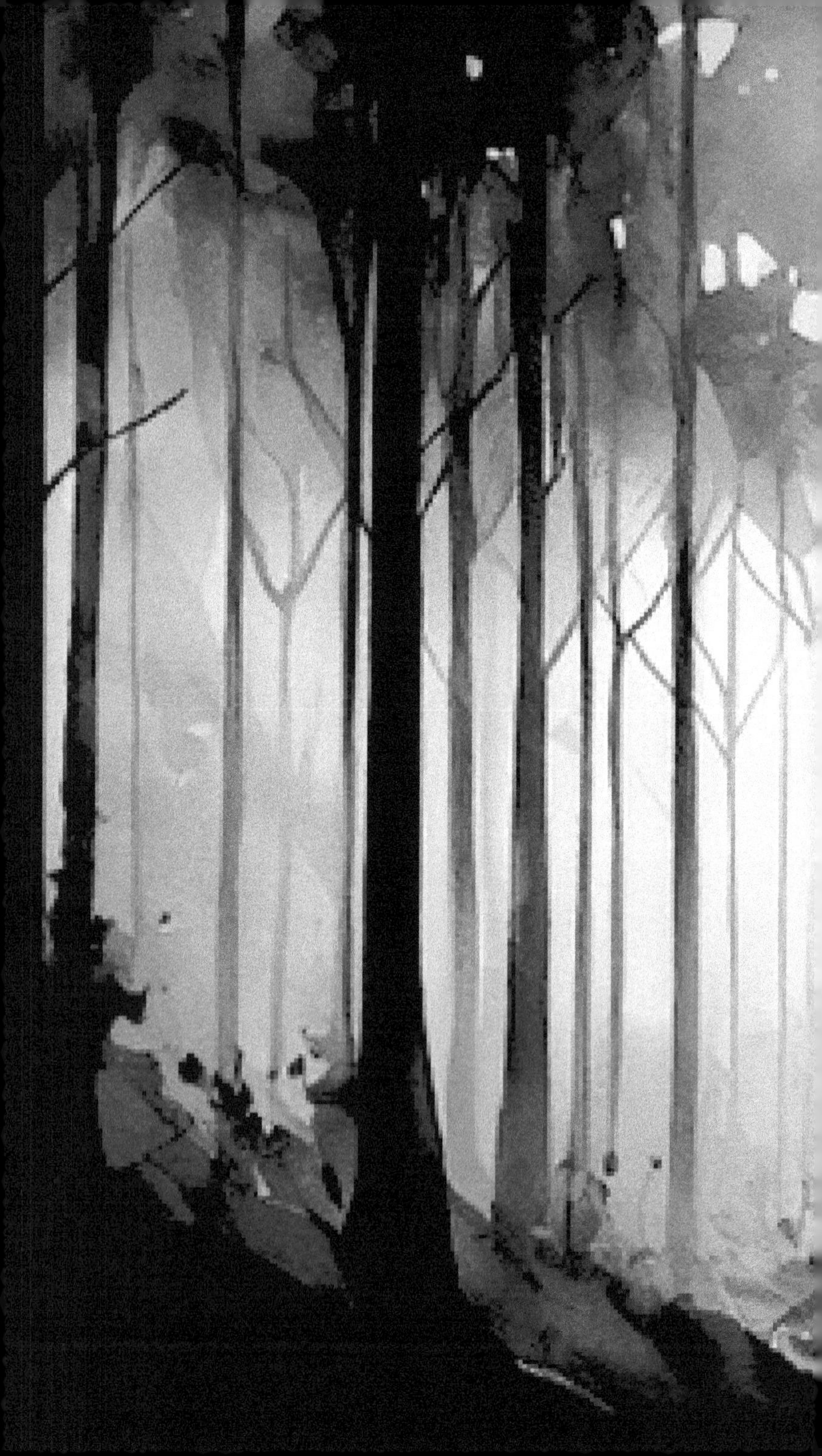

CASSIAN
40

"Where are you going?"

As far away from your nosey ass as possible.

"It's none of your business," I grumble instead, avoiding his gaze, but I can hear him tapping his finger on his chin as his eyes bore into the side of my head.

"Which means it has something to do with Adrianna," he declares, and I catch him pursing his lips out of the corner of my eyes.

Who knew the asshole vampire had a soft spot deep, *deep* down somewhere, and more than that, who knew it would make its appearance for a fae girl? Not just a girl, a princess. It's fitting for him, really.

"I said it's none of your business," I repeat, tugging on my leather jacket.

"Does it have something to do with her crying at the castle?" he asks, folding his arms over his chest. *He caught that, huh?* "Actually, what do you know about that?" he pushes, walking around me so I can no longer avoid his gaze.

"Nothing," I murmur, only partly lying as I sidestep him, gaze set on the door.

I reach for the handle, breath lodged in my throat, but before I can wrap my hand around it, he curls his fingers around my arm, forcing my attention to swing to him.

"You're not going to hurt her or put her in danger." It's not a question. It's a statement—no, a demand, one he wants me to follow.

"It's not currently my intention," I manage, giving him a pointed look that hopefully makes it clear that this conversation is done.

"Don't try me, Cassian. Just because we haven't officially claimed her doesn't mean I don't feel it in my veins," he grinds out through clenched teeth, and I shake my head at him.

"Whatever," I grunt, grabbing the handle and swinging the door open as his hold loosens.

"Cassian," he warns, but I'm already gone before I have to deal with another word. The wind whips around me as I rush to the fae building. I slow as I reach the front door, taking a moment to push Raiden to the back of my mind so I can focus on tonight.

It's easier said than done when he's such a constant headache.

Stepping inside, a few fae startle when they see me, but once they realize I'm heading straight for the stairs, they relax. Not completely, not while I'm still in their space, but enough. Taking the steps slowly, I remember what tonight is about.

The last thing I want to do is step foot on the Kenner compound, but after seeing the pain radiate from her today and the sudden bubble of horror that parted her lips when I took her to the spot where my father attacked her, I couldn't deny her.

There's not much I can offer her, but this? I can give her this.

I don't know what triggered her in her room, and I didn't want to push, but I get the feeling that it's what gave her the desire to see her mother. To understand? Maybe. I hope she doesn't have high hopes for a positive outcome. Nothing of the sort ever happens on the Kenner compound.

Reaching her floor, I'm standing in front of her door before I feel ready, but there's nothing I can do about it when she swings it open a split second later.

She looks just like she did when I walked into Janie's diner a few weeks ago. Her hair is pinned to her head and her face is void of makeup. She wears black combat pants and a white t-shirt held in place by a corset lined with daggers. Two more are clipped to her boots, and I am slightly impressed. Even with the black cloak that's draped over her shoulders.

There's no denying that danger could find us, and she's prepared, but it's my job to make sure that doesn't happen.

"Ready?"

"Yeah," she breathes, taking a deep breath as she nods, assuring herself as much as she is me.

She steps out into the hallway, rubbing her lips together nervously as her scent weaves around me.

Fuck.

Wiping a hand down my face, I turn for the stairs, needing a minute to fucking think before I slam her into the communal bathroom. Again.

Dammit.

That sounds more tempting than it should.

I don't wait for her as I race down the stairs. The fae in the lounge panic at my approach again, but I step out into crisp night air before they can get too twisted in knots over it.

Surprisingly, Addi is right behind me, body stiff as she comes to a stop before me. My hands fall to her waist on instinct, pulling her in tight as her hands lift to my chest, her fingers playing across my t-shirt as we stare at one another.

I hate that she can say so much without saying a single word, but more than that, I hate that my body reacts to her, no matter what. She could hold one of those silver daggers to my throat and my dick would still get hard.

"Are you going to start moving?" she asks, eyes dark as she looks up through her lashes at me. It's not my fault her scent is intoxicating at this close proximity.

"I was just giving you a second to prepare," I mumble, and she gives me a pointed stare.

"Right."

I start moving before she can say anything else, confirming things about me that I don't want to admit. Because she would. She's a no-holds-barred woman, and I know, if given the chance, she would make a damn example out of me.

Relishing in her body pinned to mine, I bring us to the outskirts of the compound more quickly than I expected. I release her from my grasp, despite the desire to pull her in closer.

She adjusts the cloak draped around her, lifting the hood over her head, shielding her features from view.

"Keep a step behind me at all times. Follow my directions and don't question a single thing I say. Understood?" She nods, not uttering a word. I consider pushing her for a verbal answer, but something tells me she's keeping her mouth shut so I don't get a blast of her razor-sharp tongue at my demands. "Come."

I stay in the shadows, and as agreed, she stays a step behind me. We have quite a walk on our hands, but I didn't want to risk drawing any attention by getting closer. She doesn't utter a word of complaint as we trudge through the deserted land on the Kenner compound. Trees, shrubs, and overgrown grass are all that surround us. It's my wolf's favorite place to be, even if it is the ugliest thing to look at.

The first house comes into view, and I make sure I walk the long way around it, careful not to set off any security features that I know of. Reaching out my hand, I wrap my fingers around her arm as I come to a stop, closing my eyes to listen to the noises around me.

Families are in their homes, some putting their children to bed, others bickering about inconsequential shit. All of it means nothing until a name is murmured.

Queenie.

It might be nothing, but it's the best lead I've got.

Meeting Addi's gaze in the darkness, they somehow still manage to twinkle under the moonlight. I nod, hinting for her to follow me as I release my hold on her arm, and she falls in line once again.

Inching closer to the house in question, I pin my back against the wall and Addi follows suit.

Thankfully, it's quiet tonight, but that's why I offered it. My father has dealings on Tuesday nights on the other side of town. That means wolves will either be with him or patrolling the perimeters, leaving the interior a little more accessible for us.

I wet my dry lips and peer through the window to my right. Dalton, my father's right-hand man, comes into view, and he's not alone. Right there with him is the woman we're looking for.

Turning back to Addi, I nod toward the window and trade positions with her. She keeps herself pressed against the wall, and I can hear a shift in her heart rate as she takes a little peek through the window.

"Does my woman need a foot rub?"

"I'll never say no to one," Queen Reagan breathes a heavy sigh.

Addi's hand lifts, clamping over her mouth as she takes another step toward the window. I give her a moment. It's clear her mother isn't sad about being here. I don't know whether she hoped she would be or not, but those groans are of a satisfied woman as Dalton kneads his thumbs into the soles of her feet.

"I love you, Queenie."

"I love you too, D."

Addi's gasp rings in my ears, but it's quickly overshadowed by the snap of a twig beneath her feet. My body dives into high alert, pulling her back as I take off as fast as I can. There's no time to think, to consider, to wonder. There's only time to get the fuck away as fast as possible.

I run until the familiar lights of my favorite diner come into view, not stopping to catch my breath until I hear the chime ring out over the door, confirming my arrival. Eyes dart my way, but my focus is on the woozy fae in my grasp, who is turning greener with every passing second.

"Deep breaths, Addi," I murmur, stroking her arm in comfort, and she scoffs.

"It's embarrassing how many times you've said that today," she muses, eyes pinched shut. She silently lifts her hand to my throat while resting her other palm right above my heart. My throat clogs with undeniable feelings as she repeats the same motion I had her do earlier.

It must have worked for her then, and she's leaning into it now.

Fuck.

"Hey, is that my favorite asshole?" Janie's voice pulls me from my thoughts, and I peer over Addi's shoulder to find the woman in question. She frowns, clearly noting the state of me before she points over her shoulder. "Take a seat. I won't be a second."

I nod, focusing back on Addi, who seems a little more at ease now. Wordlessly, I take her hand, tugging her along with me as I move to my usual booth. Waving for her to take a seat, I drop down into the spot across from her with a heavy sigh.

"Are we safe here?" she asks, nipping at her bottom lip nervously as she looks around the room.

"We are. My father is on the other side of town tonight, but if you would prefer to keep your hood up as an extra layer of defense, then that's fine," I breathe, keeping my voice as low as possible, and she nods. "Are you okay?" I ask, hating the words as soon as they leave my mouth.

"Fuck knows," she admits, head tipped down to look at her lap.

I can't read her without seeing her since she's mostly hidden behind the cloak. I don't like it.

"Choose something to eat and drink, and then you can talk through it," I state, hoping she doesn't argue because I can't leave here without talking to her. I can't.

Janie appears a second later, a concerned look on her face, but I shake my head, unable to share whatever this is with her. Despite her eyebrows pinching, she relents, a soft smile gracing her lips. "What can I get you guys?"

Addi looks up at her with a smile of her own. "Can I have the steak, please?"

"You liked it last time, huh?" Janie says with a widening grin, and Addi's cheeks heat.

"It's about the only reason I'm not mad about being back here," she admits, making Janie snicker.

"That makes sense. And to drink?"

"Something strong," she mutters, causing Janie's eyebrows to rise to her hairline, but she doesn't say a word as she turns to me.

"Usual?"

"Always."

"I'll have it out to you as soon as possible."

Just as quickly as she came, she disappears. Addi clears her throat, eyes fixed on mine. "She's nice."

"Sometimes," I grumble, and Addi cocks a knowing brow at me, making me roll my eyes. "All of the time," I admit, and a victorious grin curls the corner of her mouth like she just convinced me to reveal my deepest, darkest truth. Clearing my throat, I tap my fingers on the table as my knee bounces. "So, do you feel better or worse?"

"I feel numb," she admits, avoiding my gaze as her lips twist. Her eyes glaze over like she's lost in thought before she shrugs, ridding the emotions from her limbs. "She clearly wants to be there. She's in no need of being saved."

"How does that make you feel?" I ask, focusing on my breathing while keeping my eyes trained on her.

She leans forward, bracing her elbows on the table as she rests her chin on her palm. "I had a memory of her today, one I had completely forgotten until I stepped into that room again. She was happy, caring... everything you could wish for. Yet she gave it all away for a foot rub."

Fuck. When she puts it like that...

"I'm sure there's more to it than that, though. More you're not aware of," I offer, and she sighs.

"I agree, but I don't think I care to know," she admits, a tinge of defeat creeping over her as she shakes her head.

"About that," I murmur, leaning back in my seat as I try to keep myself as relaxed as possible.

"About what?"

My tapping quickens, giving away my nerves, so I quickly pull my hands into my lap, but it doesn't stop my knee from bouncing incessantly. "Did you notice?"

"Notice what?" she asks, tilting her head at me as her eyebrows pinch in confusion.

I search her eyes, unable to find a single hint of a lie in her words, which means I'm going to have to spell it out. Clearing my throat, I lean forward, matching her posture with my elbows on the table, but instead of resting my chin on my palm, I lace my fingers together, bracing for impact.

"Your mother, Queen Reagan, her ears weren't pointed, and I didn't see any scars."

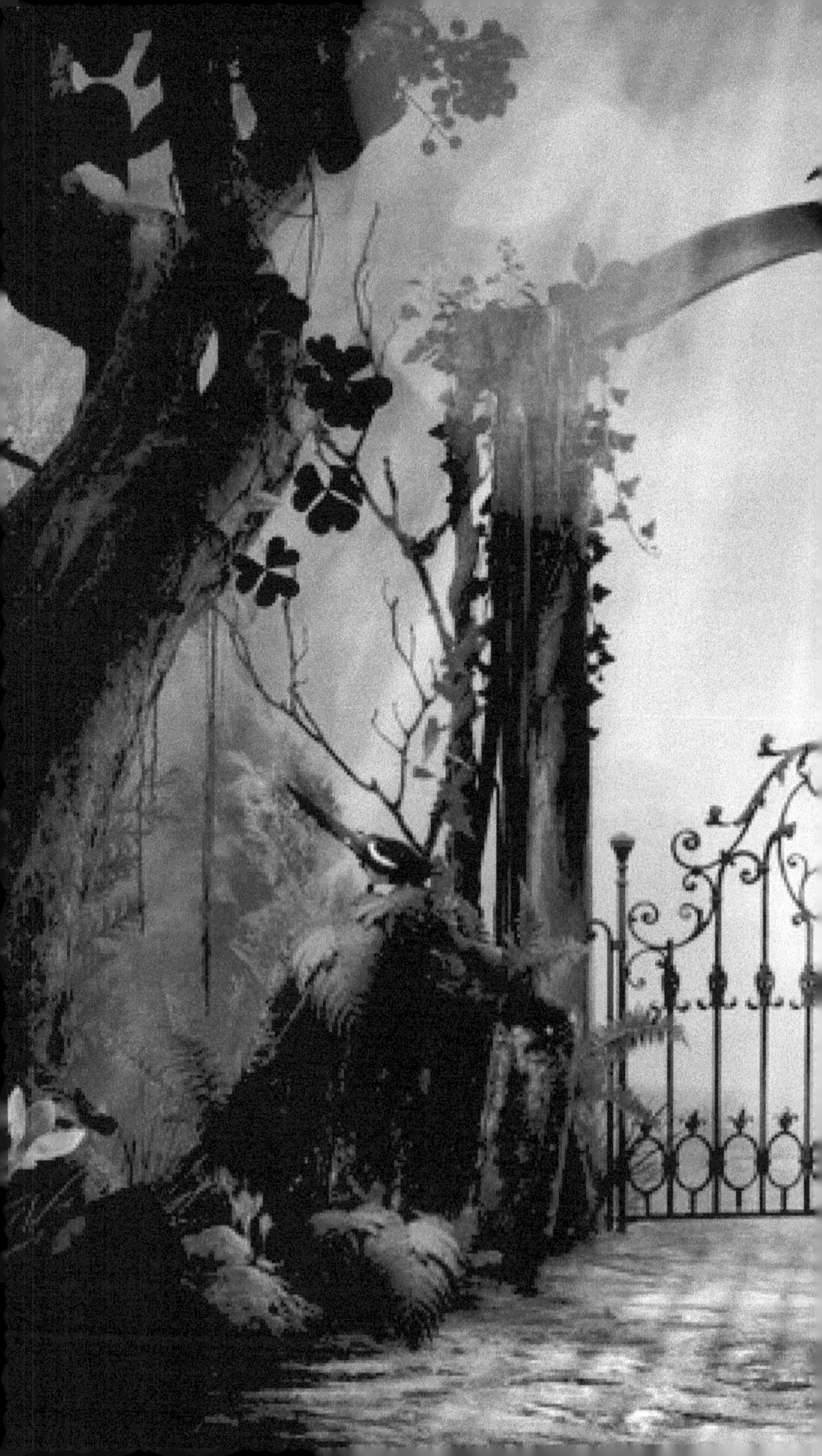

ADRIANNA

41

Her ears are not pointed. Her ears are not pointed. Her ears are not pointed.

What the fuck is that supposed to mean? I wrack my brain, desperate to revisit the memory that plagued me at the castle today to focus on her ears, but I come up empty. I try to recall what she looked like the first time I saw her on the Kenner compound, but I was too shocked to see her to even consider looking at her ears.

Fuck. Fuck. Fuck.

Thankfully, Cassian doesn't press me further. I think it has something to do with the fact that I literally felt the color drain from my face as I gaped at him in horror, confirming that the truth that just slipped past his lips was something I had no recollection of. I would call it the truth, but I'm going to have to see it myself to believe it. The gruff expression on his face tells me we won't be going back there tonight.

We eat our food in silence, the steak cheering me up a little as I continue to get lost in my mind. When I'm done, I set my cutlery down and avoid his gaze. I need to go home and wrap my head around what happened tonight. It was already bad enough that she was so… happy, carefree, and relaxed. She's no damsel in distress. She's where she wants to be, and that only confirms the taunting thoughts in my mind; she's happy without me. Without us.

I'm tough. I'm strong. I've been through enough trauma to fight off anything that comes my way, but there's a part of this that hurts my soul in a way I can't fight off. I need to talk to my father, but that's going to take some courage-building first.

"Are you ready to leave?" Cassian asks, and I dare to meet his gaze. There's no anger there, no distress, and it settles a small part of me as I nod. He stands, and Janie appears out of nowhere the second he does.

"Going so soon?"

"I don't want to risk the wrath of my father right now," he states, and I know that's not the truth; he just doesn't want to point the finger at me.

"Keep your chin up, Cass. This is a fucked up mess. Just focus on what you set out to do today, okay?" she breathes, wrapping her arms around him in a brief hug before she turns to me. "And you, keep being the badass bitch I know you are." I gape at her, but she doesn't see because she's too busy treating me to a hug too. It's only a second, but it does something to me. It makes me stand taller and embrace the *badass bitch* she thinks I am.

"Thank you," I mutter before following Cassian outside.

The night air has grown cold, and I wrap my cloak around me the best I can.

"Do you want to walk for a while or speed?" Cassian asks, and I sigh, reluctance getting the better of me.

"I need to be away from this compound, so speed it is."

He wraps me in his arms without missing a beat, and before I can brace for the move, he takes off. Pressing my head against his chest, I try to focus on my breathing to calm the nausea that threatens to overwhelm me.

We come to a stop sooner than I expect, and I'm relieved to find that I don't feel as terrible as I did earlier. Maybe that's because my body is already dealing with enough stress, and this pales in comparison, or maybe I'm getting used to it.

Taking a step back from him, I note we're by the fountain, the exact one he was at this morning dealing with two girls who Raiden said were planning to attack me. *Bitches.*

"Thank you," I breathe, a soft smile gracing my lips,

and he shrugs, the leather jacket flexing around his arms as he does.

"Don't worry about it," he insists, and I nod. Exhaustion clinging to me when he reaches for my arm, pulling my gaze to his. "What's that look?" he asks, tilting his head at me as his gaze narrows on mine.

"What look?"

"That one." He lifts his hand, stroking his fingertip down the side of my face as I sigh. "You're distant and hazy. It's not something I've seen in you before," he assesses, and I hum in acknowledgment as I avoid his gaze, hating the inability to hide my vulnerability right now. "I don't like it."

I blink up at him. "What?"

"I don't like it at all," he repeats, and before I can understand a single thing he's talking about, he grabs my waist, lifts me in the air, and unceremoniously drops me in the water fountain.

I stumble, landing straight on my ass in the water, and it sloshes up in the air, sprinkling down on me for extra measure, along with the water already pouring from the top of the damn thing.

I'm drenched, right to the bone.

"Oh my... what the fuck, Cassian?" I yell, anger vibrating through me as he stares down at me with the biggest fucking grin on his face.

"There she is."

That fucker. That absolute fucking fucker.

"I'm drenched," I exclaim, not caring how late it is or how loud I'm being.

"So am I," he retorts, and I quickly realize through my furious haze that he's in the fountain with me, the water pouring down on him as he smiles from ear to ear.

Who the fuck is this guy?

I shake my head in disbelief. "That was dumb," I grumble as he offers me his hand and tugs me up to my feet.

"No."

"No?"

"That wasn't dumb, but this is," he breathes, pinning me to his chest, and before I can question what he's talking about, he crushes his lips to mine.

I melt into him, clinging to his dripping wet jacket as he brings one hand to my throat and the other cups my pussy through my pants.

Holy. Fuck.

That move, that *fucking* move.

Fighting for control is futile. He's in charge; all I can do is succumb to his touch. His mouth claims mine, his palm grinding against my pussy as my nipples pebble, brushing against his chest.

I need him. I need him right now. I don't know whether

it's the raw desire for him that courses through me or the need for a distraction from the night's events, but I can assess that in the morning. Right now, all I can think about is feeling him.

"Don't fuck me here," I mutter against his lips, the thought of all this water makes me shudder as he leans back enough to meet my gaze.

"But somewhere?" he confirms, and I nod.

"Somewhere."

I'm bundled against his chest again, and we're moving in the next moment. I hear a door slam shut behind us as his scent envelops me, and I know without looking that we're in his room. I don't get a chance to see, though; he fills my entire field of vision. His hands move to my face, cupping my cheeks as our breaths mingle between us.

Tugging at his leather jacket, it's so wet that it doesn't budge, but I have no patience for snags like this. I need to see him, feel him, and I need it all now.

I take a step back, causing his brows to knit in confusion, but I don't bother to explain. Swiping my hands between us, I grind my teeth as I let my magic drift through the air, despite the gem on my back causing a strain. It feels like necessary magic right now.

The air swirls around us, whipping every wet piece of clothing from our bodies. With a slap, they land on the floor at our feet.

"That's embarrassingly hot," he mutters, kicking his shoes and socks off as I do the same. My magic can't do that, not while we're standing anyway. He makes a dramatic show of slowly rolling a condom down his length with his gaze fixed on mine.

I shake my head, unable to find the words as I rush at him. He catches me, wrapping my legs around his waist as I twine my arms around his neck and claim his lips. Heat burns over my skin in the most delicious way as desire fuels my every move.

He spins with me in his grasp, dropping us onto his bed with a gasp as his lips trail from mine, down my throat, and across the swell of my breasts. My back arches as goosebumps dance over my skin, elicited by his touch, confirming to him just how much I want this.

Stroking a hand down his chest, I blindly reach for his cock that's pressed against my thigh, but he grabs my wrist before I can make it. Heated eyes find mine as his tongue sweeps over his bottom lip.

"We're not rushing this," he rasps, pressing little, teasing kisses on the tips of each of my fingertips as I try to catch my breath.

"Rushing is all we know," I rasp, blinking at him as he slowly lowers his lips to my nipples, swirling his tongue around the taut peaks. I gasp, my back arching as my fingers find their way into his hair. "Please," I beg.

The inferno inside of me is incapable of dealing with the teasing. "Enjoy me next time, but right now, please, I'm begging you... fuck me."

His teeth sink into the sensitive skin around my nipple, quickly turning my gasp into a low moan as he adjusts his cock at my entrance. "Are you promising me another time?"

"You're the one who always rushes off," I retort, raising my eyebrow at him. He chooses that exact moment to thrust deep into my core.

The stretch is on the brink of pain, but the euphoria that tingles through my pussy makes it all worth it. "I'll fuck you hard and fast now, but you stay the night, and come morning, I get to feast on you," he states, cocking a brow at me. I nod, too focused on my pussy clenching around his dick. "Say it, Alpha. Tell me you'll be here in the morning," he grinds out, rolling his hips in the most delicious way as my fists cling to the sheets beneath me.

"I'll be here," I breathe, earning a quick thrust from his hips that spreads my thighs wider.

Fuck.

"Where will you be, Alpha? Tell me."

"I'll be here. In your bed. In the morning," I pant, my moans growing louder as his hips move at a more punishing pace.

It's too much and not enough all at once.

"That's it," he rasps, grabbing the back of my thighs and throwing my legs over his shoulders as he pistons in and out of me at a perilous rate.

My chest clenches tight, my face heating as my toes start to tingle.

He leans closer, perspiration clinging to his temples as he looks deep into my eyes. "Soon, Alpha, *real* fucking soon, I'm going to take this pussy of mine with nothing between us. Do you hear me?"

I clench around him, despite my mind screaming in denial, but I know he feels it because his pupils dilate beyond return and his fingers dig deeper into my flesh.

"Repeat it to me, Addi. Make me come with the words on your tongue, and I swear to take you over the edge with me."

My throat clogs, my brain trying to refuse the words, but my body wants the promise and I'm too caught up in him to deny the inevitable. "You're going to claim me, Cassian. Mind. Body. Soul. Just how you want. You're going to make me yours and fill my pussy with your cum."

"Fuck. Fuck. Fuck," he chants, his moves jagged as he chases his release at the same time he presses his thumb to my clit. It's like a trigger.

I detonate at his touch, just as he promised, before the world goes black.

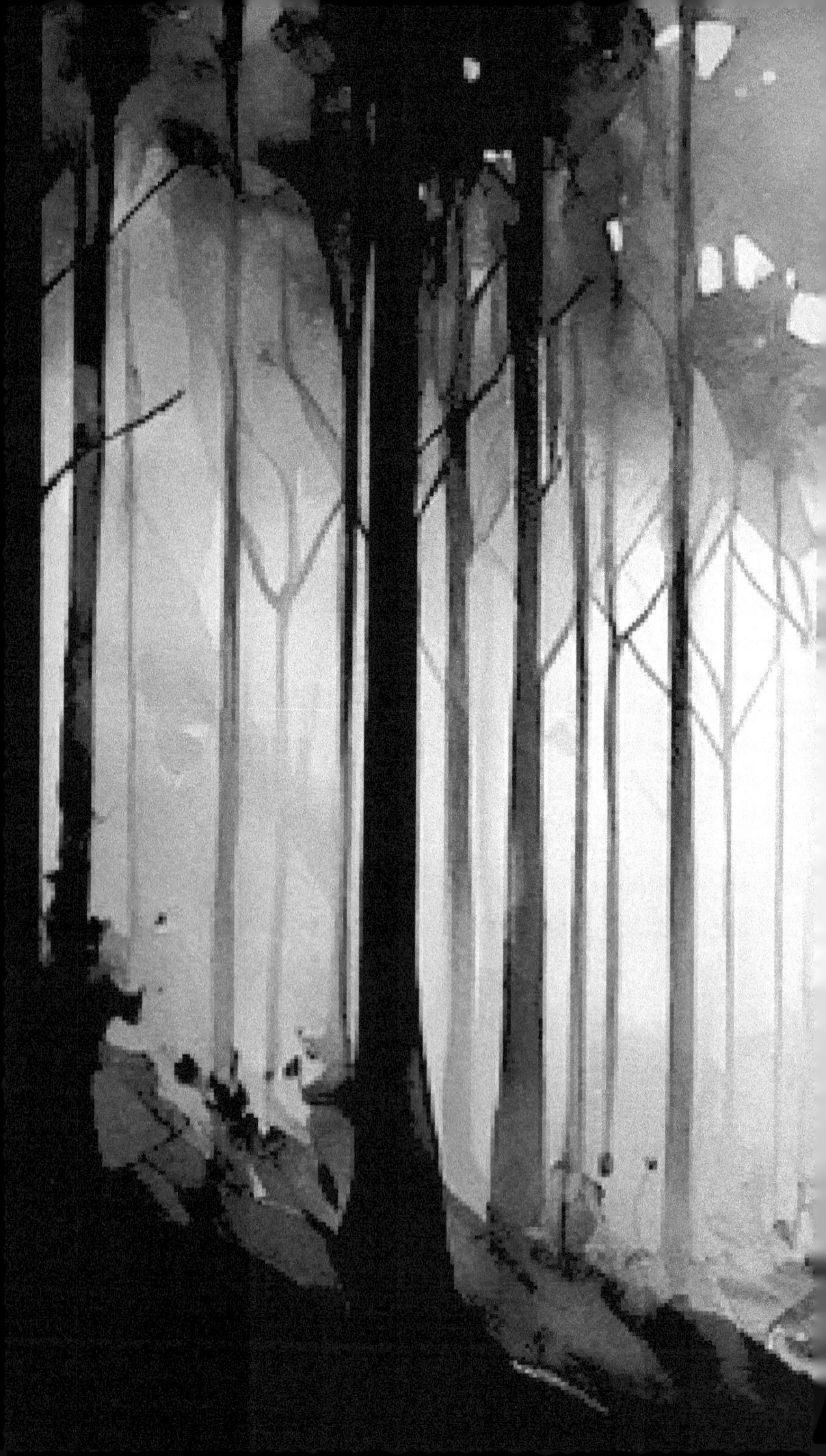

KRYLL

42

Mornings are my favorite time of day. Watching the sunrise, the rays of light breaking through the clouds, feels like I'm in another world. There's no distraction, no pressure, no drama—nothing but you, the sun, and every single one of your breaths.

Thinking about it, we're cut off from a lot of that at the academy too. We don't have to watch our every move, worrying some frenzied vampire or unhinged wolf is going to attack us. They're not the only ones, of course, but that's what I spent the most time dealing with outside the relative safety of these walls.

The frequency in which I received a message from Raiden or Cassian asking for help with a situation was weekly, on both ends, yet since we've been here, we've only had to help Raiden once.

Has it calmed down? Or is his family not keeping him in the loop anymore? He told me what he said to his mother, breaking the promise their families made. That could be part of it, maybe, but to everyone else, they're living in ignorant bliss behind the walls of the academy.

From here, my favorite view of the City of Harrows, with the castle in the distance, nothing looks out of place, but maybe that's because the dawn wards off the evil that lurks in the night and the day hasn't begun enough for the meek to step from the safety of their homes.

Taking a deep breath, I wipe a hand down my face. It's never good for me when my head starts to swim like this, with all of the possibilities and unknowns. It's against my nature to worry about anyone other than myself and my close family members, but after you've slayed origins of all kinds to protect the kingdom, you can't help but grow attached to it.

My heart clenches at the thought of something else I'm growing attached to. Or, more specifically, someone.

Adrianna Reagan.

I refuse to admit it to the others when I struggle processing it myself, but I can't stop thinking about her. The last time I was here, it was in her company. She was mesmerized by the view, just as much as I was with her, and I let it slip, let the truth barrel from my lips. Yet she didn't run.

It's a clue, really, a part of my creature. I will only be blessed to fuck the woman my creature lays claim to, and holy fuck, I think I'm feeling it when I'm around her.

My alarm buzzes from my cell phone, reminding me that I need to head back before I'm late for breakfast. Glad for the distraction, I charge toward the opening of the cave, freefalling through the sky before I shift in the air. My wings spread wide, my fingers stretch into claws, and my soul settles.

I hover high above the city below, gliding toward the academy far too quickly for my liking, but excitement buzzes through my veins at the thought of swooping past the fae building on my way to food.

It comes into view a few minutes later, and I dive down to get a closer look. She hasn't caught me looking yet, and I don't plan on her finding out, but watching her wake in the mornings is one of my favorite things to experience.

She should probably learn to close her curtains, but I won't be the one telling her that.

Hovering close to her window, I frown, my gut clenching when I don't see her there. My creature goes on high alert, my pulse thundering through me as I take to the skies again, eager to find her scent.

Lowering myself, I take a deep breath as I land on top of the wolf building, desperate to calm the panic growing inside of me so I can focus on finding her. Blinking my eyes open, I exhale slowly as a thread of her scent lingers in my nose.

It grows stronger, and when I peer toward the fountain and its surrounding pathways, I'm left speechless. I watch in surprise as she drapes a black cloak around her body, her head tipped down. To anyone else, nothing is out of the ordinary, but to me, it's the opposite.

She's not on the fae pathway to my right, although I'm sure that's where she's heading.

No.

She's hurrying down the path from the wolf building.

Cassian.

I watch her the entire time, all the way until she slips into the fae building, and the second she does, Cassian steps out of the building beneath me. Disbelief courses through me, but it's not the kind that's laced with disappointment. It feels more like hope.

Not wanting to be caught, I take off for the main academy building, landing on the patch of grass just off the pathway so I can shift back. Thankfully, I put my uniform on before I set off this morning, so I ruffle my fingers through my hair and head inside without missing a beat.

Brody is already at the table in the dining hall and I take my seat across from him with a yawn. He manages a wave but focuses on his food, and a moment later, my plate is placed in front of me, too.

I mumble my thanks, but my attention is on the wolf in question as he saunters toward the table with an extra bounce to his step.

"What's got you so happy?" Brody asks, assessing the same detail as me, and Cassian grunts in response.

"I don't know what you're talking about."

"What are we talking about?" Raiden asks, dragging out his seat and sitting with a huff. It doesn't help that he's so dramatic with the damn red cloak. He flicks and whips it everywhere like he's royalty. It's irritating as hell.

"We're not talking about anything," Cassian grumbles as the servers bring both his and Raiden's food.

"He seems chipper," Brody explains, wagging his fork at him.

"Are you sure?" Raiden retorts with a confused look, and I snicker.

"I would actually have to agree," I add, which gets Raiden's attention because usually, I would keep the hell out of this kind of stuff.

"I don't know what any of you are talking about, and you're giving me a fucking headache, so can we just eat in silence?" Cassian snaps, nostrils flaring with irritation, and I grin.

He clocks it, his jaw ticking ever so slightly as I lean back in my seat.

"I think it has something to do with a fae princess

leaving the wolf building this morning."

Cassian curses me out under his breath as Brody and Raiden kick into action, peppering him with questions he definitely doesn't want to answer. I wink at him as he glares daggers at me, but I'm up on my feet before it goes any further.

"I'll meet you all at combat. I need to speak to my brother," I holler, but they wave me off without a backward glance, too busy interrogating the lucky wolf.

I'll miss sitting beside Addi this morning, but I really do need to chat with my brother. I need someone to vent to about her, someone who might understand, so I can make sense of it all.

I keep my head down and trudge across the grounds, finding him already at the combat setup.

"Hey," he hollers, spotting me immediately and waving me over. "You're early."

"Yeah," I breathe, speechless now that I'm actually here.

My brother frowns at me, inching closer as he wipes his hands over his combat pants. "What's going on?" he asks, and I shrug, earning a pointed look from him. "Well, I can't help you if you can't give me anything to go on," he states, folding his arms over his chest, and I sigh.

"I kissed her. *Kissed* her, and I can barely contain myself," I blurt, turning away from him as I scrub a hand over the back of my neck.

"Who?"

"That part doesn't matter," I grumble, huffing in irritation at myself. I'm making it worse and I just need to spit it out. Settling my gaze back on him, I take a deep breath, exhaling slowly before I find the words. "I think she's the one."

He nods slowly. "You think?"

I pinch the bridge of my nose. *Fucker.* "I know."

"How? Tell me."

I wet my lips, searching my mind for the right words to explain any of this, but I fall short, just like I have since the moment I showed up here. "It doesn't matter. I shouldn't have come," I decide, taking a step back, but he's at my side in the next moment.

"Kryll, right now, I'm just Beau, not Professor Tora, not a member of the academy. I'm just your brother. Something is bothering you. Let me help."

Some of the weight straining my shoulders shifts as I look up at him. "I know she's the one, I can feel it inside of me, and my creature doesn't wreak havoc on me in the same way as it usually would," I ramble, sure I'm not making any sense.

"You're serious," he murmurs, eyes wide in surprise, and I nod.

"Deadly."

"I'm here for you, brother. Whatever you need. Condoms, or—"

"Shut up, Beau," I snap, shoving at him, and he chuckles as he lifts his hands in surrender.

"What? That's a brotherly thing to do."

"I'd rather you didn't."

"So, are you going to tell me who it is?" he asks; at the exact same time, a bubble of laughter echoes from behind me and my head whips around to find Addi heading toward us with Flora and Arlo. "It's the princess."

I spin back to him, my heart racing in my chest as his jaw falls slack. "Fuck. Of course, it is," he mutters under his breath, making my spine stiffen.

"What's that supposed to mean?"

"Nothing," he replies quickly, waving me off, but he must sense that it does nothing to quell the concern burning through my limbs because he takes a step closer, planting his hand on my shoulder as he sighs. "Your heart knows what your heart knows, brother. Or the heart of your creature does, and we both know it will never be wrong. I just hope it doesn't lead you into the depths of somewhere you can't return from."

THE REIGN OF BLOOD

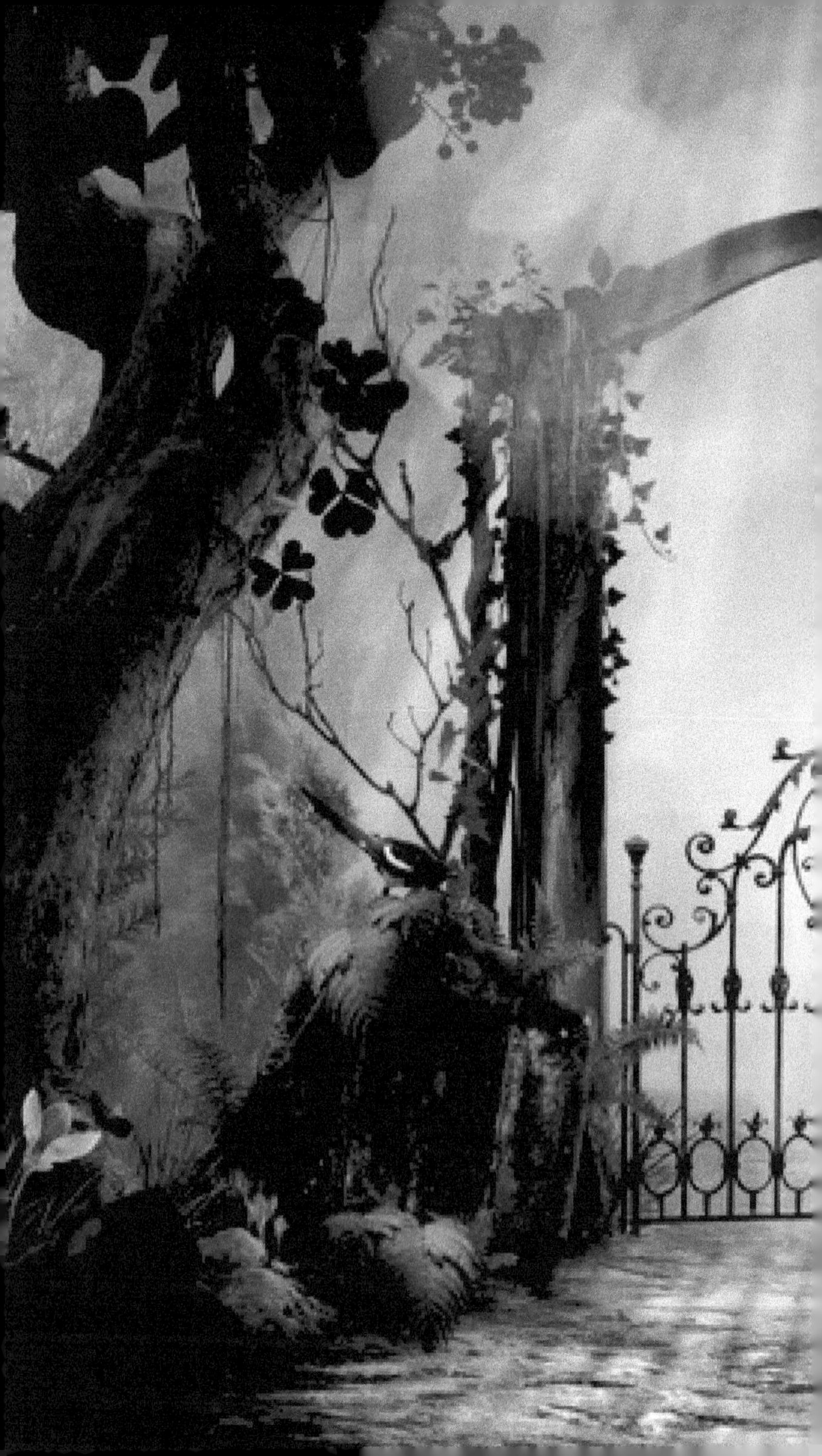

ADRIANNA

43

I stayed the night at Cassian's. I stayed the *fucking* night. He also kept true to his promise this morning, and my thighs are still relishing the most delicious ache. Scurrying back to my room this morning, I was mortified doing the walk of shame, but thankfully I didn't bump into anyone.

The embarrassment stayed with me, though, and I couldn't face showing up for breakfast this morning in fear of how anyone would react if it was brought up. So, I snacked on a cereal bar from Flora and decided to head straight to my first class.

As I step across the combat field with Flora and Arlo, I can feel eyes on me. With one glance, I spot Kryll and his brother, Professor Tora, with their gazes zoned in on me.

I raise an eyebrow at him as we near, but he shakes his

head subtly before turning away with a soft smile on his lip.

"What was that about?" Flora asks, smirking at me when I fail to give her my innocent look.

"I have no idea," I admit with a shrug, moving to join the other students who begin to gather.

"Well, just so you know, I have managed to get my hands on some moisturizing face masks, nail polish, and fluffy slipper socks for Friday night," she explains, changing the subject, and I stare at her like she's just grown a second head.

"I think I should have had a warning before I signed up for this," I muse, and she waves me off.

"I did warn you, but I'll take your place," Arlo offers, a longing look in his eyes as he stares at Flora, but she quickly shuts him down.

"Nope. Girls only."

He takes a step closer to her. "Does that mean you're going to talk about me?" Amusement ghosts over his lips as his eyes darken just a little.

"Why would we talk about you?" she asks, planting a hand on her hip as she gives him a pointed look.

"You know."

"Oh, so you're acknowledging it now?" she scoffs, and all I can do is gape at her and her sass right now.

Arlo's face falls as he takes another step toward her,

but before he can get too close, she waves him off, leaving the two of us to get some space.

My eyes are trained on her as I speak to Arlo. "Should I be concerned?"

He clears his throat. "No."

I cock a brow at him, giving him my best *don't fuck with me* look.

"Fuck, Addi, I—"

"Gather 'round; there's no time to waste when we're about to do a practice trial run," Professor Tora declares, interrupting Arlo's words.

"Save it for later," I murmur, waiting until he nods in agreement before I slip off to stand with Flora as Tora continues to explain.

"We're doing a what?" someone asks, and the professor rolls his eyes.

"We're going to do a test run of a trial," he explains, and even Kryll's eyes are wide in surprise, confirming he didn't know about this either. Holy fuck. This is kind of exciting. "So, gather 'round. We're wasting precious time," he adds, summoning everyone closer.

He wasn't joking when he said now that the ball had come and gone they would be upping the trial preparation.

"What did I miss?" Brody asks, suddenly appearing at my side with a grin. His smile is too infectious, and I can't help but grin back at him, but I quickly remember that there's more going on right now that needs my focus.

"Practice trial," I murmur, feeling a presence behind me. When I peer over my shoulder, I find Raiden looking down at me with a heated glare. Cassian stands beside me, but his gaze is fixed on Tora, paying me no mind.

For some reason, it makes my shoulders relax; feeling him act no differently reassures me of… something. I don't know what, but I like that he still remains himself, even after moments like last night and this morning. He's still a gruff asshole through and through.

"The aim of the trial is to find your way to the center," Tora explains, making everyone frown.

"The center of what?" Kryll asks, sauntering toward us with an arched brow.

"I'm glad you asked," Tora replies, nodding to someone off to the side. I think it's a mage professor. My thoughts are confirmed when the ground rumbles beneath our feet a moment later and a hedged maze appears before our eyes.

"There's a central point to this. You must work independently. Touch the token in the center and it will escort you back here. Only so many will appear, though. So if you're unfortunate not to find one, you'll have to walk your ass right back out the way you came, so I hope you remember the path you took."

"That sounds too easy," Vallie says with a snicker, eyes sparkling with a level of chaos that seems to be her specialty.

"That's probably because I haven't finished explaining," Tora retorts, giving her a pointed look, but she doesn't falter. She somehow stands taller as her friends fawn and giggle over her attitude. I still bite back a smile at the fact that Tora doesn't take her shit. It's refreshing. "Once in there, you'll face obstacles, hurdles, and challenges in the form of… each other. It's a race; get there first."

"And what are the rules for us with each other?" Cassian asks, folding his arms over his chest, but Tora simply shrugs.

His nonchalant approach sets my heart racing, and I instantly feel gazes turn my way.

He just put a target on my head for Vallie and her friends, along with at least half of the female wolves and everyone else who doesn't like that I'm the spawn of the old fae king.

My excitement for the trial quickly dies down, the adrenaline pumping through my veins fixated on getting through this as quickly as possible.

"Are we allowed weapons?" I blurt, needing verification, and Tora scoffs.

"I don't give a fuck."

I nod.

It is as if I knew this was coming when I put daggers beneath my clothes today, in case something backfired from last night at the Kenner compound.

A siren blares before anything else can be said and everyone takes off running. I stutter for a second, gaping at the carnage as people trip each other up and clamber over one another to enter one of the openings in the tall hedges.

This is so fucked.

"Aren't you going?" Tora asks, cocking a brow at me, and I scoff.

"It's not tactful to run into chaos mindlessly," I murmur, making him smirk. He nods, a flash of respect gleaming in his eyes.

"Survive, and I'll make sure that remark is put next to your name in a positive light," he states, catching me by surprise, but I don't respond as I start toward the madness. "Oh, and Addi," he hollers, forcing my gaze back to him. "Be careful with my brother."

I frown, confused by what that means, but I really don't have the time to process it right now. Shaking my head, I up my pace toward the hedges.

Stepping between the tall shrubs, I'm alarmingly aware of how much sunlight they block out. They're literally everywhere. This is going to be far from easy, even without the impending inevitability that someone is going to jump out and attack me.

Remaining alert, my hands fall to my waist, ghosting over the daggers pinned to my body as I walk to the end of the pathway. Noise and cries ring from the left. Do I follow the noise because they've figured it out, or do I attempt to take the quieter path?

A snap of a twig from behind me catches my attention and I whirl around, instinctively tugging two daggers from their holsters, but I seem to startle the human more than they have me. He halts, hands raised as he nods to the left. I don't utter a word, and he takes that as confirmation that I'm not going to attack him. He's gone a second later.

Taking a deep breath, I keep my daggers in my hands. One silver, one steel. With my mind made up, I move to the right. I manage to take four turns before I reach a dead end. Backtracking, I take a left where I had previously gone right, and it leads me down a long walkway. It feels like it goes on forever, and by the time I reach the turn at the other end, I realize I must be on the other side of the maze because the sun is no longer behind me.

I roll my shoulders back, taking in my options, and opt to move to the left since that should bring me closer to the center of the maze.

Three turns.

Dead end.

Backtrack.

Right instead of left.

Success.

Four turns.

Dead end.

Backtrack.

Left instead of right.

Success.

Fuck. This is insane. I do like that it's a solo trial though. We're meant to make it to the end by following our own gut, not relying on someone else's.

A bursting sound echoes in the distance, and I look up just in time to see a girl go hurtling through the air. My eyes widen in horror until I realize she's fae, and she did it to herself, aiming for the center.

Holy. Fuck.

Get a grip on yourself, Addi. Use your magic.

Exhaling sharply, frustration bubbles inside of me. I delve into my magic, trying to connect with the earth beneath my feet, but it instantly takes its toll on me.

This fucking kiss of amethyst.

Surviving this trial isn't about being the quickest; it's about following your gut and leading yourself to victory so you will, in turn, lead the kingdom to success. I mean, that's how I see it, but I could be completely off.

Does that mean I should use my magic to speed the process up or not?

Fuck.

Maybe I do need to think smarter, otherwise I'm going to be in here forever.

I tuck my daggers away before dropping to my knees.

I swoop my cloak aside, feeling the gem nestled into my skin.

When my father told me what to do, it sounded too simple, but I tried it that night.

The pain. Fuck. The pain.

My muscles bunch together in anticipation, instantly reconsidering what I'm about to do. Is it worth it? Fuck. Yes.

Scrunching my eyes up, I take a deep breath as my fingers skim over the amethyst, wreaking hell on my body.

Three… two… one…

"Ahhh!" I cry out through gritted teeth as pain exudes from every fiber of my body as I twist the gem.

"A kiss of amethyst can be removed, Adrianna. You yourself are one of three people alive who can do it. Only royal blood can remove such a treacherous curse, but no one but myself and Fairbourne know that. Hold that knowledge close to your chest. It won't be nice, and the pain will be excruciating, but you can do it. Use this knowledge to your advantage, though. Let them believe they have a hold on you."

My father's words echo in my head as I bite back the final whimper of pain and the gem falls into my hand.

How can something so sweet and delicate elicit such treacherous pain?

Tucking it into my pocket, I keep low, making sure

no one is nearby as I plunge my hand into the ground. I connect with the earth so quickly and powerfully that it fills me with relief and emotion.

I take a moment, embracing the magic that dances through me, so carefree, before I summon it to do as I request.

Bright green vines rise from the ground, a stark contrast to the darkness that consumes the maze. They light up a path that I know will lead toward the center of the maze. Slowly standing, I brush my hand over the first vine, watching it retreat at my touch, before I take off, repeating the same with each one I pass, not meeting a single dead end until I see a token in the distance.

Relief and pride blossom inside of me, but despite the euphoria, I take a step back, making sure no one is around as I pull the gem out of my pocket.

Fuck.

I really don't want to, but—

"There she is."

I stiffen at the sound of Vallie's voice, quickly stuffing the gem back in my pocket as I turn, but it's too late. Her vampire speed catches me completely off-guard, sending me tumbling to the ground with a thud.

She lands on top of me, pinning my arms and legs beneath her, a sinister look in her eyes, and before I can even buck my hips to get her the fuck off me or channel the air around me to push her away, she sinks her teeth into my throat.

A roar of pain burns from my throat, the feeling excruciating as it consumes me, rendering me helpless. The pain is blinding. My body wants to give in to the toxins that fill my veins, but I refuse. This isn't my time. Not yet.

Flailing my arms, I claw and fight her before I remember my daggers. Squeezing my hands between us, I manage to blindly tangle my hand through my cloak and t-shirt, wrapping my fingers around two hilts.

I don't think, and I can't see, so I swing with purpose and hope for the best.

"Ahh, you bitch," Vallie screams, her teeth finally leaving my flesh.

I swing again and again, her shrill voice tainted with horror with every passing breath, and I don't stop until she says nothing at all. She falls limp on top of me, and I shove her off with what little strength I have left.

Agony explodes through me as I try and fail to blink my eyes open.

I need to get out of here. I need to get to the token.

Rolling over, I push up onto my hands and knees, blindly crawling through the dirt as I let my magic dance over the surface, praying I can make it.

I'm ready to give in, to lay here and let the world take me when I reach out my hand one last time, only to feel something in my way. Running my hands over it, my heart quickens, hope blooming inside of me as I wildly flail my hand around until I feel it.

The ground shifts beneath me the second I connect with the token, but it doesn't ease the agony that consumes me, the terror of what will happen to me. It all stays. Even as I feel the sun beat down on me once again.

"What the fuck? Dagger, is that you?"

THE REIGN OF BLOOD

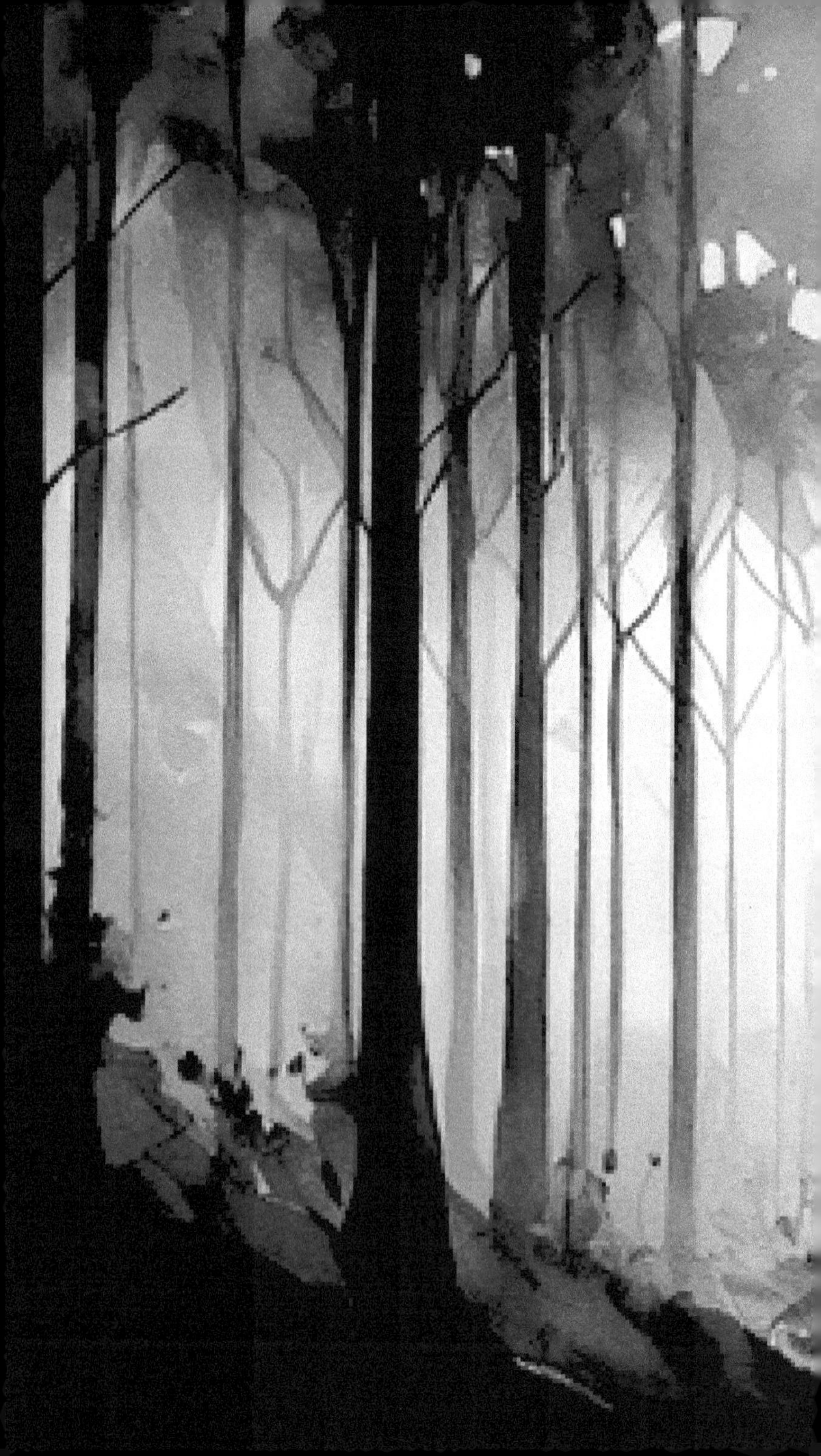

BRODY

44

I drop to my knees as I stare at the horror that is my fucking Dagger. She's covered in blood and barely conscious. Looking her over from head to toe, I quickly realize the issue. "She's been bitten by a fucking vampire," I snarl, and Raiden is at my side instantly.

"Who did this?" Cassian snarls from above me, and my gut knows the answer before it's even said out loud.

"Vallie," she rasps, eyes glazed over as she tries and fails to focus. She reaches for my hand, but it falls limp before she can grasp my fingers in hers.

"Someone fucking help me," I growl, bundling her in my arms, but Cassian takes her from my hold the second I stand.

"Where do you need to go?" he asks, not batting an eye.

"The only chance I've got of healing her is if I go to my father's coven."

"But that's on Council property," Raiden murmurs.

"It's there or nowhere," I admit, not liking the idea of it either, and he sighs.

"Fuck."

"We don't have time," Kryll snarls, hovering over my girl in Cassian's arms, and I nod in agreement. "Let's go."

Cassian takes off with her in his arms, and before I can get a warning, Kryll grabs me and follows them at high speed. There's no point reminding him I can use my own magic to get there quickly; he's already at the front fucking door of the place.

Hurrying inside, I leave the doors open as I find the healing room.

"Is it safe here?" Cassian asks, lowering her to the bed that stands in the middle of the room.

"It's the best place *and* chance I have of healing her before she fucking frenzies," I bite, adrenaline coursing through me.

I knew we should have fucked the rules and stayed with her. I should have known something like this would happen. That's what I get for thinking she was untouchable.

Fuck. Fuck. Fuck.

"Is she awake?" I ask, rushing to the far wall where all my father's tinctures are.

"No."

Dammit.

In a hurry, I ignore the mess I leave in my wake as potions, ingredients, and vials clatter to the floor.

"I can hear people," Raiden murmurs, making me still, and my gaze whips to his.

"Go watch. I need a good five minutes uninterrupted if I have any hope of saving her," I rasp, my throat clogging with emotion. To my surprise, Raiden doesn't question my order, slipping from the room with one longing glance at our girl before he goes.

"Do what you need to do, Brody. We're here," Kryll murmurs, eyes fixated on Addi's limp body, and I nod.

Reaching for the herbs first, I grind them down in my father's pot, searching for the vial of vampire blood he keeps before retrieving the essence of sage and lavender from their little containers.

The concoction looks gross, but I stick my thumb in and smear it over the bite marks on her throat.

"Ablata causa tollitur effectus. Ablata causa tollitur effectus. Ablata causa tollitur effectus. Ablata causa tollitur effectus. Ablata causa tollitur effectus. Ablata causa tollitur effectus." Panic starts to tighten my chest, worry getting the better of me, until I repeat the chant again and I note the bottom right puncture begins to heal ever so slightly. "Ablata causa tollitur effectus. Ablata causa tollitur effectus. Ablata causa tollitur effectus." I chant faster, hoping it will quicken the process, but it doesn't. Again and again and again, I repeat the precious words until each puncture wound is healed over.

"Thank fuck," I rasp, staggering back as I swipe the back of my hand over my forehead.

"Princess," Kryll murmurs, taking my place and dragging his knuckles over her cheek.

Relief floods my bones as she blinks her eyes open. She's disoriented for a moment, but when her eyes peer at mine, she's a lot more present than she was earlier.

The door swings open behind me, and I turn to give Raiden the good news but fall short when it's my father I see instead.

"Excellent, you're all here. Follow me."

THE REIGN OF BLOOD

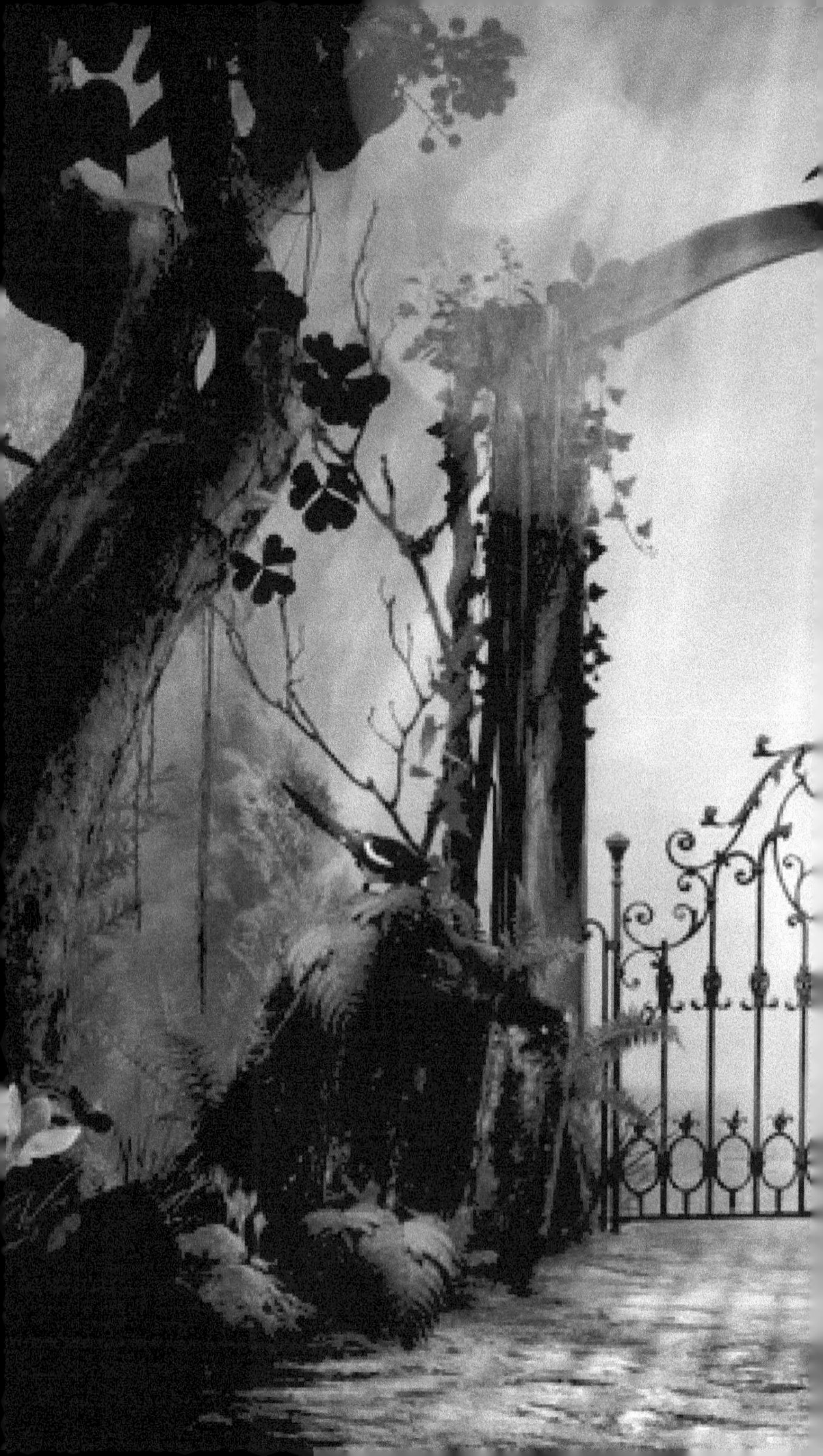

ADRIANNA

45

I feel delirious. None of this can be real, but unfortunately for me, it is.

Brody takes my hand and Kryll stays pressed against my other side as Cassian leads the way.

I press my lips together nervously, feeling the weight of the gem in my pocket, acutely aware that it's not where they think it is. I just have to hope they don't go searching for it because there's no way in hell I can get it back in place without crying in pain.

We're led down the corridor to a large open room at the far end where Raiden already waits. His head is hung low, defeat oozing from him as he stands with his hand pressed against a globe. It's only when I get closer that I realize he's chained to it.

"What's going on?" Cassian asks, pulling me from my

head. That's when I realize Raiden is not the only person in the room.

Brody's father, Councilman Orenda, stands beside Vallie's father, Raiden's mother, Professor Holloway, and Cassian's father, Kenner.

What the fuck is going on?

There are four other stands placed strategically in a circle, just like the one Raiden is attached to. Before I can consider what they're for, Brody, Cassian, and Kryll are dragged to three of them. The magic in the room is heavily charged, and I can feel it even more without the kiss of amethyst weighing me down.

"What are we here for?" Cassian grunts, his voice getting hoarser the longer he waits for a response.

Vallie's father grins from ear to ear, turning his attention to me as he ignores Cassian's question. "I'm going to assume my daughter played her part perfectly?"

"*You* orchestrated this?" Raiden snarls, anger vibrating from him as he glares at the councilman in question.

"You threatened to break the agreement," he retorts like a petulant child, giving Raiden a pointed look.

He scoffs in response. "I didn't threaten, I promised. Besides, your daughter is not in the best condition right now. That might be where you need to aim your focus," he snaps back, and I watch the color drain from councilman Drummer's face.

"See to it that this is sorted," he snarls. "I will not sacrifice my daughter for this," he adds before rushing from the room.

"Why am I here, Mother?" Raiden asks, turning his attention to her, and she shakes her head in disappointment.

"Because you threatened everything we've worked for."

"I don't really understand what you've been working for," he snaps back, and Councilman Orenda scoffs.

"Please, you're telling me Brody didn't share the facts with you?" he questions, and everyone's gaze snaps to the man in question. Puzzled looks consume Cassian, Kryll, and Raiden as they stare in confusion at their friend. "We've been researching and translating an old mage book that whispers of fated mates."

What the fuck?

"What does that have to do with us?" Cassian snaps, turning his attention to his father, who remains impassive.

"It means we worked at forcing the four of you men together and connecting you to one woman to create a connection, a power stronger than anything this world has ever seen."

"You want to connect us all to Vallie?" Kryll grunts, his nose scrunching in distaste as my gut clenches at the entire thing, but more so that it would be with her of all people.

"Over my dead fucking body," Cassian bites, anger burning in his eyes.

Brody remains quiet, his chin pressed to his chest. Why wouldn't he share this with his friends? I don't understand, but it seems there's a lot that's been kept from me.

"What the fuck is going on?" I grumble, exhausted, my body aching. I can't take all of this crap as well.

"You were acting strange before you came to me, Raiden," his mother states, lacing her fingers together as she gives him a disappointed look.

"What does that mean?" he retorts with a sigh, and she shrugs.

"It means I've been taking precautions for a while."

"Again, you're talking in circles instead of getting to the point," he snaps, losing his cool, which only plays into their hands.

"Did the stalker ever realize he had one of his own?" she asks, cocking her head to the side, and my heart seizes in my chest.

No. No. No. No. No.

"What?" he asks, head rearing back in confusion, but my gut already knows.

"You've been following him," I breathe, nausea burning the back of my throat.

"Not me personally, that's beneath me, but he's had someone on his tail, yes." She answers me so effortlessly, but the glint in her eyes confirms my suspicions.

I think I'm going to be sick.

This is worse than any pain from the amethyst or the vampire bite.

"Did you have a good time on my compound last night?" Kenner asks, pulling my attention from Professor Holloway, and I gape at him. "Because while you were there, I was a little busy myself."

The sound of a girl crying out echoes across the room as a set of doors open, and my heart sinks.

"Nora!" I yell, taking a step toward her, but Kenner lifts his hand in warning, halting me in place.

"Now, now," he teases with a wicked grin on his face, and my blood runs cold.

"Where's my father?"

"Let's worry about one family member at a time, shall we?" he retorts, and my gaze settles on Nora, who is pushed into the room in her chair, but one of the wheels is broken and she looks completely disheveled.

"Let her go," Nora snarls, staring at me with distraught tears trickling down her face.

"Nora," I rasp, my heart aching.

"I'm okay, Addi. I'm okay," she promises, but it does nothing to calm the storm brewing inside of me.

"What is it you want?" I don't turn my eyes from my sister, but they know it's them I'm speaking to.

"Want?" Councilman Orenda asks innocently, and I scoff.

"Well, of course. That's what all of this is about. Get to it," I snap, clenching my hands at my sides.

"The magic only works when combining abilities from all supernaturals," Professor Holloway explains. "Wolves, vampires, shifters, mages, and fae."

"And?" I push, wanting to hear them say it.

"And that means Vallie is no longer suitable for the position," Kenner finishes, making my muscles bunch in discomfort.

"So you think I am?"

"Actually, we're still a little unsure," Kenner retorts, pulling my gaze to him.

"How's that?"

"Since you're a half-breed, we can't fully confirm if you have enough fae magic in your veins to make it work, but you're a sacrifice we're willing to take."

"Half-breed?" I murmur, recalling the conversation last night with Cassian over my mother's ears.

"Oh, even after your little visit last night, you still haven't pieced it together, have you?" Kenner states, his grin growing wider.

"Just say it," I grind out, my nostrils flaring with rage.

"Your mother isn't a fae. She never was."

"She's a wolf," Cassian murmurs, surprise in his words.

"A Kenner wolf," his father corrects as my chest aches.

I'm part wolf? *Nora* is part wolf?

Turning to my sister, disbelief flashes in her eyes.

"I won't play these games with you. Whatever you want from me, I won't do it."

"Oh, you will, or we use your sister instead." Kenner's threat is clear as he takes a step toward me, making sure he has my full attention.

"So who will it be, Princess Adrianna, you, or little Princess Nora?"

AFTERWORDS

Ahhhhhh, I love it. I love it. I love it.

Give. Me. All. Of. The. Vibes.

This series has me hooked so damn bad, and I hope you're enjoying the journey too.

It's too much fun watching them come to life and have us in a chokehold, especially when Cassian grips our… damn.

I can't wait to continue the madness in August with the release of The Hunt of Night.

THANK YOU

Michael. It's not lost on me that I thank you in every book. Yes, EVERY BOOK, and that's a lot of books, and I don't believe you've read any of them. It's a shame really, I'm definitely nicer to you on the pages than in real life haha. I love you!

To my babies, you rock. Like for real. You definitely keep me humble, that's for sure, and you also make me thrive for so much more. I can't wait to continue stomping this earth with you guys.

Nicole and Jeni. You guys are my queens. Thank you for dealing with glitchy documents and my crazy brain. You're awesome.

Kirsty, mate. Stunning. I wish we had dicks so we could say - brother from another mother, but alas, we just act like one instead haha. You're forever the gorilla glue for this manic train. Thank you.

To my beta readers, your comments give me life. I love you words, your love for the characters, and the group chat filled with rage for more words. Thank you.

Thank you to Sarah and Lily for making everything perfect. You gals are superior.

About KC Kean

KC Kean began her writing journey in 2020 amidst the pandemic and homeschooling… yay! After reading all of the steam, from fade to black, to steamy reads, MM, and reverse harem, she decided to immerse herself in her own worlds too.

When KC isn't hiding away in the writing cave, she is playing Dreamlight Valley, enjoying the limited UK sunshine with her husband, children, and furbabies, or collecting vinyls like it's a competition.

Come and join me over at my Aceholes Reader Group, follow my author's Facebook page, and enjoy Instagram with me on the links below.

ALSO BY KC KEAN

Featherstone Academy
(Reverse Harem Contemporary Romance)
My Bloodline
Your Bloodline
Our Bloodline
Red
Freedom
Redemption

All-Star Series
(Reverse Harem Contemporary Romance)
Toxic Creek
Tainted Creek
Twisted Creek

(Standalone MF)
Burn to Ash

Emerson U Series
(Reverse Harem Contemporary Romance)
Watch Me Fall
Watch Me Rise
Watch Me Reign

Saints Academy
(Reverse Harem Paranormal Romance)
Reckless Souls
Damaged Souls
Vicious Souls
Fearless Souls
Heartless Souls

Ruthless Brothers MC
(Reverse Harem MC Romance)
Ruthless Rage
Ruthless Rebel
Ruthless Riot

Silvercrest Academy
(Reverse Harem Paranormal Romance)
Falling Shadows
Destined Shadows
Cursed Shadows
Unchained Shadows

Heirborn Academy
Kingdom of Ruin
Reign of Blood
Hunt of Night

THE REIGN OF BLOOD

THE REIGN OF BLOOD

Milton Keynes UK
Ingram Content Group UK Ltd.
UKHW050205280624
444844UK00004B/169

9 781915 203489